Reaction Shot

In the rough country of Wyoming, sometimes cattle rustlers still get a death sentence.

A ranch foreman is found dead—and, for most in Cottonwood County, the reaction is … good riddance. The investigation puts Elizabeth in close quarters with Mike and Tom—sometimes all three together—and she realizes these evolving relationships also warrant a soul-search for deeper meaning.

5-Star Praise for *Reaction Shot*

"It must be magic! The characters, their individual histories, the place and its stories, and the newest murder make these books unfold like real life dramas and tragedies. And suddenly, you aren't in your jammies reading a book, but out on the Wyoming prairie, smelling cattle and dust, right along with the indomitable Tamantha and the rest of the gang making sure the right murderer is caught!"

Caught Dead in Wyoming series

Sign Off

Left Hanging

Shoot First

Last Ditch

Look Live

Back Story

Cold Open

Hot Roll

Reaction Shot

Body Brace

"While the mystery itself is twisty-turny and thoroughly engaging, it's the smart and witty writing that I loved the best."

—*Diane Chamberlain, New York Times bestselling author*

More cozy mystery

Secret Sleuth series

Death on the Diversion

Death on Torrid Avenue

Death on Beguiling Way

Death on Covert Circle

Death on Shady Bridge

Death on Carrion Lane

Mystery with romance

The Innocence Trilogy

Proof of Innocence

Price of Innocence

Premise of Innocence

REACTION SHOT

Caught Dead in Wyoming,
Book 9

Patricia McLinn

Copyright © Patricia McLinn
Ebook ISBN: 978-1-944126-67-4
Paperback ISBN: 978-1-944126-68-1
Large print ISBN: 978-1-944126-90-2
Audiobook ISBN: 978-1-944126-91-9
Print Edition
www.PatriciaMcLinn.com

Cover design: Art by Karri
Cover image: Nicolaus Wegner

DAY ONE

Chapter One

WHEN THERE'S NOT enough real news happening, newsrooms get as restless as preschoolers fed sugar for five rainy days in a row. Not a pretty sight.

As other newsrooms are wont to do under those circumstances, the KWMT-TV newsroom devoted itself to making its own news.

I don't usually mind this self-generation of news as a sanity valve. Heck, I've participated on its fringes in newsrooms from Dayton to St. Louis to Washington, D.C., to New York.

At this moment in Sherman, Wyoming, the internal news came in the form of staff speculation about an imminent *battle royale* between me and anchor Thurston Fine.

Yesterday, Thurston announced he needed Jerry, the studio camera operator, to film a summer promo this morning.

That caused a mild stir because Thurston rarely did anything in the morning except prepare for a long lunch. Somehow—surely without effort on his part—he'd learned I'd blocked morning time with Jerry and arranged this intended bump to try to irritate me. It was all over his pampered face.

I could have squashed him on the spot. I decided on a bit longer strategy.

To meet expectations, I protested I had Jerry scheduled at eleven to shoot an in-studio interview for the "Helping Out!" consumer segment Elizabeth Margaret Danniher. Thurston pounced and said he needed Jerry at ten-thirty and couldn't possibly be done in half an hour.

Astute observers might have noticed Audrey trying to hide a grin. That's because, as today's assignment editor, she knew my interview was actually scheduled at eleven-thirty.

The less astute expected fireworks at eleven.

By eleven-fifteen, the newsroom was hyperventilating.

I rose from my desk chair, picked up my bag, and went to the assignment desk.

"Audrey, if you'd please escort my interview subject to the studio when she arrives? Her name's Odessa Vincennes. I'm going to the studio now."

"Dale, you heard her. I'm leaving that to you," Audrey immediately said to a news aide. She didn't want to be stuck in the newsroom with the action in the studio.

Condemned to miss the fun, Dale gulped. "Oh… Okay."

"Thank you."

Without looking, I knew the newsroom denizens followed me through the uninspiring hallways of Sherman's sole TV station. Past the closed door of news director Les Haeburn's office, past the certainly locked door to Thurston's posh—by KWMT-TV standards— office, past the library's seldom-used door, and, finally, down a stretch to the studio.

Michael Paycik, KWMT-TV's sports anchor and my cohort in several investigations, grinned as I passed him on my stately progress. I maintained complete and deadpan dignity as he, too, fell in behind me.

Mike's presence was a touching tribute. He'd set up an important remote interview with a baseball rookie hotshot, who'd gone to the University of Wyoming. A place not generally considered a spawning ground for Major League Baseball talent, especially since the state has no high school baseball. See the things you learn from a sports guy?

This John Smith—I'm not kidding—was tearing up the big leagues, while maintaining a steadfast concentration that precluded interviews.

Except with Michael Paycik of KWMT-TV. Turns out, as a child, John Smith followed Mike's football career at the University of Wyoming.

Mike worked connections to get the guy into a studio in Pittsburgh for his side of the interview, while Mike asked questions from here. Because, of course, KWMT wouldn't spring to send him to interview the guy in person.

At the studio door, I took a deep breath. Some might have thought it was to prepare for battle. It was to quell an inclination to laugh.

Still not looking back, I opened the door.

Do you know how many people can pack into a none-too-generous hallway outside the KWMT-TV studio? Me, either, because I didn't pause to count, especially since I wasn't acknowledging their presence. Though I did happen to leave the door open.

"—already done five extra variations beyond what Les approved, Thurston," Jerry was saying. He regularly operated the two big studio cameras and served as floor director for newscasts, in addition to other in-studio camera work.

"Then we'll do a sixth—" Thurston interrupted himself by spinning around and flashing his anchor smile, believing he'd dawdled into my time. "Have we run over? But we must finish."

His exchange with Jerry and no red light warning against opening the door—Jerry would never overlook that—said they were past finished.

"No problem." I winked at Jerry.

"No prob—?"

I paid no attention to Thurston's confusion. The usually unflappable Jerry had not winked back. He looked like the lone teacher left in charge of those hypothetical sugar-high preschoolers.

I'd prepared for this. After all, I'd extended his sentence with Thurston. I owed him.

I took a giant-sized Hamburger Heaven coffee to-go from my bag. Good coffee and with truly insulated cups. I set the still-hot coffee on a table against a wall.

He perked up—caffeine pun intended—as my peripheral vision captured the satisfying sight of Thurston deflating.

Next, I drew out three brownies from the Sherman Western Frontier Life Museum gift shop. Not only delicious, but I'd made the effort of informing their maker they were all for Jerry, none for me.

I didn't *really* think she'd try to poison me, especially since we'd reached a sort of cease-fire not long ago. But there'd been a time...

Anyway, it would be unfair to Jerry if I'd misread her. So, I'd been emphatic about who the brownies were for. She'd looked at me like I was demented, while she rang them up with no commentary.

Jerry, however, had commentary. "Yum."

"I brought a scarf to soften that wood backdrop," I told him, drawing the next item from my bag.

Most TV news sets resemble a designer's vision of the bridge for the next Star Trek series. KWMT's looks like a heart-breaking Soap Box Derby entry that falls apart nine feet into the race.

A rough wood wall serves as backdrop for far too many in-studio interviews. I'd started bringing fabrics to change up the look so viewers don't slip into a catatonic *that-again* state.

"Nice." Pretty sure that's what Jerry said. He had his head down, unwrapping brownies.

"They'll have to use a scarf over the lens for you soon."

Thurston referred to my age, which is decidedly over twenty-one. As is his, so rather risky of him.

"I wonder if that would work," I said thoughtfully. "I've heard Vaseline on the lens or shooting through a stocking as the tricks used in Hollywood's heyday. Never successful on men in my view, but you can try, Thurston. What do you think, Jerry?"

"Mmph" was the best he did around a bite of brownie.

"Whatever." Unaware of sounding like the cliché of a disaffected teenager, Thurston went back to his original tactic. "We're not done. You'll have to wait for the studio."

"Sure looks like you're done."

"We need to do an OTS."

Jerry snorted. "Over the shoulder looking at what? Me? You're not interviewing anybody, not like Elizabeth is."

"Soon, but not soon enough, you'll be replaced by robotic cameras," Thurston snarled.

"You're already a robot," Jerry grumbled as he took another bite.

The combination of mutter and brownie made deciphering his words difficult, especially from across the studio.

Thurston peered at him suspiciously.

It was no part of my plan to draw anyone else into Thurston's line of fire. I quickly covered Jerry's grumble. "You'd hate robotic cameras, Thurston. Did you see the difficulties the BBC had to start with them?"

"Of course I did," he lied.

"That's right," Jerry said around the final chews on that brownie. "Robotic cameras went rogue, panning the studio, showing people— presenters they call them—walking around the set, or an empty desk, while the one talking stood at another part of the set talking to themselves. There's one clip where the camera sneaks up behind the anchor and shows his significant butt, when it's supposed to be focusing on the weather person."

I contributed, "Or when the anchor chases the camera, trying to get in the shot."

Both Jerry and I laughed.

"When he finally does get in the shot, he's still looking the wrong way," he said. "And then where the camera's on the wrong anchor. The one off-camera keeps talking, giving the report, while the other one's taking notes and making faces. It's like a ventriloquist act."

"Ha. Ha. Ha." Thurston was not amused. "You'll have to wait, Elizabeth. I—What are *you* people doing here?"

The latter was screamed at the audience at the door, who resembled a phone-booth packing effort from the 1950s. They disassembled more easily, but no faster than the phone booth packers and, I'm guessing, with the same level of amusement.

Proving my tact, I turned my back to the studio to attach the scarf to pegs protruding from the wooden wall, letting Thurston depart with whatever dignity he dredged up. It wasn't one of his abundant resources.

I ignored sounds of huffing and puffing behind me, fussing with the scarf. The only sound from Jerry was chewing.

At last, I heard Thurston moving toward the door. I stepped back from the wall, as if judging the scarf's effect.

"Right this way, Ms. Vincennes," came Dale's voice from the hall-way.

Then, "Oh. Thurston Fine."

I turned to see him recoil from contact with the woman who'd entered the studio.

"No time for autographs. Working. Very busy. Very, very busy."

He rushed out, past the parted ranks of staffers, leaving them and Jerry fighting laughter, while I contained myself to greet my interview subject. She raised her brows, inviting comment on Thurston.

But there's battle and then there's tromping on the vanquished. I nobly refrained from tromping.

Odessa Vincennes stood straight and wore shoes with chunky wedge heels, bringing her about to my chin. She was focused, energetic, comfortably rounded, and far more practical than her exotic name.

I introduced her to Jerry, who had his laughter under control and his Thurston-sapped energy replenished by caffeine and chocolate.

We explained the interview was a lot like a conversation... with bright lights focused on you and a big clunky camera peering into your face. And KWMT had the biggest and clunkiest cameras I'd encountered, because they were the oldest I'd encountered.

No, we didn't mention the lights and camera part.

Odessa Vincennes did okay with them. Only a flicker of her eyes when Jerry repositioned.

She was justifiably enthusiastic about the program she represented. It researched local scams victimizing seniors, consulting with law enforcement and consumer affairs experts then created flyers about them.

"...we don't stop with passive information. We've teamed with other services to seniors—meal deliveries, visiting clergy, home health aides—to deliver the flyers and talk to the seniors about the information. Pilot studies have shown this increases the effectiveness."

Earlier, I'd given Jerry a quick look, asking without words if this was coming across okay on camera.

He'd responded with a slight nod, saying it was coming through fine. That was the technical aspects, though.

Most people are nervous, some disastrously. She persistently rubbed her right thumb against her curved forefinger, but out of frame. No worries there.

Nerves weren't the issue. More like she'd locked herself down and I didn't have the key.

I tried a few approaches—I'd have way more footage than I'd ever get on air. And still hadn't hit the key.

Odessa Vincennes remained out of my reach.

Maybe if I pushed a little.

"I'd like to see data from that study—"

The studio door opened.

That probably doesn't sound newsworthy. A door opened. Big deal. But the studio door opening during an interview? That was darned near earthshattering.

Jerry and I looked at each other, even before looking toward the door.

"Light's on," he said.

The first thing drummed into every TV station employee's head is not to interrupt when the red light's on.

Turning more, I saw the door opener was Mike Paycik.

Who definitely knew better.

He held up one hand to ward off being told he knew better, striding across the studio. "Elizabeth, you need to know about this. Right away."

As well as a co-worker, Mike was half of a complicated situation.

"I'm interviewing—"

"There's been a shooting at Tom's grazing association." He reached out a reassuring hand, so I must have reacted. "Not Tom. It wasn't Tom. It was the foreman from another ranch. Guy named Furman York. Looks like murder."

Tom was Thomas David Burrell, a local rancher.

And the other half of the complicated situation.

Or some portion of it, anyway, because I'm part of it, too. Though whether that makes us each a third, I'm not prepared to say.

To make it more complicated, Mike and Tom were friends. And all three of us have been involved, along with a few others, in investigating murders.

But, still, to interrupt an interview—

"They're talking to Tom. The sheriff's department."

Those words derailed the rest of my thought.

Chapter Two

"TAMANTHA'S ON THE phone for you right now. At your desk," Mike finished.

Tamantha Burrell, the heading toward fourth grade daughter of Tom.

For a frozen second, Mike and I looked at each other.

I shot up and was three strides toward the door, when I spun back. "I'm sorry, Odessa. I'm so sorry. There's an emergency and—I'm sorry. I'll be in touch as soon as I know about scheduling the finish of this." My gaze shifted. "Jerry?"

"Go. I'll take care of it here."

I didn't wait for more.

"What makes you say murder?" I demanded of Mike on the move.

"He was found out on grazing association land, dead. Sounds like they're not thinking suicide or accident, which doesn't leave much other than murder."

Mike was behind me as I reached my desk, barely aware of the few staffers in the newsroom. I concentrated on getting the phone in my hand and up to my ear.

"Tamantha? Are you okay?"

"Make them stop, Elizabeth." No tears, no shake in her voice, vintage Tamantha determination. "Fix this."

Air streamed out from somewhere that felt far deeper than my lungs at hearing her so like herself. "I need to know more before—"

I broke off because, on the other end, Tom spoke close enough to the phone for me to hear, as long as I didn't drown him out.

"It's okay, Tamantha. I told you not to bother Elizabeth."

"It wasn't okay last time. Not for months and months and months."

"This is different." By the way his voice came closer, I deduced he'd taken the phone from her. "Elizabeth?"

Deduction confirmed.

"I'm here. What can I do? Where are you? If Shelton—"

"We're at the Circle B. There's nothing for you to do. Not about that. But…" I heard rare hesitation in his voice. "My sister's out of town. I don't have time to get Tamantha to Mrs. P—" Mrs. Parens, a retired teacher and principal, didn't drive, so couldn't get to his ranch to pick up his daughter. "—and my neighbor, Mrs. George, isn't home… Would you come get Tamantha?"

"I'm staying here with you," I heard in the background from that redoubtable child.

"I'm not staying. I'm going with Sergeant Shelton to help in any way I can." Tom's words were for his daughter, for me, and for Shelton.

"Then I'm going with you," his daughter declared.

"You are not." Tom's voice reminded where the redoubtable in Tamantha came from.

"I'll be there as fast as I can," I said into the mouthpiece. I'd already stood and was dropping things into my bag. "I'm leaving the station right now."

"I'm stuck here," Mike grumbled.

"I'm driving," another voice said from over my shoulder.

It was Diana Stendahl. My friend, another member of our investigating group, and the best cameraperson at KWMT-TV.

"Then you'll get here faster," Tom said, with a faint smile in his voice, clearly having recognized the volunteer's voice.

Diana's driving speed is undeterred by pesky items like the Rocky Mountains, which would come in handy, because Tom's Circle B Ranch had more than a passing acquaintance with their eastern edge.

"We're leaving now. Tell Tamantha. We'll be there. I'll be there."

✧   ✧   ✧   ✧

"IT'S NOT LIKE before," Diana said into a silence in her truck.

"What?"

I didn't ask that buying-time question because my thoughts had been in some distant arena, but because they had been on the same track as hers ... going the opposite direction. Fearing it could be exactly like before.

"They're *talking* to Tom," Diana said. "That's what he said. Not questioning him at the sheriff's department or... anything else. Besides—"

"Do you know anything about this guy who's dead? Furman York?"

"—it's not like it was with Sheriff Widcuff not knowing his head from a hole in the ground. It's Shelton talking to him. And Russ is sheriff now."

Russell Conrad became sheriff of Cottonwood County last fall. Not long after his arrival, he and Diana became ... an item. Russ Conrad made her happy. She seemed to do the same for him. The second point didn't weigh heavily with me.

About the only thing Conrad and I agreed on was Diana.

"It's not like before. It's totally different," she said again.

"Uh-huh."

I sure hoped so. But that's not what had been in Tamantha's voice.

Chapter Three

TAMANTHA BURRELL IS not a child you scoop up and wrap your arms around. Unless, perhaps, you are her father.

I felt more like saluting her after a deputy opened the front door, admitting us to the Burrell ranch house and Tamantha's presence.

Especially you did not scoop up Tamantha Burrell and wrap her in one's arms when she is dagger-eyeing the world.

Most of the daggers were for Sergeant Wayne Shelton of the Cottonwood County Sheriff's Department. Under other circumstances, I might have enjoyed his discomfort. Right now? No.

"I came out here because I know your daddy and it's important he comes with us and talks to us about what he knows," Shelton was saying to her.

Yeah, like that would cut it.

"Why?" I asked, stepping beside Tamantha.

I also wanted to ask who and what and when, since I already knew where.

She gave me a quick look of acknowledgement, perhaps even approval, then fiercely repeated, "Yeah, why?"

Neither Tom nor Shelton blessed me with approval, though their frowns certainly acknowledged my arrival.

"You know I'm chairman of the grazing association, Tamantha. Something's happened there—"

"That guy got shot. Doesn't have anything to do with you."

Shelton glowered. Automatic reflex. He'd been around far too long to have expected the news not to be all over the county. And he knew

Tamantha well enough to be unsurprised she knew and didn't sugarcoat what she knew.

"—and I need to go help in any way I can," Tom finished.

Tamantha did not falter before Shelton's glower. If anything, her glower back one-upped his. "This is like before. You were wrong. All wrong. Elizabeth had to figure it out and make you admit it." She faced me, the daggers not quite sheathed. "You do it again. This time faster."

Without the muscles or bones of his face moving, Tom's gravity lightened, revealed by a glimmer in his eyes.

Fine for him to laugh. I'd been handed an edict and a deadline from the ruler of the universe.

"Tamantha." Her father waited until she turned to him. "This isn't like before. I can't guarantee it won't ever be, because sometimes things go … wrong. But right now, it's important I go with Sergeant Shelton and the others and tell them anything I know that might help figure this out. That's my duty as a citizen. You know about that. And it's my responsibility as chairman of the grazing association."

"Just because that man got himself shot there—"

"Tamantha."

It was the redoubtable standoff at the Circle B. Not the first between father and daughter Burrell.

She blinked first, though a small blink. "I'll wait here for you."

"You will not."

This standoff wouldn't end up in a shootout, but it might end up enduring as long as, say, Mount Rushmore. Which was what their profiles reminded me of.

I was wrong.

It ended relatively quickly, though they still resembled Mount Rushmore.

Tamantha didn't actually relent. More like she graciously acknowledged he held higher cards for this particular hand, what with being several feet taller and her father and all.

Tom did not rub it in. He said, "If it's all right with Elizabeth, she'll take you to her house. If this runs long—" He clearly expected it to. "—you can sleep over there tonight, and when I've finished with the deputies and—"

A nice touch of verbally establishing roles. Not when the deputies were done with him, instead, when he was done with them.

"—helped all I can, I will come there." His gaze flickered to me. "If that's all right with Elizabeth."

Tamantha's hand slid into mine. So unexpected a touch, I almost jumped. Her thumb rubbed against my skin.

Redoubtable was still a child.

"It is." I squeezed.

"We'll all be there," Diana added.

He declined his head, acknowledging both of us. "Now, get your things, Tamantha. I'll see you on your way before I go with Sergeant Shelton."

And if Shelton thought he'd reverse the order of those events, he didn't know Tom Burrell.

Mount Rushmore man was not about to have his daughter see him escorted away by the Cottonwood County Sheriff's Department.

Chapter Four

"WHO WAS SHOT?" I asked Tom quietly.

"Furman York, foreman of the Lukasik Ranch. Big place. East of town."

"Do they know when?"

"This morning. Sheriff's department caught a break. It couldn't have been much before he was found, around nine-thirty."

"Who found—?"

"Enough," Shelton ordered. "Be quiet or I'll take you all in."

Before I could respond, Tom said, "I'll go help Tamantha."

Shelton sent a deputy along.

Diana and I exchanged a look. Hers mirrored my concern that this was more than Shelton simply wanting information from Tom as grazing association chairman.

After several minutes of silence in the living room, Tamantha emerged first from the hall to the bedrooms, rolling a miniature suitcase that made me blink.

Its surface was like an explosion of multicolored confetti that dared any airline to even consider losing it. It was beyond neon. It was irradiated.

And completely unlike the practical clothes she wore. Practical in colors that wouldn't show the dirt and wear of ranch life. And practical in wearing them well past their prime of fit and form.

Tom picked up this resplendent bag with one hand, his other arm around her. Through the living room, out the door, across the porch. The two of them in sync every step of the way despite the difference in their strides.

At Diana's vehicle, he buckled Tamantha into the back seat.

She didn't even complain about being treated like a baby. On the other hand, she didn't deign to reply when he told her to be good. They didn't hug, but exchanged a long, level look.

To Diana and me he said in a low voice, "I'll call." The unspoken rider was *When I can.*

As we drove out, Tamantha looked back to where her father stood, watching the vehicle, with one hand raised, until trees and a curve around a low hill cut off the view.

Unspoken thoughts filled the passenger compartment like a heavy gas.

To change the subject that hadn't been mentioned aloud, I said, "That's a great suitcase, Tamantha."

"It rolls."

"I saw that."

"Not much good on the ranch, but it's good when I stay with friends in town."

"That makes sense. Was it a present?"

"My Grandma Burrell gave it to me."

A prickling at the bridge of my nose provided an early warning of tears. I'd learned to pay attention to it to ward off crying on air, during interviews, or other inopportune moments. Like in front of this child.

Tears. Because her father's mother gave her a present expressing joy and color, when I hadn't believed there was any relationship there at all.

Certainly, I'd heard almost nothing of Tom's relationship with his parents, nor theirs with Tamantha. Though both Tom and Tamantha were close with his married sister, who lived not far over the border into Montana.

"What a great gift to get from your grandmother."

"Yes. She said to select what I wanted and then she got it for me and had it delivered in a big box. Not wrapped, but plenty of paper around it inside the box."

Her tone was far too matter-of-fact to allow for wistfulness. Another attack of prickling at the bridge of my nose acknowledged the collapse of my dreams of a grandmother who nurtured this girl's wild, colorful side, perhaps even in the guise of exotic wrapping paper. Instead, going with the practicality of direct shipping.

Except, the reality was better, because it turned out it was *Tamantha* who nurtured that wild, colorful side.

She chose the confetti explosion and she used it, apparently with pleasure, when it didn't involve her father being interviewed by the sheriff's department.

"Great choice. I love it." I cleared my throat, catching a glance from Diana. "It suits you."

"Of course. I picked it."

MY THOUGHTS WENT to the situation with Tom, Mike, and me.

We—Mike and I, then Tom and I—had become friends and part of this group of friends, while mutual attractions brewed underneath. Bringing the attractions out in the open—testing them, so to speak— had been the idea behind starting to date recently.

Maybe it would have helped if the dates happened frequently and close together. Maybe then the compare and contrast hypothesis would work.

That didn't happen.

Duties at KWMT-TV kept Mike busy, with the wrap-up of local spring sports seasons, the beginning of rodeo season, full-throttle pro basketball, hockey, and baseball seasons, and football off-season. "I'm a well-seasoned guy," as he said.

Duties at the Circle B Ranch kept Tom busy, with the end of calving, the beginning of branding, the ever ongoing fence-repairing. Plus his road construction business and his rampant civic activities.

Add in my settling into my new-to-me house and the fact that when our calendars' open spots meshed, we often applied them to getting together as a group with Diana, Jennifer Lawton, other friends, plus now and then Diana's honey Sheriff Russ Conrad, her kids, and Tamantha … and you have a sprinkling of dates each over the past month-plus.

"Elizabeth," Tamantha said from the back seat.

For our return, Diana dropped her speed a notch. Still, I braced against the dashboard as I turned toward the back. Diana's truck had seat belts and airbags, of course, but I wasn't above helping them out.

"This man was shot at the grazing association." Tamantha did not make it a question. "That's where the clues are."

"Maybe. All we know for sure is Sergeant Shelton needs your dad's help figuring some things out about what happened."

Not bad. I'd avoided *shot, killed, murder, suspect,* and *questioning.*

Unimpressed, she *humph'*d. "That's where we should be, at the grazing association. To figure this out fast."

"No way, Tamantha."

I thought I heard a *Good* from Diana under her breath.

"You always want information. That's what you say all the time. That's where the information is."

Tamantha had a point…

"No. We're going to my house, where we'll wait for your father to finish, uh, his business with the sheriff's department."

"There isn't any information at your house."

Not yet. But I could work the phones while she was there. Heck, she'd probably help me dial if she thought that would speed things up.

"And," she continued, "I know how to get there. We go there a lot. I pick the flowers, but only after Mike said I could. We could go right now."

Sidetracked by flowers at the grazing association and why Mike had the say-so over them, I replied a bit slowly. "I promised your father to take—"

"Care of me. The best way is to get this figured out fast. So Daddy is home."

"Tamantha, I am not taking you to the grazing association, that's final."

"Then *you* go. You go and get the information you need like you always do. I'll stay at your house. I'm old enough to stay by myself and—"

"You're not staying by yourself." Now I heard *Uh-oh* from under

Diana's breath. I hurriedly added, "That's final." It sounded weak.

"Shadow—"

"Or with my dog."

"That's silly. But if you go to the grazing association to find out things and get my daddy home, I'll stay with Mr. and Mrs. Undlin."

"You know them?" This time I'd swear my words were followed by *Goner* from Diana's sotto-voce commentary.

"Of course. They'll be happy to help."

TAMANTHA WAS RIGHT, of course.

My next-door neighbors, Iris and Zeb, did know Tamantha—no surprise. First, almost everyone in Cottonwood County knew everyone else. Second, I already knew her father thought highly of the Undlins.

Also, she was right about their willingness to look after her. They were delighted to have Tamantha stay at their house until I returned.

"Are you sure? I can't tell you exactly when I'll be back."

"Not necessary. Not necessary at all. Let us know if you'll be past her bedtime and we'll tuck her up in your guest room and stay there until you come," Iris said.

Tamantha punctuated that with a look that clearly said the arrangement left no excuse for slacking and I better not come back until I had a lot of information or, preferably, the whole thing figured out and her father in the clear.

Iris softened Tamantha's look by adding, "I was thinking of making doughnuts. Would you like to do that, Tamantha?"

"Yes, I would. I've never made doughnuts before."

She sounded as if her sole desire was to add doughnut-making to her resume. However, I've seen her eat doughnuts and she was no slouch.

As we left, I heard Tamantha casually mention to Zeb that Shadow was alone at my house and it seemed a shame to wait until she was ready for bed to see him.

I suspected doughnuts were also in Shadow's future.

Chapter Five

I BROKE THE silence in Diana's truck cab once we'd cleared town.

"What was that look for when I was talking with Tamantha about her suitcase?"

"Mmm. Thinking about Tamantha, how she's growing up. The bag's a good sign, but…" She cut me a look. "Being extraordinary's not necessarily easy. Especially at her age."

"You mean being accepted by other kids? She doesn't seem to have trouble there. If anything, she's a leader."

"Yes, she is. On the other hand, I've seen with my two a period when what kids accept as 'normal' shrinks. Happens at the same time their self-confidence plummets. It opens up later, thank heavens. Now, *there* Tamantha won't have any trouble. In the meantime, small shifts in her—let's call it style—could make that narrower period easier for her."

"Her *style?* You think Tom getting her to wear something other than old jeans and older sweaters would ease her way?"

"I don't think *Tom* would have a clue."

Her emphasis made me edgy, though she had a point. Beyond a couple decent suits, he was strictly utilitarian.

"He dresses okay for what he does," I said. "So does she. I mean, jeans and sweaters are practical for her."

"You said *old* jeans and *older* sweaters a second ago. In fact, she's a not-yet fourth-grader wearing mom jeans and grandma sweaters."

"If anyone can pull off the look, it's Tamantha."

"The point is, should she have to? Do you want her to have to?"

My answers to her spoken questions were easy.

No, she shouldn't have to if she didn't want to.

No, I didn't want her to have to if she didn't want to.

Then came my question in response to her unspoken statement that I should do something about it.

Why me? How am I supposed to take care of this?

Maybe Diana didn't catch that internal bleat, because she continued. "Do you want her to be dressing like this in middle school? Tom's gun-shy, what with Mona…"

Tamantha's mother and Tom's ex-wife, now deceased, had fancied herself a fashionista. In that and other ways, she had not provided a model any who cared about Tamantha wanted the girl to follow.

Belatedly, my bleat burst out as, "Well, I'm not the one to get him to change. Or her. What will probably happen if I try to guide her is I'll start wearing mom jeans and grandma sweaters."

"She *is* strong-minded. As we just saw." She looked over at me with the last sentence.

"Yeah, I know. Tamantha manipulated me." Then a much more cheerful thought than being outmaneuvered by a not-yet fourth-grader struck me. "Maybe I let her because deep down, I want to see what's going on."

"Of course you want to see what's going on. Though it had nothing to do with what happened. Do you want to know where you went wrong?"

"Turning around when she said my name?"

She chuckled. "Not quite. You did well when she proposed all of us going to the grazing association. But then she distracted you from your first, blanket *No* by dividing the blanket into pieces. No, she couldn't go to the grazing association. No, she couldn't stay alone. Even as you said no to those, you implicitly said yes to *your* going to the grazing association, to leaving her with somebody. Step by step, she got you to where she wanted you to be—right here, on your way to the grazing association."

I swore. "She should be negotiating in the Middle East."

"Oh, this was pretty basic kid tactics."

"I'm a patsy? Is that what you're saying? Why didn't you stop it? Why didn't you save me?"

"Because I wanted to go with you to the grazing association. Notice I didn't volunteer to look after her."

I gave her a look of admiration. "I never realized you were that sneaky."

My phone rang.

"Thank you," Diana said modestly. "Aren't you going to answer? I thought you were past dodging your parents."

What was this? *Hit Elizabeth Margaret Danniher With the Truth Day?*

In fact, I hadn't dodged my parents. Not lately. They had stayed with me for three and a half days before heading farther west for Yellowstone Park.

We'd had a good visit. A very good visit.

We're not a family that feuds or fusses, but I often experience internal tension in the company of my parents and older siblings. Love isn't the issue. Neither is liking. It all stems from their seeing me as a nine-to-thirteen-year-old (depending on their mood) not overly blessed with common sense and me seeing myself as a passably functioning adult.

There'd been far less of that tension in my parents' recent visit than I'd experienced before.

One evening, Diana hosted a cookout at her ranch house, where Mom and Dad met a lot of my Wyoming friends. We went to the Sherman rodeo and had chocolate pie at the Haber House Hotel dining room another evening. They connected with my next-door neighbors, Iris and Zeb.

Oh, and they petted, treated, and fussed over my adopted stray dog, Shadow. In further proof he was putting his antisocial ways behind him, he lapped it up.

Mom and Dad would stay with me another few days—duration not yet specified—after Yellowstone and before their drive back to Illinois.

I looked forward to their return, tamping down any uneasiness over whether the outbound visit had been a fluke.

"It's not my parents." Score a point for honesty that I didn't try to deny I had, at some points since my arrival in Sherman, dodged them. "It looks like a station number. Not one I recognize."

"Maybe it's Thurston, calling to apologize. Or Les, calling to assign you to cover the murder."

The second possibility was as unlikely as the first. Les Haeburn, officially the station's news director, spent more of his time placating Thurston than directing the newsroom. He largely left me alone, since my new contract from last fall gave me considerable latitude.

With a smirk about Diana's Thurston and Les speculations, I answered the phone.

"Elizabeth, it's Jerry. You need to come to the station."

"I'm sorry for walking out mid-interview and leaving you to deal with—"

"No problem. I want you to see something. Maybe I'm totally wrong, but... I think you need to see this, you and Mike. I couldn't catch him in time or—"

"Jerry, I can't get away. And I don't know where Mike is."

I'm not sure he heard that because he seemed to be involved in a conversation taking place in the background on his end.

He came back to say, "Okay, we have a solution. Might take a while."

"Whatever works, Jerry. Thanks. I've got to go now. Thanks again."

Chapter Six

DIANA TURNED OFF the highway, then from one dirt road to an even rougher one, seemingly knowing where she was heading.

Much of Cottonwood County sat on the Jelicho Table, a stretch of relatively flat land, driest on the eastern edge where it blended into the semi-arid Bighorn Basin.

Ah, the Bighorn Basin. That presents issues to elevate the blood pressure of print journalists everywhere.

The sheep are Bighorn—one word. The county and town are Big Horn—two words. The sheep had no say, the town and county got to decide for themselves.

Then there are the mountains, river, and basin. Depending on the governmental source and, apparently, mapmakers' whims, you'll see either spelling, and sometimes both.

Broadcast journalists are fortunate—they sound the same.

However, we broadcasters get our come-uppance on the western end of Cottonwood County, where the Rocky Mountains, specifically the Absaroka Range, bring the Jelicho Table to a jagged conclusion.

Although more formal sources mostly divide between "ab-SOR-o-ka" and "ab-SOHR-kuh"—with a whole lot of variation on how "O/Oh" sounds—we have a persistent strain of "ab-sah-RO-kuh" pronouncers in our listening area.

No matter how I pronounced it, to some segment of our audience, I'd be the outsider who hadn't bothered to learn local ways.

I do my best to not venture into such dangerous territory. So, what I viewed through the back window of Diana's truck as we headed east across the Jelicho Table, those were the Rockies.

"Will we be at the grazing association soon?" I asked.

"We're here."

"That last turn? I thought there'd be a sign or something."

"Two turns before. Expecting a sign like the one at the country club? Maybe landscaping with a rock wall? It's not that kind of group. Only the land matters."

"They lease?"

"Not much. Most associations have some deeded land, this one is almost all deeded. They don't like being subject to lease prices rising."

Before I could ask more, we came to the end of an extensive line of vehicles, nearly all pickups, parked along the dirt track.

Not something I would have expected before my move here, but those pickups provided information.

Pickups, like cowboy boots, fall into classes in Wyoming.

There are very few of the fashion statement type—which is mostly what you see in cities, especially east of the Mississippi.

Then there are Sunday-best pickups, saved for plan-ahead occasions. Vehicles that leave from their starting point shined up, even if they seldom reach their destination in that state. It can take a trained eye to distinguish fresh dirt or mud on a recently shiny vehicle from the long-standing variety, but it's quite clear to Wyomingites. It can be a social solecism to arrive to some functions with old dirt, while fresh dirt is perfectly acceptable.

The next variety—the working pickup—goes to town for business or casual pleasure, never fancy. Old dirt is perfectly acceptable. If these trucks are clean it's because it happened to be time for that chore.

On the bottom—perhaps the most important—rung are the ranch trucks, so-called because they seldom left the ranch. Their dirt is old and honorable, as are their rust, scratches, scrapes, and screeching doors. They're battle-scarred warriors, afraid of nothing, even if, at times, they aren't able to get out of situations their willing spirit and optimistic drivers get them into.

As Diana and I started walking forward from where we'd parked, we passed mostly ranch trucks.

Except at a roundup or helping with branding, the people of Cottonwood County didn't usually congregate in ranch trucks. They kept their beasts-of-burden ranch trucks on their ranches ... carrying burdens.

But what brought them here had been so urgent their owners stopped work, jumped in their ranch truck, and drove straight here.

Closer, we saw that inside this deep layer of ranch pickups sat a bevy of official vehicles, mostly SUVs, with trucks and vans sprinkled in.

It took getting closer still, past where the curve of a slight swell of land had masked them, to see two more pickups—one working and one a ranch truck.

The working truck bore the name Lukasik Ranch on its green door. The other had no name on it, but I recognized its faded, dented, and pummeled blue surfaces from scoping it out as a potential shield from imminent gunfire last year.

Fun times in Cottonwood County.

As we cut through the ranks of parked pickups, shifting that swell of land to a new angle to reveal more behind it, my attention skidded past the two isolated pickups to an unexpected sight.

A square house to our right.

The structure itself wasn't that surprising, though its solitary situation here, amid what even I recognized as grazing land, was.

Carrying ghost traces of once white paint on its walls and porch, it resembled the last outpost of a deserted civilization. The pyramidical hipped roof sagged at one seam. The symmetrical windows to either side of the front door glinted with glass, the one on the side of the building we could see was boarded up.

The surprise was a riot of roses growing around the house, up the walls and over the porch, like a fairy tale rose thicket to protect—or imprison—the princess. They stubbornly bloomed in a true red far darker than the pink wild roses I knew from growing up in Illinois.

I admired their courage, at the same time they made me sad.

At some point someone carefully planted these bushes for the vibrant red and green against a white house. The white had mostly worn away. The red and green scraggled wildly.

And, now, in a further indignity, police tape attached to the post holding up the left end of the porch.

At that instant, a second unexpected sight drew my attention—the athletic stride of Mike Paycik, headed between scattered vehicles for us.

"What are you doing here, Mike?" Diana asked.

"Got a ride with Jenks after my interview ended."

Past Mike, I saw KWMT-TV's senior cameraman raise a hand in greeting, which we returned. Jenks hoisted his equipment bag—camera out and at the ready—and headed toward the police tape.

That explained Jerry's reference to *not catching* Mike—he'd already left the station.

"Hoped I'd get to look around before you two got here, until Jenks said that had to be Diana coming up behind us like a bullet. You almost beat us here."

She ignored the comment on her driving. "Glad the station's on the story."

"No thanks to Thurston. He turned the police scanner off again to get his beauty rest. Right after you two left for Tom's, Pauly—" His part-time sports stringer. "—and I had to get on that interview. As it was, I got there a minute after the line opened and I thought Pauly would keel over from fear I wouldn't show up. It wasn't until after finishing the interview that I could tell Audrey about this."

Distracted as I was, I asked, "How'd the interview go?"

It was a coup and it was important to Mike.

"Went well." He grinned as he tipped his head, indicating we should follow the path Jenks had taken toward the activity. "Went real well. John was a little nervous at first, but we talked a couple minutes about Wyoming and connected about the weird stuff you encounter when you first leave."

"Like escalators?" Diana said, touching on a past discussion.

"Hey. You know there are two in all of Wyoming, but—"

"I do know, since you told us."

"—turns out John had been on both before going pro, so he was ready for the big leagues. Anyway, afterward, the team's media guy called almost as soon as we'd finished, all excited, saying nobody else had gotten much of anything from John except *Bull Durham* cliché quotes—you know, *We play them one game at a time* and *There's no I in team.* The media guy wants to get clips to their local network affiliate, maybe some other cities in the league, on their website, stuff like that. Haeburn will go along. *It's only sports.*"

That last part was a credible imitation of our station manager.

"We're not even going to run the whole interview until the weekend. I get snippets in the next few days." Mike concluded, "You look confused, Elizabeth."

"Not about any of that. It's no less than I expected and when those other stations get a look at your work, they'll be knocking at your door. No, don't deny it. John's not the only one ready for the big leagues." Glancing toward the house again, I added, "But I am confused. I thought a grazing association was like a ditch."

I'd learned about irrigation ditches and their importance to Wyoming, especially ranchers, as the conduit for essential irrigation. Also about organizations called ditch companies, which united the landowners who shared a ditch, and the ditch boss responsible for the water getting where it belonged.

From what I'd heard, grazing associations ran along similar lines, with a group of ranchers going together to buy or lease acreage for grazing—dividing costs and sharing benefits in the same proportion.

This house represented something I hadn't expected, since all I'd heard about grazing associations was ... well, grazing.

"Sort of similar," Mike said. "What's confusing?"

"Grazing associations have clubhouses?"

We cleared the last pickup as I gestured toward the house and the entire scene before us.

From its anchor on the house's porch post, police tape extended toward our left, forming a large, lumpy off-limits oval. Within it, an expanse of screening blocked all view of an area about the size of a large pickup truck. Crime scene personnel came and went from behind the screen.

Everyone else's attention focused toward that screening.

Everyone else included Shelton talking with Tom near a knot of law enforcement from multiple jurisdictions, judging from the variety of uniforms.

Another group, this one civilian, congregated well to our left, near where police tape enclosed those first two pickups in its thin, yellow arms.

My attention pulled away from the scene when Mike laughed, because that familiar sound had an unexpected edge to it.

He looked back in the direction we'd come, leaving me the back of his head to try to decipher the edge.

Diana glanced at him, perhaps she'd heard it, too. When she spoke, though, she gave no sign of it.

"It's not a clubhouse, Elizabeth. This used to be part of a ranch. When the owner sold, he got more money selling parcels to various buyers than he would have for the place as a whole. This section wasn't as sought after. The association got a good deal on the land. This house came with it. It's used for supplies and such now."

"How have the roses survived with nobody living here?" I wondered.

"There's a spring—that's why they picked this spot for the house."

I expected local knowledge from Diana. But Mike, who'd been away playing college and pro football for a decade and a half, being the source for that information had me asking, "How do you know?"

I caught Diana taking another glance at him.

Without that I'm not sure I would have heard anything deeper in his tone. "Because my great-great-grandparents started this ranch and built that house, my great-grandmother planted those roses, and my grandmother tended them until the day she died."

"This... this is your family ranch."

Chapter Seven

I STUMBLED OVER the words and felt as if I'd nearly stumbled physically, too.

Or possibly blundered. Right into his past.

The huge house he lived in and its surrounding substantial acreage, which he leased to nearby ranchers, were purchased with earnings as an NFL player with the Chicago Bears, supplemented by good investments. I knew that.

I also knew he'd grown up on a struggling family ranch that his father sold.

Leaving that family ranch had broken his boy's heart. It had nearly broken his relationship with his father, too, though that seemed to have improved, if not completely healed.

He had never told me the family ranch's name, never detailed its history, never indicated what part of the county it was in, even.

One other fact I'd known about Mike's family ranch was it was broken up when his father sold it, so it no longer existed as a ranch for Mike to buy back with his football money, instead of the one he had now.

Standing here, on what had once been Paycik land, it struck me I didn't even know if he'd tried.

"This was part of the family place." The care he took to make his answer offhand undercut the attempt.

"This was where you grew up?"

"*Here?* No."

His emphatic dismissal struck us all as funny.

One of those moments that wasn't truly funny, but with the group reacting as if it were, it became funny. And relieved the tension.

When we were done laughing, he said, "It didn't look quite this bad then, but no, our house—and the place where my grandparents lived when they got older—is over that ridge." He pointed to the southeast. "Grandma came back to fuss with the roses almost every day. They were really rare around here when they were first planted and surviving like they have…"

"They're amazing."

They also explained Tamantha's comments about picking flowers here with Mike's permission. The ranch had been sold, but to some the roses still belonged to the Paycik's.

"Yeah. Most days Grandpa came back with her. They left some of their things here, including an old record player and records. With the wind right, you could hear the records playing, and they'd dance together on the porch. I watched them a few times until Mom caught me." His faint smile faded and he cleared his throat. "Good to see the roses still here. Though the circumstances…"

Mike turned toward the crime scene, shutting the door on memories. Following his lead, so did we.

I saw Tom still in the company of Sergeant Shelton near a section of police tape fluttering busily.

They stood in earnest conversation at the western side of the police tape enclosure, facing away from us. With any luck, that would continue.

Small groups of civilians dotted the northeast curve of the police tape ring. More men than women. They wore cowboy hats—the majority—or ball caps, shadowing their eyes from the bright sun.

"Grazing association members?" I asked with a nod toward that group.

"A lot of them are. Not all," Diana said.

I recognized a few from events around the county, including a search for a missing man last fall. One who'd been involved in that search, though, I'd already known.

Plus, he wasn't part of the group. He stood just inside the police tape under the watchful eyes of two deputies, Richard Alvaro and Lloyd Sampson.

He was a rancher named Hiram Poppinger, widely known as an eccentric. When Cottonwood County, Wyoming, calls you eccentric, that's saying something.

It was his battered ranch pickup I'd recognized.

Inside the tape, the screening cut off the view from north to south. Whatever it masked—and it was a pretty good guess it included a body—was in an otherwise open area.

"Is Hiram Poppinger in the grazing association?"

"Yep," Mike said.

"Yet, he's been separated. And look where his truck is."

"Inside the crime scene. He found the body?" Mike suggested.

I moved slightly closer to Hiram and his escorts, not directly facing them, showing no overt interest.

Even without looking at him, I had an image of a bright reddish-orange vest encasing Hiram's torso—startling the eye against his otherwise subdued, if not downright drab attire—burned into my retina. Somehow, it suited him. It reminded me of portraits of men in the American Revolutionary era with their button-straining waistcoats. In those times, a pot-belly indicated the wearer's wealth—enough to eat to develop a potbelly—and I found that subtle bragging rather endearing.

I put aside Hiram's sartorial choices and shuffled another foot closer.

This could get tricky.

Not only to avoid attention from Alvaro and Sampson, plus Tom and Shelton, but now a third threat I'd spotted on the far side of the civilian group.

It was Needham Bender, publisher and editor of the local paper, the *Sherman Independence*.

I liked and enjoyed Needham as a person. I feared and respected him as a rival newshound. Especially because the *Independence*'s reporting in its twice-weekly editions frequently scooped KWMT-TV.

I didn't want Needham zooming over here—which he would do if he thought I was on to something—and hearing anything Hiram said.

Of course, at the moment, I couldn't hear Hiram.

"Mm-hmm. Hiram finding the body could explain a lot," Diana murmured as she and Mike joined me in my new position.

In fact, Diana took an extra two steps toward Hiram.

Naturally, Mike and I had to do the same to hear her next words. "You know, this grazing association's one of the county's strongest."

"Is it? That's interesting." No risk, no potential gain. I added two more steps. The trio inside the police tape came into range of my peripheral vision. "Out of all the grazing associations in all the counties in all the world for this to happen, huh? And there must be a good number of them in Cottonwood County."

"There are." Diana matched my steps and added another. "Lots cross county lines, too."

"Ah," I said softly as Mike and I joined her, because Hiram Poppinger's voice was audible now.

Lloyd Sampson said something to Hiram, who cocked his head like a grumpy, alert, overfed robin in that reddish vest.

"*Victim?* Furman York's no more a victim than a rattlesnake would be. And I'd sooner see him lying there dead than a rattlesnake. If anybody's a victim, it's me. Kept here all day, wastin' my time when I got better things to do. Told you everything there is to tell."

"You haven't explained why you were in that building," Sampson said. "If you took something and Furman York caught you—"

"Him? Catch me stealin'? Hah. Besides, what's in there worth stealin'? You saw I don't have none of those supplies they keep there in my truck."

Richard Alvaro kept his voice too low to distinguish words.

Hiram spat in apparent disgust. Well away from any target, so he was behaving himself. "I already told you, I didn't shoot him. Don't know why Shelton's got you two on me like white on rice."

He received no response. That never bothered Hiram Poppinger.

"And takin' my gun is damned high-handed. Officious, that's what it is. I ain't even fired my gun. Even fools like you can tell that and know I didn't shoot that snake."

A sound followed. That familiar, faint indrawn breath in preparation for someone to speak.

But no words came.

I caught movement in the farthest reaches of my peripheral vision. Without turning my head noticeably, I slued by eyes toward it.

Richard Alvaro's hand was retracting, while his fellow deputy's arm was slightly rebounding, as if from being poked. Or lightly punched.

Interesting.

"Persecution, that's what this is. I was the one as called you," Hiram continued.

"You don't get a gold star for that," Alvaro said. "Calling law enforcement when you find a body is your responsibility as a citizen."

"Could've walked away and pretended I didn't see a thing and you couldn't've proved otherwise, with him over here and in that bit of depression in the middle. If it hadn't been for a glint off that gaudy buckle he wore, I wouldn't have climbed up here and seen what I seen. Where he is, could be nobody'd've seen him for a long, long time. You'd've been dealin' with a skeleton that wouldn't get you any clues at'll. You should be thankin' me for lettin' you get it fresh, so to speak."

Neither deputy followed that suggestion.

"Should've known this is how it would be. Police, deputies, game wardens, you're all alike. Makin' life miserable for the ordinary citizen. You tell that Shelton that I won't stand for none of his nonsense. You tell him—"

A new pickup arrived, distracting Hiram's discourse.

Unlike the others, this pickup didn't park at the end of the line. It drove up the center of the open lane to park right next to a sheriff's department vehicle with a swirl of dust that sent tendrils into the civilian group. I caught a glimpse of the driver's white hair.

"*Him.* That's all this needed," Hiram said. He spat again.

Neither words nor expectoration was necessarily a severe indictment of the new arrival. Hiram didn't think much of humanity.

On first impression, though, I might be inclined to agree with him about this newcomer. Because the geometry of our positions meant his grand entrance drew unwelcomed attention to Diana, Mike, and me.

In fact, Tom and Shelton couldn't look toward the newcomer without spotting us.

Maybe they'd be distracted enough by the pickup door opening and...

Nope.

Chapter Eight

WHICH BURNED HOTTER, Shelton's scowl or Tom's?

Tom's. His aimed all at me. Shelton's spread across the three of us.

Tom took half a step. Shelton held his arm, not physically stopping the other half a step, while advising against it.

The movement directed Hiram's attention our way. "*Them.*"

His disgust drew looks from Alvaro and Sampson.

No sense trying to keep a low profile now. I started toward Hiram.

"You can't talk to him." Alvaro stepped in front of the much shorter rancher. "This isn't the beginning of a beautiful friendship, breaking all the rules."

Beautiful friendship? Breaking all the rules? What was he talking—? Oh. *Casablanca?* My reference to *Of all the grazing associations*, replacing *Of all the gin joints…*

I was impressed. First, he'd heard me. Then, he'd connected the reference.

"Elizabeth." Tom made my name a reprimand.

"She's fine," I told him, knowing his main interest. "Tamantha's with the Undlins, making doughnuts. In fact, we're here on her orders."

His scowl eased by a modest percentage at the last sentence.

Shelton's deepened. "Now obey my orders and get out of here."

"We're behind the police tape, not interfering with your scene. Freedom of the press, Sergeant."

"Doesn't give you any right to be on private property."

"Grazing association property," I shot back. "Tom?"

Tom held my gaze a moment, adjudicating my appeal to his authority, then looked away. Following the direction of his gaze, mine landed on Hiram Poppinger.

"Tom's worried about him." Diana's conclusion matched mine.

"Shouldn't he worry about himself?" Mike muttered.

"Yes," I said.

"He knows he didn't do anything."

Mike and I looked at Diana. She gave a slight nod, confirming the unspoken part of her comment would go something like, *but he's not entirely sure about Hiram, who might have gotten himself into a mess.*

"If Hiram…" My part in this unspoken exchange added …*did this and we start investigating, we're not pulling punches to save him.*

"Of course." Diana's nod emphasized her silent addition of *Tom wouldn't expect any different. And if you or anyone has doubt about… oh, anything… this clinches it. Because Tom's more convinced Hiram didn't do this than he is worried that he might be accused of it.*

"Okay," I said. *Yeah, well, how about people worrying what he might be accused of? Not me. Other people. Like his daughter.*

"I think I got that." Mike took off his cowboy hat, wiped his brow and put it back on. "But I sure would like to go back over it."

Diana patted his arm. "We will later."

"Are you three done muttering over there?" Shelton demanded.

"No. But we'll take a timeout." I looked at Tom. "We left it in your court."

"They can stay." His straight, hard look added, *But they better get something done.*

I preferred Diana's non-verbal communication to his.

"Thank you. Now, if we can ask a few questions—?"

"No," Shelton snapped. "Alvaro, Sampson, move that tape. Get these people—these spectators—back."

With the police tape putting us out of conversational range, I looked around and spotted Cagen, a reporter for the *Independence*, among a knot of people nudged back by the police tape. Leaning forward to see around a man with a potbelly, I searched for Cagen's boss without success.

When I straightened, Needham stood beside me, watching with bright-eyed interest.

He knew exactly what I'd been doing.

"That was quite the get-together at Diana's for your folks. Pretty much all the most interesting people in the county." He considered for a beat. "The most interesting who aren't entirely eccentric."

"I didn't think my parents were ready for what Cottonwood County has in the way of top eccentrics."

He grinned. "Nice people, your parents. Can see a real blend of them in you. Proud as Punch of you they are."

I knew they were. Sometimes, though…

That could wait for another day. One without a possible murder.

The sheriff's department certainly treated the scene like a murder. Caution or a reason they weren't sharing?

As if following my train of thought, he said, "Lean pickings on the information front, huh?"

"What do you know about this, Needham?"

"Like you, just got here. Wouldn't think accident, based on this response." He tipped his head toward the scientists behind the screening.

"Shelton told me once that Hiram Poppinger's a lousy shot."

"That screen's not covering sniper distance. Wouldn't need to be much of a shot."

"What about the victim?"

"Dead man is Furman York." I noticed he didn't say victim. "Foreman of the Lukasik Ranch, which belongs to this grazing association."

"Did you know York?"

"Wouldn't say I did."

"So, not a friend?"

He confirmed what I'd picked up in his careful words. "Wouldn't say a friend, for sure."

I turned to him. "What are you not telling me?"

"Lots." He smiled. "For starters—"

Even before a voice interrupted Needham, he'd stopped, because his attention had gone to somewhere over my shoulder.

I turned, too.

Movement among pockets of observers outside the east end of the police tape caught my eye. Clumps coalesced, forming an identifiable center around one man, while maintaining ragged fringes of those not persuaded to be drawn in.

That one man had white hair combed back and flowing to his collar. The white hair glimpsed from the late-arriving pickup, I guessed.

He was tall and thin. Tall, with more of the height coming from his legs and neck than most people. Thin, of the kind that gave me the impression I could see the ridge of his femur press inside against loose-fitting jeans. The sort of bony thinness of Abraham Lincoln that brought to mind the word *gaunt*.

Not that he otherwise reminded me of Lincoln. That honor belonged to Tom. And, coming from Illinois, I know my Lincoln.

With Lincoln, my attention went to his eyes. With this man, my attention went to his mouth, thin and wide.

"Norman Clay Lukasik," Mike said in a low voice. He'd come up beside me when Needham and I shifted our attention to the newcomer. "Furman York worked for him. Though you could say it started the other way around."

I'd heard Lukasik owned a major ranch. He was a defense attorney. He'd long been in demand around the region for high-profile cases. Frequently with the kind of client that made you think, "Who on earth would defend *him*?" Or, not to be biased, *her*?

Before I could ask Mike how and why Lukasik had worked for York, the lawyer raised his voice to courtroom levels.

"Furman York was not a happy man. Despite all the tonics here of open spaces—" His long arms spread wide. "—blue sky—" Those arms now stretched up as if he held the blue heavens aloft. "—and good companionship." He encompassed the gathering with one sweeping arm. Then, with a glint that invited his viewers to join the joke, he swept the other arm, indicating cattle in a nearby field.

A few chuckles rumbled briefly, then faded.

With their fading drawing away any element of levity, Lukasik solemnly continued in a low, throbbing voice, "We shall all hope that his eternal rest brings him the peace he, sadly, seemed to lack in life."

No one joined his hope by word or gesture, though shifting of work boots raised the dust to a level that might indicate discomfort.

As if unaware of the reaction, which I doubted, Lukasik raised his voice again. "This is abominable. For a man's body to be left on the dirt like an animal. I demand he be accorded the respect that would be given to an animal."

Had he misspoken?

Didn't he want his former employee to be treated *better* than an animal?

Or did he mean it the denigrating way he'd said it?

I picked up a murmur of *animal*—impossible to trace its source. It sounded less like the murmurer's objection to the treatment of York than confirmation that the description fit.

Norman Clay Lukasik reminded me of an old-school actor my parents had taken the family to see when I was a kid. He'd projected his voice to every corner of that theater.

This guy managed the trick even outdoors in Wyoming, with lusty competition from the wind.

"This is *my* employee who has been murdered. My long-time employee." He started with long strides toward the police tape, aiming directly for where Hiram Poppinger stood between the two deputies.

Lloyd Sampson said, "Sir, you need to stay back."

Lukasik ignored him. "The foreman of Lukasik Ranch, operating in his capacity as *my* ranch's representative. *My*—"

"My crime scene."

At Shelton's flat words from a distance, Alvaro stepped directly in front of Norman Clay Lukasik, only the tape separating them.

Lukasik stopped advancing.

He was smart enough to recognize he might have gone through or around Lloyd Sampson, not Alvaro.

Then he compensated for stopping by projecting his voice even more.

"Furman York was my trusted foreman—"

Hiram, his mouth working like he'd swallowed something sour, snorted. I thought at *trusted*, rather than *foreman*.

"—for more years than many of you have been alive. Not—" He dropped his voice. "—including you, Sergeant Shelton."

Shelton remained impassive at the possible slight. Though how it could be a slight when the speaker's trunk clearly had more rings around it, I didn't know.

"My foreman," Lukasik belted out.

"Impressive," I muttered to Needham. "I wouldn't want to be standing next to him."

"Not even his best performance. Should have seen him at the beginning, in all his glory." The dryness of *his glory* would fan a wildfire.

Hiram tried to advance, stopped when Lloyd clasped his arm. Richard still separated him from Lukasik.

"The foreman you're boo-hooin' about didn't do diddly squat for your cattle numbers. How long you been stuck at near enough the same number to make no difference? Some foreman. Anybody who'd hire Furman York to clean out a barn, much less be foreman deserves what he gets. More like foreman of your playpen than a real ranch. Ranching's not your business, not your livelihood. Never has been. Not like the rest of us."

"Good thing it's not my livelihood. With the herd barely staying even, much less growing like you'd expect from the births, it's no way to get rich. Don't understand how you all do it. Oh, that's right—" Lukasik smirked and his voice turned sharp. "—you don't."

He jerked his head toward Tom. "Burrell with the paving company, that neighbor of his working at the airport. Makes us all part-time ranchers." That effort to include himself in their community twanged with insincerity. "Your other jobs just aren't as lucrative as mine."

Ah, now that sounded sincere. And self-congratulatory.

"None of us puttin' murderers back on the street, either," Hiram snapped. "We can live with ourselves."

A low sound like a vibrating wire indicated agreement from others. No one spoke it, though.

The upper corners of the lawyer's lips retracted. "I have no trouble living with myself when someone I represent to my fullest ability is found not guilty by a jury of his or her peers. That's what our justice system is all about. Innocent until proven guilty."

"Or until you buy off a juror."

"Watch it, Hiram." Sharp and short, those words sounded nothing like Lukasik's others. Out of control? Or a deliberate effect? "I've been thinking a case out of criminal court could be interesting. Slander has a lot of appeal. And those few acres of yours would make a nice little addition to my ranch. Have to be brought up to my standards, of course, which the house couldn't be, so the bulldozer—"

"Why you—" Hiram's surge forward stretched Lloyd's arm to the max. The deputy held on.

Good thing he doesn't have a shotgun now, I thought.

Didn't need to say it, since I saw similar thoughts reflected in other faces.

Tom was right. Hiram might be in trouble.

Chapter Nine

CONFIRMATION OF THAT came far faster than I could have guessed.

Though not immediately.

"Get him over there, away from the tape," Shelton directed Lloyd. He told Lukasik, "You get back, too. Quit with the stump speeches."

Before Lukasik could object, Shelton turned his back and gestured for Tom to return to where they'd been at the start.

With a self-satisfied smile convincing enough to mask that he obeyed Shelton, Lukasik pivoted away from the tape.

Almost as if by accident, he pivoted in our direction.

"Ah, representatives of the media. Michael Paycik, good to see you, even under these circumstances."

"Norman." Mike's handshake was nearly as brief as his greeting. "These are co-workers from KWMT—Elizabeth Margaret Danniher, Diana Stendahl. You know Needham."

Needham crossed his arms over his chest and stared at the man.

Lukasik smiled, unperturbed.

After the lawyer acknowledged Diana with a nod, I came under the spotlight of Lukasik's gaze.

I'd dismissed his eyes too easily.

They weren't Lincolnesque, yet they had power, along with his mouth.

"Elizabeth Margaret Danniher." The way he said it had me searching my conscience for wrong-doing. For a fraction of a second, still long enough to recognize his power.

Power stemming from a talent and expertise at eliciting the response he wanted.

Good thing I had experience and skill at resisting.

"Sorry, you have the advantage of me." I extended my hand. A handshake can convey considerable information.

A flicker of annoyance showed in his face. Good. It put him off balance.

Not long, though.

He had experience and skill at resisting, too.

He met my hand with his large one—bony, pampered.

"Norman Clay Lukasik, owner of the Lukasik Ranch where this poor soul so brutally murdered worked. Also a practitioner of law."

His handshake was firm and accompanied by his left hand gripping around my forearm. Lightly, but conveying it could tighten if he chose, intimating he could maneuver me as he chose.

Without releasing his handshake, I stepped sharply to the side— not away from that hold by his left hand, toward it. Fast enough that he couldn't adjust and it bent his left wrist back sharply, possibly painfully. He released that hold.

We ended the handshake at the same time.

His metaphorical man-spreading tactic, trying to take up all the space in the Jelicho Table to make me feel small and insignificant, hadn't worked. Unlikely he'd give up. Something to look forward to with our next encounter.

"Do you know for a fact he was murdered?" I asked.

"Ah, facts." He dismissed the paltriness of facts and possibly me, with an open-handed sweep of his arm, returning to group of civilians.

I might have been tempted to make him pay for that dismissal—of facts, not of me—except activity claimed my attention.

One of the scientific types came from behind the screening and gestured for Shelton to join him.

Shelton said something to Tom, who remained where he was, then went to the scientific type. He listened for some time, all the while staring at Tom. Absentmindedly? The closest place to rest his eyes? Or with intent?

Even after Shelton gave a brief nod and the scientific type returned behind the screen, he remained where he was.

Shelton dropped his head for a beat, then, as he raised it, he surged forward.

Not toward Tom.

Not toward us.

Hiram.

"Turn around, Hiram," Shelton said abruptly.

"What for?" The older man didn't move.

"To put handcuffs on you. You're going to the sheriff's department.

"What for? Because I'm tellin' the truth? If that isn't just like you deputies. Tryin' to shut up somebody tellin' the truth."

Shelton sent Alvaro a look I couldn't interpret. Alvaro, though, didn't look confused.

"Because we're detaining you as a material witness. You said you know things. And we want to know them, too. You won't turn around? I'll cuff you in front."

Shelton reached for the older man's arm.

Hiram put both hands behind him, like a naughty kid.

Alvaro secured one handcuff faster than I could see or Hiram could feel. He had to work harder for the second, with Hiram reacting.

So that had been the communique from Shelton.

"Hey! Hey!" Hiram protested. "You dirty ba—"

"Watch it, Hiram, or you'll make me testy."

Shelton had been testy as long as I'd known him. Apparently, he thought he had at least one more level of testiness to achieve.

We—along with the other observers—watched them load the still-protesting Hiram into a sheriff's department truck.

Shelton returned to Tom, exchanging words we couldn't hear.

They stepped out of the police-taped area on the opposite side from the spectators and started along its perimeter, heading east, before disappearing from sight because of the screening.

The vehicle holding Hiram started, pulling attention back to it.

It drove overland to avoid other vehicles, and the knot around Norman Clay Lukasik loosened with a shifting of feet. Perhaps recognizing he was about to lose his audience, he made it seem as if he'd broken up the gathering. He clapped one man on the shoulder and said for us all, "Rusty. Glad you're here. I wanted to talk to you."

The rest drifted away, with a few mini-knots lingering.

They acted as if taking Hiram Poppinger to the sheriff's department settled everything.

Shelton's intent?

With a word to Mike and Diana, I moved away to call the Undlins. Zeb answered.

"They're both elbow deep in doughnut dough. Tamantha maybe a little higher than her elbow. First batch was quality taste. These two weren't pleased with the shapes. I won't argue."

"Sounds good, Zeb. I, uh, wonder…"

"Yeah," he groused without heat. "I'll put the speakerphone on and hold it near Iris."

"Hello, dear," his wife said a bit breathlessly. "Everything's fine."

"We're leaving the grazing association soon. I could come back now, but—"

I heard Tamantha's emphatic *No*, then more words. She must have been at the other counter, because her usually precise words were muffled. Iris said, "Tamantha says you should not come back. You should keep working. When we finish with these doughnuts, we'll have supper, something nutritious like a good salad, because they have been nibbling more than a bit—yes, salad for you, too, Zeb. You've been way past nibbling. So, you see, everything's fine here, Elizabeth. You keep doing what you need to do, we'll be with her at your house if it gets to be her bedtime."

I'd said good-bye and was reporting this update, while Mike salivated remotely over Iris Undlin's doughnuts, which he'd previously sampled, when a voice from behind us said, "Those do sound good."

We all spun around.

An excellent reminder to be aware of who was around us when we talked. This had been innocuous doughnut talk, but you never knew.

"Jennifer, what are you doing here?" Diana asked.

Jennifer Lawton possessed computer skills—and a network of

likeminded buddies—that largely went to waste in her job as a KWMT-TV news aide, but were integral to our group's investigations.

"Didn't he tell Elizabeth I was coming out with Walt when Audrey sent him to cover the shooting? I could have sworn he did."

"Who?" My question was distracted, because I'd spotted Shelton and Tom, now on the east side of the police tape loop, heading toward the first clump of official vehicles. Spectators left in a steady stream.

"Audrey sent Walt?" Mike's disapproval came through clearly.

"He's all right," Diana said. "More than all right."

Jennifer said, "Audrey tried to persuade Thurston to come out. Of course everybody knew he wouldn't and we were right. Too much dust, bad for his hair, he said."

Fighting upstream against Walt's competence or Thurston's obsession with his hair, I asked, "Who could you swear had told me you were coming?"

"Jerry. When—"

"Why would Jerry tell me you were coming?"

"I'm telling you. I told him I'd bring something out to you. He'd asked me for your number and I listened while he told you he wanted you to come in to see something. You said you were busy—and I knew what *that* meant. What was it that guy said in those movies you made us all watch last month, Mike? The ones with the guy in the hat."

I heard them in the background of my attention, as Tom got in the front passenger seat of Shelton's vehicle, with the sergeant taking the overland route to jump ahead of civilians.

"The game's afoot. And it wasn't *those movies*. It was the entire collection of Basil Rathbone as Sherlock Holmes. To show you computers do not solve all mysteries."

"I like the newer guy. He uses computers."

Tom wasn't in custody. But if he'd driven here and Shelton insisted on him leaving in an official vehicle...

"Benedict Cumberbatch? He's good. No Rathbone, but—"

"Hey," I interrupted, the official vehicle out of sight, leaving behind no answers to my wondering. "Quit with the movies. What about this something you told Jerry you'd bring out to me?"

"Oh, yeah. He was wound up about some footage. I loaded it on my phone."

With Jennifer holding her phone, we scrummed around her, trying to block the glare of the sun.

The camera focused on Odessa Vincennes' face as I began my question about verifying what they put in the brochures delivered to seniors. Then came Mike's interruption.

There's been a shooting at Tom's grazing association.

The break before his next words seemed shorter than in real life.

Not Tom. It wasn't Tom. It was the foreman from another ranch. Guy named Furman York. Looks like murder.

On the small screen the woman froze, not blinking or moving while my abrupt departure was caught as a blur in a corner of the screen. She stayed that way another full minute, until Jerry's voice came on saying, "Sorry Elizabeth had to leave for that emergency. As she said, she'll get in touch with you—" He turned off the camera.

We all remained huddled around Jennifer's phone, as if awaiting more.

"I don't get it," Jennifer said. "Why was Jerry wound up about this? That woman was surprised, so what?"

Mike shrugged agreement. "Shocked at a murder in little Cotton-wood County."

"Or maybe she'd heard about your reputation for attracting them, Elizabeth, and then to have it played out in front of her..." Diana suggested.

"Very funny. Jennifer, did Jerry say why he wanted us to watch this?"

"Something about Lady Charlotte and a curse."

"Lady Charl—? *The Lady of Shalott?*" I heard my voice rise with surprise. *Jerry* knew Tennyson?

"Maybe. Who's that?"

Absently, I explained about the lady in the tower, cursed to weave reflections of the world, until she dares to look directly at Lancelot. Then the curse really gets busy, the mirror cracking, and the lady dying before she can reach Camelot and Lancelot.

"They thought that was a good story?" Jennifer said indignantly. "Just because the woman *looks* at a guy she dies? Why shouldn't she look, huh? That stinks."

"I agree," Diana said as we all started toward her truck. "But the point now is we're not seeing anything extraordinary in this footage. We'll have to ask Jerry about it. What next? Do we go to the station to ask him? Or go to O'Hara Hill to see Mrs. P?"

Caution settled over Jennifer. "Mrs. P? What for?"

Diana didn't answer directly. "We should go see Mrs. P if Elizabeth wants to understand about Norman Clay Lukasik and Furman York."

I perked up at that. "If there's history I should know, tell me."

I remembered now that when I asked her at Tom's if she knew anything about Furman York she hadn't answered.

She shook her head. "It's from well before my time. I could only give you half-remembered rumors. Probably the same for Mike."

"Is there a lot to know?"

"Quit trying to lead me into telling you more." This was the problem with good friends. They knew your tactics. "For the core history, Mrs. P is the absolute best source."

"Let's go see Jerry," Jennifer suggested.

"That's not a bad idea," Mike said as we reached Diana's truck and he invited me to ride shotgun. Appropriate, though maybe not the best term under the circumstances.

That didn't distract me from amusement at Jennifer and Mike being wary of visiting their former teacher and principal. Barely five feet tall, the woman still wielded a big stick—literally in the form of a long pointer and figuratively in the memories of her former students.

"We couldn't get to the station before he's occupied with prep for the Five. We might catch him between newscasts, but there's no way we can do that *and* get to O'Hara Hill, because I need to get home to see about Tamantha. Mrs. P is the winner."

Chapter Ten

JENNIFER DIDN'T CONCEDE. "If Hiram's the killer, the sheriff's department already has him, and there's nothing left for us to do."

"That's a big if," Mike said.

"A *very* big if." Three looks came my way.

"Why'd you say it that way?" Jennifer asked.

"I noticed something. It could mean a few things, including nothing. I want to think about the best possibility more."

"That's it?" Mike asked. "You want to think about it more? Not tell us what it is?"

"Yep. I need to think it through."

"That's mean," Jennifer declared.

"It's payback for saying she needs to talk to Mrs. P," Mike said.

I could, of course, have easily refuted his accusation with logic. However, something else had caught my attention.

"Diana, you're awfully quiet." Also, she'd taken off from the grazing association at sub-supersonic speeds.

"Deflection," Mike muttered.

I ignored that. "Diana?"

"Leaving the grazing association, I thought I recognized a vehicle from the station parking lot." She looked in her rearview mirror. "Can't see it anymore."

No surprise she couldn't. Her truck and the others kicked up cones of dust behind us like the parachutes that brake land-speed-record-setting cars.

I wasn't about to keep her talking about the topic. Not while she was driving. Especially with striking out toward the western part of the county where the roads' degree of difficulty jumped up because, along with being narrow, rough, and frequently unpaved, they started the precipitous climb toward the Rockies.

I would, however, keep talking to distract *me* while she was driving.

"We know how, where, and when—approximately, anyway—on this shooting. Before we get to why or who did it, let's start with the other who—who is this guy? The victim. Furman York. Beyond being a ranch foreman at the Lukasik Ranch. And connected, through Lukasik Ranch, to the grazing association that Tom's chairman of. Needham started to tell me when Lukasik intruded. There must be some stuff you can tell me before we get to Mrs. P's."

At the unexpected silence, I slued around in my seat to see Jennifer, who shrugged, and Mike, who looked out the side window.

"Okay, you guys, spill it."

Looks zinged around the inside of the truck, all of them avoiding me.

"I don't know about him," Jennifer said. "I thought that's why you're all insisting on going to Mrs. P's."

"It is a long story. There's a lot of history to it." Mike's evasiveness said he wasn't going to be easy to draw. He confirmed that with his next sentence. "Besides, we need to think it through."

Payback.

With a fairly open and even stretch of road ahead—I tried, "Diana—?"

"I didn't remember a thing about him initially. A few things at the grazing association stirred memories of hearing stories as a kid. Mrs. P is the one to give you the background. The rest of us were too young to know details."

"Especially me," Jennifer said. "I don't know any details at all."

Zeroing in, I held her gaze. "Let's start with what you *do* know."

"What everybody else knows. He—"

"Wait for Mrs. P," Diana interrupted.

"If you tell me what you know, we'll spend less time at Mrs. Parens' house and that will trim the chances of your aunt spotting us there," I said to Mike.

His Aunt Gee—Gisella Decker—and Emmaline Parens were long-time next-door neighbors and had a relationship intricately balancing rivalry, cooperation, and mutual respect. A trip to one house required either a trip to the other or silent reproach to compensate. It was brutal.

"Ha," he said with a carefree laugh. "She won't spot us at all. She's at a convention for a couple more days."

"What kind of convention?" Jennifer asked.

"Dispatchers. The actual convention's done. She and her cronies stay over a day or two. They say it's to compare notes and such from the classes, but I suspect it's to drink margaritas. Either way, she's not around to see us at Mrs. P's today, so she can't get on me—us—for not seeing her."

Rats.

"C'mon," I pleaded. "What'll it hurt if I know a little beforehand."

"No," Mike said solemnly, as if this were his real reason when he'd already revealed it was payback. "I agree with Diana. Get the whole story at once. We might give you bad information that would start you down the wrong path."

"You think I'm not capable of sorting through what I'm told?" I asked sweetly.

"Not saying that, but why not get the full and accurate story to start by waiting a little longer? When we get to O'Hara Hill, we'll drop you off at Mrs. P's. You have a good talk with her, and we'll wait at Ernie's—"

Before I could protest his plan to avoid having his feet held to the fire by his former teacher and instead go nosh at one of the few restaurants in that part of the county—though still very good—Diana did it for me.

"We all need a refresher on that history." She kept talking over Mike's groan. "If we're trying to figure out what happened today, we all need to know as much as possible."

Chapter Eleven

EMMALINE PARENS GREETED us without surprise.

She proved her grasp of our motivation—and the efficiency of the county grapevine—when she escorted us into the front room of her small, tidy house. This room's walls were lined with Cottonwood County history and school photos, floor to ceiling.

"We came from the grazing association," I said, mostly to relieve her of the burden of starting the topic.

"Of course." She picked up the pointer that never failed to make Mike nervous, even though she focused on me now. "You are familiar with the history of Rock Springs, are you not?"

That came out of left field.

"Which Rock Springs?" I doubted Mrs. P would mention one outside of Wyoming, but surely others around the country made it a reasonable question while I tried to figure out what this had to do with a man being killed at the grazing association this morning.

"Rock Springs, Wyoming. It is in the southern part of the state, along I-80, and in the western third. Here." Her pointer connected with a spot on a large wall map.

Oh, *that* Rock Springs.

I had nothing.

Ripping off the bandage, I shook my head. "Not familiar with its history at all."

A faint groan came from the direction of Jennifer at this open invitation to Mrs. P.

"From its founding and beyond, Rock Springs, Wyoming, boomed with railroads and mining, as did, indeed, much of the state."

"Rock Springs has another claim to fame," Mike said. "Before he became a famous outlaw, Butch Cassidy worked there as a butcher—that's how he got the nickname. Butch. Butcher. Get it?"

"Got it."

Mrs. P corrected him. "That is *possibly* how he attained that nickname before becoming an *in*famous outlaw. More pertinent to its history as a community, Rock Springs was the site of a mob attack on Chinese miners in 1885, in which nearly thirty were killed, while their homes and businesses were looted and burned."

"The Rock Springs Massacre." Jennifer appeared surprised she remembered that.

Mrs. P nodded once at her former student, remaining solemn. "A deplorable example of striking out at a minority in times of stress. However, it is more recent events that prompted me to ask if you are aware of Rock Springs' history, Elizabeth. In the late 1970s, another boom and its attendant ills took hold of the town. In this instance it was oil. Corruption and illicit activities formed the greater part of the town's reputation in that period. In 1978, the head of law enforcement shot one of his undercover officers in the head while they were in a car with two other officers."

"An officer was shot by his supervisor? With two more officers right there? Holy—" I bit it off. Holy moly wouldn't do the circumstances justice and Mrs. P would object to anything stronger.

"It was all over the news," Mike said. "*Washington Post, 60 Minutes, New York Times.* You should've seen all the coverage."

"*Now* you remember all this?"

He was unabashed by my accusatory question. "It was well before my time. I did a project on it in high school."

As if that excused him.

"Indeed," Mrs. Parens said, "Michael produced a colorful project, albeit one that called for greater care in separating verifiable information from sensationalistic speculation. The head of law enforcement was tried for murder. His defense maintained the dead officer had been reaching for his gun and thus the defendant shot in self-defense.

The jury acquitted him, perhaps on the basis that he was an extraordinarily fast draw and thus able to draw, shoot, and kill the other officer, whose hand was not on his own gun."

Whoa. Self-defense when the other guy didn't have a hand on a gun? Mrs. Parens' historical references seldom slid into boring, but this might be the best yet.

Still, I tried to keep my head on the current case.

"What does this have to do with—? Was Norman Clay Lukasik involved in the case—?"

"He was not," Mrs. Parens said even before the math in my head sorted dates and ballpark ages. "What prompted that question?"

"Association, I supposed. Sounds like the kind of case he'd defend and he was at the grazing association. Said today's victim was his employee. Foreman."

"I cannot provide any corroboration, though neither can I envision a reason for him to be untruthful on that point. I can, however, share with you other background if you are interested."

Chastised for wandering from her lesson plan, I responded with a heartfelt, "Absolutely."

"Norman Clay Lukasik *was* involved with a case in O'Hara Hill approximately thirty years ago that stirred comparisons, especially as to the level of sensationalism, with Rock Springs."

"*O'Hara Hill?* But it's…" Tiny. Sleepy. Boring. I decided against any of those. "So peaceful."

"It was, indeed, peaceful before that period. And it is again. It was not at that particular time. Have you wondered why O'Hara Hill warranted a sheriff's department substation?"

That was where Mike's Aunt Gee reigned as head dispatcher, with deputies rotating through on temporary assignment from the main office in Sherman, both to learn this part of the county and to be schooled by Gisella Decker.

She ruled the substation so absolutely, I'd never given the reason for its existence a thought. It was like gravity. It operated smoothly without needing to think about it.

"Because it's the second largest town in the county?"

"That might be the explanation people now would like to present." A glance in the direction of Aunt Gee's house intimated one of the people she referred to. "However, at the time the substation was established, it was because O'Hara Hill was known as the Rock Springs of Northern Wyoming. Also, our town temporarily had a larger population than Sherman. It shrank after the promised oil was found to be both less plentiful and less accessible than early speculators believed."

"There's oil near O'Hara Hill?"

"West of town," Mike said.

Since west of town essentially meant the Absaroka Range of the Rocky Mountains, I understood the accessibility issue.

"As you study Wyoming history since its formation as a territory—" Mrs. Parens' gaze moved across each of her former students before resting on me. "—you will recognize a pattern of boom and bust that has endured into the present. The cycle affects cattle ranching, although not as dramatically as it does mining and oil production, including the sharp decline in coal leading to near ghost towns in parts of our state.

"O'Hara Hill is fortunate to have avoided that fate. It was not clear at all that it would. The boom brought on by oil speculation swept over us with the force of a tsunami. As with a tsunami, the immediate effects are dramatic, however, the aftereffects can be more enduring and detrimental. When the boom busted—or in my tsunami metaphor, the waters receded—debris, destruction, and devastation remained for years.

"However, I recognize from your restlessness—" Unfair. I'd moved on the chair. No fidgeting at all. "—that you are eager to connect these happenings to the current matter drawing your attention."

On the other hand, her unfair accusation opened an opportunity to hurry this along... "Tamantha is staying with me—well, with the Undlins right now—while Tom talks to Sergeant Shelton."

Grimness slid into Mrs. P's expression. "Is Sergeant Shelton talking with Thomas as the equivalent of the earlier phrase used by the

British that a person was helping the authorities with their enquiries?"

Jennifer sat up. "What does that mean? They say that in old movies when it's clear they suspect the heck out of the guy. It wasn't at all the way *we* help the sheriff's department with their investigations."

"They wouldn't say we help," Diana muttered.

"It's a euphemism," Mike told Jennifer. "They used it when they were questioning somebody, but weren't ready to arrest him yet."

Jennifer swiveled to me. "They're going to arrest Tom?"

"No." I said it with absolute certainty, built on a foundation of doubt and fear.

Irrational doubt and fear.

Pretty sure it was irrational.

Just because the previous hierarchy of the Cottonwood County Sheriff's Department had demonstrated its ability to have its head where it did not anatomically belong for extended periods of time did not mean this one would.

I hoped.

I glanced at Diana, probably for reassurance that Sheriff Russ Conrad would never do such a thing, since she knew him so much better than the rest of us.

She didn't meet my look.

Not reassuring.

"Thomas shall not be arrested," Mrs. P proclaimed. I wished Shelton and Conrad were subject to her declarations. Throw in the county attorney, too. "However, I now have a clearer understanding of your impatience."

She straightened her already erect posture and went into teaching mode … which wasn't all that different from her other modes.

"Under the influence of rampant oil speculation, O'Hara Hill erupted into a landscape of rapidly constructed buildings best called shanties. Their redeeming quality was that when the bust followed, they proved relatively easy to dismantle and nature has largely covered their scars. These shanties housed offices, shops, restaurants, bars, and other establishments. Workers drawn by the lure of employment took accommodations in their vehicles, tents, at times on the streets, though that, most often, was as a result of their consumption of alcohol or drugs.

"As you likely can imagine, most of this influx of population was male. In addition, a number of females arrived who provided entertainment of various sorts, some public and some private. A much smaller number of females came as office employees of the more stable companies drawn by the speculation. This last group had the most difficulty acquiring suitable housing. While their bosses could afford the exorbitant rents being charged by our townspeople, these office workers' pay was insufficient for that. Some rented as far away as Sherman or even Red Lodge, then joined together for the drive here each day, with all the inconveniences such a car-pooling arrangement can inflict for those expected to work as long as their bosses considered necessary.

"Through attendance at our local churches, a few found rooms with families who would not otherwise have considered opening their homes to strangers, even with the inducement of rent."

"Aunt Gee," Mike said, frowning. "I remember hearing something..."

"Yes. At that time, Gisella had recently been widowed. She rented a room to a fine young woman in a mutually beneficial arrangement. Leah Pedroke provided Gisella with company, for they were quite compatible, as well as extra income as she prepared to provide for herself."

Uncharacteristically, Mrs. P paused, appearing caught in memories the rest of us did not share.

"On a Saturday in late August, Leah called to tell Gisella that she had to work late and would miss supper. When she had not returned home by midnight, Gisella called the office. No one answered. Gisella knew where the supervisor of that office rented a room and called there. He said they had dinner brought in and worked steadily until Leah left at ten-thirty, shortly before he did. Now deeply concerned, Gisella called the sheriff's department in Sherman.

"She also contacted several of us in the area. We all hurriedly dressed and searched the route Leah normally walked to and from the office. We were joined by the supervisor, Mr. Erwin, and others among the companies' managers. We found no sign of her.

"By the time the sheriff's department vehicle arrived, it was nearly dawn. The bars were officially required to close hours before that, however, with no law enforcement on hand, they frequently shifted to what they termed private parties, generally in the back rooms of the same establishments.

"The largest of such circumventions of the law was concluding, with the inebriated participants exiting into an area we were searching. Expressing their willingness to help and ignoring all pleas not to, they trampled any effort at organization, as well as any potential evidence."

She drew in a breath.

"An hour later, Leah Pedroke was found in high weeds between the back of that establishment and another. She had been raped and strangled."

It wasn't a complete surprise. From Mrs. P's demeanor and tone, this story had been destined for an unhappy ending.

It clearly still hit Emmaline Parens hard.

Hard to imagine Aunt Gee's reaction.

Mrs. P drew in a breath, then released it slowly.

"Her murder became a *cause célèbre*. It provided media outlets obvious and colorful angles for their reportage. It was during this period, to facilitate the investigation, that the sheriff's department opened the substation." She couldn't resist slipping in that fact of county history.

"Last one to see her," Mike murmured. "Story about working late."

"Indeed, they investigated her supervisor quite carefully. However, two other young women had seen Leah leave, waving to them as she passed by the open door of their office next door. Shortly after, these same young women gave that supervisor, Mr. Erwin, a ride to the most popular bar as they left for their housing in Sherman. Numerous witnesses stated the supervisor had one drink, then left in the company of two other men renting rooms in the same house. As those three entered the rental, they encountered the owner of the house next door, searching for an errant dog. That homeowner had lived his whole live in O'Hara Hill, had no connection with the supervisor or with the oil companies. He attested to the supervisor's whereabouts until shortly before Gisella's phone call to him."

"The investigation stalled?"

"Not at all. The sheriff's department found their suspect quickly. A young man originally from Texas who had come here seeking employment in oil. He had been in that bar drinking much of the day. He left shortly before the time Leah left her office. He returned some time after eleven o'clock and before midnight. He rapidly drank himself to near insensibility. Multiple witnesses described him on his return to the bar as disheveled, buttons missing from his shirt, and marks on his face.

"A button of the same size, color, and form as those on his shirt was found near Leah's body. The marks on his face matched a ring she wore. In addition, two witnesses said he had worn a belt with his jeans before his absence from the bar. He did not have one on after."

"DNA?"

Mrs. P's mouth pursed slightly. "It was not as prevalent at that time. Further, the sheriff's department did not preserve the crime scene, nor did it collect evidence as it should have." The lines in her face deepened. "After the trial, I understand the department destroyed what evidence it did gather."

I interrupted in surprise. "They can't do that. They have to wait for the appeals."

"The issue of appeals did not apply in this case. The defendant was found not guilty. That defendant was Furman York."

Chapter Twelve

"**THE GUY WHO** got murdered today was the one who killed that girl?" Jennifer asked. "Wow. I really *didn't* remember details. If I ever knew them. I knew he was a bad guy, not that he murdered somebody way back."

"He was found not guilty," Mrs. P said precisely.

Mike said, "Yeah, found not guilty, and then he went to work for the lawyer who got him off."

"Norman Clay Lukasik got Furman York acquitted of murder?" I knew the answer before I finished my question. "Had York worked for him before the murder? Was he already foreman of the ranch?"

Diana shook her head. "Lukasik didn't buy the ranch until later."

"Diana is correct," Mrs. P said. "Norman Clay Lukasik left Cottonwood County almost immediately after the verdict, establishing his practice with a base in Denver. Three years later, he purchased what is now Lukasik Ranch. Furman York returned at the same time, as an employee of the ranch."

"Had he worked for Lukasik somewhere else in the interim?"

"I do not know what his employment status was while he was away from Cottonwood County. Nor do I know what motivated him to return. There was considerable disapproval of his presence. County leaders appealed to Norman Clay Lukasik to end Furman York's employment. He declined without any explanation or shred of consideration for sentiment of county residents, indeed without noticeable courtesy."

A new stiffness in her jaw pointed toward the conclusion that she'd been among the county leaders that approached him.

"Numerous letters to the editor appeared in the *Independence*. The sheriff's department was called upon on numerous occasions when residents' disapproval gave way to physical expression. A series of fires at the Lukasik Ranch only ceased when it was forcefully brought to the county's attention that such events endangered the members of our fire department."

Mike said, "Boy, I don't remember any of that."

Jennifer frowned. "Me, either. I only know Furman York's worked at Lukasik Ranch for as long as I can remember. Way, way back, even when my brother and I were little kids, my parents told us to stay away from him. Far away. It was like he was the boogeyman or something. As a little kid, whenever there was a scary man in a story, that's who I thought of."

"Probably because most people in the county never stopped thinking he was guilty of murder," Mike said.

"Yet he was acquitted," I said. It seemed so unlikely after the story Mrs. P told. "How did that happen?"

She kept her lips closed in a firm line.

Diana said, "There's a persistent rumor that someone or, possibly, several someones on the jury were bribed."

"Oh, yeah," Mike said. "I'd forgotten that part. And Hiram was on the jury."

"**PEOPLE THINK *HIRAM*** was bribed to get Furman York off?" I demanded, trying to reconcile that with their attitudes toward each other at the grazing association.

Could that be a motive? Killing York to keep him from revealing Hiram had accepted a bribe?

A scenario burst into my head. Hiram operating under a load of guilt for all these years finally reaching a breaking point. Taking justice into his own hands.

Having seen him in action, I had no problem imagining him taking something into his own hands, including his idea of justice and his loaded shotgun.

Could I see him waiting decades?

Diana interrupted my internal questions. "I heard Hiram was a main source for the rumors about bribery. He wouldn't do that if he'd taken a bribe." She paused. "Even Hiram wouldn't do that."

"Maybe we shouldn't bother investigating this guy's murder. Sounds like he finally got what he deserved," Jennifer said.

Now Mrs. Parens spoke. "That is the way of vigilantism, Jennifer. Murder as the perpetrator's solution to their problems or discomfort is unacceptable. It should never go uninvestigated."

I might remind her of this statement that next time she balked at coming too close to the edge of what she considered gossip.

"The idea is that if the murder goes unsolved, other people suffer, too," Mike said. "Being suspected when they didn't do anything. Like Hiram."

That did not appear to alter Jennifer's views. "Maybe he did it."

Diana leaned closer to her and said quietly, "There's another reason. Tamantha's worried about her daddy. We all know he had nothing to do with it, but the gossip…"

Jennifer relented. "Yeah. Okay."

If Mrs. P noticed that exchange, she gave no indication of it, appearing lost in her own thoughts or memories.

Mike said, "How did Lukasik get York off? Even if someone on the jury was bribed, Lukasik needed some argument about reasonable doubt for the juror to hide behind."

Mrs. Parens blinked, instantly back with us.

"Norman Clay Lukasik made a great deal of the mistakes made in the search. He particularly highlighted the unchecked number of people involved in it. We ordinary citizens intent on searching for a young woman were not aware of forensic issues at that time. As I said, the sheriff's department's methods were rudimentary and ours…"

That trailed off in a fading voice quite unlike Mrs. P.

Before any of us could react, she re-squared her shoulders and picked up briskly, "There was not the broad dissemination of information on crime, on detection methods, on forensics that there is now, especially in O'Hara Hill. We were concerned that she had fallen somehow, was lying somewhere injured. We never considered... We were far more innocent of such things at that time.

"Norman Clay Lukasik also returned incessantly to the participation of the supervisor, Mr. Erwin. Despite the evidence brought forth by the prosecution that he could not have committed the crime, Norman persistently raised him as an alternative suspect. He was particularly stringent in his cross-examination of Gisella about such matters, as if she had been in charge of the search.

"She could have been perceived as taking charge in that search, which was essential in the absence of any presence or guidance from the sheriff's department. She was not, however, responsible for any faults in its process."

If the others reacted the same way I did, the following silence resulted from a reluctance to make her self-conscious of such support for her rival and friend, even decades after the fact.

"The jury must have seen through all that, though, didn't they?" Jennifer asked.

Mrs. P's expression became ... *careful.*

Under no circumstances would her lips be loose enough to sink a rowboat, much less a ship. Now even a toy paper boat would be safe.

"I cannot say what the members of the jury saw or didn't see. They found the defendant not guilty."

"What was the reaction to the verdict?"

"Disbelief. Outrage." Mrs. P using sentence fragments signaled extreme emotion. "Sorrow for Leah's family, who had been here throughout the proceedings. Also sorrow for Gisella."

Mike leaned forward, elbows on his thighs. His expression hidden from us.

Mrs. P cleared her throat.

"Gisella and Leah Pedroke had become quite close in a short time. During the trial, Leah's parents stayed with Gisella, going together to the courthouse each day. She remained in touch for many years afterward, indeed until their deaths."

I looked at Mike. So did Diana and Jennifer.

He looked at his hands, clasped between his knees. "How'd Aunt Gee take it?

"Gisella took it very much to heart. If she had not already started her training as a law enforcement dispatcher when the trial began, I cannot envision how she would have absorbed such a blow. That purpose helped her greatly."

It was never easy—at any age—to recognize that figures from your youth, whom you always considered impregnable, were not.

"Mrs. P," I started, drawing the others' attention to me. "What about the attitude toward Furman York around the county now?"

"He has been widely viewed as a man who committed murder, yet escaped punishment and who, given an undeserved second chance, squandered it by being a poor neighbor."

Wow.

For once, Mrs. P had not held back on what to my mind—much less hers—amounted to gossip. Or at least generalized sentiment picked up from casual conversation. And since she didn't care for generalized or casual conversation, that said a lot. A whole lot.

Might as well go for more.

"What about Norman Clay Lukasik? How is he viewed?"

"The view of Norman Clay Lukasik would be as varied as the individuals of this county. Some admire his successful law practice, others do not."

That vague response announced I'd gone a gossipy-ish question too far. Backtrack, backtrack, backtrack.

"You attended the trial?"

She nodded.

"Every day?"

A single nod.

"What were your observations of Norman Clay Lukasik as a defense attorney?" Her lips parted and I hurried to add, "In addition to what you've already told us."

She closed her lips for thirty seconds.

"He showed determination throughout the trial, as well as confidence, despite testimony that knowledgeable observers said should have diminished his confidence greatly.

"Further, he was well-prepared, as demonstrated by his ability to recall details at any moment. At times, that ability appeared to lead him to change a line of questioning abruptly."

"Was that effective?" Diana asked. "Or did it get him into trouble?"

"In most instances it was effective. I remember only once when it might be considered to have drawn him to act precipitously by underestimating his adversary, which, as you termed it, *got him into trouble.*"

"When was that?" Diana followed up.

"That occasion was when he cross-examined Gisella. Under Norman Clay Lukasik's questioning the previous witness had been pulled into what could have been construed as an admission of illicit involvement with Leah. There was nothing of the sort occurring and it was not at all what the witness had meant, although persons who did not know the people involved could have come to that erroneous conclusion.

"Gisella had testified extensively under direct examination, providing a great deal of information important to the prosecution's theory of what happened. Even an inexperienced observer would have expected Norman Clay Lukasik to immediately revisit that material in detail in an effort to reinforce the possibilities of another interpretation of the night's events that he'd previously introduced. He did not.

"When he rose from behind the defense table, his bearing was markedly different from the other times. He did not pause to draw in the jurors, nor did he ease into the questioning, making the witness relax."

"If he was smart, he knew Gee wouldn't relax."

Mike's mutter earned a slight uptick at the corners of Mrs. P's lips. She did not otherwise respond.

"He made me think strongly of the stalking behavior of a barn cat my family once had that was the best mouser of my experience, perhaps because it so thoroughly enjoyed the hunt."

Her expression lightened suddenly. "However, no cat would ever mistake Gisella Decker for a mouse, which Norman Clay Lukasik apparently did, to his detriment. He attempted to pounce, disconcerting her into an admission which might reinforce the erroneous impression left by his cross-examination of the previous witness. She would have none of that. By her answers and expression, she made clear to any who might have been unaware that he was attempting manipulation of her testimony."

"We should read the transcript."

"I'll get it," Jennifer said, making a note.

"The transcript will be unable to do justice to Gisella's domination of Norman Clay Lukasik," Mrs. P said simply. "However, you should understand, all of you, that other than that one instance, he was relentless, even, at times, ferocious in the pursuit of his goal."

"Was he persuasive enough to have legitimately swayed any member of the jury?"

"That is impossible to answer, Elizabeth, for it would require being inside twelve other human beings' brains, to have lived their experiences."

"Did he persuade you that there was reasonable doubt of Furman York's guilt?"

"He did not."

I nodded, satisfied.

Because I now felt confident about accepting a working premise that York was guilty of murdering Leah Pedroke—no matter what the verdict was. Also because, believing in his guilt as she did, Emmaline Parens could be nudged along to share more information than usual. With care and caution, of course. Let's not get wild and crazy here thinking Mrs. P would pour out all secrets, opinions, and memories.

"Anything else about Lukasik?"

"He greatly enjoyed the attention of the media, which proved a harbinger for his subsequent cases."

Was that what Needham had in mind? *Not even his best performance. You should have seen him at the beginning, in all his glory.*

"Jennifer, you appear to have a question."

Mrs. P's statement turned all attention in that direction.

"Sort of. Didn't you say Furman York was in O'Hara Hill in the first place because he was looking for a job in oil?"

"I did."

"Then how'd he become a ranch foreman?"

Mrs. P bestowed a look of approval on her. I might have, too.

"He sure didn't begin as foreman," Mike said. "Started as a hand. Not a good hand, from what I always heard. Probably needed a job. No one else would have hired him then. Maybe—"

"And even fewer now," Diana said.

"—he and Lukasik bonded during the trial."

A bond that didn't mature until three years later, when Lukasik bought the ranch? Unless he'd done other work for Lukasik. Before I could raise that, Diana had another question.

"Why stay here, where people believe he got away with murder? He could have gone anywhere else."

"Maybe he liked shoving it down people's throats that he got away with it," I suggested.

"Sounds like his kind of move," Mike said.

"But that's not what I meant about him becoming a ranch foreman," Jennifer protested. "What I meant was why cattle, when he'd been working in oil?"

"That," I said, "is a terrific question. And your first assignment, Jennifer. See what you can find out about Furman York before he came to Cottonwood County. Unless…?"

Mrs. Parens shook her head. "My information is limited to what appeared in the *Independence* at the time."

"A rundown of what was in the *Independence* back then would save me time getting started, Mrs. Parens," Jennifer said.

"As I stated, he was from Texas. Born there, as well as receiving what education he had there. He had previously been employed in the oil industry. He was not well-regarded by those he had previously worked for or with. My understanding of their objections was that his errors in judgment and impulsiveness endangered others. That reputation followed him here to O'Hara Hill and was widely spoken of before Leah Pedroke's murder."

"Interesting," I said. "I thought the West was known for letting people reinvent themselves. For accepting people as they present themselves."

Mike grinned. "Sort of a what happens in Vegas stays in Vegas for the entire region?"

Mrs. P's cool look silenced him. "One might wish that all that *is* Las Vegas would stay in Las Vegas."

"Not a slots or shows fan, Mrs. P?" I asked.

"No." That ended that topic. "I cannot speak for all of the western region. However, I can tell you, Elizabeth, that it is true that Cottonwood County and, I believe, the rest of Wyoming, accords newcomers the opportunity to prove who they are."

"In other words, they get a shot here, but if they screw up, that's that." I tilted my head, getting another angle in the map of Wyoming on Mrs. P's wall. "What's interesting is whether that's the result of a sense of fairness—wanting to offer second chances—or because Cottonwood County doesn't think what happens outside of Cottonwood County is important enough to count?"

"The latter is possible," she acknowledged. The lines in her face seemed to deepen as I watched. "It is very possible. However, it is certain that if wrongdoing occurs in Cottonwood County, it is not forgotten or forgiven."

AS WE SAID our good-byes, Mrs. Parens delayed me with a light touch to my arm.

"Elizabeth."

I turned back to her.

With the others gone ahead, she said, "I have another thought to share about the barn cat my family had."

At her uncharacteristic pause, I said, "The excellent mouser."

"Yes. It also was a thoroughly unpleasant animal. None of the other animals on the ranch would go near it, no cats, dogs, horses, or cows. The humans, as well, gave it a wide berth. It not only enjoyed the hunt, it enjoyed the kill."

Chapter Thirteen

"**WHAT DID MRS.** P say?" Mike asked as he held open the truck's front passenger door for me.

"That Norman Clay Lukasik is a dangerous adversary and we should be careful."

"She'd already said that. The stuff about relentless and ferocious."

I met his gaze. "She upped the ante."

Mike whistled softly.

ERNIE'S WAS THE oldest restaurant in O'Hara Hill. Essentially also the sole restaurant in O'Hara Hill, unlike the oil boom days Mrs. P had told us about.

It also had good food.

When Mike suggested we stop there for dinner before the drive back to Sherman, he sold the idea by adding, "We could pick up news. Or at least rumors and gossip, and you always say those can be helpful, Elizabeth."

All true. But he really wanted to go for the burgers and fries.

Since the rest of us were hungry, too, he received no argument.

Ernie's décor is mostly the result of wherever there was space on a wall when a new item arrived. It tells the history of the place and its town in enough layers to delight an archeologist. It's a look several chains have tried to duplicate without rising above the level of plastic trying to duplicate a tree.

After we'd found a spot among the tables on the left side—the right side was reserved for an impressive bar that ran from near the entry to the back of the room—and ordered, I got up to examine a group of photos on the wall behind the front door and near where the bar began.

Unlike the rest of the restaurant's wall-hung collection, these represented O'Hara Hill's history in roughly chronological order, as reported by the dates noted on most of the photographs.

Something had caught my attention as we'd sat at the table. I wanted a closer look.

In contrast to Mrs. Parens' collection, this display could not be moved wholesale to a museum. It was an informal and idiosyncratic gathering. The photographs jumbled individuals in various poses around the restaurant with landscapes, town events, a news article or two, and snapshots and postcards stuck into the corners of more formally framed pieces.

And it included not a single item from the period we'd heard about from Mrs. P.

I went from top to bottom again, in case those years had been misplaced.

Nope.

Back at the table, I reported my observation, concluding, "It's like those years didn't exist or the restaurant didn't exist during those years."

Mike frowned. "I don't ever remember Ernie's not being here. We'd come see Aunt Gee, and sometimes we'd come here for lunch or supper. I always got a chocolate milkshake. Only time I got to have them. I was a kid, but I'd remember if there was a gap in chocolate milkshakes."

"The photos say it was here before and it was here after, and you'd think with the town booming that business would be great and they'd have marked that period."

"Maybe with all the competition from the pop-up restaurants, bars, and other, uh, facilities, Ernie's had to close temporarily," Diana suggested.

"Or they didn't want to remember—"

Mike broke off as the door opened.

Jack Delahunt entered and received the Cottonwood County version of the "Norm!" greeting on the old TV show *Cheers*—without looking at him, the stool-sitting lineup of regulars along the bar to the right and most of the diners at tables nodded briefly and silently. That way they acknowledged his arrival without placing any obligation on him to reciprocate.

Jack was the long-time foreman of a big cattle operation butting up against the Montana state line. Mike had worked for him summers when he was in school.

If Jack walked in and went straight to a stool—usually the same stool, apparently left open for him—without speaking, no one would speak to him, including the bartender as he placed a beer in front of him. I'd seen exactly that happen a few times while eating here. At least twice he'd never spoken a word before leaving with a general nod to the bartender and whoever else cared to catch it.

Today, as he came in, he looked toward us, then raised his hand to the bartender and pointed to our table.

"Jack, come join us." Mike half-stood, aiming for an empty chair from a nearby table.

Had Mike missed that Jack had already invited himself, or was he certifying the welcome the man had assumed? Correctly, as it happened.

On a sudden suspicion, I asked Mike in a low voice, "Did you call and tell him to meet us here so I'd be satisfied this was a good use of our time?"

Palm flat on his collarbone, he protested, "Me? When would I have had time to do that? Besides, no need. Jack's here most every night."

Jack beat him to the chair, succinctly asked the table's occupiers' permission with a single raised eyebrow, received an equally succinct nod in return, which he replied to with a tug on his hat. Consider it Wyoming sign language.

Jack spun the chair around with an easy twist of his wrist, inserted it between Diana and Mike, and sat.

He nodded to Diana, me, and Mike, leaving a slight pause before nodding to Jennifer.

Mike got the message. "Jack, this is Jennifer Lawton, our colleague at the station."

Jack ignored that identifier and went straight to the important matter in Cottonwood County. "Faith and Kent's daughter," he said. "Known them and your uncle Rob most their lives. Good people."

"Yes, sir." That was a rare deference to age or authority for her. I wondered which it was.

The bartender arrived with Jack's beer. He drank deeply.

Then, with the social niceties addressed, he rumbled, "Shame about Furman York."

Both of Mike's eyebrows rose.

Jack nodded. "Shame it didn't happen a lot sooner. At birth, say. Would've saved this world a stretch of misery."

"Because he killed that girl way back," Jennifer said wisely.

"That was the worst. But he had being no good down to a science. My ma had a saying—begin as you mean to go on, and he sure went by that."

"You had dealings with him, because of the ranch?" I asked.

"Couldn't entirely avoid it once Lukasik made him foreman. Cattle can make for a small world. Mostly good folks. Can't always sidestep any who aren't." I had the impression Jack would have spit in disdain if we'd been outside.

I was glad we weren't outside.

Was the disdain for York? For Lukasik? For York being a lousy foreman? Or for Lukasik putting him in that position?

Before I could formulate a question to negotiate among the possibilities, Mike asked one of my questions, "What kind of foreman was he?"

"Bad kind." Jack Delahunt clearly took personally what he deemed a besmirching of the title he occupied with pride and integrity.

I got that. I'd felt that way now and then about some individuals identified as journalists.

"How bad—I mean in what way?" Mike asked.

"Bad with cattle. Bad with horses. Bad with hands. Bad with vehicles. Bad as a neighbor. Bad with his employer's money. And lazy." Jack continued, "Not entirely stupid, though, which made it worse. A cautious man clapped his hand on his wallet the second Furman York came into view. Even so, heard credible accounts of his roping in otherwise cautious men. You know he was involved with that fella over in Dakota who ripped off all those people?"

"I heard that rumor." In an aside to me, Mike added, "Feedlot operator who took friends, neighbors, fellow ranchers for millions with reports of phantom cattle. Consider him the Bernie Madoff of the West."

Another nod from Jack. "All those and family, too. Man ripped off his *family*. Going to take them decades to recover and those are the lucky ones who can get back on their feet. And it was more than rumor. Heard all about it from law enforcement over that way. They were darned near sick about how that fella only got a few years in prison."

"Those otherwise cautious men... Anyone specific?"

Jack gave me a level look. "Not firm enough to tell a reporter."

I wanted to know. Of course, I wanted to know. The itch to keep at him gnawed at me. The knowledge that the only thing it would firm up was his determination not to share kept me from scratching that itch. For now.

"How widely known was it that York might have been involved?" I asked.

"Thinking someone might have decided to hand out more direct justice?" Approval tinged that. "Not impossible. But with the folks who were hurt the worst in Dakota near the head guy, more likely they'd do something to him. York was involved more around the edges. Not to say he couldn't have been cooking up somethin' else with that piece of—" He swallowed the epithet along with a mouthful of beer. "Nah, I'd say Furman York going to his just rewards today is more likely the result of something closer to home."

"That old murder? But—"

Cutting across Mike with, "And something more recent," Jack had all our attention.

He made sure of that with a pause before speaking a single word. "Rustling."

He said it quietly, yet I could swear the word caught the attention of everyone in the place.

There are some words that vibrate loudly in a group sensitive to them no matter how softly spoken. I once saw a similar reaction when someone mentioned a book title that included the word assassinate in a roomful of Secret Service agents.

No head-turning gave away the people in Ernie's, but the abrupt stillness and silence couldn't be an accident.

Jack continued, "Not a word I say lightly. There's been trouble with rustling these past few years, up to Canada and down through Texas. Ranchers have lost a lot of money. Mostly small operators who can least afford to have three, six, eight go missing.

"Lot of the rustlers doing it for drug money. Had a new hire get hauled in last month. Usually spot the signs of a druggie. He slipped by. Earning his pay wasn't enough for him. He and some others took a trailer from a repair shop, scooped up a dozen head from a few places and went east to sell them. Then put the trailer back. Would've gotten away with it, too, if the guy at the repair shop hadn't noticed the trailer that had been clean as a whistle wasn't the next time he looked. Law enforcement put together reports of the missing cattle and the hauler being used."

My thoughts snagged on logistics. "A rustler takes the cattle and then what?"

They all looked at me like I'd asked what a sound bite was.

"They sell them," Mike said. "And keep the money."

"Thanks, I figured that. Where? How? Who buys them? They'll have other people's brands on them. Won't the buyers be suspicious? Don't the brands give them away?" I asked.

"West River it would."

I knew the individual words Jack spoke, but looked to Mike for the phrase's translation.

"West of the Missouri River," he said. "You must have seen a sign when you crossed the Missouri on I-90 in South Dakota saying you were entering the livestock ownership inspection enforcement area."

He had to be kidding. First, I'd made that drive a year and a half ago, when I moved here. Second, the trip was with my parents, who had not yet given up the notion that I should move back into my childhood bedroom and remain there until transferring to a retirement home.

Across South Dakota, I'd been fighting to hold onto my autonomy and adulthood, not watching for road signs that sounded like gibberish to me—then and now.

Apparently recognizing his comment as misguided, Mike continued, "Most folks just call it West River. The Missouri about cuts South Dakota in half. West River and East River have a lot of differences—geography, roads, agriculture. For instance, mostly farms in East River, ranches in West River. The biggest difference might be how they handle brands. West River, brands are required, but not East River. And East River livestock markets aren't required to get proof of ownership. Some do, but…"

"Some don't," Jack said grimly. "And for not asking questions, they get a good price, gain a fatter margin. Do that enough and you're sitting pretty."

"How about for the rustlers? Is it lucrative?"

"Yep. Hardly costs the rustlers anything. A bag of feed to gather the cattle, fifteen minutes to load 'em in a hauler, then they're on their way to an East River auction. Get there, settle up, and they're headed back next day."

"What makes you think Furman York was involved with rustling?"

"Same thing that makes me think a skunk stinks."

That clearly sufficed for him. Wouldn't for law enforcement.

For us? Might be enough to start digging. Nowhere near enough for a conclusion.

"Anything consistent with the rustling, Jack?"

He nodded twice at Diana. "Always close to a highway."

"Quick getaway," Mike muttered.

"Right. They look for spots they won't be seen doing their stealing and can get on their way fast when they're done. Particular kind of spot. The smart ones look for that."

"He was foreman of a big ranch. Why take the risk of getting caught rustling?" I protested.

"Money."

"Was he into drugs like those others you talked about?" Jennifer asked.

"Not that I heard. Drink and women, sure. Gambling, yeah." He took another long drink of beer. "Thing is, being foreman's sort of what you'd call a glass ceiling when it comes to advancement."

I blinked at *glass ceiling*, but got past it fast. Just because I didn't know West River didn't mean he didn't know glass ceiling—possibly indicating his knowledge base was broader than mine.

"He'd get raises, I suppose, but not big jumps. He'd moved up as far as he could in the Lukasik outfit without kicking the old man or his son out. Hell, he had more power than the son. Norman Clay Lukasik hardly ever questioned what York did, even when… Well, wasn't the way I'd run an operation."

"Wait, wait, go back. What son? Lukasik's or—?"

Jack hiked one eyebrow. "Lukasik's kid. Never heard of York having any. Gable Lukasik."

"Is he involved with the ranch?"

"Sure. Works when he's needed. Helps out other folks, too. Not a top hand, not worthless. Works hard. Getting better. Hell of a lot harder than York ever did."

Yet he'd worked under York as foreman? I wondered how that went over with the son of the owner.

"I know Gable," Diana said. "He helped coach Gary Junior's summer baseball team a couple years. Nice guy."

Good. Diana could provide more information later.

I turned to Jack. "You said you never heard of Furman York having kids, how about relationships. Married?"

He shook his head.

"Involved with somebody?"

One shoulder rose, denying knowledge and declaring lack of interest.

Knowing how to get information out of sources is a vital skill for journalists. Knowing which source is a good match for what information is another important skill.

Jack was not a good source for digging into York's personal life. Maybe Diana's acquaintance Gable Lukasik would be.

"Jack," I said, "you were talking about York being foreman and not getting big raises, is that enough to drive him to take the risk? Surely he'd lose his job if he were ever caught."

"Most owners would let him go on rumors of rustling," Mike said. "It's not tolerated."

"Lukasik's not most owners," Jack grumbled.

I asked, "Do you think Lukasik's involved in—?"

"Whoa." Jack shoved back. "Don't go turning a calf into a bull. Never said anything like that."

Jack had been talking so openly I'd almost forgotten about Ernie's eavesdropability. Both the ease of hearing other conversations and the penchant of customers to capitalize on that ease.

"Sorry. I wasn't putting words in your mouth. Simply following the idea up the chain of command. We're all clear you didn't add him to the conversation, I did." Hoping that placated him, I brought the topic back to the main thread. "The talk about York being involved in… uh, selling cattle he didn't own. Does anyone have proof?"

"To take to court? What good would that've done? There was plenty of evidence he killed that girl years back and he got off scot-free."

He certainly had no issue expressing that opinion.

"Did you know York then? Or Leah Pedroke? Or Lukasik?"

"Didn't know them. But everybody knew about her getting murdered that way."

"Jack," Mike asked abruptly, "is there a reason Ernie's doesn't have photos or memorabilia from the years O'Hara Hill was in the throes of that oil boom?"

"Yep. The reason's Dorrie. That's Ernie's wife."

We waited. One of us less patiently than those accustomed to the ripening time required from some Wyomingites' conversations.

"Did they know Furman York? Or Leah?" I added, thinking about her renting a room from Gee so nearby.

"Might've."

That evasiveness said yes to me. "How—?"

"Tell us about the pictures, Jack," Diana interrupted. She nudged my foot under the table.

Fine. Message received.

It still took Jack another couple beats to start talking.

"Ernie got oil fever. Told Dorrie he was closing the place because he was about to make his fortune in oil and no reason for a millionaire to work as hard as he did. She said he was loco. A few other things, too. He said things back. Pretty soon he signed somethin' that gave her fifty-one percent if she kept this place running, but with something in there about he could buy back to even."

"He was back with his tail between his legs soon enough. Course Dorrie'd worked like crazy all that time with all the business during the boom. Nobody wanted to work ordinary jobs because they were all going to make their fortune in oil—trying to find a hand worth a nickel during those crazy days..." He shook his head.

"Ernie comes back, but with no money to make it even. She reminded him 'bout every day, along with all she'd done to hold onto the place. Until one day, about five years after, he went pure haywire and starting pulling down every last one of the pictures on that wall and slamming them into a pile. Dorrie comes tearing in from the back screaming at him. Makes him pick up those pictures and take them off to be fixed and framed." A slow grin pulled one side of his mouth. "Somehow the photos from those couple years got lost and never did make it back on the wall.

"The two of 'em never have spoken on it since to my knowing."

Chapter Fourteen

AFTER JACK LEFT our table, I said we should try to talk to Ernie and Dorrie.

Both were very busy—Ernie in plain sight behind the bar as he supplemented the bartender and handled payments, Dorrie identified by a voice in the kitchen from glimpses when the door swung wider than usual.

Solely to stretch our time in hopes they'd become free, we all ordered dessert except Diana, who showed a lamentable tendency to not view our sacrifice in its true light.

In the end, though, we admitted defeat. Neither Dorrie nor Ernie would have free time to chat any time soon.

"Still, this visit to O'Hara Hill gave us plenty to think about," I said when we were all buckled up in Diana's truck.

"Yeah," Jennifer said, "like who Scott is and why everyone talks about him getting free."

"It's scot with one t, like a person from Scotland. But without a capital S. It has to do with an old word for taxes. It comes from getting away without paying a tax."

"How do you know all this stuff without Googling, Elizabeth?"

"Let's get back to what Jack said," Mike said from in front of me.

I'd asked to switch seats, thinking I wouldn't see the road with his broad shoulders ahead of me.

"Right, motive," I said. "It could provide motive to anyone he might have rustled from—if, in fact, he did rustle. How do we find out who might have had cattle rustled?"

"Most would report it to law enforcement, the brand inspector," Mike said.

"Which?"

"Either or both, depending on circumstances. If there's physical evidence to be processed, say, the sheriff's department would be better. Brand department's often underfunded. Still, worth reporting."

"I'll check the records," Diana said before I could ask.

"Great. Tell me more about this East River, West River stuff."

They did for much of the drive, expanding on what Mike had said.

As we neared the station, I said, "So, we need to talk to Ernie and Dorrie, check who might have been victims of rustling lately, take another run at getting information from Lukasik, and—" I watched Mike. "—get with Gee about the murder of Leah Pedroke."

A sigh lifted his shoulders, but he said nothing.

Asking Gee to relive the pain of that time wouldn't be fun.

Diana pulled into the KWMT-TV parking lot so the rest of us could retrieve our individual vehicles before reconvening at my house.

"Wait. Before we split up, tell us about Lukasik's son, Diana. What's his name?"

"Gable. Nice kid—well, not a kid. He must be in his mid- to late twenties."

"Mid-twenties? Lukasik looks like he could have grandchildren that age," Mike said.

"Yeah. His wife was a whole lot younger."

"Was?"

"She died several years—No, must be getting close to ten years ago. Car accident, I think."

"You knew her?"

"More like knew who she was, recognized her if I saw her in town," Diana said. "She wasn't involved in activities, so Leona wouldn't be much help."

Leona D'Amato covered KWMT-TV's version of the society beat, which meant she worked part-time and some of that time went to filling in as anchor. Because Thurston Fine knew she hated covering hard news, he didn't worry about her taking his job. She could have if she'd wanted it.

"Her death was really hard on Gable. I heard he doesn't have a good relationship with his father." Diana's brow wrinkled. "Even while Gable was volunteering, helping the kids out—and they adored him— you could tell he was down. Then I saw him, oh, a month ago? Maybe two. And he looked happy. Genuinely happy. And I was happy for him."

"What changed?" Mike asked.

Diana flashed a grin at him. "A woman, of course. I don't know who. Want me to ask around, see if I can find out? Though why Gable's dating life would be of interest—?"

"Yes, ask," I said. A love interest might be another way to approach Gable if the Lukasik family front united under the stress of Furman York's apparent murder.

At the same time, Jennifer said, "Gary will know."

Diana looked around at her in surprise. "My son? He doesn't care about dating, especially not who a former coach might be dating. He barely notices Russ and me."

"Oh, he notices. And he'll know," Jennifer repeated, her toes curled around the line of smug without quite crossing it.

Diana gave her a long, thoughtful look before taking out her phone and hitting speed dial.

Gary Junior answered, "Hi, Mom."

"Hi. I've got you on speaker with Elizabeth and Mike and Jennifer."

We all called *Hi* and he replied. "Gary, remember Gable Lukasik?"

"Sure. Is this about the foreman from his ranch getting killed?" His young voice drew taut. "Gable didn't have anything to do with it. He's a good guy."

"Don't worry. We're trying to clear up some background. What I'd actually like to know is who he's dating."

Matters of innocence and guilt, of murder and justice faded beneath the teenage lament of "Oh, *Mom.*"

His older sister's voice came from the background. "Don't be a dweeb. Tell her, so they can figure things out."

"You should talk, all the hysterics you had because of some purse—"

"Gary. Jessica," Diana said in her Mother Voice. "Do you know who Gable's dating?"

"Yes."

Before Jess, who must have come closer to the phone to make her voice that much clearer, could say more, her brother jumped in.

"Some new teacher at Sherman Elementary. Came in mid-year."

"Asheleigh. Her name is Asheleigh with an 'e' in the middle. And they're *really* serious," Jess added, asserting her superiority on this sibling battlefront. "They're going to get married."

"You don't know that," Gary declared. "You don't know them."

"I hear things. And I listen. Unlike some who—"

"Jessica. Gary," Diana said. "Stop squabbling. Thank you for the information. Are all your chores done?"

They unified momentarily in a, "*Ye-es.*"

"Great. Don't stay up late. You both have things in the morning."

"We know. We're not babies. Well, I'm not." Last point to Jessica.

"Go to bed. Both of you. Good night. I love you." She hung up as their good-nights started to degrade toward bickering. "They used to get along so well."

"It's the age," Jennifer said. "Adam and I were like that at their age. We got over it after a few years."

Diana's mouth twitched. She said solemnly, "Thank you for that hopeful prediction, Jennifer."

IRIS OPENED MY own back door to me with a smile. "We heard you drive in. Pity you still can't park in the garage."

Between the previous owner's furniture and mine brought from the East Coast, closing the garage door counted as a miracle, much less getting my SUV in. At least the house wasn't jampacked.

I planned to sell much of the spillover at a neighborhood yard sale coming up later this summer. Already, I'd contributed more than my share to a neighborhood storage facility in anticipation of the sale.

"Someday, I'll live that dream. Others are coming behind me, Iris. Probably to the front door."

"Don't fret. Zeb's at the front to let them in. We made coffee for you all—decaf and regular. And there's a platter of doughnuts on the counter."

"Thank you. That's kind of you. Thank you and Zeb for everything. Is Tamantha asleep?"

"No thanks necessary. We had a grand time. She's in bed. Don't know about asleep."

"I'll just check on her."

As we wished each other good night, Iris stepped back to let me pass her. But I had another obstacle to overcome.

My dog.

Shadow was stretched out on his side with his back to the closed door to the guest room.

His head rose at my approach, checking who came, while repositioning to jump up if necessary.

"It's okay, Shadow," I said, barely above a whisper.

He stood, walking under my free hand for a stroke as I used the other to quietly turn the door knob.

The faint hall light striped across the dark room.

Tamantha Burrell was not a girl to fear the night.

Or the brilliance of her bag, which formed a kaleidoscope at the foot of the bed.

Even in sleep or pretend sleep, she presented a determined presence. Was I a chicken for being grateful she was asleep or feigning? Either way I was grateful.

Because we hadn't accomplished nearly enough to satisfy Tamantha.

Tomorrow wouldn't be any better, I feared, unless we came up with enough plans tonight to hold her off.

✧   ✧   ✧

"WE HAVE LOTS of people we need to talk to, starting tomorrow. In the meantime, let's organize what we have," I said as I passed the others in the living room—comfortable around the coffee table in front of the unlit fireplace—on my way to pour myself a coffee from the pot on the kitchen counter.

It's a small house, making it easy to talk from the kitchen to living room at a volume that won't stir anyone in the guest room.

And, yes, it's worth mentioning a fireplace being unlit even at this time of year. It was Wyoming.

Mike answered, "We've got doughnuts—they're great—nuts, chips, and coffee. I think this'll hold us for a while."

"She meant what do we have about Furman York being shot." Diana held out the doughnut platter, its contents noticeably diminished, as I sank into the upholstered chair next to her. Mike and Jennifer occupied opposite corners of the couch.

"Not sure we've got much," he said.

"The history Mrs. P told us, especially with so many people believing he killed Leah Pedroke," Diana offered.

"Yeah, but why would that get him killed after all this time?" Jennifer asked.

I tipped the half of the doughnut I hadn't yet eaten—they were excellent, if not perfectly shaped—at her. "Exactly. Not to mention *who* would have killed him because of that."

"Hiram," Mike said immediately. "Sounds like he's maintained Norman Clay Lukasik bought someone on the jury and York got away with murder."

"There's a fundamental flaw with the theory," I said. "One person on the jury being bribed could have prevented Furman York from being convicted, but how could one person get him found not guilty? It would be eleven and one—a hung jury."

"You mean to get him off, Lukasik had to bribe all the jurors, which would mean Hiram was bribed, too?" Jennifer asked.

"Possibly there's something in between. But—" I groaned. "—we'll have to talk to Hiram."

"We've got the prime suspect in jail, where we can't talk to him, not to mention we have no idea why he might have chosen to kill Furman York after all these years. What does that leave us?" Mike asked.

"Prime suspect? Tom doesn't think Hiram's guilty," Diana protested.

"Oh, yeah, those telepathic communications you guys had out at the grazing association. I got the impression you didn't think Hiram was the prime suspect, either, but no idea why. Not to mention there'll be folks who consider Tom a strong suspect. What he thinks won't carry much weight with them, including some we know who wear a certain uniform."

Frowning, Jennifer protested, "If Tom's a suspect, people should pay *more* attention to him saying Hiram Poppinger didn't do it, because it would help him to have people suspecting Hiram."

"That might be logical, but people don't always think that clearly," he said gloomily, then popped a piece of a doughnut in his mouth.

"If all these doughnuts are making you negative, we're going to have to cut you off."

At my threat, he grabbed two more from the platter and put them on a napkin by his elbow as far from the rest of us as possible. "Facing the facts," he said when they were secured and he'd swallowed his mouthful.

"The facts include that we can hope Tom has more to tell us when he's done talking with the sheriff's department—" I refused to consider the alternative I saw flicker across their faces. "—and in the meantime we have at least one other place we can start. Jennifer, you'll do a full workup on the victim?"

She snorted. "Some victim." Before I said more, she added, "Yeah, yeah, it's on my list. The quick look I took shows a *lot* of coverage during the trial. Besides—"

"Which reminds me," I said, "did you put following up with Ernie and Dorrie on the list? And Aunt Gee when she gets back."

"*Besides*," she repeated with emphasis as she typed, "we know where Furman York's been and what he's been up to for years. No mystery there to follow up on. He's been here, pissing off people in Cottonwood County. For-*ever*. If that was going to lead to murder it would've happened way back then."

"We've dug into other people who've spent decades pissing off people." Diana continued, "Jack Delahunt's reaction when Elizabeth asked about Lukasik possibly being involved in the rustling was interesting."

"It was." I put down my coffee mug. The better to reach for another doughnut before Mike emptied the platter. "He seemed to want to put big distance between York and Lukasik over this—particularly his making any accusations—with the question being why. Sense of justice? And—"

"Jack's a real fair man," Mike said.

"—he's sure Lukasik isn't involved? Or—"

"Afraid the lawyer will sue his ass off." After a beat of silence, Jennifer looked up from typing. "What? Wasn't that what you all were thinking?"

Pretty much.

She had another point to make. "I want to go back to why York didn't move on after he was found not guilty. Oil was a bust here, then why not go elsewhere? Oil guys can earn big money." She'd briefly dated an "oil guy," who'd been a long-time friend. "Why switch to cattle? Working on a cattle ranch isn't known for bringing in big bucks."

"Yeah, and sudden change from oil to cattle at—what?—late twenties? Doesn't happen much," Mike said. "Sometimes, maybe, if somebody wants solitude, wants to hide away from the world... But this guy was thumbing his nose at the world—the world that believed he'd killed Leah Pedroke. Put down *Not the brightest bulb in the lamp*, Jennifer."

Against the tide of chuckles, I said, "It sounds like he was bright—at least cunning or crafty—about a lot of things. With a blind spot in assessing other people. So the interesting question is why."

Possibly catching my seriousness, Diana said, "Or not caring. All the way back to Leah. When he attacked her, he probably thought she'd keep quiet. She fought back."

"That's good, Diana. What we need now is to find who knew Furman York well. I wonder if Jack would have ideas about who he associated with."

"I'll give him a call tomorrow," Mike said.

I nodded, acknowledgement and thanks. "Lukasik Ranch should be a source of information. His close friends on the ranch and people there should know who his friends are off the ranch."

"How about Lukasik himself?" Mike asked. "He sure seemed to be trying to pull off his version of the Mark Anthony burying Caesar speech today. What? You didn't think I had Shakespeare in school?"

"Mrs. P," Jennifer murmured wisely.

"Putting Shakespeare aside for the moment—sorry, Mrs. P," I said to the ceiling. "—I had another question. What about tire tracks at the scene? Could the sheriff's department—"

A knock at the front door stopped my words.

"Tom?" Mike asked.

I was already on the way to the door.

I opened it without looking—I was becoming a true Shermanite.

"Tom. How are—?"

He stopped me with a slightly raised hand. I shut my mouth, stepped back, and let him in.

Chapter Fifteen

TOM DROPPED HIS cowboy hat on the bench in the mini entryway. Without that brim's shadow, his tiredness showed as sharpened grooves around his mouth without any of the lightening usually provided by lurking amusement.

This change wasn't solely from today's events.

They'd triggered memories of another time, other questionings by the sheriff's department. The same ones that had frightened Tamantha enough to call me.

Yes, frightened that redoubtable personage.

Before he had to ask, I said, "Tamantha's fine. Sound asleep in the guest room. I checked on her not long ago."

"I'm going in to see her."

"You might wake her…"

"I'm going in."

I didn't try to stand in his way. Instead, I ushered him to the door—as if he couldn't have figured out where it was in my small house, even if he hadn't known from helping me move in.

Shadow, still on lookout at the door, was already standing. One look that identified the newcomer and he stepped back, too.

I pushed the door open.

Shadow followed Tom in. I stayed where I was.

"Daddy," Tamantha said immediately, sitting up in bed.

Had she heard his knock at the front door? His voice? Sensed him? Always been awake? Listening to us in the living room?

Two strides, bent over, and he had her in a hug. Tamantha

wrapped her arms around his neck and buried her face in his shoulder.

I'd say that was a sign that Tamantha Burrell was truly still a little girl, except I'd had an impulse to do the same thing when he walked in the front door.

I pulled the door closed and returned to the living room, where the others sat in solemn silence, none of us inclined to pick up where we'd left off.

Instead, Diana replenished the doughnut platter from a secret source Iris entrusted to her, Mike filled the nut bowls without an unacceptable number going astray into his mouth, I refilled all our coffee mugs with decaf in acknowledgment of the hour and poured an added mug for Tom, Jennifer topped off the milk and sugar containers, then shifted her seat to cushions in front of the fireplace, leaving the corner of the couch for Tom.

We'd all settled back into our places when the guest room door opened and Tom and Shadow came out.

As Tom headed for the open spot on the couch, I noticed Shadow did not return to in front of the guest room door. Instead, he took up one of his favorite places—a patch of floor not far from the front door, facing that barrier to the outside world.

My father, on first seeing Shadow lie there, had identified it as a herding dog guarding the pass, with his flock safely behind him.

I wondered if Tom realized what a compliment it was to him that Shadow figured Tom could handle the job of guarding the inside approach to Tamantha, allowing Shadow to take up his more usual perimeter sentry spot.

I doubted it.

From Tom's grunt as he sat, and the long, thirsty drink of coffee, he had other thoughts and needs on his mind.

"Do you want something more to eat? A meal?" Diana asked.

That promised a little high for my kitchen. "Sandwich," I amended.

"No, thanks. They brought in supper at the sheriff's department. This is good." He picked up a doughnut, observed the oblong shape but did not comment on it. "They're keeping Hiram in custody."

His even delivery provided no rough edges to try to catch onto for potential meanings behind that bare fact.

If that had stopped me, I never would have asked half the questions I've asked in my journalism career.

"Why did they keep you so long?"

"Wait. First tell me what you all did after leaving the grazing association."

Supposed the man deserved a break from answering questions.

We told him. Each of us contributing some.

When Mike repeated Jack Delahunt's information about rustling, Tom said a single swear word. Softly enough that anyone listening from the guest room couldn't possibly hear, yet vehement enough that those of us in the living room understood the depth of his reaction.

Palm up, he invited us to continue.

At the end, he gave a noncommittal, "Huh."

Leaving it to me to ask, "What does that mean?"

"Wait. Thought I heard you asking a question before I knocked."

An essential skill in interviewing, especially politicians, is to remember where you were when they tried to sidetrack you to what they wanted to talk about or spin you away from what they didn't want to talk about.

"Yes." Saying that gave me half a beat to remember. "I was asking about tire tracks at the scene and whether the sheriff's department could have gotten a lead on who was there from tracks?"

Mike, Diana, and Tom shook their heads.

"Tough in a spot like that. Dry, windy, and open," Mike said. "Even if the tires made impressions on the dust, a good amount would blow away before the scientists got there."

Somehow that sounded like a quote. "Did you talk to your aunt? Call her between the station and here?"

As head dispatcher in O'Hara Hill and senior dispatcher for the county-wide system, Gisella Decker knew most of what the sheriff's department was doing and all that it should be doing. Since the new sheriff had aligned those two much more closely than his predecessor, Aunt Gee had become more parsimonious about sharing information with us.

"Maybe."

"But she's at a convention," Jennifer protested.

"Doesn't mean she doesn't know everything that's going on in Cottonwood County." I didn't take my eyes off Mike. "What else—?"

"It's more than the general conditions." Tom cut across my words, for all the world as if he were protecting Mike from harassment. As if Paycik couldn't stick up for himself.

See what I mean about an odd triangle?

Tom continued, "Hiram parked where an earlier vehicle would most likely have been. There're two prime spots by the house—where York's and Hiram's trucks were. Any time two trucks are there, that's where they're going to park."

"Was that why Hiram walked up that little knoll and found York? He parked beside York's vehicle, didn't see anybody, started wondering?" Diana asked.

"Wouldn't be surprised," Tom said.

"Why wouldn't he say that, instead of that stuff about catching sight of something shiny?" I asked.

"Might have also seen something shiny," Mike said.

Trying to bring this foray into Hiram Poppinger's possible thought processes back on track, I asked, "How about other ways of getting there?"

Mike's brows rose. "Helicopter? Hot air balloon? Motorcycle— Hiram might not be as likely to drive over those tracks, though the problems remain with the conditions. Not to mention no sightings of helicopters or hot air balloons."

"What about horseback, smart aleck?"

Mike turned to Tom, inviting him to answer.

"Members haul their horses." He went silent a beat, then shook his head. "Trailers mostly park on the approach road. If there was anything, the sheriff's department would have seen them and secured that area, too. Besides—"

"Someone could park on another road on the property and ride across to where York was shot, right? Horse trailers are out on the roads all the time."

"Horse trailers aren't uncommon, but they're notable," Diana said. "Somebody'd be sure to see one coming or going, wondering what they were doing. Next person they saw they'd ask if so-and-so was thinking to sell his paint, because they'd seen him hauling it when the spotter knew so-and-so wasn't working a herd at the time. And then it would be all over."

Tom added, "Not to mention it starts to sound like premeditated. Somebody knowing or getting York to that spot. Setting up to have a horse trailer some distance away—which it would need to be so it's out of sight—to ride over there to shoot him? I don't think so."

"Why not? A surprise attack—"

"Wouldn't be a surprise, either," Mike picked up. "You'd hear a horse coming. And if somebody got York there on purpose, wouldn't he be on alert?"

Tom's turn again. "He was on alert with a whole lot less call than that. No, Elizabeth, think you're going to have to reconcile yourself that the killer was there in a vehicle and the tracks are gone."

"More like the sheriff's department has to reconcile itself to that. I was just exploring possibilities." That isolated spot. Was that truly fortuitous for the impulsive killer? In the meantime, there was something else to follow up on. "Explain your *Huh*, now, Tom."

He pulled in a breath. "Furman York's distant past is a different direction from what Shelton and the sheriff appear to be pursuing."

At the mention of Sheriff Russ Conrad my eyes shifted to Diana. Mike's did, too.

She growled. "You've been with me every second since we found out about this murder and you know darned right well that, in addition to keeping my word to keep the two areas of my life separate, I haven't had any more opportunity to pump Russ for the sheriff's department's thinking than I've had to blab what we've been doing to him."

"Too bad," Mike said. "About the pumping part, not the blabbing part."

"What about you, talking to Gee?" she retorted.

"She didn't know anything. Said she'd been too busy to find out details. Threw in the stuff about tire tracks like she was thinking out loud."

Diana pointedly focused on Tom. "What direction do *you* think they're taking?"

"The grazing association. With a side order of me."

Aware of his daughter in the room not far away, I resisted the urge to shout my question like a White House press room scrummer.

"*You? Why?*"

He turned to me. "You know about grazing associations?"

I gritted my teeth.

In keeping with the theme of the White House press room under every administration and every press secretary I've ever known of, that was not responsive to the *why* I'd asked and he knew it.

I didn't give a rat's patootie if Russ Conrad, Wayne Shelton, and every other member of the Cottonwood County Sheriff's Department devoted every second to looking into the grazing association.

Also something Thomas David Burrell knew.

But he was determined to tell it his way. And his resemblance to Abe Lincoln's good-looking cousin wasn't the only reason he reminded me of Mount Rushmore. He can be about as easy to move as that pile of granite.

With assumed ease, I said, "I know a grazing association isn't exactly like a ditch." Or a country club, so they didn't have clubhouses. I skipped that part of what I now knew.

"Not exactly like a ditch." He tipped his head in a single, deadpan nod. "Ditch company's roughly based on geography. Even when it's not, you don't have a choice of who shares a ditch. A grazing association's voluntary. A group of like-minded ranchers getting together for mutual benefit." He considered. "Starts that way, leastwise. What can happen over time, though, is you get another generation coming in, not getting along with old-timers, or a couple of the same generation butting heads. It's not so like-minded after a while."

"Does that describe you and Norman Clay Lukasik? Different generations, butting heads? Or merely not like-minded?"

"It's no secret Lukasik and I don't see eye-to-eye. And that extended to Furman York."

"If you don't like him, why not get rid of him? Lukasik," I added quickly. I must be tired to use the infelicitous *get rid of* where it could be mistaken for a reference to the murdered man. "You're chairman of this grazing association, right? And you said it's voluntary. There's got to be a way for the group to oust a member."

"Getting rid of him or anybody else gets complicated." His mouth twisted into a grim smile. "You heard he's a lawyer?"

"Oh, yeah, I've heard. His profession and style figured largely in the history from Mrs. P this afternoon."

"With Mrs. Parens telling it, you have a good introduction to the man." He looked around at the others. "I didn't know much myself until becoming chairman of the grazing association. Turns out, right after he bought into the association, shareholders decided to accept his offer to revamp the bylaws for free. They thought they were getting a gift horse they didn't want to pass up. More like the Trojan horse. He's got twists and turns added to the agreement that make it real difficult to move him out."

"You looked into it?"

"It's been looked into a few times. Twice under my father." Apparently in response to the raised eyebrows surrounding him, he added, "He was chairman when the Lukasik Ranch was allowed in. They recognized their mistake soon enough. By then the damage was done."

"Your father isn't a fan of one of Cottonwood County's most famous citizens?"

"I think you'll find the few who are fans are those who don't have dealings with his ranching operation."

"Mrs. P had a different take. She indicated some in the county don't approve of his legal tactics or, I suppose, his choice of clients."

"Some don't. But since he's been plying his trade outside of the county for the past several decades—"

"Became too big a fish for Cottonwood County. At least in his eyes," Mike said.

"—worry about that aspect faded. Especially with him being famous."

"In other words, he's liked better when he's not here?"

"Pretty much. Except, as I said, when it comes to those of us who have to deal with his ranching operation. Some even have thought that if he came back and took the reins from York the issues would go away. A few were hoping Gable—"

He asked the question with a pause. We all nodded we knew about Lukasik's son.

"—might be an answer. Green, but seems like a good enough guy. Trouble is, York was clearly the boss, leaving the son no authority. No sign the father intended to change that."

"And you're not among those who believed the problems would go away if Norman Clay Lukasik took charge."

He hitched one shoulder. "I had a few passing thoughts about us jumping from the frying pan into the fire, considering Lukasik's ways. But there's no way of knowing how it might have turned out. Couldn't get over the first hurdle of getting Lukasik to take charge. Or even to check what York was doing. Lukasik's been told issues in the past— started well before this rustling—and never made a move to fix them. Matter of fact, what with the way he angled the association agreement, pretty much nobody can call him to account for such problems short of law enforcement."

"What problems?"

"Furman York. And rustling."

My mind was working over the implications when Mike asked a question that drove all other thoughts underground.

"Tom, have you been hit by the rustling?"

Chapter Sixteen

"YEAH."

"Bad?"

"Bad enough."

Mike swore.

Diana said, "When? How bad?"

I said, "You didn't tell Shelton that, did you?"

"I did."

"Why? Now you have a motive," Jennifer spoke my thoughts exactly. "We were thinking the rustling motive took attention right away from you. Weren't we?"

"We were," I said grimly. "We were not bargaining on you blabbing your potential motive to Wayne Shelton the first chance you had. No wonder they kept you so long."

He appeared remarkably unaffected by our disapproval. "Wouldn't have mattered if I told Wayne or not. He'd have known soon enough. As it happens, he knew already. If it's a motive, I already had it. Might as well get it out in the open."

"You've been in on what we've been doing this past year and more and you still don't know that's not how it works? You keep motive to yourself."

"Why? Besides, even if Wayne didn't know, you all would find it out soon enough. As you said, I've watched you in action."

And then we'd have had to decide whether or not to let Shelton know. Had Tom, darn the man, intended to protect us from that decision-making or was that an accidental byproduct of his overactive honesty?

Didn't matter. He'd handed over a motive wrapped up with a bow.

I pushed my hair back. "First words out of your mouth to Shelton, you told him Furman York backed a truck up to your land and loaded some of your cows onto it and sold them as his?"

"No."

"No? But—

"That wasn't first thing I told Wayne. Though… Look, I might as well repeat what I told Wayne."

He took another drink of coffee. I got up to bring the pot to refill his mug and offer it to anyone else, with Diana and Mike as takers.

"Clyde—"

He questioned us again—mostly me—about whether we knew who that was.

We—I—did.

Clyde owned a neighboring ranch to Tom's Circle B. He was one of the ranchers Lukasik had dismissed as part-timers for his job as a mechanic tending the mini-fleet of rental vehicles at the tiny airport.

"—told me he'd seen some of my brand mixed in with Lukasik's on the Lukasik Ranch a couple days ago. Clyde had gone there to get back a horse trailer York borrowed months ago and never returned. He ran into Gable—Lukasik's son—at the home ranch. Gable told Clyde where to find Furman York and directed him to a tucked away pasture Clyde had never known about. York was not best pleased to see him. Wanted to know who sent him, muttering about firing his ass.

"York being that worked up made Clyde curious, so he looked around real close without seeming to. Snapped a couple pictures with his phone of a Circle B cow who'd miraculously given birth to a Lukasik-branded calf."

"What?"

He held up a hand to hold off my question. "I went over there yesterday and sure enough. York tried to make out it must have been a mistake made in the fall at the grazing association, when we separated out cattle. Pure bull, since we mostly have individual pastures. He knew it. I knew it. He still tried to brazen it out. Said since he'd fed the cows all winter, they should get to keep the calves. We had some words."

Diana shook her head. Mike made a sound of disgust, then asked, "What did you do?"

"I'd gone with a horse trailer. I saddled up and trailed them to Paul Chaney's place until I could arrange to trailer them home."

I said, as calmly as I could. "Explain all that for the Easterner in the room. Except the part about you having words with York the day before he gets himself murdered and that last part—you trailed the cows to a friend's ranch because you thought they'd disappear if left in York's keeping. That I understand."

"It's another way of stealing cattle. You get a mother cow that's not your brand in the fall. After she drops a calf in the spring, you slap your brand on the baby, and that calf becomes part of your herd," Tom said.

"But if the mother cow still has the other brand...?"

"Exactly. It's a darned, uh, gutsy thing to try. And the thieves are feeding all winter. Course that's not much of a problem when your boss is paying for the feed and labor."

"Eventually, wouldn't someone spot the cow having the wrong brand for the ranch it's on?"

"Probably," Mike said. "Ranchers notice things like that."

"They're downright nosy. If calves aren't branded according to what the cows are, somebody's going to ask how come," Diana said. "Was he going to try to hold onto them? Sell off the cows when the calves could be taken off them?"

Tom raised one shoulder. "I plan to ask around, see if he could have done this to other ranches other years. Pull it enough times and you've got a nice bump up in your herd. If you don't get too greedy."

"The grazing association counts cattle on and off, doesn't it?" Diana asked.

Tom grimaced in apparent pain. "Supposed to. That rotates around and Lukasik Ranch's been in charge the past year, which meant York."

"Fox guarding the hen house," Mike grumbled.

I pulled them back to an earlier point. "Tom, you said if he didn't get too greedy, but according to Jack Delahunt, York *did* get greedy. And you weren't surprised by what he told us."

He looked up from his coffee mug and for the first time a filter of amusement softened the lines around his mouth and eyes.

And then the infuriating man took a drink of coffee. *And* said, "Good coffee."

"Iris made it, not me, if that's what you're getting at. Now quit stalling."

Amusement left.

"Adding in what Jack told you, I suspect Furman York was going around hitting association members—not the fancy touches like he did with my cows' calves. Directly at the home ranches. Me, Clyde, the Chaneys, others. Cattle's taken at night from somewhere hard to spot from the home ranch."

"That's despicable," Diana said. "Using knowledge of your neighbors to steal from them."

"Doesn't get much lower," Mike agreed.

Tom reached for another doughnut. "That's pretty much what Wayne said."

I gawked at him. "That's what Wayne... Let me get this straight. First you told him about how you had this dispute *yesterday* with York over his poaching calves and—"

"Rustling," came as a quartet.

"Rustling. A dispute over his taking some of your mother cows so their babies would be born on the Lukasik Ranch and branded before you caught them at it.

"And then—*then*—you told him that you, along with other members of the grazing association, have had more head outright stolen, and you believe York took them east and sold them where paperwork isn't required and it's possible to find livestock lots that follow the Don't Ask, Don't Tell business plan. Am I right so far?"

"Yeah."

"And you told Sergeant Wayne Shelton of the Cottonwood County Sheriff's Department all this?"

"Pretty much."

"Pretty much," I repeated.

"Didn't say it as strong as you put it. Didn't know then what you all heard from Jack. All I had was a suspicion York might also be involved with rustling direct from grazing association members' land."

"Anything else?"

"Yeah. No alibi. I was alone, checking cattle on my own place. No way to prove it."

"Of course," I said bitterly.

"But why are you worried, Elizabeth? Tom's not the main suspect, because Hiram Poppinger is," Jennifer protested.

I responded with my own question to him. "Do they really think Hiram shot Furman York?"

Mike answered instead. "He was there. With a shotgun."

"Hiram with a shotgun at the grazing association might work in the Cottonwood County version of *Clue*. It's not enough for reality. Not nearly enough. And Shelton's too smart not to see that."

"Might not be his call." Mike carefully did not look at Diana.

I brought it out in the open. "Sheriff Conrad? Maybe, but he's probably too smart not to see that, too. And I sure hope he's too smart not to ignore Shelton."

Diana declined her head in mock thanks for the semi-compliment to her honey. And, I suppose, by extension to her, since she'd picked him.

"But," Mike continued thoughtfully, "we don't know the county attorney. Could Jarvis Abbott put pressure on the sheriff? Shelton, too, for that matter."

"Conrad and Abbott worked together before coming here, so you'd expect them to listen to each other. Maybe holding on to Hiram is a ploy to lull the murderer into thinking the coast is clear and somehow that's going to make him or her expose him- or herself."

"Maybe." Mike didn't believe it.

"Hiram didn't kill York," Tom said.

I spun on him. Did the man not understand he pushed himself to the top of the suspect ladder by bringing Hiram down a rung? "What evidence do you have of that?"

I half expected him to say none, he just knew. Or that Hiram wasn't capable of it, which was a stretch.

"How he was acting, especially when we first got there. He was fretting and cussing about needing to get on his way, he'd done his duty, and a man had the right to have a life. It didn't cross his mind they could suspect him. Even later, when you all were there, he didn't really believe it.

"Heck, at the sheriff's office, he was still peeved at them interrupting whatever he had planned today. I had to lean on him to call James." James Longbaugh was a lawyer of all trades in the county and the master of every one I'd seen him try so far. "Hiram said he wasn't putting money in Longbaugh's pocket for nothing. Nothing—that's how he sees this."

I wasn't convinced, but it was a far better argument than I'd expected.

Apparently presenting it depleted Tom's energy, because he sat back with the top of the couch back supporting his neck and closed his eyes.

No one responded. We all seemed caught in the waves of weariness emanating from Tom.

Until Jennifer sat up abruptly.

"Wait a minute. What was that you said on the way to O'Hara Hill, Elizabeth? Something about Hiram's gun."

"Right," Mike perked up. "What you *said* you had to think over."

"I did have to think it over. And you guys got plenty of payback with not telling me about Furman York's past and his relationship with Norman Clay Lukasik before they were foreman and ranch owner."

"Tell us about Hiram's gun," Mike ordered.

"I don't know for *sure* it's about Hiram's gun."

"Tell."

I recounted what Hiram had said about the deputies taking his gun being high-handed and he hadn't fired his gun. Diana and Mike nodded, confirming they'd heard that.

"Tom, I think you were too far away to hear that."

He lifted one shoulder an inch. "Didn't hear it or don't remember."

"Well, he said it. Next came hearing a sound as if someone were about to speak. Then motions. I looked over and caught the end of Richard pushing or lightly punching Lloyd's arm to warn him off. As if he knew what Lloyd would say and he didn't want him to."

"That's it?" Mike asked. "You caught a bit of movement and you might have been mistaken. Even if you weren't, Richard could have been telling Lloyd to knock off just about anything."

"Like what?" Jennifer demanded.

"I don't know." Pushed by her eye-roll, Mike said, "Picking his nose."

"Gross."

"Like I just said, I don't know. But it could have been anything."

"I don't think so," I inserted before Jennifer responded. "Timing was too perfect. That's what I had to think through, whether it fit the one thing that occurred to me right off. I had to let it roll around in my head."

"And? What's the result of this internal pinball game?" Diana asked.

"I believe my first impression was right. That—"

"You never told us your first impression," Mike complained.

Jennifer reached up from her floor cushions to backhand his upper arm. "She was about to. Be quiet, Paycik. Go ahead, Elizabeth."

"We can't know for sure," I acknowledged. "With the way it happened and the timing, I'd say the most likely thing it meant was Lloyd was going to say it didn't matter that Hiram hadn't shot his gun."

All of them frowned.

Jennifer spoke. "Why wouldn't it matter that Hiram hadn't shot his gun? It has to be important. York was shot, wasn't he?"

"We don't have confirmation he was shot—"

Tom interrupted. "He was shot."

"How do you—?"

"Saw him. Screen came loose in the wind before they had it secured. He was shot."

I said, "That's got to help Hiram, since he wouldn't shoot someone in the back."

"He wouldn't." Tom didn't open his eyes. "But York wasn't shot in the back."

As I sucked in a new supply of oxygen, I realized that somewhere deep down, I'd nursed the hope York *had* been shot in the back. Because no one who knew Tom Burrell even a little bit—say the way the new sheriff knew him—would believe he'd shoot someone in the back.

"York was shot and that means Hiram's gun has to be important, especially whether it was shot or not," Mike said.

I shook my head.

"Hiram's gun wouldn't be important if they already knew it wasn't the murder weapon. And that's what Richard didn't want Lloyd to give away—to Hiram, to us, to anyone else listening."

"How could they already know Hiram's gun wasn't the murder weapon?"

"Easy. They'd know Hiram's shotgun wasn't the weapon if the fatal shots were from a handgun or a bazooka or—"

"Bazooka?" Mike interjected.

"—anything else different enough from Hiram's shotgun that it not being fired said nothing about whether or not Hiram could have killed York with this other, hypothetical weapon. If the injuries weren't consistent with his gun—"

"They were," Tom said. "Consistent with Hiram's shotgun or a thousand others in the county, including mine."

"So Furman York was shot with something consistent with Hiram's gun, yet they already knew it wasn't his gun, well before ballistics or anything? How is that possible?" Diana broke off and looked at me. "Unless...?"

"Exactly. They know Hiram's gun isn't the murder weapon because—"

Mike made a noise of discovery. "Got it. Because they already *have* the murder weapon. And it's not Hiram's gun. But then why aren't they going after whoever it belongs to?"

They were following the same mental route I had. "Those are things I've been trying to sort out, though there hasn't been much quiet time to work on it. Off the top of my head..."

"Off the top of your head...?" Mike urged.

"We shouldn't get too attached to this theory," I warned. "But what if they know Hiram's gun wasn't the murder weapon because they know the gun that killed Furman York belonged to York. That would also explain why they aren't going after anybody."

"York's gun... Why didn't Hiram see it when he found the body?" Mike asked.

"It was under the body."

"Oh. That's good," Diana said. "And the deputies didn't find out until the scientists moved York. Tom, did they move the body at all before we got there?"

His eyes slit open, he said, "Yeah. There was some talk about moving York. Shelton made sure I didn't hear the rest."

I nodded. "We'll need to confirm Hiram didn't move the body when he found York, looking for a pulse or something."

"We're saying this York guy was shot with his own gun?" Jennifer asked.

"That's one possibility. The sheriff's department *could* have the weapon and it's not York's, though they know who it belongs to—raising the question Mike asked of why the heck aren't they going after the owner. Or they have the weapon and *don't* know who it belongs to, which is more likely. Though I still think York's gun being the murder weapon is the top theory."

"Tom, have you seen York with a shotgun?" Mike asked.

"Yes. Keeps a couple in his truck and carries one a lot of the time, even just walking out in pastures."

Jennifer frowned. "If the sheriff's department knows Hiram's gun isn't the murder weapon, why are they holding him?"

"If York's gun is the murder weapon, it means anybody could have taken it from his truck or grabbed it away from him and shot him, including Hiram," I said. "They'll do gunshot residue tests and such on him to help rule him in or rule him out."

"Did they do those tests on you, Tom?" she asked.

"Yep."

"What were the results?"

"They didn't say, but there should be residue. Shot at a coyote near some calves early this morning."

"You got it?" Mike clearly expected the answer to be yes.

"Nope. Got away."

"But they let you go and they're holding Hiram," Jennifer said.

"Shelton's irked at him," Mike suggested.

I said, "Or he didn't want Hiram giving away things he'd seen when he found the body."

"Oh, yeah, that makes sense," Diana agreed. "And it applies even if all or any of the other possibilities are true."

Tom's mouth twisted. "Could be any of what you all mentioned. Or maybe they want to make sure they keep Hiram alive."

We all turned toward him.

"How?" Jennifer asked.

"To keep the murderer from taking out Hiram, setting him up as a scapegoat, hoping everyone accepts that he shot Furman York and the sheriff's department would end the investigation?" Diana mused.

"That wouldn't end the investigation," I protested. "If Hiram was murdered, it would shift to his murder and the murderer would be even worse off because the potential fall guy was gone."

"Wasted, so to speak," Mike murmured. At our groans at the grim play on the word's alternative meaning, he added, "Sorry."

Tom stuck with the main thread of the discussion. "There are a lot of ways to die that don't look like murder or are real hard to prove are murder."

Mike nodded slowly. "A lot of ways on a ranch, especially for an old hot-head like Hiram, leaping before he looks."

Chapter Seventeen

I'D BROUGHT DOWN bedding for the couch, told Tom where things were in the bathroom, and asked him a second time if there was anything else he might need.

"Thanks. I'll be fine here."

We stood across from each other. The coffee table between us ... along with exhaustion, the knowledge of his daughter's presence nearby, and Mike's presence, not nearby.

"Good night, then," I said.

"Good night."

I was almost to the doorway that led to the stairway to the master suite when he spoke.

"Elizabeth."

I turned to him.

"Jenny's starting to sound like you." He still slipped sometimes and reverted to the nickname he'd been calling her most of her life, though less and less in front of her.

"Like me?"

"Yeah. Earlier, when she remembered what you'd said about Hiram's gun, she said *Wait a minute* like you do a lot and it sounded exactly like you."

I remembered her saying that and I knew I said it, but I hadn't made the connection.

Dryly, I asked, "Is that a good thing or a bad thing?"

"A good thing," he said. "Definitely a good thing."

DAY TWO

Chapter Eighteen

THE MORNING BROUGHT a horrifying revelation.

Tamantha was a lark.

I am not.

And I'd stayed up, doing a preliminary pass on the top layer of research on Furman York that Jennifer had shared. That content, as well as the limited gap between closing my eyes and opening them pretty much eliminated the already slim chance I'd had of waking up happy today.

Last thing I needed was a morning person.

Not only a morning person, a singing one.

I discovered those weaknesses in Empress Tamantha as I came down the stairs and turned the corner to see her and her father in the kitchen.

Also the girl couldn't sing.

Well. She couldn't sing *well.*

Because she sure was singing with enthusiasm and volume, and what she was singing was *Oh, What a Beautiful Morning.*

She had finished declaring musically that everything was going her way, when she spotted me.

"Morning, Elizabeth. Do you want Daddy to fix you scrambled eggs? It's his specialty. I finished mine. And now I'm going over to see Iris and Zeb."

"Mr. and Mrs. Undlin," Tom corrected.

"They said to call them Iris and Zeb. I'm doing what they asked."

He frowned at her.

She smiled back, having won that round.

She left, practically skipping, while singing *Surrey with the Fringe on Top*, accompanied by the back door slapping closed after her.

"She thinks everything's settled because I'm here. I'll have to talk to her later." Tom lifted the pan he'd clearly used for eggs. "Want some? Hope you don't mind."

"Don't mind. Glad you did. But none for me. Just coffee."

Tom poured me a cup of coffee.

"Thanks," I muttered after the first mouthful of my true lifeblood.

"Thank yourself. You had the timer set up."

I shook my head with a modicum of effort. "Not me. Must have been Iris." After several sustaining sips, I belatedly asked, "Eggs? Didn't think I had any."

"Iris."

"Ah." More coffee, and I added, "*Oklahoma!*, really?"

He shrugged, a faint grin fanning creases from his eyes. "She picks up the music at the library. We had to talk about *I'm Just a Girl Who Can't Say No*, but I preferred that talk to the one about *Molasses to Rum* from *1776*."

I grimaced. "Explaining the slave trade. Tough." Another sip from my mug brought another thought. "I wonder if she knows about *Sweet Charity*. Great songs."

He frowned at me suspiciously. Apparently his education in musicals was coming from Tamantha's explorations of them and she hadn't reached that one yet.

"Hey, big spender, spend a little time with me," I filled in.

Realization flooded his eyes. "Don't you dare, Elizabeth."

I widened my eyes in utter innocence, then ruined it by spluttering into my coffee.

As I raised my head and met his eyes, my breath stuttered.

We remained like that. This morning, last night, his arranging a sleepover for Tamantha for our not-going-to-happen date, shimmering between us.

My phone rang.

Grateful or disappointed or both, I reached for it. Gesturing a slightly apologetic acknowledgment of interrupting ... *something* ... after I'd clicked to answer.

Tom tipped his head, accepting the inevitability rather than my apology.

"Hello? Elizabeth?"

"Yes. I'm here."

"It's Jerry. From the station. Did you see the footage? Thought I'd hear from you."

"Sorry. We went from one thing to another all day and into the night. We did look at the footage on Jennifer's phone—and thanks for sending it out with her—but, honestly, Jerry, we didn't see anything remarkable."

"I wondered..." Before I needed to ask what he'd wondered, he continued, "Okay, then you've got to come in here and see it on the screen. Tell me then there's nothing remarkable and I'll quit bugging you."

Even if I hadn't owed him the courtesy as a colleague, I was curious now.

Jerry was not the flight of fancy type. Being the main studio camera operator, put him in contact day after day with Thurston at his most dictatorial, because there was a camera involved, a nice big camera he considered all his. Jerry held onto his sanity by being unflappable. Stolid, even.

"I'll be there."

"Good. I won't rest easy until you see this and see what I see."

I hung up.

"Jerry. From the station," I explained.

"Figured."

"Wants me to come in and look at footage on the monitor there. Us. You want to come? I'm going to call the others..."

"Need to get Tamantha squared away."

"Of course. I'll just..." I lifted the phone.

He nodded and took the egg pan to the sink.

✧ ✧ ✧ ✧

DURING THE SHORT drive to the station after calling Jennifer, Mike, and Diana, it hit me what an odd time it was for Jerry to be there.

He'd worked the Ten last night and would do both newscasts today. To be there at this time of the morning made for a short night last night and a long day today.

Diana was leaving her truck when I pulled in to the KWMT parking lot behind Jennifer, arriving to work her scheduled shift. Before I was out of my vehicle, Mike arrived in his posh SUV.

Diana headed toward the main doors, then waited there for the rest of us to catch up.

She pointed. "Isn't that Thurston's car?"

The red sedan was distinctive enough to be sure it was. Thurston at work this early was odd enough to disbelieve our eyes.

"What would he be doing here now?" Mike asked.

"I was wondering—" I noticed Jennifer had also been about to speak, but I'd started first and she didn't interrupt. "—the same thing about Jer—"

I broke off because Diana, the first to pass the exterior set of double glass doors into the vestibule before the interior set, had stopped abruptly.

"Something's up."

Past her shoulder, I saw Thurston, red-faced and waving his arms, shouting into the newsroom bullpen from the spot where the hallway led to his private office. The scattering of staffers at their desks or transfixed in transit to somewhere all stared at him, motionless.

"If Thurston catches wind that we're looking into York's death, he'll delay and derail us any way he can," Mike said. "I watched the Ten last night—"

He meant he'd recorded the newscast on his home setup. I used to do that for every newscast at my stations until I came to KWMT. Couldn't take the punishment of watching that much Thurston. But it was smart of Mike to do it. To check on Pauly, his stand-in last night for the sports segment, and to critique himself on a regular basis.

It was part of why he was getting better and better.

"—and you would not believe how he botched it."

I would believe it. I also agreed with Mike about Thurston trying to delay and derail us. "Let's hold up out here and see if it blows over."

"You mean if he'll blow over. He's such a blowhard, shouldn't take long," Jennifer muttered.

It didn't.

With a final, dramatic gesture, and his voice loud enough that we heard the climactic "...jobs will be lost!"

He spun on his heel—actually a little farther around than he wanted, because he had to backtrack a step to start down the hall.

Diana eased one of the interior doors open and when we heard the emphatic slam of the door to Thurston's inner sanctum, we entered.

That slam released the newsroom from its spell, so our entry was covered by conversation, movement, and laughter. A lot of laughter, though kept at a level that would not penetrate Thurston's office.

"What's going on, Audrey?" Diana asked the assignment editor/producer as she passed us going the opposite direction.

"An impressive Thurston hissy fit, even by his standards." She was gone before we could get more from her.

Leona D'Amato, the reporter with the Cottonwood County's society beat, came within reach. I held onto her arm.

"What was Thurston's hissy fit about?"

"Didn't you hear? This was Act Two. In last night's Act One, he screamed at Les for most of the time between the Five and the Ten."

"What about?"

A lot of times he screamed about me, not a fact I'm ashamed of. But I hadn't even been in the office.

More important, as far as he knew, I didn't have any interest in the murder of Furman York. Thurston claimed rights to all lead stories. Then he failed to report them halfway decently. Heck, he often failed to pronounce the names right.

If he'd gotten out of his cushy office and gone to the scene yesterday, he would have known I was *very* near this big story. That couldn't explain these hissy fits, though, because Thurston didn't do on-the-scene reporting. Remember? Too hard to keep his hair perfect in Wyoming's windy outdoors.

"About how Les had to fire anyone who has sent or in the future sends Thurston clips of those robotic camera bloopers. Too bad you missed it. Thurston was practically foaming at the mouth."

"Robotic camera bloopers?" I asked innocently.

Not innocently enough.

"You set him up?" Leona's question held no criticism. Possibly a bit of approval.

"Mmm. I might have let him set himself up."

"Even better." Definitely approval.

Quickly, I explained the background of yesterday's studio show-down, when she'd been out of the newsroom.

"If Thurston gets vindictive, throws his weight around and gets anybody fired…"

I absolutely didn't want to contribute to others losing their jobs.

"He can try. He won't succeed. That's why it bothers him so much. The videos must have started right after you left. By the time I came in before the Five yesterday, they'd found the easy videos of the robotic camera goofs and were competing to find more—bonus points for any not previously seen. Then they emailed him using really bad spoofed email addresses, like Hiring@TopTenStation.com. What idiot would think that was a legit email and open it expecting to find info on a job?"

"Thurston," Diana said.

"Exactly. The emails kept flowing in and with Les not here yester-day—again. Has anyone else noticed our fearless leader is here less and less?—"

I had. Nods from Diana and Mike said they had, too. There was no time to discuss that detour before Leona resumed.

"—Thurston went for the direct attack. Came flying out of his office, pushed aside that sweet news aide, Dale, then started ranting at everyone."

"What did he say?"

"That he would not stand for being attacked this way. That he knew who was sending these demeaning emails—not clear if he meant demeaning to the robotic cameras or him and, besides that, he has no clue who's sending the emails. He'd be shocked that some of his sycophants have been the most prolific. Nice to his face, kick him in the behind when he turns around. Anyway, he was threatening jobs again, this time saying *he'd* fire them personally. Maybe he got confused in all the excitement and forgot he doesn't have hiring and firing authority."

"The man's a maniac," Mike said.

"True. Right now, though, he's a maniac with a hot interview."

"Who?" Mike, Diana, and I chorused.

"Norman Clay Lukasik."

While the rest of us still tried to catch our breath at the idea of Thurston with that hot interview, Leona added, "Probably the biggest name in lawyers between east LA and west Chicago. And you know it's his foreman who—oh, of course you know. On the case already?"

No need to answer what she clearly knew. Instead, I got out, "*Thurston* got an interview with Lukasik? He called Lukasik and—"

"No," Jennifer interrupted. "Lukasik called him. I started to tell you before. Dale emailed me last night. I didn't read it until this morning."

Poor Dale. Forever yearning after Jennifer, who remained apparently unaware that her fellow news aide's epistles with news and information he thought she might be interested in were his version of love letters. Which she left languishing in her inbox overnight.

But I was less focused on Dale's unrequited adoration than the news that Norman Clay Lukasik had called Thurston.

Thurston thought he'd achieved a coup, scheduling the interview.

I'd bet Lukasik got what he wanted out of it, though.

I patted Jennifer's shoulder as she dropped her belongings at the desk where she'd be working. "Don't worry. We'll tell you all about it if there's anything to tell from what Jerry wants to show us. Stick with your work. Don't get in trouble. We might need you later."

"Are you kidding? I want to see this, too. Give me half a second to get things rolling."

"C'mon," Mike called from the open door of the editing booth. "Jerry's waiting."

We crowded in.

Actually, crowding would have been two of us. We packed in.

Jerry had me sit a little to the left. "Same angle you were at during the interview." Diana sat to the right. Mike was in back and hanging over us for a clear view. Jerry reached in for the controls.

The door started to open, eliciting, "Occupied" from all of us.

The door continued opening. As much as it could. Jennifer squeezed in sideways. "They won't miss me for a few minutes, especially since I transferred calls to my cell. Pretty dead this hour, anyway."

Jerry took over. "Okay, I'll start it with your last question, Elizabeth. It's all reaction shot. That's how we'd set it up and it kept rolling."

I would have fidgeted in impatience if there'd been room. We knew all this from what we'd seen on Jennifer's phone.

Admittedly, everything was much clearer in this size. Against the scarf-softened background, Odessa Vincennes' face held center stage. It had been a postage stamp on the phone screen. Now it was slightly larger than life.

My voice came on, asking Odessa how the group selected and verified material to include in the alerts. Her response. Me beginning to ask for the study. The door opening. Jerry saying the light was on. My starting to tell Mike I was conducting an interview.

Then him saying, "There's been a shooting at Tom's grazing association." His footsteps as he crossed the studio to me. "Not Tom. It wasn't Tom. It was the foreman from another ranch. Guy named Furman York. Looks like murder."

In the footage there was a beat of silence.

In the editing booth it was followed by varied sucked-in breaths, then Mike's soft whistle.

When the footage ended, we all stared at the screen a moment longer.

"*The Lady of Shalott*," Diana murmured.

"That's exactly what I said." Jerry spoke with justifiable vindication.

"You're a Tennyson fan?" I asked absently, my brain processing what we'd seen.

"Me? Nah. It's my wife quoting something about the Lady of Shalott all the time."

"The mirror crack'd from side to side; 'The curse is come upon me,' cried the Lady of Shalott."

"That's it. That's it exactly."

"Your wife's the Tennyson fan?" Diana asked.

"Nah, not her, either. But she sure does like Agatha Christie and books like that. There's one about a mirror cracking and that's where she learned that bit. Real taken with it, she is. As I said, she says it a lot. This—" He gestured toward the screen. "—is the first time I saw what it meant."

A shiver went across my shoulders. As if that motion had been the start of turning toward Jerry, I did that and said, "Let's see it again."

We watched it five more times.

"It's weird. Mike says there's been a murder, there's some reaction at the start, and then her face like ... empties," Jennifer said.

"Can you stop it on that first expression, Jerry?"

He did.

I understood why we hadn't seen it on Jennifer's phone. It was all in the eyes.

Odessa's overall expression was one of surprise.

Almost as if her brain said that was what was called for and produced it.

But her eyes... Her brain didn't rule her eyes.

Diana nodded. "That moment at the start... I keep thinking of the word beatific."

"Like beautiful?" Jerry asked. I thought Jennifer shot him a glance of gratitude that he'd asked the question.

"No. It's supremely happy. I associate it with angels. A sort of exalted happiness."

Looking at the screen, I said, "This is not angelic. More... triumphant?"

"Exalted triumph. Yeah," Diana said.

"What's even creepier is the next part. Jer?" Mike invited him to advance a few frames.

He did and stopped precisely on a sharp, clear view of eyes without expression, without life.

"It's like someone unplugged her," Jennifer said.

"Good one," Mike said. "What do we know about her?"

"Not much. She was sent by the group raising money for consumer alert flyers to be distributed to the elderly in the county, along with meals and other assistance. It was an info interview on that effort. I researched the group and the program behind the fund-raising, didn't look into her."

"Think we should?"

"It might be a sidetrack, but if only for our satisfaction, let's find out more about this woman. Her background—"

"On it," Jennifer said.

"—history, where she's from, if she has any connection with Furman York or murder or … well, anything that might explain that reaction."

"And what she drives," Diana inserted. I raised an eyebrow at her. She answered with, "The vehicle at the grazing association I thought I remembered from here. A long shot, maybe—"

"Got it," Jennifer said. "This is more like it. Instead of boring Furman York."

We started to stir. We'd have to unpack carefully and in the same order we'd packed to get out of here.

"Thank you, Jerry. Especially for your persistence."

He winked at me. "You can pay me in brownies and coffee."

Chapter Nineteen

NONE OF US said anything until we were in the parking lot.

At best, newsrooms are hotbeds of eavesdropping. KWMT-TV's newsroom had the deeper drawback of the shadows of Thurston Fine and Les Haeburn.

The camaraderie in the bullpen had risen exponentially in the past year, while Fine retained several adherents. More dangerous were the ones who presented themselves as part of the new attitude, while scuttling back to report to Fine, huddling under the shreds of his patronage.

Haeburn?

He had no adherents. He had only Fine.

Or Fine had him.

Hard to tell.

One theory was that Haeburn did whatever Fine wanted—or mostly did—because he intended to attach himself to coattails as Fine ascended.

I found that theory deeply flawed, because I couldn't imagine any decent station manager not seeing through Fine's fatuous exterior right to his fatuous interior.

No, if Haeburn had a brain, he'd attach himself to Mike's coattails, because he had talent, ambition, and the right amount of connections—enough to open doors, not so many that he was dismissed when he got inside the door.

However, Haeburn didn't have a brain.

Which left the theory that he took the easy way out by letting Fine have his way.

We stood in the parking lot, our clothes and hair streaming before a brisk west wind, to discuss.

Not much of a discussion.

"Strange reaction."

"Could be nothing, but..."

"Need to find out more about her before writing it off completely."

"So, what's next?" Jennifer asked.

"I have to work," Diana said.

Mike gusted out, "Suppose I should, too. Hey, aren't you scheduled now?" he belatedly asked Jennifer.

"Yeah. I could get Dale to fill in for me, if there's something important." She looked at me hopefully.

"Not important enough to pull you off your shift, especially since Dale worked late last night. Besides, you have work to start on already."

"What about you?" Mike asked me.

"I'm going to call Odessa Vincennes to schedule the end of our interview—" That drew nods all around, recognizing that would be a great opportunity to pump the woman about her reaction to the news of Furman York's death. "—then do a little grocery shopping."

This time the nods were joined by grins.

Chapter Twenty

ODESSA DIDN'T ANSWER her phone. I left a message, sufficiently vague that she would need to call me back if she wanted to know what I was talking about.

My phone rang as I pulled into the Sherman Supermarket's wide-open-spaces parking lot, built for mega-pickups and people who didn't like to be fenced in.

For about two seconds I congratulated myself on crafting a message that got such a prompt response. Then I saw the call was from my parents.

"Hi. Having a good time at Yellowstone?" I answered.

"It's amazing. Stunning," my mother's voice responded. With that talking-from-inside-a-tin-can quality—or lack of quality—that said she had speakerphone on. "We should have brought you children here as a family. I can't believe we never made this trip then."

"Accident-prone daredevils, thermal springs, canyon, forest fires," my father said in the background, presumably from behind the wheel, since I heard road noises.

"Nonsense," Mom said firmly, rewriting history. "Our children would have gotten so much out of a trip here. I'm going to strongly recommend that Rob and Anna bring the children—maybe this summer."

Dad groaned.

Mom willfully misinterpreted it. "Your father has been absolutely mesmerized by Old Faithful, Elizabeth."

"Saw it erupt four times, Maggie Liz," Dad exulted in the background.

"And we've seen the canyon and thermal springs and buffalo—"

"Bison," I corrected on behalf of Mrs. Parens' efforts to educate humanity on the difference. Not loudly. Maybe Mrs. P would have another shot at her when they came back through Cottonwood County on their return trip to Illinois—after a satisfactory conclusion to this murder investigation, I hoped.

"—deer, elk, wildflowers, mountains—oh, and so much more. Maybe we'll come back out with Rob and Anna."

That might be a record fast transition from considering suggesting to my brother and sister-in-law to a definite trip ... and coming with them.

Dad said, "Rather take you off someplace alone, Cat."

"Now, Jimmy." Her voice had a grin in it, though. "The Lake Yellowstone Hotel has been lovely, Elizabeth. I'm so glad you recommended it."

Uh-huh. Did Mom realize she'd connected being off someplace alone with Dad with the hotel, which had the bedrooms, which had the beds... Nope, wasn't going there. Even though I suspected my face wore a bit of a grin at the moment. They were pretty cute together, my parents.

"And I'm glad you're both having a good time."

"Oh, we've had a wonderful time."

Had? Not *having?* "But—"

"We thought we'd head out tomorrow."

"Not too early in the morning," Dad said.

"Jimmy." That level of scolding wouldn't stop a butterfly, much less a bison. "Not too early and spend the day leisurely, getting back to your house about dinner time. We'd—"

"Tomorrow?"

"—like to take you out for dinner. Yes, tomorrow."

Did I say cute?

Only when they weren't driving me nuts.

Especially by planning to arrive on my doorstep while we were trying to figure out who killed Furman York.

"You shouldn't miss a chance to spend time in Cody on your way back. There's a great museum—the Buffalo Bill Center of the West—and the Irma Hotel there was built by Buffalo Bill Cody. There are good restaurants and shopping. You shouldn't miss it. You can go straight there from Yellowstone, have a nice few days. I'll make reservations for you. Let me do that. I'd like to do that. Stay four or five days, then come back here to the small charms of Sherman."

"I don't know…"

"Really you need to see Cody. You can't have come all this way and miss it. And I'd love to treat you after all you did for me while I was transitioning from New York, moving here, and everything." That included the collapse of a career not long after the dissolution of a marriage. "Please."

"Jimmy?" Mom asked him.

"The girl wants us to see Cody, I think we should visit Cody." *Yay, Dad!* "She was right about Yellowstone and the hotel, wasn't she?"

Mom giggled softly.

Yeah, they were pretty cute.

✧   ✧   ✧   ✧

I DELAYED ENTERING Cottonwood County's center of culinary staples and delights to call Jennifer.

"If I have Leona send you a couple hotels and several restaurants in Cody, can you make reservations over the next few days?"

"What? You're going to leave now?"

"No. It's for my parents."

"But they're at Yellowstone."

"They're leaving in the morning."

"Oh. *Oh.*"

"Exactly."

"Sure. I can slip in making reservations, no problem. Soon as I get the places from Leona."

I called Leona next.

She answered with, "Busy."

I explained concisely, without getting into why I wanted to stall my parents' return to Sherman. She didn't ask.

"Will get those to Jennifer."

"Thank—"

She hung up before *you*.

I HAD MY packages of Pepperidge Farm Double Dark Chocolate Milano cookies in my shopping basket. Wished I could open one now to stoke me for what I was about to face, as the previous customer trundled out of Penny Czylinski's checkout lane with a "Bye now" sendoff.

Listening to Penny was like buying one of those five-dollar boxes at an estate sale. For the chance of finding a treasure, you endured the certainty of taking home junk. You paid for the privilege. And you did it over and over.

"Well, hi there, Elizabeth. On the trail, aren't—"

I lunged in with, "Do you know Odessa Vincennes?"

"—you. Figured. Told Carol Sue yesterday you'd be on it. Words barely out and news of Elizabeth Margaret Danniher being at the grazing association comes streaming in with all the rest. Pity for Tom Burrell. If he thinks he can come in here singing *Love Me Tender*—"

Tom? No, she couldn't mean Tom. Had to be part of her indiscriminate pronoun use.

"—going to find out he's mistaken. Won't have that. Him singing in here. Not that."

My brain skipped from *Love Me Tender* to Tamantha's morning warbling. The two pieces didn't connect, slowing me in picking up the threads of what Penny was saying.

"…and can't expect much different with that apple not bouncing far from the tree. Like my granny said—"

I threw in a name, hoping it would bob up downstream in her flow. "Lukasik."

"—at least they don't ruin another couple. That woman's as original as him. And—"

"Lukasik and—?"

"—that's mighty original. His shenanigans—well, you know. You've been in the middle of them. With—"

"Wait, go back. The woman as original as him? Who? Odessa Vincennes?"

"—him shooting—shooting off his mouth and shooting off a gun, though can't hardly fault him for that—"

My hopes spiked at the reference to shooting. For a blink, connections among Odessa Vincennes and Norman Clay Lukasik, then Lukasik and a gun, specifically shooting it, flared brightly.

"—when they were trying to steal from him, which you saw yourself. Course, that's not the way you're supposed to go about things, even when they deserve it and taking care of things himself's more direct like and satisfying. That one's slippery as soap…"

Hopes splattered around me. The gun, the shooting, fell back to earth. Her reference to my witnessing an attempt at stealing, connected to my early months in Cottonwood County and made the *him* in this episode of Penny's scattergun pronouns Hiram Poppinger, not Lukasik. And I saw no way to connect either man with Odessa Vincennes. Unless Penny knew of an aspect I didn't…

"…talk to the old man. Not—"

Darn. I'd missed parts. Always dangerous to think while listening to Penny.

"What old man? Hiram?"

"—that he'd know everything, because he chooses not to. First one didn't do it. Slide, sliding back to where he'd started. Hated that worse than anything. Needed another one and did it again. Him?" she scoffed. "Old man at the ranch. Knew that nice wife of his, too. Strange friends, real friends. And the boy. Turned around, though. Happy now. Hope it lasts for him. Not likely, considering the complications," said Ms. Sunshine. "Sins of the father shouldn't, but do, and wider than fathers. Well, bye now. Hi, there."

I stumbled out of the end of the checkout lane, feeling I hadn't gained anything. Except cookies.

✧   ✧   ✧   ✧

BACK IN THE Sherman Supermarket parking lot with one of my packages of Pepperidge Farm Double Dark Chocolate Milano cookies already open, optimism resurfaced along with an idea.

I called Tom's cell.

From the background noises he was driving his truck—not his ranch truck, because the engine noise wasn't loud enough for that.

I explained about Odessa Vincennes, starting with yesterday's interview and ending with the footage Jerry had shown us, while skipping the side issue of Thurston Fine. I finished with, "Do you know Odessa Vincennes?"

"No."

"Hah. Finally found someone new enough to Cottonwood County to have slipped through the web you and your cohorts have spread."

"Slipped past me, probably not Mrs. P."

That deserved a heel-of-the-hand-to-forehead thunk.

"Of course. If her daughter's a teacher…" Retirement had not cut Mrs. Parens off from the school system information network. "I'll have to try her. In the meantime, I need your help deciphering Penny's references to locals."

"You're usually good at translating her yourself."

"Getting *better* at translating her, but as I said, these are local references. She was hopping around talking about Hiram, and then about a woman. I thought she meant Odessa."

"Then what do you need me for?"

"Because, the more I think about it, the more I think Penny didn't mean her. Here's what she said." I repeated, as precisely as I could, Penny's comments about the old man at the ranch and having an odd friendship with a nice woman. "Not Hiram?"

"Not Hiram and not his ranch. Unless Penny was referring to something else entirely, I'd bet on Kesler, who works on Lukasik's ranch. Kesler's worked on the place most of his life from what I know. And the nice woman was Lukasik's wife. Heard they were close before she died."

"Oh?"

"Not that way. Kesler was like an uncle to her, maybe a granddad."

Lovely for them, less promising for me. I moved on. "So, if he's the man, the ranch is Lukasik's, and the woman is the deceased Mrs. Lukasik, then the boy must be the son, Gable, right?"

"Seems likely. Don't know it for a fact."

"Thanks." We ended the call.

Adding the people Tom had identified to my mental who-to-talk-to list shot Lukasik Ranch to first among places I needed to visit.

The question now came down to whether I waited for my colleagues to be free of their pesky jobs versus how much apologizing I would have to do for not waiting for them.

Chapter Twenty-One

I OPTED FOR apologizing.

My SUV's navigation system informed me I'd reached the Lukasik Ranch and still had a stretch to go to reach the home ranch.

I finally spotted a handsome ranch house by a creek bed, with a cluster of working buildings well to the side and behind a screening of trees in the distance. That view also informed me the distance would take considerable time to traverse, with all the bends and curls in the road ahead.

But I was fortunate.

After a few bends and curls, I came into a long valley. Straight ahead as the crow flies, but not as the road went, was the home ranch, seeming no closer than it had at that first glimpse.

On my left, at the far side of a pasture greener than most I saw in this area, I saw a distant cowboy on horseback. Too far to call to. Past a couple of roadside cottonwoods, however, I came to a cowboy off his horse, doing something to a cow I preferred not to focus on too closely, all near to the fence that divided the pasture from this road.

I pulled over and got out, taking my time until the cow rumbled away and the man turned toward me.

By his movements, I'd expected a much younger man. By the creases in his face he could have been well into his eighties.

"Hi. I'm looking for Kesler."

"You found him. Who're you? What do you want?"

I extended a hand over the fence, hoping he took off the decidedly unlovely glove he'd been using with the cow. "Elizabeth Margaret

Danniher. KWMT-TV."

He took the glove off and shook my hand—crunching the bones slightly.

His expression did not convey delight or even neutrality at discovering my identity.

I pulled out the big guns fast.

"Penny from the supermarket—"

"Penny. There's a good woman."

"She is." Over his shoulder, I saw the rider across the paddock watching us. "She sent me to talk to you."

"Penny did." A statement, not a question, and filled with skepticism.

Justifiable skepticism, I had to admit, considering Penny's indirect mode of communication.

"Not that succinctly. But that was the gist."

"Gist."

Bolstered by the mildness of this repetition, I said, "She said you could fill me in on a few things. In fact, she said you were the best possible person to give me background."

He spit. "You mean blabbing all over about people so you can figure out who killed Furman York and make another one of those TV programs? Why would she think I'd want to do that?"

Skipping arguments about truth and justice and how one person's murder going unsolved hurts us all, I said, "So that the wrong person isn't charged."

That caught him. But he approached it sideways. "Like who?"

A gamble to guess whom he might be worried about without more guidance.

But how much time did I have to be subtle? He hadn't exactly welcomed me. As much as I wanted to push Kesler, that risked he'd close the door completely. Plus, I feared my alone time with him was running out. The other rider turned toward us, advancing at a slow trot.

"Hard to tell who might catch the attention of the authorities. Say, someone known to have argued with him shortly before he was killed."

His face hardened. "Furman York was forever arguing with some-body. Pure chance of who was the last one when he got himself killed. Cottonwood County Sheriff's Department should be able to figure that out."

Too bad Shelton or Sheriff Conrad, wasn't here to hear that.

Agreeing with him, though, wasn't a good tactic for what I wanted.

"Maybe. But once something like that points in a direction, they're bound to dig deeper. Find out things otherwise innocent people might not want found out."

He squinted at me, not giving an inch.

There had to be a way in with him. Time to toss spaghetti against the wall and see what stuck.

"How long have you worked here?"

"Long time."

"The same long time Norman Clay Lukasik has owned this ranch?"

"Pretty close."

That meant a lot of overlap with Furman York.

"Did Lukasik bring you here from somewhere else? Did you al-ready work for him?"

"No." His tone said *No way in hell.*

One piece of stuck spaghetti.

"Did you know Furman York before coming here?"

"No." And didn't bother to hide that he hadn't wanted to know York at all.

"Who were his friends on the ranch?"

"Hell if I know."

"You must be aware of who he spent time with, went for a beer with after work. Or friends outside of the ranch."

"Didn't keep his social calendar."

The approaching rider slowed his horse to a walk. Kesler didn't turn, didn't shift his eyes, or betray any overt indication awareness of the newcomer's presence.

I was sure he knew, though.

Now he'd braced for more on York. Time to switch gears.

"Penny said—indicated—" I corrected the word with a smile. "—the Lukasiks' son basically grew up here, works on the ranch now. Not just being the owner's son. Good worker?"

"Yep."

"Some say he—Gable—is getting more and more valuable when the ranching community works together. Roundups, branding and such."

"As long as he's not mooning after that girl."

Jessica Stendahl, Penny, and now Kesler. This must be some romance.

"Growing up, he spent a lot of time with his mother here at ranch, right?" A silence was as good as a *yep* with this man. "Penny told me about Mrs. Lukasik being a very nice woman." No need to spell out Tom's interpreter role. "And her tragic accident."

"Real nice lady. Nobody better say different in my hearing. Real shame about her dying. Especially for her boy." He shifted, recognizing he'd given away more caring than he'd intended. "Didn't know a lick about ranchin', but a nice lady."

"Kesler?" the rider said from half a dozen yards away.

He didn't turn. "Nothin' for you to worry about, Gable."

The rider came on anyway, and swung out of the saddle, taking his cowboy hat off as he did.

I employed a friendly, harmless smile while I studied him.

Gable Lukasik had his father's height, with flesh on his frame.

Despite the cowboy attire, including working boots, gloves, and hat, he had a vaguely preppy look. It might have been the hair—shiny brown, it came away from a peak at the top of a thoughtful forehead and did a smooth side sweep. A bit longer on top than a lot of Wyoming men, but trimmed on the sides and back.

He had a round face. Not pudgy, soft. Like a layer of cushioning between him and the outside world. An attractive face, prevented from lapsing into *cute* by the gravitas of dark brows over deep brown eyes.

I widened my harmless smile. "Gable Lukasik? I'm Elizabeth Margaret Danniher, from KWMT-TV. Came out here to your ranch at Penny's suggestion. You know Penny, right? So, you'll understand I'm terrified that if I cross her, she'll cut off my cookie supply. She'd never let me starve, but she might torture me by limiting my chocolate access."

Kesler muttered, "Foolishness."

Gable smiled. "For me, it's tortilla chips. Cut off my chips and I'd fold at the knees."

"Exactly." We were compatriots. Fellow travelers in the wicked world of carbs.

"I've seen you on the news," he said. "I pay attention when you're on."

"Thank you." I meant it. A modest compliment, yet genuine. "You work here on the ranch, right?"

I could try to ease him into talking about the operation of the ranch, and from there, possibly, to an indication of whether he knew of York's rustling activities. Though the latter probably would have to wait until we were away from Kesler's clam-like influence.

"I do. Not sure how much help I am, though."

"You'll do." That, I suspected, qualified as an extravagant compliment from Kesler.

Gable's eyes warmed an instant, then went flat. "Suppose you're out here about York?" he said to me.

"I am. In fact, I was just about to ask Kesler if he saw Furman York yesterday morning. I'll ask you both now."

"Nope," Kesler said.

Gable frowned slightly. "He must have gotten up earlier than usual. The truck he uses wasn't here when I left to check out some fence a little before nine."

"Alone?"

"Yep."

"How about you, Kesler? Where were you yesterday morning?"

"Doctoring cows." He jerked his head north. "Next pasture up."

"Alone?"

"'Cept cows and my horse."

"We're not much help." Gable looked faintly apologetic. Kesler didn't. "What other kind of information are you after?"

"Background. Get a feel for where he'd worked so long. Those who worked beside him and—"

"Heads up."

My first inclination to be irked at Kesler—bad enough he'd been no help, but now to interrupt my foundation-laying with the alternate—faded as I followed the jerk of his head toward the road from the home ranch.

A green pickup with the same logo as the one I'd seen at the grazing association barreled toward us with a plume of dust boiling behind it.

With neither Kesler nor Gable scrambling out of the way, I felt honor-bound to hold my ground, too. But I was grateful the truck had good brakes when it nose-dipped to a stop a yard from us.

Norman Clay Lukasik sat behind the wheel.

Not for long.

He seemed to catch hold of the top of the door frame and swing out with it, as if he didn't have time to exit the normal way.

It brought him among us startlingly fast, never even disturbing his cowboy hat.

"Don't leave on my account, Gable." His words mocked, rather than extended an invitation.

Chapter Twenty-Two

THE SON HAD adjusted his hold on his horse's reins in gloves that matched Kesler's for stain and spatter, as if preparing to mount. "Better get back to work."

"Stay," the father ordered.

The older ranch hand grunted. Gable glanced at him.

Lukasik didn't. He didn't look toward his son, either, clearly assuming he would be obeyed. He focused on me, watching me watch them.

The second my gaze came to him, Lukasik said, "Digging up dirt?"

"Background," I said equably. Nothing bothered a goader more than not being goaded.

"Nothing here for you to add to your *background*."

"Don't be so modest." My dryness matched the day's non-existent humidity level. "Everyone knows you represented Furman York when he was found not guilty of murder."

Taking my suggestion at face value, he said, "I did keep him from the gallows, metaphorically speaking. Not another lawyer could have pulled it off."

"He must have been grateful to you."

I had a momentary impression of tightening around his eyes, suppressed in record time. They talk about micro expressions. This—if it existed—was a nano expression.

"Ah, yes. He was. Most grateful." He paused to build anticipation. "But not so grateful as to refuse a paycheck."

His dry smile started his own chuckle. No one joined him.

Kesler continued his getting-nothing-out-of-me pose. The look the younger Lukasik sent the elder lacked all familial affection and admiration.

One thing for sure, Lukasik senior expected to be the center of attention. Seeing what came of going along with that expectation, I asked, "Did he do good work for that pay?"

"Of course. Otherwise, wouldn't have kept him for years, made him foreman."

"Yet you said that under him as foreman your herd only stayed even, didn't grow. Doesn't that concern you?"

"Not at all. Long as this place pays for itself—No, doesn't even need to do that. Long as it doesn't cost so much I can't afford it, that's good enough. It's a place to visit now and then that offers a change from the office and courtroom. Gable's the one devoted to this place."

He tossed that in as an aside, almost as if it indicated a weakness in his son.

As a human being, the apparent discord in a father-son relationship struck me as sad.

As a journalist and digger into murders, I knew a lead to follow up on when I saw it. Especially since Gable's reaction to his father's arrival plastered a big neon arrow in the sky over his head.

I also knew not to do it now, with them together. The time to tackle Gable would be off on his own, when he wasn't strung tight by his father's presence.

For now, I continued asking Lukasik senior about York.

"How did York feel, after the passage of years, about having been on trial for murder?"

"Shouldn't you have a camera rolling and a microphone in my face when you ask questions?" He didn't wait for an answer. "Furman blamed TV for his predicament."

Despite myself, some of my reaction must have shown.

Lukasik chuckled. "Not the little local station here." His ersatz reassurance didn't cover his pleasure at dismissing KWMT-TV. "No, he blamed *60 Minutes*."

Had he missed the real cause of my reaction? Or had he purposely detoured toward television egos because he'd picked up my disgust at his categorizing a young woman's murder as a *predicament* for the man charged with her murder?

"*60 Minutes* didn't do anything on him," I said with confidence.

I would have heard about that. Probably from half the county. Definitely from Mike, Diana, Mrs. P, Aunt Gee, and probably from last night's research before sleep knocked me out.

And yet, after those assured words and thoughts, a crackle of *Could I have missed it?* doubt hit my nerve-endings.

Followed immediately by a recognition of Norman Clay Lukasik's power.

I needed to think more about that. Later.

Lukasik watched me, his eyes dark and avid, his mouth smiling faintly.

I said evenly, "Furman York felt the piece *60 Minutes* did on Rock Springs influenced Cottonwood County's view of him."

"Very good, Elizabeth Margaret Danniher. He did. Yes, he did."

"He felt that way at the time of his trial? Or in the years since?"

"Both. If anything, more strongly as years went by."

"Then he didn't know the people of Cottonwood County." And hadn't learned about them in the decades he'd lived here.

"Oh? You present yourself as an expert on the people of Cottonwood County? Yet you're a newcomer, aren't you?"

"I am, having been here a little over a year. It took only a fraction of that to recognize Cottonwood County does not look to TV—local or national—to form its opinions. Furman York spent how many decades here, yet you say he didn't recognize that?"

"But then you're a smart, sophisticated, educated, and worldly young woman. Not at all like Furman York."

I verbally stepped around that pile of ... compliments. "What was Furman York like? You must have known him well, all the years of his working for you, not to mention representing him in a murder trial."

"Not to mention getting him acquitted," he edited in a murmur that still would carry to the corners of a courtroom. "But as I said before, I can't say I knew him well. Not sure anyone truly did."

Classic distancing from an unsympathetic character. Though Lukasik clearly hadn't done that when York was alive. Was it cynical to think that was because York had been useful to him in life, but wasn't in death?

Not too cynical to explore.

"You knew him well enough—and trusted him well enough—to have him run your ranch."

"Business. Purely business. A very different connection from the kind that would lead to a crime like this. He was my client and then he was my employee." More distancing. "I'm too busy a man to cultivate buddies."

"Who are his buddies?"

"I have no idea." His eyes widened as he spoke, as if it had never occurred to him that York might have buddies. "Kesler, you have any idea? Gable?"

Both shook their heads, Kesler looking straight at Lukasik and Gable with his head down.

"There you have it. A man either without buddies—" Lukasik twisted the word. "—or without his buddies being known by us."

More wriggling away from his connection to York. "Yet you spoke so eloquently of him yesterday."

"On his behalf as a human being, who did not deserve to be shot down, perhaps over a dispute with someone who appears to view himself as a demigod in this county."

He meant to rile me with the not-so-oblique accusation of Tom.

I was unriled.

However, two interesting things. First, that he wanted to rile me, which could be a significant reaction because I'd gotten too close to *something* or could be an automatic reflex. Second, that he'd used a description that fit himself far better than Tom.

"I don't believe the sheriff's department knows what might have led to this murder yet. What about you? What do you think led to York being shot?"

"Me?" His opened hand pressed to his heart. "I am merely a bit player in this event."

As much as I didn't believe that, he believed it less.

"Another one," Kesler said.

When we all looked at him as a result of the *non sequitur*, he jerked his head toward the ranch road again, this time in the opposite direction.

He was right. Again.

No vehicle in sight yet, but another dust plume tracked its progress from the entrance and toward us.

Whether it was aversion to dealing with whoever might be coming or taking advantage of his father's distraction, Gable mounted easily, turned, and left a view of his back and his horse's rump.

The arriving truck came at a reasonable speed and stopped a safe distance behind mine.

The two men might not have recognized the truck, but I knew from a slight change of atmosphere that they recognized the man who got out of it.

Tom Burrell.

Chapter Twenty-Three

"OH, GOD, HE'S here to moan again about something or other." Lukasik didn't modulate his courtroom voice.

Tom heard, didn't react.

His arrival surprised me, but didn't displease me. Antagonism can be a great truth-finder and, under Lukasik's mocking, antagonism poked its pointed head.

"Kesler," Tom said.

"Tom."

"Lukasik."

"Burrell."

Four flat names, yet the first two held respect and the last two none.

"What's the matter now, Burrell?"

Tom looked at Lukasik silently.

"Come, come, surely you have complaints to lay at my feet. What sin against the sacred communal order of cow patties have I committed now?"

"You've committed most of them, even though you're hardly ever here."

"My vital responsibilities take me far beyond the aroma of cow patties. I have no time for such—"

"You want to leave the grazing association? We'll be happy to oblige. Won't even charge you the fees you put into the agreement years back. But, as it stands now, you're a member of the grazing association and membership carries responsibilities. Especially when there are issues—"

"Not my issues. You said yourself I'm hardly ever here."

"Furman York is your employee—

"Was."

"—and was when the problems arose. You have responsibility for—"

"Bull. A gas station owner can't be held legally liable if his clerk goes out and robs another gas station."

That sounded darned close to an admission of knowledge of rustling. Yet it wasn't.

Tom's eyes narrowed. "He's got ethical responsibility if the other gas station owner gives him strong proof and he chooses to keep putting that clerk in a position to commit more robberies. And the law will frown on it if this first gas station owner spreads his arms and lets the thieving clerk hide behind him."

Norman Clay Lukasik came upright in a snap. He winced, nearly squelched it. Couldn't be sure if whatever caused the wince or his failure to stop it sharpened his tone as he closed the gap to Tom.

"Look here, son—" He slathered the word with sneer. "—you better watch what you're saying. You understand?"

"I understand that I haven't said anything I'm about to take back."

They stood, not nose to nose, but nearly cowboy hat brim to cowboy hat brim. Tension tightened the tops of my shoulders.

Lukasik made a chuffing sound that might have been laughter, smiled—not pleasantly—and stepped back. "As long as we understand each other."

"I understand you."

"Listen—"

"This is gettin' to be a regular party," Kesler said.

"What the f—" Lukasik swallowed the word we all heard anyway. "—are you talking about, old man?"

In what was rapidly becoming a familiar gesture, Kesler jerked his head toward the road, this time past Tom's truck. I turned. Here came another vehicle heading toward us and eventually the home ranch.

No. Several vehicles. All from the Cottonwood County Sheriff's

Department.

Another change of atmosphere behind me.

As I adjusted to turn my body for a better look without corkscrewing my neck, I spotted Gable Lukasik opening a gate from astride on the far side of the pasture and riding out. Continuing the turn, I encountered wooden expressions from Kesler, Lukasik, and Tom.

Nothing to read there, so back to the sheriff's department parade.

The lead vehicle swung around Tom's truck and my SUV, while the rest stopped behind. That lead vehicle continued to us, effectively blocking Lukasik's truck unless it backed up.

Sergeant Wayne Shelton got out.

I was becoming a connoisseur of men making exits involving modes of transportation. Lukasik had gotten out of his truck with a swing, Gable departed on horseback with stealthy smoothness, Tom left his truck with studied deliberation, and now Shelton hopped out of his four-wheel-drive. His short stature required that from the tall vehicle, his innate dignity bleached any hint of comedy from the move.

Innate dignity didn't improve his temperament, however.

"What are you doing here?" he demanded of me.

"My job." Before he could introduce petty facts about whether my nominal boss at KWMT-TV also saw it as my job, I continued, "Interviews. A very interesting conversation with Mr. Lukasik."

"Please, call me Norman."

His words aimed at me, the gleam in his eyes focused on Tom.

No reaction from Tom.

Shelton had a reaction, which centered on me. Aren't I lucky?

"Interviewing folks is my job in this investigation and I want to follow up some things with Mr. Lukasik. Kesler, too. So, you get along, both of you."

"Both of them? Shouldn't you hold onto Tom Burrell? Question him? After all, as you know, he's the one who exchanged a certain kind of pleasantries with Furman most recently," Lukasik said.

"Furman York told you about that, did he?" I asked Lukasik. "So you knew the subject of those pleasantries. When did York talk to you? What did he say? Was anyone else there? Were you, Kesler?"

"Not me."

Lukasik spoke almost on top of the ranch hand's words. "Furman relayed the tenor of the interaction, not its substance. He knew I have no interest in the running of the ranch. He was, however, concerned enough by threats of personal violence made by Tom Burrell the day before his death to tell me of those."

"Did you see him yesterday morning?" I slid in.

"No. Not until I was called to the scene where his dead and blood-ied body—"

"What were you doing in the morning?"

"You—better yet the authorities—should be asking Burrell for his whereabouts for—"

"The authorities know my whereabouts."

"Odd you don't want to tell us what you were doing yesterday morning," I said neutrally.

Lukasik's eyes sharpened, but his voice came easy.

"I was in my office, working on a case. From the time I finished breakfast until being informed my foreman had been shot.

"Naturally, when the sergeant here asked if I knew of any enemies Furman York might have, I immediately relayed the information to him about Burrell's threats against York and he went directly to question Burrell over the ... *issues* between them."

That speech played like verbal tap dancing. Shuffle-ball-change away from Lukasik possibly knowing about rustling. Sideways riff to Tom's confrontation with York. Stamp to seal Tom as a suspect.

The muscles along Tom's jaw ticked. The bones of his face showed strongly, as if the bedrock inside surged toward the surface. "I don't settle issues by killing."

Without moving, he seemed to loom over Lukasik physically, de-spite Lukasik being slightly taller.

I blinked, trying to reset my impressions.

Shelton stepped in. "Nobody official's saying you do settle that way, Tom. We're checking everything and everyone. Not taking any one person's say-so. But there's others've said you and Furman York had words. Yeah—" Shelton's palm-out raised hand would have stopped any protest if Tom had tried to make one. He didn't. "—you're not the only one that tangled with him. Long line, stretching way back to the beginning."

"Really, Sergeant, harking back to ancient history in a blatant avoidance of the obvious is—"

Shelton cut off Lukasik with a look and repeating emphatically, "Stretching way back."

He redirected to Tom.

"No getting around it that, for all those words Furman York had with people stretching way back, he didn't die right after any of those other words. He did after yours."

Before Lukasik had time to score follow-up points, Shelton returned to him.

"We're here to search—"

"Your people already searched Furman's rooms yesterday."

"Wider search. Pursuant to our investigation."

"Sergeant—"

"Don't get yourself in a twist. We have a warrant."

"A warrant? My goodness." Lukasik smirked.

"Yes. All nice and legal."

I bet it was. I bet Shelton had made absolutely sure it was for Lukasik's viewing pleasure.

"Go on, you two," Shelton said to Tom and me, "get out of here. We have professional investigating to do."

"Professional?" I repeated. "So far all your investigation has done is put Hiram Poppinger in jail. Which reminds me, Sergeant Shelton, I want to talk to Hiram."

"You can't. Prisoner. Now, git."

We did. Partly because Tom had hold of my arm and I am far too dignified to descend into a physical tussle. Especially one I won't win.

Mostly because, as Shelton turned away with his parting shot, I'd caught a speculative gleam in his eyes.

Chapter Twenty-Four

I HAD NO time to parse the meaning of that gleam because Shelton must have signaled to the waiting sheriff's department vehicles. We had to step smartly to the edge of the road to give them room.

The driver of the first official vehicle to pass us was Richard Alvaro. He raised a finger off the steering wheel, acknowledging us without anyone else being able to see it.

Tom touched his hat brim in an almost equally subtle response.

I waved broadly. Continuing to wave after Alvaro's vehicle passed, so the next in line saw me.

"Want a bullhorn, too?" Tom muttered.

"Do you have one?"

He expelled a would-be dismissive breath, but couldn't suppress the fanning of lines at the corners of his eyes. So he changed the subject. "Get what you wanted by coming out here?"

"No. Of course I didn't. Not with you and Shelton lumbering in like indiscreet elephants."

Especially since I couldn't define what I'd wanted. Except everything of any significance whatsoever. In other words, short of someone falling to his knees and admitting to shooting Furman York, I wasn't getting what I wanted. It's what sent me on to the next interview, the next bit of research, the next question.

I had the eerie feeling he'd read my thoughts or knew some other way that I wouldn't have been completely satisfied even if he and Shelton hadn't arrived.

I switched gears as the last official vehicle passed and we resumed the walk to my SUV. "What brought you out here, anyway?"

"Deduction." At my lifted brows, he added, "What you asked me about what Penny said. What I answered. How your mind works. And everybody else being at work at the TV station."

"I've been doing this a long time, Burrell. I don't need an escort to conduct an interview. You can't tell me you think Lukasik would knock me off in broad daylight on his own ranch."

"No, I don't think he would." He held my gaze. "Doesn't mean I'd trust him not to, Elizabeth."

"That's melodramatic." I raised a hand as he started to reply. "Okay, okay. You're entitled to your opinion. But now that you've achieved your goal of ending my talk with Lukasik, are you going to stand here and chat?"

"Maybe."

He'd made no move to open the SUV door or otherwise hurry me into my vehicle. No follow-through was a most un-like-Tom-Burrell situation. As was *chatting*.

"*Ah*. Got it. Because remaining here bugs Lukasik."

He said nothing.

"It'll also bug Shelton."

"Collateral damage."

"I'm good with that. Small price to pay for bugging Lukasik," I said.

"Tell me what was said before I got here."

"I'll have to repeat it all when we're all together."

"I'll corral the food while you do that."

Who could pass that up? Not me.

I told him.

"...stonewalled by your friend Kesler, a glimpse into what appears to be a strained—at best—relationship between father and son Lukasik, and a view of the father's professional skills. But what I didn't get was insight into the victim. Nor did I get any leads on York's friends or associates." I eyed Tom. "Was York part of the ranchers' guild?"

"The ranchers' guild," he repeated between amusement and caution.

There'd been an element of truth beneath Lukasik's mocking reference to a sacred communal order of cow patties. As highly individual as the ranchers were, there also was a sense of community. Loosely knit, but strong.

"You know. Branding, roundups, moving cattle up the mountains and down the mountains." I rattled them off as if I knew more about these activities than observation and listening.

"Wouldn't say he was. Lukasik's place is big enough it doesn't need as much mutual aid as us smaller operations who pitch in to help each other. Now and again some of their individual hands come along. Informal. Because they know folks from around."

"But not Furman York."

Subtlety would do nothing. Blunt instrument all the way. "His choice or because people didn't want him there?"

"Can't say."

I huffed.

"Really. Don't know, Elizabeth. When he joined up with the Lukasik Ranch, I was a kid. Not looking at much beyond school, basketball, and the Circle B. By the time I came to noticing what was happening in the county, it was settled that York didn't mingle with ranchers or hands."

"Who did he mingle with?"

"Can't say—I mean, I don't know. Could ask Badger."

Badger was the bartender at the Kicking Cowboy in town. It was one of those in-between bars. Not seriously bad, yet a hint of seediness made the careful feel like they were living dangerously.

"Good. Known associates, enemies, anything you can pick up about him."

"Yes'm."

"Are you sassing me?"

He laughed. Almost like his old self—no, almost like the self he'd become in the past few months.

"What about Gable?" I asked.

"If there's anybody from the Lukasik place helping other folks,

Gable's the first. Works hard and willing to learn. Can't ask better than that."

Hoping to hold onto his improved mood, I asked, "Why's it called the Lukasik Ranch, when yours is the Circle B? I've noticed some ranches use the name of the brand, others the name of the owner."

"Depends on the history, who started the ranch, who has it now, and who's talking. Talking with somebody who knows the reference as well as you do, you're likely to say the Smith place or the Jones place.

"More formal references, it gets more complicated. A place that's been around a long time, keeps the same home ranch, pretty much the same acres, it's going to be called by the brand a lot. Especially where more than one person or family owned it to start, so the brand covered all of them. Or a company owns it now, you call it by the brand if you're referring to the home ranch, by the company if you're talking about the whole thing, see?"

What I saw was my simple question had no simple answer.

"Which did Lukasik do?"

"He bought out a place that'd been the G-Bar-T brand for nearly a hundred and fifty years, then he declared it the Lukasik Ranch."

"It's interesting," I said, "he makes a point of putting his name on the ranch, on the trucks, but doesn't show interest in the other aspects. Seems like his wife did and his son does. But he's indifferent to the… the—"

"Ranching."

I nodded. "He likes what Lukasik Ranch means to other people. But he doesn't care about the ranching part of it. He said it flat out. Also, it stands to reason or he wouldn't have put someone as bad at it as Furman York in charge. That's unusual in a ranch owner, isn't it?"

"Different people feel differently about ranching. A lot depends on when you're hit—when you get the bug. There're phases."

"Phases? Like the moon?"

He looked up to a blue sky with no sign of the moon. "Sort of. When you get hit can decide how bad you get it. How much you'll care. How much you can take."

I waited, knowing he wasn't done.

"How much heartbreak you'll take," he said at last.

"The heartbreak didn't scare you off from ranching."

"No."

The syllable vibrated with something more. The heartbreak hadn't scared him off because he had an affinity with heartbreak?

It wasn't that he couldn't be happy. But did he trust it?

The only happiness he really trusted now was Tamantha.

I veered away from the concept of Tom Burrell's happiness.

But, in retrospect, I could have done a better job of changing topics.

"Mike came back to ranching. Even knowing the heartbreak from losing the family ranch as a kid."

He cut me a look. "He'd been caught at a real tough stage that—"

"Phase," I corrected.

A glimmer of a smile. "Phase. Kids usually like the ranch when the balance of chores and fun tips toward the fun. A lot fall away from loving it when they get a little older and the balance shifts. Especially somebody like Mike, who'd gotten big enough, strong enough, tough enough to do a lot of work young. Can feel like working's all you do. But you get past that and you start seeing the rest. Mike got a glimpse of the rest. Then they lost the ranch."

"What do you mean, a glimpse of the rest?"

He *huh*'d, saying it was a good question without a good answer. "Might be it's different for each of us."

He wasn't getting away with that. "Tell me what it is for you."

Silence. But not his never-going-to-tell-you silence. "Ever hold two contradictory feelings at the same time? Like you knew they couldn't both be true, yet there they were, inside you?"

Had I ever...? I was looking at one and we'd just been talking about the other.

All I said was, "Yes."

"Well, with ranching, it's like this swell of huge all-encompassing pride of ownership, like your heart's too big for your chest because it's yours. You're its, too, though. It holds you."

He shifted, looked away, adjusted his hat, then looked down at me.

"Isn't this supposed to be about Furman York?" he asked.

His retreat didn't surprise me.

"It is. We told you about Jennifer's excellent question about why he switched from oil to cattle. If he'd gotten the cattle ranching bug early, why go into oil? Unless. Maybe, he got the ranching bug from being here in Wyoming."

"Not likely when he'd been exposed to ranching early in Texas and didn't take to it."

"Also not likely getting bitten by the ranching bug suddenly a few years after his trial?"

"No. Another thing. Most of those who get the ranching bug don't dream of working for somebody else. Even as foreman."

"Jack Delahunt—"

"Jack's a special case. He's a cattleman. Taught himself to be a good businessman, too. That's put him in a special situation. Now, York, he reached his level of incompetence early on. Turnover's real high on the Lukasik Ranch as a result."

"But Kesler said he'd been here from when Lukasik bought the ranch."

"Before. He worked for the previous owners."

So Kesler's *pretty close* about working on the ranch as long as Lukasik had owned it meant he'd been here longer than Lukasik. Sneaky.

A tuck formed between Tom's brows. "Suspect Mrs. Lukasik asked him to stay on. Take Gable in hand. Teach him to ride, about ranching. At least enough he wasn't a danger to himself."

"Is Kesler a top hand?"

"Sure was in his prime."

"Would he have made a good foreman?"

"Yep."

"Yet Lukasik chose someone lazy and not good with cattle or people. Does Norman Clay Lukasik strike you as stupid?"

"Some other adjectives, not that one."

"And yet that's who he's had as foreman of his ranch. Why?"

"That's where you're the expert, Elizabeth, finding out why."

I WASN'T FEELING like much of an expert at figuring out the death of Furman York. Nor several other matters.

"You and I are off for getting together tonight, I suppose," Tom said.

That was one of the matters.

"I'm sorry. I think the others will expect—"

"No need for sorry. Not your doing."

Before I could respond, a rider came into sight, trotting along the fence line toward us.

Kesler. Not Gable.

"Tom. Wanted a word. Section of fence at the Dry Fork property needs work before it opens."

Tom lifted his head to acknowledge hearing Kesler, then turned to me.

"Where you going next?"

"I haven't decided."

"Get somebody else to go with you."

"Tom—"

"You're the one says two pairs of ears are better than one. Get someone else to go along with you," he repeated. "You're poking into hornets' nests. I know—can't stop you. Just remember, one of the hornets is a murderer. Want you to stick around, 'specially now you owe me a date."

✧   ✧   ✧   ✧

TOM AND KESLER dwindled in my rearview mirror.

Dating two men at the same time is not all it's cracked up to be.

Actually, I don't know that anyone's ever cracked it up to be anything, so maybe it *is* all it's cracked up to be.

As I mentioned, the scheduling is a bear.

Mike and I tried the movies—once—in Sherman, trading commentary with our heads close together and our hands meeting in the popcorn. Holding hands when the popcorn was gone. But no more than that, with many pairs of curious eyes on us.

After that, we went to Cody a couple times. For a movie (not great) and dinner (great.) Another time we had Sunday brunch in Cody, then spent the afternoon at the Buffalo Bill Museum. We also spent a day searching for furniture for his sprawling, mostly empty house—something other than a mega-couch, TV, and workout equipment.

That made it more homey to watch movies at his house, sharing popcorn, trading comments with our heads close together, and doing more than holding hands.

Tom and I spent time at his ranch, often with Tamantha, including riding horses to a gorgeous valley well above his home ranch where we all had a picnic. One day, we drove over the state line to Red Lodge, Montana to visit with Tom's sister, Jean-Marie. She looked after Tamantha, while we had a nice dinner at a historic hotel that could teach Sherman's Haber House Hotel a thing or two.

Another time Tamantha stayed with Mrs. George, their neighbor, while we went to a talk by an author we both liked at the Cody library. After Tamantha went to bed, we sat outside on his deck, watching the stars, talking, and being silent.

I swore I saw a bedroom curtain twitch. It was like having a curfew and a fourth-grade chaperone.

And then there were times when we—me and one or the other of them—would start to plan time together and instead broaden it to include the entire group.

Did I enjoy the time spent with each of them? Hugely.

There's something about being with another person for a concentrated period of five, eight, ten hours that either makes, breaks, or deepens the connection.

Deepen, in both cases.

Both.

Have I mentioned complicated?

✧　✧　✧　✧

AN INCOMING MESSAGE pinged not long after I started the trek on the ranch road back to the highway. When I reached that intersection,

I stopped and read the message. It was from Diana.

Rather than working the rest of the day and using her lunch hour to keep a dental appointment, she was taking the afternoon off. Barring dental catastrophes, she'd be available by two-thirty if I wanted company.

I messaged back "Sure" and arranged to meet her then.

I also mentally juggled the order of what I'd do next.

Not even Tom could object to my going alone to my next stop.

Chapter Twenty-Five

I CALLED NEEDHAM Bender and invited him to lunch.

"I accept. But instead of us going where we have to watch what we say, how about you get takeout for three, I'll call Thelma to set the table, and we'll meet at the house."

"Sounds great."

On the way, I placed a call to a source in the Washington, D.C., area who'd become a kind of friend over the years. The call might find him at FBI headquarters or at the FBI lab in Quantico, Virginia, depending on his duties.

"Hi, Dex. How are you?"

"The ranch foreman shot on grazing association lands appears to be quite straightforward, Danny."

I smiled. Both at his telephone manner—talk about straightforward—and the use of the nickname we'd established back when I was a well enough known national reporter that talking to me could have gotten him in trouble. The nickname spread among colleagues, friends, even family. But, oddly had not caught on here in Wyoming.

Or maybe not so oddly. Maybe that was a nickname for a different person.

"There are one or two points," I told him.

"Of interest to me?"

"Let's find out."

I described the scene and the scenario.

"You don't believe that man shot the ranch foreman," he said at the end. "Why?"

"Tom? No, I don't believe—"

"The other one. The one who called authorities."

"Oh. Hiram. I could believe he'd shoot a man."

"But not this man?"

"I could believe that, too, but… None of this is scientific…" I told him about Hiram, the deputies' interplay and the logic behind thinking it wasn't someone else's gun. "…York's gun seems most likely, but Hiram would have blabbed if he'd seen it, so… Could it have been under the body?"

"Yes."

"Have you seen that happen before?"

"Yes."

"There's another thing, they screened off a larger area than right around the body." I hesitated. If I hoped Dex would jump in and make a guess, I should know better. "Any ideas?"

"I could not posit any without examination of the crime scene photographs at the least."

Fat chance I could get those out of Shelton. The shots Jenks took for KWMT would have the screen covering the area we were interested in. "Sorry, no crime scene photos, Dex."

"Do you have other evidence?"

He meant that would interest him. "No, sorry. I'll—"

He hung up.

You either hated Dex or loved him. I grinned as I finished. "—talk to you later."

Needham, his wife, and I had salad and burgers from Hamburger Heaven. Needham complained about the lack of fries, but I knew Thelma worried about his cholesterol. Besides, she added dessert of homemade angel food cake and fresh strawberries drizzled with dark chocolate.

As soon as she presented it, along with coffee, she insisted on clearing the rest of the table and leaving us, "So you two can talk freely."

"You know I tell her everything anyway," Needham said to me.

"I figured."

"Never mind, the pair of you," she scolded with a smile, pushing the swing door to the kitchen with her backside.

"Well?" Needham invited before the door's first rebound swish.

"Did you cover the murder of Leah Pedroke or the trial?"

Needham's gray eyebrows hiked toward his receding gray hairline. "That's the angle you're pursuing?"

"Can't say we have an angle. We have bits and pieces. Would like to have a few more, by hearing what you have to say about it. If you were around then."

"Oh, yeah, I was. Didn't own the *Independence* yet, but covered both stories, along with doing most of the other jobs around the place."

"Was that the first time you crossed paths with Norman Clay Lukasik?"

"No. I'd covered some of his cases. At that point, he wasn't nearly as good as he thought he was." He stroked his chin. "Still isn't. Not sure he could be that good. Or anybody else, either."

"Maybe he can't be as good as he thinks he is, but there is one thing about him."

He raised his brows, inviting me to continue.

"He has power. In fact, a superpower when it comes to being a high-profile defense attorney."

"Superpower?" He sounded amused.

"He's excellent at raising doubt."

His amusement vanished. "Explain, Elizabeth."

"You agree he's excellent at raising doubt?" He jerked his head, agreeing without liking it. "Not the reasonable kind of doubt a juror must get past to convict Lukasik's clients, but the unreasonable kind that could make those around Lukasik—juror, prosecutor, judge, witness—doubt himself."

Or herself.

"That would always give him a second path to a not-guilty verdict. Attack the evidence on one level and undermine everyone's certainty on the other. Even if it lasted only a second or two, how many— especially jurors—let an instant of deep self-doubt manufactured by Lukasik bleed over to their verdict? After all, if they doubted themselves, how could they not doubt their judgment about the evidence? And wasn't that reasonable doubt?"

"Insidious," Needham said.

"Part of his power. Part of his talent and expertise at eliciting the response he wants."

"Also known as manipulation."

"Oh, yes. He's a grand manipulator. Did he get the York case by chance?"

"No. It went to Haus."

"Jay Haus? The divorce lawyer?"

"Back then he wasn't settled into family matters. Just starting to practice, wet behind the ears. Lukasik didn't have to do much persuading to get him to give it up, though how he got Haus to say the things he did about his inexperience... True, though you don't often hear lawyers talk like that. Ah. Your superpower theory."

"That's it." I smiled at him. "So Lukasik went after the case. Did it look like it would make him a name?"

"Not a good name. Not around here. Not the way people felt about what happened and Furman York."

"How did they feel?"

"It was a shock when that girl was killed. Stranger to most in the county, of course, but a young woman like that, every appearance of being an upright citizen, working hard. Pretty to boot. No denying that tugged at people. And then Gisella Decker's connection with her."

He tipped his chin.

"Rough time she'd had with her husband dying like that—"

Like what?

"—and everybody knew it."

I shook my head. "I can imagine how hard that was for Gee."

"Don't know about it, do you?" If he'd been wearing suspenders, he'd have hooked his thumbs in them and rocked back and forth in high delight with himself.

I could deny him his satisfaction or I could find out what he knew—some of what he knew.

No contest.

"No, I don't. What happened?"

"Well, now, that's still the question, isn't it?"

"Needham," his wife called from somewhere else in the house. "Stop teasing Elizabeth."

"Always rushing a story. She's as bad as an editor cutting from the top."

I chuckled, which drew a fleeting smile from him.

"It was a single truck accident. Off the road, into a steep ditch. No sign he hit anything. Just went off the road. No brake marks, no skids. Smashed up the cab bad."

"Medical event?"

"No history. No sign on the postmortem."

"Suicide?"

"They ruled it an accident. That didn't stop some from drawing the other conclusion and wagging their tongues. Hard on Gee. Strong as she is, it was real hard. Losing her husband, her life turned upside down, compounded by the questions, the not knowing." He rubbed his chin. "Not knowing, for a woman like her…

"She'd started coming around, training to be a dispatcher. Even more when Leah Pedroke rented a room from her. They got on from the start. Brought life into Gee's house. They'd bake together. Gee taught her things. Leah brought plants for the garden. A shame. A real shame."

We sat in silence for a moment.

Needham heaved out a breath. "But would that cause the death of Furman York yesterday?"

I lifted a shoulder. "It's an avenue to explore. So are more recent events."

He side-eyed me. Waiting.

"You know about the reports of rustling."

"I didn't say—"

"But you don't have enough to run a story or you would have. And neither of us particularly likes that angle because it points at Tom as a possible murder suspect. Although there are others who had cattle rustled. The Chaneys, Clyde, for instance."

"That wouldn't make me much happier," Needham grumbled.

"Well, what about Hiram Poppinger? Do you think he could have shot Furman York in the chest?"

"Yep, I do. In a fit of anger, in a scuffle. What I can't imagine is him denying it up, down, and sideways. But you know there's something else…"

I waited while he either considered what or how he'd tell me.

He started, "There was a guy ran a feedlot over in Dakota—"

"Bernie Madoff of the West?"

"That's the one. Thing is, I've heard rumbles York tried to pull in a few people here. Never approached Tom, but tried the Chaneys, who told him to get lost on general principle. That couple who bought the Pecklies' place, the McCrackens? They've started running cattle in a small way. Well, Sam McCracken starts asking for all this financial information and York couldn't run away fast enough."

"But someone else didn't?"

He exhaled shortly. "Clyde wrote a check. The guy was on the way to the bank with it when law enforcement took him in. That's how close-run it was from Clyde. He blamed Furman York, as he had full reason to."

Chapter Twenty-Six

I **DROVE TO** the dentist's office a block off Cottonwood Avenue and spotted Diana emerging. Perfect timing.

As I pulled over to pick her up, two women emerged from opposite sides of a little silver car parked four spots down the street.

Recognizing the older one, I did something I never would have done in most places I've lived. I jumped out of my SUV, leaving the door open and the engine running.

"Odessa Vincennes, how wonderful to run into you this way."

She recoiled momentarily.

The younger woman with her slowed, then looked back, surprised when she realized Odessa had fallen behind.

"I left a message, apologizing for cutting short our interview so abruptly yesterday. And—"

"Yes. No problem. No problem at all. Excuse me."

She'd restarted at higher speed, clearly intending to walk past me.

With the double benefit of plenty of experience at walking-and-talking with interview subjects and significantly longer legs than Odessa, I pivoted and moved along with her, catching a look between her and the younger woman.

Warning?

"Hi, I'm Elizabeth Margaret Danniher," I said to the pretty, younger woman while I kept up with the elder and we all came together on the broad sidewalk. "I was interviewing your..."

"Mother." She returned my smile tentatively. She was medium height, which made her taller than her mother. Slender, with enough curves to avoid boyishness. Hair streaked to be a bit blonder than nature had established, fair skin, and blue eyes. Concerned at the moment.

"Of course. Your mother. It's a pleasure to meet you…"

"Asheleigh," she supplied. Unlike her mother, she was almost too easy to nudge into answers.

Her name registered in the next fraction of a second. "Asheleigh?" Could it be? The Asheleigh with an 'e' described by the Stendahl kids? Also the girlfriend of Gable Lukasik? The dating possibilities for their age group couldn't be expansive in Cottonwood County, which certainly made it possible. "Are you a teacher?"

"I am. How——?"

"I met your boyfriend, Gable Lukasik, this morning." If that led her to think Gable had been my source, that didn't worry me.

"Oh." Her face glowed at the mention of his name, adding credence to Jessica Stendahl's report that they were *really* serious.

"It was actually the news about the Lukasiks' foreman being shot that interrupted my interview with your mother."

Just call me Elizabeth the Glow Killer.

Asheleigh paled. This look from daughter to mother carried nervousness. I gave her a break.

"Odessa, I'd like to schedule a time to finish our conversation, so we can get the information about the program out to our listeners."

"I'll call you about that. Soon."

"As long as we're both here now——"

"Can't. Sorry. We have to get to the dentist. We have appointments. Right now."

She cut across behind me, hooked her daughter's arm, and steered her to the dentist's office.

"We'll talk soon," I said brightly, the last word spoken to the closing door.

Diana watched me circle around the front of the SUV.

She climbed in and closed the passenger door. "That was interesting. You sure know how to make friends. Nothing like making someone eager to see the dentist."

I did something else I wouldn't do in many places I'd lived—I made a U-turn. "You recognized her?"

"Oh, yeah. Her face and her voice. Also caught the bit about Gable Lukasik being her daughter's boyfriend. Interesting. Could that explain her reaction? The connection to her daughter's boyfriend? If she misunderstood...?"

"You heard it." I turned west on Yellowstone Street. "Mike was clear about the name. Never mentioned Lukasik or Gable. Even if she knew Furman York was the foreman of the ranch of her daughter's boyfriend's father, would you expect that reaction?"

"No. Think she'll call you?"

"No."

"Are you going to tell me where we're going?"

"O'Hara Hill. Hope to talk to Ernie and Dorrie."

"Hope? They'll be there. They're always there. Whether they'll talk is another matter. Did you call ahead?"

"That's why I didn't call ahead. Didn't want to give them a chance—"

My phone rang. ID said it was Jennifer.

"—to say no or plan their responses." I answered, "Hi Jennifer, what've you got for us?"

"Us?"

"Diana's here."

"How'd you get away?" Jennifer asked Diana. After the explanation, Jennifer added, "Sheesh, Mike and I are the only ones stuck working."

"Tom—" Diana started.

"No, he told Mike that he and Elizabeth were out to the Lukasik Ranch earlier."

Diana cut me a look. I returned it with limpid innocence, saying to both her and Jennifer, "We'll tell you all about it when we're all together. But there's nothing earth-shattering. Certainly nothing that changes the direction or order of what we're doing."

"What direction and order?" Jennifer asked.

"Gathering information, focusing on the victim."

"Well, there's plenty of information on him, like I said last night. I'm still pulling it. There's so much from the trial it's going to take some organizing. Not doing as well with that Odessa woman. Found lots about the group she's part of."

"What group?" Diana asked.

"They print warnings about scams, especially those preying on seniors and distribute them to groups doing home visits or delivering meals."

"What a great idea."

"It will be if they get funding," I said. "They did a trial run, but the county's budget to help seniors is strapped. That's why I wanted to have her on, hoping it would raise their profile and get more funding or donations."

"The station should sponsor it. In connection with 'Helping Out'," said Diana.

"Can't you just see Haeburn agreeing a.) to spend money on helping people and b.) having it possibly reflect well on 'Helping Out' or me."

"Go over his head. Go to—"

"Hey." Jennifer's sternness stopped us. "Do you want to talk about this group and 'Helping Out' or the murder?"

"The murder," Diana and I said meekly.

"Actually, there isn't much to tell. As I said, lots on the group. Not much on her. She moved here in February. She and her daughter have an apartment. I have the address and phone number if you want those."

"Send those to me. And that's a good start, Jennifer."

"Nothing before here, though."

"We have something more about her daughter." I told her about Asheleigh Vincennes being Gable Lukasik's girlfriend.

"I'll try the daughter and see if that will open up things."

"What about Odessa's vehicle?" Diana asked. "Any luck with that."

"Oh, yeah. A two-door Toyota. Bright blue."

"That's it. That's the one I saw in the station's parking lot, then at the grazing association. Seemed odd. Not getting out of the vehicle. Just sitting there. I was pretty sure it was the same woman when Jerry showed us that footage. The vehicle clinches it."

"So what she went out there? So did everybody else in the county," Jennifer said. "By the time Walt and I got there we had to walk forever to reach the scene."

"That's a valid point. Suppose it would be natural to be curious." Diana deflated a bit.

"Not everybody who was curious had the Lady of Shalott look," I said.

Diana rebounded. "Yeah. And now we know she was out there. Though that's not the vehicle she was in at the dentist."

"You saw her, too, Diana?" Jennifer's voice rose in accusation. "You two arranged to talk to—"

"Hold on," I said. "We just happened to see her going into the dentist's office with her daughter. I'd called Odessa, she didn't return my call, and seemed to prefer the dentist to me."

"True." Diana chuckled. "Anyway, the car we just saw could be her daughter's. She was driving."

"I'll check," Jennifer said, only partially mollified.

Diana described the car.

To prevent future bad feelings, I told Jennifer we were going to O'Hara Hill to try to see Ernie and Dorrie before they got busy.

"That's okay. That'll be about all that old stuff."

I couldn't entirely disagree with Jennifer's priorities.

Odessa Vincennes' reaction to Mike's news of Furman York's death had made her worth looking into. Discovering her daughter was Gable Lukasik's serious girlfriend either made it understandable—if you didn't agree with Diana—or even stranger.

For now, I voted for stranger.

"Keep on checking on Odessa Vincennes' background, too."

"Will do."

Chapter Twenty-Seven

ERNIE AND DORRIE greeted Diana with pleasure, me with openness, and sat with us at a table toward the back.

Ernie reminded me of the actor Ben Johnson, with a brush mustache and eyebrows to match, a rumbly, western voice, and eye-squinting lines dug deep into tanned skin.

Dorrie had short, determinedly dark hair with a line of girlish, short bangs across her forehead. The determination of her hair color, though, couldn't hold a candle to her jaw. She could have shared it with three or four folks not blessed in the jaw department and had plenty left over.

"Did either of you know Furman York back then? Before the trial and everything." Tactful way to refer to murder, but I didn't want to discourage them from talking to me if he'd been friendly with York.

"Yeah, I knew him a little. Mostly from playing cards."

"And drinking," Dorrie said. "Bunch of little boys acting like truants from school. Wouldn't give 'em all the liquor they wanted, so they'd go from here to those shanty bars that popped up like mushrooms."

"York was one of those?"

"Not often," Dorrie said. "He went straight to the loose bars. Didn't want to waste time eating when all he was interested in was getting a skin full."

"The lady asked me and you just said he hardly came in here."

"Go right ahead. Tell her all about your dear friend."

"He wasn't no dear friend of mine. And you know—"

I stepped in to keep this from completely derailing. Sometimes back and forth between sources can reveal more than direct answers. But this seemed to be heading toward revealing more about their marriage and history. Certainly more than I wanted to know.

"What kind of card player was he?"

Both of them blinked at me. With a second blink, a light went on in Ernie's eyes.

"That's a real interesting question, Elizabeth. Most times he was kind of all over the place—no discipline, you know? But then he'd get ticked off at somebody who won a pot he thought he was going to win and Furman would turn into one of those dogs that latches on and won't let go. All focus. All on one thing. It was like he didn't care anymore about winning, he just wanted the other guy to lose. Sometimes it wasn't just that night, either. He'd go days and days, following the poor guy who'd ticked him off, doing his best to make him lose. And you know, he did pretty good making some of those guys lose."

"But eventually he'd get over it? Move on?" Dorrie asked.

Ernie cocked his head. "Move on, yeah. To the next guy who ticked him off. Pretty much let go of one guy because another one came along more recent like. Did it once to me and as soon as he was on to the next guy, I didn't ever play with him again. There were plenty enough games around to get in on, no need to tangle with him."

The militant glint returned to Dorrie's eyes, indicating her temporary detour into poker's character-revealing aspects had ended. "Plenty enough games around to lose your money in, you mean."

Again, I stepped in quickly with a question.

"Have you encountered him much in his years at the Lukasik Ranch?"

"Nah. Not the type to stop in here or go to county events. Might've seen him in Sherman now and then, not to pass the time of day with."

"Did you know Leah Pedroke? Maybe encounter her in the office where she worked?"

"Sure did. I was in there most days, trying to catch on with them right off when—if the boom hit. Good outfit."

I suspected he was aware of Dorrie's scowl, but neither of us looked at her.

"What was she like?

"Good worker. Spoke real pleasant to just about everybody. Sweet thing. Too sweet, really, for dealing with those oil toughs."

Dorrie's snort communicated her disdain for oil toughs, reminded Ernie he'd experienced a spell of madness when he tried to become one, and added that she'd like to see one of those so-called toughs coming after *her.*

Ernie paused, perhaps to make sure she had no further non-verbal comment—probably a wise move.

"She handled most of them real well," he said. "She'd give them that cool look like they'd get from their mommas and remind them to treat her like a lady. Trouble came with those who didn't have the right kind of momma or any momma at all. Because all they saw was a pretty face with a body that would turn an altar boy into—"

He coughed to break it off under his wife's stare. Then reset his conversational path.

"Not at all sure she'd have known how to deal with someone who didn't behave himself after one of her looks, if you know what I mean."

"She did," Dorrie said abruptly.

Ernie and Diana looked as confused as I felt. "She did what?" I asked.

"Have a momma of the right kind. A momma, daddy, sister, and brother."

"How'd you know that?" Ernie gaped at her.

"Leah told me about them. Came in here a couple times when she first arrived and saw I was near drowning." She side-eyed her husband, a reminder that he'd caused that predicament. "After that, she pitched right in. Had no restaurant experience, but knew her way around a kitchen and caught on quick. Talked about all her parents taught her. They'd taught her well. She was a good young woman. A kind person." Tears came into her eyes while her chin remained firm.

"I never knew you—"

"You weren't around."

Ernie winced, as if he felt the impact of those three flat words more than everything else she'd said on the topic.

Dorrie turned to Diana and me. "Told her parents so when I went to see them at Gee Decker's and give them the checks she'd never take for helping me. Couldn't afford much, considering, but it was some." She sighed. "Helped with the cost of their coming out here to see that worthless scum get tried. And then he got off. Almost like the girl dying all over again."

DORRIE TOLD US more about Leah helping her. Both confirmed that the general sentiment was that York got away with murder through bribery, with the wide-ranging theories about how unhindered by proof. Other than that, neither she nor Ernie expanded beyond what Mrs. P had said.

Two messages to call as soon as I was available awaited when I turned my phone back on after Diana and I left Ernie's restaurant ... with only a small carryout bag each.

Mike and Tom. In that order. So that's how I returned their calls.

Mike answered with, "Where are you?"

"Diana and I are driving back to Sherman after talking to Ernie and Dorrie."

"Hi, Mike."

"Geez, I missed that, too? Hi, Diana."

"Too?"

"Don't act all innocent. Tom told me about you going out to Lukasik Ranch, Elizabeth. And how you were talking to Lukasik, and nosing around about York's friends."

"Did he?"

"Nosing around's my term, not his," he added quickly.

Another example of them sticking up for each other.

Tom first appeared in Mike's childhood world as a high school basketball star, though Mike's athletic success exceeded Tom's. A long time ago they'd come to the equality of mutual respect.

"Did he tell you I said I'd fill everybody in at the same time?"

"Yeah. And he didn't give me any details for the same reason." He groaned. "If I didn't have to do these lead-ins for the other stations that wanted pieces of the interview, I could have shaken free this afternoon."

"How many stations, Mike?"

"Four. Plus Chicago—I knew some of those guys from when I played—wants me on live for intro and outro for the interview. So I'm tied up until five." That would cover the end of a five o'clock broadcast in Chicago, which was an hour earlier than Wyoming. "And then I might as well stick around for the Five here. Les is grumbling around the shop this afternoon and it'll keep him off my back a while."

"That's tremendous exposure, Mike. You've got to be thrilled about that."

"Way to go," Diana added.

"Yeah, I know." Underneath I could tell he was excited. "But you're going to have this all solved before I get into it at all."

"Not likely. We'll bring you up to speed—and we'll all share what we learned."

"Can you wait until after the Ten, because one of the stations is West Coast and another station—I forgot about that, so it's five total. Anyway, D.C. wants me to do a fresh lead-in for their late broadcast— in the news segment, not sports—so I'll be working straight through."

"If the others can't wait that late, I promise to fill you in no matter how late it goes."

"Okay. Thanks, Elizabeth. That's when I'll tell you what Jack said when I talked to him." He sounded much more cheerful, probably because he'd remembered he had information to hold hostage in order to get ours. "And hope I'll get a chance to contribute more after this rush."

This rush—this interview could be a career-maker for him.

"Go knock 'em dead, Paycik."

He clicked off.

We drove in silence for a few moments.

"Is he as good as I think he is?" Diana asked.

"Yes."

"He'll leave here?"

"Yes."

"How do you feel about that?"

"I don't know."

She blew out a breath. "You better find out."

I drove several more miles before placing the next call.

Chapter Twenty-Eight

TOM ANSWERED WITH, "Hear you two've been in O'Hara Hill, talking to Ernie and Dorrie."

So I didn't even need to tell him Diana was with me and listening.

"How do you know that?" I wasn't surprised. More curious about which branch of the Cottonwood County grapevine transmitted this time.

"Mike messaged. Says we're going for another late-night discussion at your place tonight."

"If you can't because of Tamantha—"

"She's fine. Has a sleepover tonight. Already scheduled." A sleepover scheduled the same night we'd had a date scheduled... I jerked my thoughts away from that when he added, "Remember Clyde?"

"Your neighbor. Member of the grazing association. One of the people who had cattle rustled, presumably by York." As well as another run-in, according to Needham. But I wasn't bringing that up right now. "That Clyde?"

"Yep. Wants you to come by and hear what he has to say."

"He wants us to or you want us to?"

"Both."

"Okay. Are you going to tell us what it's about?"

"Nope."

He then gave directions to Diana that lost me after "Turn off the highway—you know where."

"Something else," he said when he was done. "I talked to Badger."

"Great. What did he say?"

"No way," Tom said, at the same time Diana gave me a you-had-to-know-that-wouldn't-work grimace. "When we're all together, just like you."

"I have a question—at least an observation—that doesn't need to wait until we're all together."

His reply nicely balanced wariness and amusement. "What's that?"

"You've never been this gung-ho about investigating."

Before anything came through the phone from Tom, Diana said to me, "I'm betting you aren't the only one Tamantha told to get busy."

"Oh-ho. And you were going to set things straight with *her.*"

He sighed. "Are you two comedians coming or not?"

"We're coming. We haven't even started with the jokes, but we're coming."

DIANA GUIDED US easily to where two ranch trucks kept company along the side of the road.

I parked behind Tom's truck. As we walked past it, the men finished placing tools and a roll of barbed wire in the back of one truck, presumably Clyde's.

Tom made an economical introduction of "Elizabeth, this is Clyde. Clyde, Elizabeth," as he pulled off work gloves. Diana and Clyde said their hellos with congenial nods. Clyde pulled off only his right glove to shake my hand.

He was a few inches taller than me, with a chin beard growing gray and brown in a distinct pattern, like a dog's markings. The outside corners of his eyes turned down, so when he squinted, they became crescents.

A silence fell.

Silence can be a powerful tool for an interviewer, pulling truths or revelations from reluctant interviewees.

This silence felt as if it had the potential to last forever.

"So, Clyde, Tom tells us your sharp eyes spotted some of his branded cows with calves carrying the Lukasik brand."

"Yep."

"How did you happen to see them?'"

"Went to Furman York to get my horse trailer back. Used it months ago for that ugly brute of his Bonedrin." He shook his head. "Knew a call wouldn't get him to bring it back, so went to get it. Came up on young Gable and he told me in general where York was.

"Got there and didn't see anybody. Followed this little track and there he was, off in a draw on the Lukasik place I doubt half a dozen people in the county know about. When I got there, York and a new hand they'd signed I wouldn't trust around a polecat, much less cattle, were branding calves.

"Never seen York work so hard. Never seen him turn so green when he spotted me, either. Wanted to know right off who sent me there. Told him I didn't know the hand. Seemed familiar, but couldn't identify him."

Clyde allowed himself a tight smile.

"He was that eager to get me out of there, he even agreed on the spot to take me to the trailer—and for once he did what he said he would. Probably afraid I'd return to his hidey-hole. But I'd seen what he'd tried to hide. Circle B cows."

"When was this, Clyde?"

He rubbed his chin. "Two days before yesterday, it was. Got with Tom right off."

"And I confronted York the next day at the grazing association. He'd already unloaded some of my cows with their calves branded Lukasik, but caught him with more in the hauler."

"Took video, too," Clyde added.

"Were you there?" I asked him.

"Yep. I took the video."

Diana asked Tom, "Have you shown it to Shelton?"

"Not yet. Been busy." His head tipped toward the fence. "Did mine before we came over here."

I asked, "The rustlers tear down fencing to get the cattle out?"

"Not always." He might have left it at that, until I popped up my eyebrows sharply in impatient questioning. "A lot put the fence back so it's not noticed right off. These thieves left it gaping."

Adding destructiveness to theft.

I turned to Clyde. "You're one of the grazing association members who had rustlers hit you here, on your home ranch?"

"Yep. Others before. Tom and me most recent."

Diana asked, "Have you talked to the others, Tom?"

"Not yet. Was there something else you wanted to say, Clyde?"

I waited for the story about York luring him into writing a check to the Bernie Madoff of the West, only to be saved by a fluke of timing when law enforcement made the arrest.

"Strange thing about this? They could have hurt me a lot worse if they'd taken my registered Angus from the next pasture over."

He jerked his head toward an up-sloping area past the side fence, where five cows grazed peacefully.

"They're high-performing purebreds," he said with pride. "Don't get me wrong, the rustlers hurt me plenty. But it could have been worse. Could've been a whole lot worse if they'd taken them, too."

Tom nodded in silent agreement.

"Could the rustlers have known about them in the dark?" I asked.

"They'd have known," Clyde said. "Rustlers don't come blind to a spot in the middle of the night. Too risky. They know ahead of time where they're going to hit and how they're going to do it. That means they find the spots in daylight. Know where there's not traffic that somebody going by could spot them, where they can't be seen from a house, not even reflected light."

I nodded wisely to all this, as if I'd known rustlers cased the joint, so to speak.

"But you're still leaving those—the Angus—out here?"

"Sleeping in my truck," Clyde said. "Got a couple of the dogs out, too. They'll raise a fuss if anybody comes 'round. It's only 'til I can get fences up on a section near the house. The airport wants me today and with this loss I can't say no to any work they're willing to give."

"We'll get that done, Clyde. Tomorrow suit you?"

"More than suit, Tom. But—"

"I'll make a few calls. Let you know when. If you're at the airport, get your dad to come by and keep us on track."

"He'll do that. He'll definitely do that, the old buzzard."

And thus was passed the danger of giving or receiving gratitude.

Chapter Twenty-Nine

TOM FOLLOWED US to my house, where we found Jennifer sitting on the front step with her device—no doubt giving orders to her cyber cohorts.

Once inside and supplied with drinks, I asked Tom, "Couldn't rustlers easily miss those Angus? Someone that far away spotting them as valuable livestock…"

He eyed me. "It's not just recognizing they're Angus. It's registered, high-performers."

"See? That makes it even more of a stretch."

"Not for a cattleman."

At first, I thought that was meant to put me in my place. I started to twist my mouth in acknowledgment I wasn't a cattleman.

Halfway there, I stopped.

"Rustlers aren't cattlemen? I mean, I know you said York wasn't, so you're saying that even if he'd seen them other times—"

"He had."

"—he wouldn't know they were more valuable. But… How can that be?"

"Rustlers are after the money, not the cattle. Jack told you last night, a fair number are feeding a drug habit, like people breaking in and stealing TVs or computers."

I sat back. "They're thieves."

"Yeah." He said that like he didn't get my point.

"There's this view—I guess it's the romanticism of the West—that rustlers aren't thieves like the guy who knocks over a convenience store is."

"Romanticism of the West," he repeated with his own twist.

"Yes. Accept it. It's real. At least real as far as being imbedded in people's imaginations can be, which is pretty real. And rustling's part of that. Rustlers, highwaymen, pirates, art thieves. All of them perceived as more romantic than criminal."

"Not to the people they steal from."

"It's not about the reality. It's the perception. Except in this case, it might be about the reality and not the perception. The reality is rustlers who don't know cattle, who are after the money, first, last, and always." I pulled a mini-legal pad out of my bag. "Let's go over all the episodes of rustling you know about."

"I can take notes—"

"I want your hands free to do searches to get any incidents we miss, Jennifer."

Diana picked up the pad. "I'll take the notes."

I turned to Tom. "You've always suspected Furman York?"

"Yeah."

"Anything more than prejudice?"

"Is it prejudice to know what a man's capable of?"

"Especially after the confirmation from Clyde," Diana said.

I didn't answer directly. Clyde was not an unbiased source, according to Needham. Nor had he shared the bit of history. "Okay, let's get to work."

TOM PICKED UP the pad, looking at the list of nine incidents carefully, though he already knew what was on it, because he'd helped create it.

The two incidents he hadn't contributed, he'd heard Jennifer share as a result of her searches.

At the moment, she was creating a spreadsheet to put the list into, having taken a photo of the list to work off of.

The list hadn't told me much, but I could tell it spoke loudly to him.

"Not prejudice now," he said softly.

"Why?"

"A lot of grazing association members on that list, aren't there?" Diana asked.

"There are. And six I know for a fact had run-ins with Furman York. The other three, I don't know about. I can find out fast enough. Along with the dates we don't have firm."

"Do that."

Pulling his phone out, he took the pad with him out to the back yard.

Diana and I refreshed the drinks. I made more lemonade.

As Jennifer finished typing, she explained she had columns for name of rancher, name of ranch, number of cattle taken, date of rustling.

She tapped buttons, rearranging the listings.

Tom returned and gave Jennifer three more names, as well as filling in dates and details on several entries.

"Look." She tapped keys and the list sorted, jumbling the names, while sequencing the dates. "Or I can do it by—"

"Wait. Go back to the dates," Tom said.

He leaned forward, looking over her shoulder. As he straightened, he clasped her shoulder and squeezed. "Good job."

"You've spotted something—what?" I demanded.

"It started in the eastern part of the county, like it leaked over the eastern county line. If you plotted those reports by date on a map of the county, you'd see it creeping west like an advancing army. Except one blank spot. Lukasik Ranch."

"Wait. Just a second." Jennifer tapped a few more buttons. "This sorts by dates first, then number of cattle taken. That trends up."

"Nice." I scanned that column. "He was getting bolder—"

"Or more careless," Tom said.

"—and greedier as he went."

"The blank for Lukasik Ranch... Did Lukasik know? Was he in on it with York?" Diana asked.

Tom rubbed at the back of his neck. "I don't like the man, but why would Lukasik get involved in rustling? He's got a name, a career that would all go up in smoke. For what?"

"Money? Maybe he's not as rich as everybody thinks." I paused after saying that.

"Got it. I'll check his financials—only what's public." Jennifer didn't even look up. "This is interesting and all, but what does it mean to the investigation? Unless you think all of the people who had cattle rustled killed him, like that movie on the train where a bunch of people stabbed the murderer of a baby, not knowing which was the fatal blow."

"Too bad Mike can't ask Aunt Gee how many times he was shot," Diana said.

"Once," Tom said.

My thoughts hadn't left an earlier point.

"You said these rustlers aren't cattlemen, Tom. And Furman York wasn't part of the ranchers' guild."

"Yeah."

"What about Norman Clay Lukasik? Is he a cattleman?"

"No."

"Part of the ranchers' guild?"

"You mean joining in at roundups, branding, helping out? No."

"Would you call Lukasik a rancher?"

He answered without inflection. "He owns a ranch."

Ah, Thomas David Burrell, I'm on to you. At least a little.

In his own, understated Wyoming way, he'd just shouted, *Hell no, he's not a rancher.*

I kept coming back to that question—why would someone who didn't care for ranching own a ranch?

"What next?" Jennifer asked. "I mean I can get the gang started on Lukasik's financials, and keep on the rest of it, including York's timeline, but I mean overall."

Expelling a breath, I said, "We sure would be better off if we could talk to Hiram and the only way to Hiram is through James Long-baugh."

I was aware of the others' gazes aiming toward Tom and joined the crowd.

He had his head down, placing his glass on a napkin on the coffee table. "Already called James."

I wasn't totally sure he'd said what I thought I'd heard. I had to play the words through my head a second time before I said, "Really? Voluntarily?"

"Knew it was coming when you said out at Lukasik Ranch that you wanted to talk to Hiram. Going through his lawyer's the only chance at that, so..." He shrugged and sat back on the couch.

We waited. At least a second or two.

Then Jennifer beat me to the next question. "What did he say? James Longbaugh. What did he say about talking to Hiram?"

"Said he'd have to ask Hiram. And he'd message me after he did."

"When was that? When do you think he'll get an answer from Hiram? How much longer—?"

Those were all Jennifer's questions. She had the bases covered, so I could watch Tom. He was enjoying this.

"Got a message just before I came in."

"What? And you didn't tell us? What did he say?" I beat Jennifer to it this time. But she expelled a breath on an empathetic, "Yeah."

"You—" He looked at me. "—and I are scheduled to meet James at the jail in half an hour."

"You?" Jennifer repeated in a not completely flattering tone, directed at Tom.

"No, no, that makes sense," Diana said. "Both Hiram and James know Tom better than they do any of the rest of us. He might even have some influence over Hiram."

"Don't count on it," Tom muttered.

"Wait a minute. Shelton approved this?" I asked.

Tom raised one shoulder. "Or James talked him into it. Wouldn't be happening without Wayne's okay."

"Interesting time. Late in the day. Like maybe they don't want a lot of people around? Who picked it?"

"James said Wayne set the time. If you don't like it, you can say no thanks."

"Hah." Shelton would only say yes if he saw a benefit to his investigation. That was okay if it also got us what we wanted.

"Mike's going to have a conniption," Jennifer predicted. "Already feels he's missing out on everything."

Diana picked up her bag. "No problem with me. Drop me at the dentist's office for my truck and I'll go home and see my kids, feed them supper. This should be good, actually—surprising them to see what they're really doing when I'm not there."

"I'll stay here and check in with the rest of the gang."

Jennifer's casualness caught my attention. "No hacking. I—"

"Why do you always say that?"

"Because your *gang* scares me and—"

"I thought you liked them."

"Most of them." That didn't mean I trusted even the ones I liked. "And this time you'd be using my internet connection, which means the authorities or the black hats or whoever else would come after my poor, innocent, little cyber footprint."

"If you'd let me do more security around your—"

"That's not the point. No hacking, period, for your sake and because your nice parents would hate visiting you in prison. And especially no hacking here, at my house, for those reasons and because I don't want my nice parents to have to visit *me* in prison."

"Nobody's going to prison," she scoffed.

"Jennifer."

"Fine, fine. I won't hack from here."

I think she'd just pulled a Tamantha on me.

Chapter Thirty

WE ENTERED THE sheriff's department to see James Longbaugh talking with Wayne Shelton at the end of the hallway, back where they dispensed something only sadists would call coffee.

"Hi, Wayne," I said with a big smile, all for the edification of the desk deputy named Ferrante, whose life ambition centered on denying me access to Shelton.

Shelton scowled, but Ferrante couldn't see that. He could only see my cheerful wave as I led Tom down the hallway.

After greeting James, I said to Shelton, "This is going to take a while. You know Hiram, and you can't expect us to get in and out fast. It's going to take time to open him up."

He jerked one hand and tipped his head in an impatient and dismissive gesture.

Better than I'd hoped for.

"Get in there and sit."

James led us to the larger of two interview rooms. He gestured for me to sit in the middle on one side of the table in the room.

"Don't expect much," he said.

"He's not talking?" I asked.

"Oh, he's talking all right. All about how he's not going to talk because the sheriff's department is determined to ruin his life. But he's not answering questions."

Tom frowned. "Not telling you what happened?"

"Not what happened, not why he was there, not why he appears to have been inside that house at the grazing association, even though he didn't take anything. He suspects I'm part of the conspiracy. Good thing you called me, Tom, because he used his one phone call for something else, won't say what. The good thing is he hasn't refused to see me." He considered a moment. "Maybe a good thing. Maybe not."

I patted the lawyer's arm. "Hang in there, James. You've had difficult clients before."

Tom pretended not to notice us looking at him.

The door of the small room we sat in opened and Lloyd Sampson escorted Hiram in. He wore a jail jumpsuit and handcuffs. But no leg shackles and his cuffs were in front. That qualified as downright casual treatment if they considered him a murder suspect.

While Lloyd took Hiram to the chair on the opposite side of the table, Shelton followed them as far as the doorway.

"We'll be watching you." He jerked his head to a mirror on the wall behind Tom, James, and me. On the other side of the wall, it became a window in an even smaller room used largely for storage.

"No sound," James warned.

"No sound," Shelton confirmed.

When the door closed behind the deputies, I smiled warmly at the prisoner. "Hi, Hiram."

He grunted.

Off to a great start.

"Hiram, you know we want to talk to you about things that only you can give us information on."

The lines in his face shifted, reminding me of a stubborn newborn.

"We're researching and we've heard from many other people. You, though, have a unique perspective, because you were on the jury of the trial for the murder of Leah Pedroke."

Stubborn gave way to shock.

He listened as I outlined what I knew of the trial and the case— without using York's or Lukasik's names, which required a few verbal loop-da-loops. Worthwhile to avoid his defenses cutting off communication.

"...and then the not guilty came in," I finished neutrally, watching him.

Four breaths, then a fifth. Nothing.

When he spoke, I had to tamp down a jolt.

"I ain't never taken a bribe. I did my civic duty and they put me on that jury and I sat there and listened to everything they said—the prosecutor guy and Lukasik and every one of those witnesses, even when it was boring as hell. So boring I'd like to fall asleep. Didn't let myself. Stayed awake the whole time. And then we get into that jury room and the talking and talking and talking. You wouldn't believe it. Little room. All those people yapping away. Hour after hour."

"You know some people believe the defense bribed a juror?"

"I ain't talking about that. Haven't and won't."

"Okay, Hiram, we'll leave that." His fisted hands eased. "When you found Furman York, what did you do?"

"Whaddya think I did? Pull out my gun and shoot him? The sheriff's department's checking that up one side and down the other. Still got my gun. Had it long enough now I should start charging them for rentin' it. Because they ain't ever going to find any evidence I used it to kill that bastard York, because I didn't."

If my theory based on Lloyd Samson's reaction and Alvaro's suppression of it was right, though, Hiram could have used York's gun to commit the murder.

"Let me rephrase," I said smoothly. "What did you do when you found Furman York's body?"

"Whaddya think I did?" he repeated. "I called the sheriff's department to report a dead body at the grazing association."

"Did you check him for a pulse?"

"Pulse? Clear as certain he was dead. Didn't have to play patty-fingers with him to know that with the big hole in him."

"Did you touch him at all or—"

"You think I'm an ignoramus? Think I never seen *Dateline* or those others? Everybody knows you don't move the body. Don't move it. Don't mess with it. Don't touch it. Nothin'. And that's what I did—nothing. 'Cept call the sheriff's department and sure as hell wish now I hadn't done that."

Playing to his *Dateline*-fueled confidence, I asked, "Knowing about crime scenes, did you notice any footprints or—?"

I stopped because he'd cocked his head like a grumpy, alert, over-fed bird again. This time a Baltimore Oriole, considering his jail jumpsuit's hue.

"First smart thing you asked me, girl. Smarter than the crowd here ever asked. No footprints. But there were marks like something swished one way, then the other, over and over."

"Like what?"

"Don't know. Except way too wide to be reins. Wider than a hal-ter, even a saddle strap? Saddle blanket maybe?"

Reins, halter, saddle strap, saddle blanket... "Do you have reason to think someone was there on horseback?" Tom had shot that down, but—

"No." Grumpiness overtook alert. "Didn't say that, did I? Just said the marks were made by something wider than reins or a halter and such."

"Right up to York's body? Or was there an area close to him that—"

"Right up to his dead carcass. And all around him."

"How far out?"

"Five, six feet."

"What else did you see?"

"Nothin'. Not a darned thing. Just Furman York with a hole in his chest and blood around him on that swished ground."

"The weapon?"

"That woulda been something to see, wouldn't it? And I said noth-ing. Nothing is nothing. No gun. No footprints. No killer. Nothin'."

No weapon.

Taken away? Or still there, under the body?

Wiping out footprints could match either possibility.

Wiping all around indicated the killer's footprints in several places, as they would be in a fight.

"Why did you go to the grazing association yesterday, Hiram?"

"Picking up a wrench I'd left there," he said promptly.

"A wrench." I kept every iota of disbelief out of my voice, despite the flood of it in my brain.

"My favorite wrench."

James sighed. The sigh of someone who'd heard this story before and told the teller it didn't pass a believability test.

"Left it in the old Paycik house by accident last time I was there. Went to get it back. As I returned to my truck, I saw that gleam up on that little knoll the drive goes around. Went up to see. That's when I spotted Furman York. Dead. Dead when I saw him. Dead before I got there. Don't know why anybody thinks otherwise. I didn't kill that piece of grime that was worth less than the cow dung left on my boots from last winter."

Gee, I wonder why the sheriff's department suspected him. Especially combined with his finding the body.

"Where's the wrench now, Hiram?" I asked.

"On the front seat of my truck, unless one of them deputies stole it."

Toss up of whether the detail of the wrench's location added credence to his story, resulted from happenstance that he had a wrench on the seat of his truck when he was first asked why he'd been at the grazing association, or offered evidence of premeditation by a mind that thought retrieving a favorite wrench sounded like a good alibi.

After a short silence, Tom said quietly, "Clyde said he expected you were out there on his behalf. Something about a favor."

Hiram half huffed, half clicked his tongue. "Well, if he told you that, why'd you ask me all these darned-fool questions?"

Tom didn't point out he hadn't asked the other questions, I had. I didn't either, even to say I hadn't been privy to Clyde's comment about a favor.

Tom's reason might have been gallantry. Mine was recognition of James' heightened interest, which told me we'd ventured away from Hiram's script.

"What was the favor?" the lawyer asked. I appreciated his alchemy that turned a possibility into a fact. Good questioning technique.

Hiram's eyes slued sideways, apparently looking at the blank wall. "Told him I'd help him. Taken some losses lately, he has." He cagily avoided the R-word. "Told him not to do anything just yet. I'd have a word with York. Never got the chance, considerin' he was dead."

My opinion of Clyde's common sense nosedived. Nose dove?

What is the past tense of nosedive? Let's say plummeted.

This might explain how York and the Bernie Madoff of the West had so nearly taken him.

"And he listened to you?" James asked.

"Course he did. Why wouldn't he?" Hiram demanded.

No one replied.

He clearly misinterpreted the silence, saying with satisfaction, "Even you types know I got my ways."

We did. That's why we were speechless.

"And I do him a favor, he does me a favor."

I recovered enough to ask, "What favor did you want him to do for you?"

"Somethin' as none of your business."

I glanced at Tom and James to see if they saw what I saw—Hiram Poppinger blushing.

A phrase from Penny teased at my memory. *If he thinks he can come in here singing Love Me Tender.*

Could she have meant Hiram? But how would Clyde figure in?

Besides… *Hiram*—?

Absurd.

"His favor to you—?" James started.

Hiram lurched up, his blush turned purple. "Done here. Done. And don't you go reporting this—"

"Reporting what?"

"—or jabbering about it. I got things to do. Go. Go away."

It was almost funny, him shooing us out of the interview room, like he owned the place.

Except the interview ending wasn't funny.

He pounded on the door, quickly opened by Lloyd. Very quickly.

I studied Lloyd. His face had no words streaming across it proclaiming, *I listened in on your conversation.*

He closed the door as soon as Hiram cleared it, leaving Tom, James, and me to look at each other.

"No clue what set him off." The lawyer expressed the sentiment in the small room with no indication he'd intended an investigatory pun. "But you sure got him to say more than he had to this point."

Chapter Thirty-One

WE SPENT A futile stretch in the break room, while Shelton tried to get us to share everything and I tried to get him to share everything.

"Lloyd, see these people out," he finally snapped.

Interesting.

Shelton mostly had Richard Alvaro deal with us if he did any delegating, because Lloyd was more porous than Richard.

I gave Lloyd a smile as I stood and slid my hand inside his arm, like he'd offered to escort me at a cotillion. He blinked in surprise, then the tops of his ears pinkened.

"That's so kind of you, Deputy Sampson." I dropped my voice low—too low for Shelton to hear—and tipped my head toward Lloyd's as we walked down the hall with Tom and James behind. "I'm nearly exhausted with Hiram talking our ear off. You know how he can be."

Lloyd mirrored my actions, dropping his voice and leaning his head closer. "Sure can. That's why it was weird him refusing to talk before. Wouldn't say a word once we got him to the office. Seems to have loosened up some."

I remembered that gleam in Shelton's eye at Lukasik Ranch. Had he agreed to let Tom and me see Hiram in hopes we'd act as lubricant to get him to talk.

"He has. He surely has." I patted the deputy's arm as we parted at that door.

"What was that about?" James asked once we were all outside.

I looked back at the door. "I'm not sure. I'll let you know if I figure it out."

"And if she thinks you should know," Tom said.

"If it concerns my client—"

"Tom's pulling your leg, James, in hopes of making me trip. It's nothing directly concerning your client's legal position. I promise."

He had to be satisfied with that.

Tom made a major detour from the sheriff's department to my house by going the opposite direction and arriving at the Sherman Supermarket.

"Want to come in or stay in the truck? I'll be a minute."

"I'll stay."

I thought I'd have more time to run back what Hiram said, but, true to his word, Tom came out almost immediately.

A stock boy carried a six pack in one hand and a grocery bag in another, putting them in the back seat of the pickup. Tom put the two covered trays he carried on the back seat, preventing them from sliding forward by wedging a tool I didn't recognize from floor to ceiling in front of them.

He returned to behind the wheel.

"So this is your version of rustling up the food for tonight, Burrell?"

"I can take off plastic wrap with the best of them."

"They had it waiting for you?"

"Penny."

It was long past her usual shift, so he must have arranged this earlier.

"I'm always surprised this place is open at this hour." Actually, it stayed open until eleven, which I knew from a few emergency cookie runs after a newscast. "Considering most stores in town close early."

"Serving the after-work crowd."

I raised my eyebrows at the widely spaced vehicles—all pickups—in the lot.

"Ranchers quit work when last light goes. You get a good order from a rancher coming in for a stock-up, and that makes it worthwhile staying open."

I looked at the profile of the man beside me.

Growing up in Illinois, Abraham Lincoln's portrait resided in every grade school classroom I attended. I never quite shook the feeling Abe was the presidential version of my patron saint.

Thomas David Burrell bore a resemblance to the sixteenth president of the United States. Tom's bone structure was more refined, his nose less substantial, his hair not as unruly. Somewhere between Daniel Day-Lewis as Lincoln and the real thing, yet all himself.

I sidestepped the thought that desire and a patron saint didn't mix, and addressed what made me turn to him in the first place.

"Yet here you are, working after sunset on something entirely different."

He glanced to his left, then pulled out into the empty road.

"Tamantha," he said, in full and eloquent explanation.

A good reminder of priorities. His daughter was worried about him. He'd do whatever he could to put her mind at rest. Even give up prime ranch time to chase after threads he hoped would tie up a murderer.

It wasn't the Gettysburg Address, but then it was a lot shorter.

Chapter Thirty-Two

"HURRY UP," JENNIFER called as Tom and I entered my house. "Thurston's interview with Lukasik is about to come on. They teased it before break and this is the last commercial."

Diana was there, too. "Hope you don't mind us turning on the TV."

"Of course not." I'd already deposited the trays on the kitchen counter, leaving the heavier liquid refreshments to Tom, and joined them in front of the TV.

The establishing shot of Thurston at the anchor desk faded to a one-shot—the camera in tight enough to see only Thurston's head. Which was how he thought the entire broadcast should air.

"Tonight, I have an exclusive interview conducted today with world-famous defense attorney Norman Clay Lukasik, Cottonwood County's most famous son."

"Mike's as famous as him," Jennifer grumbled.

"And far more popular," Diana added loyally.

Lukasik's face came on the screen. With the camera adding weight he looked somewhat less skeletal. Needham's phrase came into my head. *A bunch of bones strung together.*

"KWMT-TV's viewers are grateful to you for coming to me to bring your thoughts to all the listeners out there."

"I'm honored, Thurston—" The view switched to a two-shot, to include Thurston. It also showed that the interview had been conducted in his office, with a huge promotional poster of him visible on the wall between them. "—to talk to a journalist of your caliber at this difficult, difficult time. This horrible tragedy."

He was talking Thurston's language. Empty hyperbole.

"It is, indeed, a horrible tragedy, this difficult time for you."

Figures Thurston would goof and twist the phrases around to make Lukasik having a difficult time the horrible tragedy. Unless his sycophantism believed that and he'd said what he meant.

"It is an extremely difficult time as well as an important time," Lukasik intoned.

"*Still* a two-shot?" I muttered. Generally interviews are introduced by the interviewer, then concentrate on the interviewee. Not in Thurston World. I consciously unclenched my teeth.

"For me, for the Lukasik Ranch, for all who work at Lukasik Ranch, all who are associated with Lukasik Ranch, and for Cottonwood County."

Lukasik World vs. Thurston World. A battle for the ages.

"Surprised he didn't call it Lukasik Cottonwood County," Diana said.

"What matters now is justice and the correct functioning of the legal system I have spent my career toiling in. The adversarial relationship that hammers out the truth on the forge of the courtroom."

"Oh, brother." That came from under Jennifer's breath.

"I call on all the citizens of Cottonwood County to rise up with the truth, to share whatever they know about the tragic death of the long-time foreman of Lukasik Ranch. Because justice and truth are the bulwarks of the legal system to which I have devoted my life, as well as because of my devotion to Lukasik Ranch, as well as this, the home of my youth, I am offering a reward for information."

Thurston looked around, undoubtedly in search of the camera. He so seldom filmed outside the studio, he was lost. "Ah, yes, information they can call into the Cottonwood County Sheriff's Department at ... Well, uh, to the number on their website."

Still in the two-shot, something crossed Lukasik's face. As if he'd grimaced from the inside without anything on the outside moving.

"Tell me, Norman Clay Lukasik, about your long-time foreman, uh, Furman York, so tragically killed yesterday."

Lukasik's face arranged into solemn planes. "He was with Lukasik Ranch for many years. He worked beside so many of my employees, who have benefited from their time at Lukasik Ranch, and, I am proud to say, a great number of them used their experience in my employ as a springboard to achievement."

Jennifer, with hands poised to take notes, said under her breath, "Is he ever going to say anything about York?"

"Furman York contributed greatly to that by delegating—"

Tom made a sound.

"—allowing those he supervised to constantly add to their skills and take on new responsibilities."

"In other words he made others do the work and take any blame?" Diana asked rhetorically. "One of those *It's not my fault—ever* types."

"Bull's-eye," Tom muttered.

Jennifer typed.

On the screen, Thurston shook his head. "A loss. A true loss to Cottonwood County. I am happy, Norman Clay Lukasik, to bring your important words to all our listening audience." He turned to where he thought he'd have eye contact with the camera. He was almost right. "We'll have more of this important interview tomorrow at five o'clock. Tune in then for more of what Cottonwood County's most famous son told me exclusively."

"Was that *if?*" Jennifer demanded.

"Shh."

The shot cut back to the live one-shot of Thurston at the anchor desk.

"Be sure to tune in tomorrow at five for the rest of my exclusive and important interview with Norman Clay Lukasik, who came to me to bring his important and exclusive news to you, my audience on KWMT-TV, Sherman, Wyoming."

"Why'd he repeat all that?" Tom asked.

"Because he forgot what information was included at the end of the piece, because he didn't bother to listen to it again after it was edited."

"Or he wanted to say all of it again because it sounded—what was the word?—*important*," Diana suggested.

"Or that," I agreed.

Mike burst in the front door, his eyes on the TV screen, which had gone to commercial. "Did you see it? Did you see it?"

"Just ended," Diana said. "But—?"

"What are you doing here?" I asked.

Not heeding our questions, Mike's face fell. "No. It couldn't have. It's too early."

"Oh, you mean sports? Nah, hasn't been on yet," Jennifer said.

"Then what—? The Lukasik interview? Saw it in the editing room. Awful."

"Even worse on-air," Jennifer told him. "Thurston repeated the outro nearly word for word live."

"Hold it." I raised my hands. "How can you be here now—"

"I finished all the spots for the other stations."

"No, I mean KWMT's sports hasn't been on yet."

"Thurston had one of his fits after the Five, said having Warren and me in the studio live would prevent him from doing his best work with the Lukasik thing. Les made us record our segments. And he's not going to include a 'previously recorded' bug."

"That is an all-time low."

I agreed with Diana, but since Thurston Fine and Les Haeburn continually dug deeper with their lows, there'd be other opportunities for commentary on that. My question followed another tack. "Mike, you saw the whole interview in editing?"

"No. Just tonight's."

Darn that meant we'd have to watch or record tomorrow's newscast. Just in case Fine accidentally got Lukasik to say something interesting.

"You think there'll be anything useful in tomorrow's?" Diana asked. "Tonight's was content-free."

"Doubtful," Mike said cheerfully. "So, what was it all about? Lukasik grabbing a spotlight?"

I shrugged. "Like Pavlov's dogs hearing a bell? He sees the possibility of publicity and can't resist? Could be."

"Can he think a reward will really make a difference?" Diana asked.

"How? A witness? Not likely there was a witness when York was shot. Somebody the killer talked to? I know that happens, but this fast?" Mike asked. "Maybe Lukasik just wanted to annoy the sheriff's department."

Jennifer, who hadn't participated in the speculation, twisted around, looking into the kitchen. "Was that food you brought in? I haven't had any dinner. All Elizabeth has is peanut butter and cookies. Not even peanut butter cookies."

Before I could protest that I also had yogurt, as well as a freezer unusually supplied with leftovers from my parents' visit, Mike said, "I haven't eaten, either."

"Am I the only one who managed to have a meal?" Diana asked.

Tom and I nodded.

"See?" Jennifer said. "Can we eat now?"

Tom said, "Thought we'd wait 'til after sports. Got more of your interview on, don't you, Mike?"

He grinned. "Yeah. Thanks."

"How did you guess that?" I asked Tom.

Mike grinned wider. "I might have said something."

We all grinned back at him. Who could resist?

When the sports segment came on, though, he turned a serious gaze to the screen. In the lead-up I watched him assess himself with professional regard.

I shifted my attention when the interview came on. It was only a short piece of what he had—Thurston didn't allow sports or weather to interfere much with his camera time. Didn't matter. The quality showed through.

Mike was even better than I'd expected. Had I not been paying attention to his progress? Taking it for granted?

Those questions had produced no answers when Mike said, "That's it. Let's eat."

Chapter Thirty-Three

"SINCE YOU'RE DONE eating, Elizabeth," Jennifer said, "start telling us everything you found out, since you did lots today that you haven't told anyone else."

After that it seemed petty to say I'd been eyeing the cookies included with the sandwich makings and finger-food vegetables.

I started the *everything* while Diana helped Tom with the minimal cleanup in the kitchen.

I'd covered the phone message to Odessa Vincennes, my parents' new schedule, the highlights with Penny, the start at Lukasik Ranch, and reached the point where Gable Lukasik rode over, when Diana placed a plate of cookies on the coffee table.

The woman's a mind-reader.

Fueled by cookies, I told them the rest from Lukasik Ranch, finishing by asking Tom, "You want to add anything?"

"You covered it."

"What about what Kesler wanted to talk about?" Diana asked.

"Grazing association business. Not related."

Jennifer asked, "Does Shelton really consider Tom a suspect?"

"No," he said.

"Yes," I said. "He has to. Because of exactly what he said about York dying so close after the two of them having words. I'd say it was good news that Tom's not his prime suspect, except Shelton making Hiram the number one suspect is not one of his shining hours."

Could I be that wrong about Hiram? Could he have committed this murder?

Yes, the answer came. He could have.

But did I really think he had?

That remained undecided.

"What did you get from Hiram?" Mike asked.

"Wait, wait," Jennifer said. "You're jumping ahead. Way ahead. After you left Lukasik Ranch, what did you do, Elizabeth?"

"Lunch with Needham and Thelma. The tiny bit to add about Furman York is that Needham didn't like him and thought he was guilty of killing Leah Pedroke."

"Well, that's no surprise," Jennifer said.

"No. He did have one surprise." I glanced toward Tom, then told them Needham's account of York getting Clyde to write a check and his close call.

"Wow. York tried to con him and then rustled from him? That's got to be motive," Jennifer said.

"I have an idea that guy was arrested quite a while ago," Tom said. "So that check business would be, too. Check the date of arrest, Jennifer."

Had he already known about the check? He didn't say.

He was right about the arrest, though. Jennifer found it seven months ago.

Seven months to let go of anger? Or to have it build up?

I told them, "Needham also said something interesting about Hiram—that he could see him shooting in anger or a scuffle, but couldn't see him denying it after."

"Needham shoots and scores," Mike said. "Hiram's more likely to proclaim he did it with good reason and everyone should agree with him."

"I know that's been his approach on less serious charges. Murder might make even Hiram think twice," Diana said.

I agreed. With Jennifer's expression indicating she stood beside Mike, I decided to detour that divide—and they said I'd never learn diplomacy.

"After lunch with Needham and Thelma, I picked up Diana at the dentist's office."

"And saw Odessa Vincennes and her daughter, Asheleigh—with an 'e' in the middle. Right." Jennifer tried to hurry us along. "Then, after that—"

"Hold up, you didn't tell me about talking to Odessa Vincennes," Mike said. "Tom, did they tell you?"

"Bare bones."

"There's not much beyond the bones," I warned.

Despite Jennifer's obvious impatience, I described that encounter, with Diana sharing her observations.

"Can you believe Odessa's daughter is dating Lukasik's son?"

The rest of them looked at me blankly.

"I mean, the daughter of the woman I just happened to be interviewing at the moment Mike comes in and says a ranch foreman has been killed is the mother of the woman the son of the ranch owner is dating. What are the chances? I know the dating pool isn't very big—"

"Try a puddle. What are the chances around here of something like that happening? Not bad, not bad at all."

I'd had similar thoughts earlier. Diana's observations now underlined and boldfaced them.

Jennifer slid into the gap. "I confirmed the daughter does have a silver car." She grimaced. Not, I suspected at the concept of silver cars. Grudgingly, she added, "Got her middle initial from it—T—so that'll help narrow searches. I want to hear the other stuff you all did, but as long as we're talking about her, I might as well update you where we are with Odessa Vincennes."

"Great." I upped my enthusiasm level to offset Jennifer's glumness.

"Not great. In fact, not much at all. She moved here with her daughter when Asheleigh with an 'e' in the middle got the teaching job here mid-school year. The two of them rented one of the apartments they put into that big old house by the B&B. She started working for the senior assistance group soon after. It's a paid position, not volunteer. But she's paid even worse than the station pays me, so it might as well be volunteer. If I got into the group's system I could get her references, former address—"

"Jennifer."

"All right, all right. I said *if*. Following the obvious, straight line on Odessa, we're not picking up anything before here in Wyoming. We'll fan out next, seeing where we can pick up her thread.

"In the meantime, we started tracking the daughter. Baby steps. Just found out she graduated from Penn State with a major in elementary and early childhood education."

"How'd you find that?"

"Came across a piece in a newspaper from a little town in Pennsylvania. That 'e' in the middle of her first name helps, though we check other spellings, too. She was doing a program at their local school as part of a special class on teaching. Guess it was a big deal in their town. It said she was raised in Maryland. That's a good lead. I'm looking for her there and I've started searching for the mother in Maryland. No success so far. But it's early. Also throwing in Pennsylvania for Odessa."

"Why?" Mike asked.

"Figured if the mom moved out to Wyoming with her—"

"Good figuring, but please don't mention a mother moving here with her daughter to my parents when they come back through town."

"—maybe she moved to Pennsylvania while the daughter was in college."

Diana responded to my interjected plea, which Jennifer hadn't talked over while also not taking it seriously. "Don't worry. They won't move here, because they'd have to leave your siblings in Illinois."

"True, but they're married and settled. That leaves only my brother, Steve, who moves about every four months, so they'd spend most of their time packing and unpacking, or me."

Diana shook her head. "They have grandchildren in Illinois. You can't compete."

"Still, don't give them ideas." I turned back to Jennifer. "You've made progress. Don't give up."

"Who said anything about giving up?" She dismissed the possibility, just this side of affronted. "There are lots and lots more things to try. Takes time to get through them all. Same with Furman York. So, what happened in O'Hara Hill?"

"Anything on York?" Tom asked.

Jennifer half-swallowed what seemed destined to be a martyred sigh. Clearly, it really bothered her not being along on today's O'Hara Hill trip and wanted to hear what she'd missed.

If she hadn't been so good at digging up background, she wouldn't have as much to share and we'd get to our report sooner.

This didn't seem the time to console her by pointing that out.

"We found bits and pieces of Furman York—"

"That's grim," Mike said.

"—before he came to Wyoming." Jennifer ignored him. "Born in Texas. Youngest of seven kids. In trouble with the police as a kid."

I opened my mouth to ask how she'd seen juvenile records, then thought better of it.

"Starts showing up in regular police reports, mostly bar fights. Pops up in Alaska. Followed by records in Montana, North Dakota, New Mexico—all oil jobs—but with gaps, so he could have been other places, too." She looked up. "A couple assaults on women."

"Sexual assaults?" I asked, thinking of Mrs. Parens' account yesterday as well as Ernie and Dorrie today.

"Assault and battery. Only hit the surface so far. He moved around a lot. Not just place to place, also company to company. Some places don't match up with a company and vice versa, so we need to fill in those dates on his timeline. I'll send you all we have so far."

"Good work," Diana said.

"Thanks. *Now*, can we hear about you two talking to Ernie and Dorrie?"

Diana and I related what they said in the order they'd said it, then came back to Ernie's answer to my off-the-cuff question about what kind of card-player Furman York had been.

"Maybe it fits," Mike said, "if he'd had a similar interaction with Leah Pedroke. Say, he thought she'd done him wrong or dismissed him somehow or led him on. Could that have triggered his killing her?"

"That's an interesting idea," Diana said. "It would fit with what they said about him and what Dorrie said about Leah, how she'd give guys a look that would make them straighten up if they'd had a good momma."

"Doesn't sound like Furman York was one who had a good momma, which might mean that look had an entirely different effect," I said.

"But does what happened thirty years ago help us with his murder now? York getting killed, not his killing Leah Pedroke, is the one Tom—" Jennifer broke off, glanced toward Tom, frowned, then looked at her lap as she determinedly finished, "This is the one we're dealing with now.

"It gives us another piece of York's background. And every piece advances us, even if it's by telling us what's not important."

She didn't raise her head.

"I was thinking," Tom said slowly. Jennifer didn't look at him, but the rest of us did, prepared for him to say something to put her at ease. "I was thinking about your Penny riddle, Elizabeth."

"You already told me the solution. That's why I went to find Kesler at Lukasik Ranch."

"A different part of her riddle. You said Penny was talking about Hiram and a woman."

Chapter Thirty-Four

"*HIRAM?* AND A *woman?*" Mike repeated.

"He did blush…" I said.

"*Hiram?*"

"You have a thought about it, Tom?" Diana asked.

"Yep. Hiram and Yvette."

Not only did I know whom he meant, but it triggered a cascade.

Elvis. Romance. Hiram Poppinger blushing. Yvette.

They streamed through my brain like Penny's mismatched pronouns, somehow making sense amid the jumble.

That didn't mean I accepted it without confirmation. "How do you know?"

"Yvette? Yvette who?" Mike asked.

"You know," Jennifer told him, "the one who thinks she forced Elvis to fake his death because she loved him too much, Elizabeth told us about her weeks and weeks ago."

"Oh. Right. You met her at a wedding you went to with Leona."

"Yes," I confirmed. "But, Tom … why? Why would you think Hiram and Yvette…?"

"Because of what Hiram said about doing a favor for Clyde by talking to York. And Clyde doing a favor for him—"

"By talking to Yvette," Diana finished off. "Makes sense, since they're family."

"Who's family?"

"Clyde and Yvette." Diana raised a finger, drawing lines in the air. "Clyde's mother was a cousin of Yvette's father. That makes Clyde and

Yvette second cousins. But closer than that, because Yvette's father was raised by Clyde's mother's family after his parents died."

"I thought Clyde was related to Dirk Seger," I said. Dirk and his wife, Krista, owned Sherman's solitary bed and breakfast. She also happened to be related to the owner of KWMT.

"He is," Tom said. "By marriage, anyway. Clyde's wife is Dirk's older sister. Half-sister."

My head hurt. "Good heavens, this county's genealogy is a nest of snakes."

Mike reached for three more cookies. "Well, the good news is Yvette getting together with Hiram should ease the heat on Elvis. He can finally quit pretending he's dead and come out of hiding and not have to worry about Yvette."

Ignoring that happy aspect and somewhat grudgingly, I said, "I suppose it might fit with what Clyde said and with Hiram's reaction."

"Right, we're finally at you two talking to Hiram." Jennifer accompanied her brisk statement by brushing cookie crumbs from her fingers in apparent preparation for typing.

"No, we're not. We still have Clyde," Mike objected. "Let's hear that first."

"He didn't say a word about Hiram." I looked directly at Tom. "With that and the check he wrote, we need to look at him more closely."

"Let's hear what he did say," Mike said.

I gave the broad outline, Tom and Diana gave the technical rustling details.

Mike whistled. "Can't get away from York rustling from grazing association members as a possible motive."

"Couldn't that be a defense?" Jennifer asked. "Defending your ranch, like some states have for defending your home."

"Even if it were, it wouldn't cover going to the grazing association, confronting York, and shooting him," I said. "Besides, what we have might be enough evidence for a suspect to *believe* York was rustling, but it's not enough evidence to *know*. I want to know if he was or not. And if he was, to be able to prove it."

"So do I." Tom's quiet voice reminded me we weren't trying to build a defense—for him or anyone else—but were looking for a killer. Partially for justice, partially to exonerate him. Of course if we consulted Tamantha there'd be no partially involved. "Then I'd like to shove the proof down Lukasik's throat."

That last statement's slide from the height of disinterested pursuit of truth into the muddy reality of disliking someone, eased the mood.

More cookies and coffee refills also helped.

"Now Hiram," instructed taskmaster Jennifer.

I obliged, with Tom's contribution limited to nods, until I reached the end.

"Something I want to know," he said to me, "is why you asked Hiram if the marks were right up to the body?"

"First, because the best reason I could think of—" I mentally apologized to Dex for skipping his contribution to this point, but the less I brought him up—even to this group—the better. "—that explained the killer brushing out the marks was a scuffle. Going right up to the body's consistent with that.

"And the other reason I asked about the marks being right up to the body was to test my thoughts about the gun. Hiram says he didn't touch the body, says he didn't see a gun, says the marks went right up to the body. That all fits with the Sampson-Alvaro interplay, with them already having the murder weapon because it was under the body, and with it most likely being York's gun. Because, again, it if had been somebody else's gun, Shelton and his buddies would be going after that somebody else."

Mike said, "How would the gun get under York? He fell on his own gun? Suicide? That's far-fetched with someone sweeping around his body. Accident? Someone wanted to wipe out they'd been there?"

"Possibly. Or someone swept at the dirt because he or she killed York and put the gun under his body."

"That's weird," Jennifer said. "Why would anyone do that?"

"I don't know why—" *Yet*, I hoped. "Hiram knows more. But he's not sharing. We need to talk to him again."

Tom closed his eyes.

"Couldn't it have happened another way?" Diana asked. "Say York didn't die right off, but staggered. The killer's dropped the gun and—"

"Why would the killer have dropped the gun?"

"Horror at killing York." Diana ignored Jennifer's snort and kept going. "The killer's dropped the gun, York staggers toward the killer, and he or she pushes York away, causing him to fall. On top of the gun."

"Like an accident? Like York just happened to fall on it. So the gun being under York doesn't mean anything? Well, that doesn't get us anywhere," Jennifer complained. "We're going backward."

I argued, "It might keep us from going too far down a wrong path. We need to keep possibilities open. Jennifer, will you look particularly at where Furman York was and what he was doing between being acquitted and when he returned to Cottonwood County to work on Lukasik's ranch."

"Okay."

"Why?" Mike asked.

"Murder's usually about the victim. Jennifer's picked up enough from his childhood and before he came to O'Hara Hill to see a pattern. How he acted here since he returned also fits. Between the not guilty verdict and returning here to work on the ranch is the gap in Furman York's life we don't know anything about yet."

Jennifer said, "We'll keep filling in details for that earlier part, but make this gap a priority. When was the trial exactly?"

"Mrs. Parens will know. And check real estate records for the sale of the ranch."

"Got it. What about York's friends? Aren't most people killed by someone they know?" she asked.

Mike raised a hand. "I called Jack Delahunt, and he says he doesn't know of anybody he'd call York's friend."

"The guy's got to have some associates," I protested. "Besides, could he have pulled off the rustling on his own?"

"It'd be a lot easier with help," Mike said. "Jack did say there were rumbles about York being associated with a couple guys from Big Horn County who don't have the best reputation." Big Horn was the next county east of Cottonwood.

Tom spoke up. "That fits with what Badger told me."

"For Pete's sake, when were you going to share that you got information from him?" I demanded.

"When the topic came up or nobody else had anything to say, whichever came first."

"I'm half tempted to report you to Tamantha. She wouldn't stand for such dilatoriness."

"Dila-what?" Jennifer asked.

"Procrastination," Mike said.

Peacemaker Diana kept to the point. "Tell us now, Tom."

"Badger says Furman York was known to drink with some of the Lukasik Ranch hands at the Kicking Cowboy, but not often. The hands came in regular. It was York who didn't come in often. The past few years even less."

"Darn. Not surprising, I suppose. But I hoped if we found his drinking spot—"

"Hold up there. Don't close the gate yet. Turns out Badger has a buddy who works at a place across the county line—the eastern county line."

"Where the rustling in Cottonwood County started," Diana said.

Tom dropped his head slowly in confirmation as he kept talking. "Badger and this buddy were talking the day York was shot and the other bartender says York was a regular there. Had two, three guys he drank with. Not one of them somebody Badger's buddy said he'd introduce to his worst enemy."

I perked up. "Where is this place? What are the names of these guys York drank with? Does the buddy know where they work? Live?"

"Before you go charging off," Tom said, "none of us goes tonight. It's late. And we have to wait for the Pickled Cow to—"

"The *what?*"

Tom correctly deduced I'd heard the name of the bar. "—open tomorrow. Even then, it's a long shot. York's group wasn't the kind to pay with credit cards or otherwise be free with their names. The bartender didn't even know the name York and he thought Fur-Man was a nickname. He only put it together with news of the shooting because he'd seen him driving a Lukasik Ranch vehicle.

"Better to wait. Bartender's talked to Big Horn deputies and if some of York's group comes in, he'll call and let them know."

"Then he calls Badger," said Optimist Mike. "And we hear through Tom."

"I dig. Tom waits for a phone call," Jennifer said with a bit of attitude. "What are the rest of you going to do?"

Easy choice for the top of my wish list. "Try to get Gable Lukasik off by himself so I can pump him about his father."

"Nice," Diana said, but she didn't truly disapprove.

"Anything from your kids?"

"My entire crop from dinner with them is that Asheleigh's cute and she and Gable are really, really serious."

I twisted my mouth. "After Gable, I don't care how long a shot it is, I'll follow up with Badger's bartender friend—"

"Not alone," the guys chorused.

"—because we can't wait around for—"

"I'm going with you," Mike said. "Or I go alone."

"I'm going." I didn't mind his coming. A second pair of ears did help, but the first pair of ears would be mine. "Tom? What do you plan to do?"

"You mean besides trying to talk James into talking Shelton into letting us back in to talk to Hiram again?"

I COULDN'T SLEEP.

My reason said Tom wasn't a serious suspect. Something else wouldn't let me sleep.

Why this hadn't happened last night, I couldn't imagine. Unless it had something to do with his being in the house. If the sheriff's department had decided to take him in... Well, at least I'd have known right away.

To keep my mind off visions of Thomas David Burrell's possible arrest—*unlikely arrest*—I searched for an instance when I'd felt like this.

Examining those memories, I realized I usually combatted concern with reason, fear with action.

Then my memory produced a previous instance.

Before my wedding to Wes, my ex for the past year-and-a-half, I had fretted about the weather. We had contingencies in place. Even better, every forecast from every source—and I checked them all—predicted fine weather. Still, I fretted, and worried, and couldn't sleep.

The weather was perfect.

The wedding was perfect.

I'd wasted all that effort worrying about the wedding. I should have worried about the marriage.

DAY THREE

Chapter Thirty-Five

THE PHONE WOKE me.

Never my favorite thing—being awakened, especially by the phone. I grabbed it off the bedside table and glared impartially at the time and the notification that Mike Paycik was the caller.

"What? It's seven-thirty-eight in the morning and you guys left six hours ago. This better be good."

"Aunt Gee's back from her convention."

✧ ✧ ✧ ✧

I CURLED INTO the passenger seat of Mike's posh SUV, huddled around the warmth of the half-consumed Hamburger Heaven coffee he'd handed to me as soon as I got in.

Mike glanced in the rearview mirror, to where Jennifer slept in the back seat. He'd informed me that she hadn't hesitated or complained when he called her. Just said she'd be out in front of her parents' house waiting when he came by.

Diana had passed up this morning jaunt in favor of breakfast with her kids, then reporting for work on time.

Tom said he needed to get some things done early today. The subtext being that he intended to slip in ranch work before Tamantha got home and gave him hell for not keeping his nose to the investigative grindstone.

Mike turned toward me, and grinned.

"It's going to be a sunny, warm day. Could hit ninety, Warren said."

He referred to Warren Fisk, the station's weatherman. Warren didn't have as much success fighting off Thurston's constant efforts to trim weather and sports as Mike did, so the weather report often came across as telegraphic headlines. Mike might be reporting Warren's forecast literally: *Warm, sunny day. Could hit ninety. Back to you, Thurston.*

"Tell me when it gets there. In the meantime, it's cold. And it can't be called sunny, because the sun's barely up."

"Been up for hours. Ranchers have been up even longer. Nothing like seeing the sun come up over a growing herd of your own cattle on your own land."

"Maybe if you stay up all night to watch the sun rise, because otherwise you need to go to bed right after the Five O'clock news to get enough sleep. Have you thought about that when you wax lyrical about running your own cattle? Because you can't do that if you're the hotshot sports guy who does the Ten O'clock—or Eleven O'clock broadcast if you're on one of the coasts. Not to mention your cattle will be a long way away from Chicago or D.C. or wherever you end up."

"I might not."

I nodded. "Well, you don't have to. You can go on owning the ranch, leasing out the land."

"I meant I might not move up in sports broadcasting."

"Oh, yes, you are."

"I could stay here and—"

"No."

He blinked as if I'd slapped him. Then his grin flashed. "You're not the boss of me."

"I'm not, but your talent and ambition are. You're having a career, Paycik."

"Ranching's a career, too."

Not one you've been pursuing.

I didn't say it. Not sure I'd fully recognized the truth of that until this second. But even as I did, I knew he had to recognize it for himself.

"You feel like ranching has had a hold on you?"

"That's exactly it. It grabbed onto me young."

"Right, Methuselah." I downshifted on the sarcasm to add, "Tom was telling me yesterday that the ranching bug can hit people harder, depending on the circumstances."

"He should know," he said with passable lightness.

"Must have been tough going through losing your family ranch the way you did. Was your grandmother—" I searched for a less harsh way of asking. "—still tending the roses when that happened?"

"No. She'd died a couple years before. Grandpa used to go sit on the porch and listen to the records they used to dance to."

This wasn't a good time to deeply probe his feelings about his family or how those and other elements factored into this future. Not with Jennifer possibly waking any second. Not with me struggling with my daily morning fog.

He slanted a look toward me. Started to say something, then stopped. After another moment, he opened his mouth again.

"Do you want to hear about Aunt Gee getting back early from her convention?"

I sipped more liquid warmth from the Hamburger Heaven cup. "Yes. Yes, I do."

✧ ✧ ✧ ✧

ON OUR ARRIVAL, Gisella Decker ushered us into her kitchen and informed us we were hungry.

She's the only person I've ever known who can cook and still have her kitchen clean enough that at any point in the process a tech team could move in and make semi-conductors.

We'd already eaten fluffy scrambled eggs, with biscuits fresh from the oven. Then batches of waffles, which Mike consumed nearly as quickly as Gee and the waffle maker produced them, with minimal help from Jennifer and none from me.

Oh, okay. I had a couple.

Now Gee had started something that required vigorous chopping.

"Are we ever going to ask about the murder," Jennifer leaned in and whispered to Mike and me.

He tried to shush her with his mouth full of waffle and syrup. Not successfully.

Jennifer sat up and said loudly, "Was the convention fun?"

"It was highly educational, as it always is. We are in sessions all day, learning—or teaching—specific methods, updates in technology, and wellness for ourselves and co-workers among many topics. But perhaps the most beneficial aspect is touring nearby ECC—that's Emergency Communication Centers—to glean ideas from how others organize and operate their centers to carry back to our home organizations.

"One we saw this year has a structure that I found most interesting. They share space with traffic management and the emergency operations group, in addition to being back-up for other jurisdictions. As soon as I've developed a detailed plan, I shall strongly recommend that Cottonwood County establish similar approaches."

Her eyes gleamed with anticipation.

Forget strong recommendation, this was as good as done. And Gisella Decker would be in charge of it before anyone knew what hit them.

"Sounds like a great plan, Aunt Gee," Mike said.

"I had intended to gather more detailed information on their process, but of course, I changed my reservations to return as soon as possible after I heard the news," Gisella Decker said.

"Why? Why come back early?" Jennifer asked with the lack of fear of the young.

Gee didn't even turn from chopping cooked chicken breasts.

"To assist the investigators, of course."

Mike, Jennifer, and I looked at each other.

Again, Jennifer voiced the question. "The sheriff's department or us?"

"I shall share all the appropriate information I possess with the authorities."

"What about us?"

This time only Mike and I exchanged a look—one that shared the same thought. We weren't ever coming to ask Gee for information again without Jennifer along.

Not only were her direct questions getting answers, but Gee hadn't even turned around from her chopping.

"That will depend on what the authorities say."

Those who didn't know Gisella Decker might interpret that as meaning she would follow the authorities' instructions about whether to share her information beyond them. More likely, it meant she would decide what to share with us based on whether the authorities—in other words, Shelton and Sheriff Conrad—investigated as thoroughly and as quickly as she wanted them to.

Jennifer the Intrepid said, "The sheriff's department hasn't shown any interest in Furman York's past."

Gee stopped chopping and turned toward us, raised knife in hand.

"What have they shown an interest in?"

When the tip of the wicked looking knife pointed toward me, I obeyed its order and said, "Hiram Poppinger and Tom Burrell."

She gave a kind of growl that would have sent me running if I'd been Shelton or Conrad. I might run anyway.

"Why?" she demanded.

The other two looked at me.

Gee returned to her chopping while I explained about Hiram finding the body.

Then Tom's conflict with York, what we—and Tom—thought York had been up to, and the timing. By the end of relating all that pointed at Tom, I had to admit it wasn't entirely unreasonable for the sheriff's department to look at him.

"Though they should be running that arm of the enquiry strictly to eliminate him." Unsure if those words fit with what I'd said aloud or only with what I'd been thinking, I quickly added, "We're examining the past. Whether the solution lies there or not, it seems likely Furman York's character is important. So that's where we're starting."

"Yes." Her voice rang like a deep bell foretelling doom. "I am aware you spent considerable time visiting next door."

Mike tried to look innocent, but shifted in his chair, picked up his glass of milk, put it down, and adjusted it precisely in the center of its coaster.

"Mike insisted Mrs. Parens was the best source for the history of what had happened that I didn't know anything about," I said. "Diana agreed."

As long as I was getting payback, might as well get two for the price of one, since they both withheld information from me.

Over her shoulder, Gee looked down her nose at Mike. "Did they?" Then she turned to me, knife still in hand. "So, now you've come to me to fill in what shreds of information you believe Emmaline Parens might have unintentionally omitted."

Uh-oh. I might have unleashed a tiger. Before she struck, I took a gamble.

"Not at all. I doubt Mrs. Parens would unintentionally omit anything she thought we might benefit from knowing unless she considered it gossip."

I gambled by making an appeal to the mutual respect and honesty that stood shoulder to shoulder with their rivalry. It was a calculated gamble.

"But each of you," I continued, "has an individual perspective on events—individual, yet equally perceptive—so we get the most well-rounded and complete picture by hearing from you both."

"Humph."

It was a complicated *humph*. It said she knew soft-soap when she heard it. But it also said that, whether by accident or design, I'd hit a truth.

I concentrated on making my face convey *By design, by respectful and appreciative design.*

"I will tell you one thing that Emmaline Parens never would. If I could murder, Furman York would have died many years ago."

"*You?* We weren't—You aren't—"

Mike rescued me from shocked incomplete sentences. "We'd *never* consider you, Aunt Gee."

"You should. You should look at everyone with a murder. But you will find—if you check thoroughly, as the sheriff's department should and shall—that I was far away from the grazing association lands where he finally met his end and I was in the company of many disinterested people who will attest to that."

Gee's gaze met mine and my shock slid away.

That was contradictory, because what I saw in her eyes made what she'd said about Mrs. P click.

Not that she *couldn't* tell us that if Gisella Decker could murder Furman York would have died many years ago, but that she never *would* tell us.

So Mrs. P knew it to be true. How could she know that unless she'd been witness to Gee's desire to murder York and her inability to do it?

I doubted I'd ever know for sure.

For once, I accepted not knowing. I accepted that what Gisella Decker had felt—felt now—and what Emmaline Parens had passed through with her in the heat of its origins was for them alone.

I cleared my throat. "Take us through your knowing Leah Pedroke, Gee. Please."

She turned, transferred the last of the chopped chicken to a large bowl. She washed the cutting board and knife, then got out a bunch of celery. *Whack.* She and her knife cleanly removed the base in one stroke.

As she washed the ribs of celery, she began to speak.

Chapter Thirty-Six

GEE'S ACCOUNT FOLLOWED the skeleton of Mrs. Parens' story, without including any emotion. No mention of her husband's recent death. Factual account of the oil boom in O'Hara Hill. Leasing a room to Leah Pedroke as a business arrangement. Her renter's failure to return on schedule. The search for the young woman relayed in police report dryness.

Except she never faced us.

Mike shook his head slightly. He was concerned.

His aunt would resist mightily being yanked out of automaton mode and Gisella Decker with her heels dug in would not be budged.

On the other hand, perhaps she could be lured with a carrot to where she could not be driven.

A carrot in the form of professional shop talk.

"Once the sheriff's department arrived that night, did they conduct the investigation well?"

"With Jimmie Careb as sheriff?" she asked with characteristic— and relieving—tartness. "No. Started off okay with the first officer on scene. He was an old-timer. Hadn't moved with the times, but he had common sense, experience, and worked hard. Then Jimmie Careb showed up, throwing his weight around when it dawned on him there'd be reporters on hand."

"What kind of sheriff was he?"

"He set up to talk to reporters right where Leah was killed *before* they finished searching the area. Didn't have the science we have now, but a simple search? You want to know what kind of sheriff he was?

Taught Robert Widcuff everything he thought he knew."

"That's an indictment if I ever heard one."

"Jimmie Careb *should* have been indicted. He was the mold, Robert Widcuff merely the knockoff copy."

"Yet you still chose to sign up as a dispatcher with the sheriff's department under him. I'd have thought you'd stay as far away from that operation as possible."

She turned, leaving the knife behind this time. Her hands on her substantial hips proved nearly as intimidating. "When there's something wrong, you can run the other direction for fear of the spray getting on you, or you can dig in and try to make it right. Like those stables that guy cleaned as one of his miracles."

I wrestled with that a moment. "The Labors of Hercules? The Augean stables?"

"Did it in a day, right?"

"I think so. He rerouted a couple rivers. He needed to because the livestock was supposed to be divine and thus produce prodigious amounts of, uh, dung." Now *that* had stuck in my memory.

She snorted. "Don't care whether they were divine or not, I've seen cattle *dung* and it's nothing compared to what was in that sheriff's department then. Took me—and others, including you and Mike and the others at the end with Widcuff—to clean it out, but it's cleaned out now. That's what counts."

"And now Furman York is dead." Did someone view that as a punctuation mark on the misjustice of the Leah Pedroke murder verdict?

Someone who'd cared about that young woman and who abhorred misjustice?

Involuntarily, my head jerked up.

But Gee had said she couldn't...

The thought floated through my mind that if Furman York had been killed by anyone trying to figuratively muck out a particular corner of the Augean Stables, Norman Clay Lukasik's life might not be worth much, either.

That thought struck a nerve, like banging your elbow. It zinged around as if hugely serious, yet I couldn't see how.

"About time he left this earth. Sure wasn't doing any good on it. Not that a murder can be ignored, but if one could be, this would be it. Should have been in prison these past decades, instead of slithering around here like he's been, doing heaven knows what."

"Like allegedly rustling?"

She expelled a "Huh" that put allegedly in its place. *Of course he was. Sounds just like him.* "No good that one. Every way, shape, and form."

"Had you met him before ... before the trial?"

"No. Haven't met him since, either. Made sure of that. Our paths didn't come close to crossing often. When they did... Well, I saw him entering the supermarket when I had a cart half-full. I left that cart and prepared to walk out the door. Penny stopped me with one hand and pointed him out the door with the other. He laughed. Nasty, nasty, nasty. But he went.

"I can't suppose he was barred from there every time, but at least that once, he knew he was not fit to be around decent people."

"Did you know about his connections to the grazing association?"

"I knew the ranch for which he worked belonged to that grazing association, despite efforts to change that. I did not, after the passing of Leah's parents, keep an awareness of his activities, with the grazing association or anything else. Wayne Shelton knew my sentiments about having the man in our county. I left it to him to ensure no other young woman became York's victim. To Wayne's credit, none has. And now none will."

She poured the results of her celery chopping into the large bowl and deftly set up four more ribs in a row on the board.

"You said after Leah's parents passed. When was that, Gee?" I asked.

"Ten years after Leah's murder. Their two other children had left home by then. Leah's siblings had moved on. Young people are resilient that way. Her parents did not move on. After Leah's father died—the second to die—I received only a clipping of a newspaper notice. I wrote back, but never received a response."

"Did that surprise you?"

"It did, a little. When Leah's parents stayed with me during the trial, I saw them as a strong, connected family. But—" She briskly whacked through the celery. "—people react differently, move on differently, heal differently."

I wondered about Gee. The death of her husband left her with questions, followed by a young woman she'd cared for whose murder left the taste of bitter injustice. Gisella Decker certainly moved on. But had she truly healed?

"Leah's parents stayed with you? During the trial, you mean?" Mike asked.

"Yes." Whack. Another precise cut across the ribs of celery. Whatever she was making would have plenty of crunch.

"Tell us about the trial."

"It was like the officer I mentioned as first on the scene and Sheriff Careb. The old, stolid way of doing things unable to stand up to the flashy and underhanded."

"The county attorney of that time and Norman Clay Lukasik?"

"Precisely. The county attorney set forth a solid case. But he did not know how to contend with Lukasik's theatrics and misdirection.

"That Lukasik kept harping on Mr. Erwin, who was Leah's boss. Didn't matter that the county attorney had brought in those girls who'd seen Mr. Erwin leave *and* dropped him at the bar. And then the men from the bar who were with him every minute until they all went to where they were living. And Roland Fuller out looking for his dog saw them arrive. Mr. Erwin had an alibi practically minute by minute. But those were mere facts."

She looked even grimmer. "Which Lukasik tried to make sound mysterious and suspicious, succeeding all too often with the weak-minded. While his client sat there smirking—despite all the evidence of his being out of the bar during the time Leah must have been attacked and killed, and looking like he'd been in a fight when he came back, and that button tying his shirt to the crime scene for heaven's sakes."

She sucked in a deep breath, clearly having lost the thread of that sentence. However her grammar had tangled, her point remained straight.

"Did he persuade anyone?" I asked.

"Nobody with half a brain," Gee said emphatically, picking up the knife again, but not returning to her chopping. "All razzle dazzle and repeating perfectly ordinary words as if they were significant and suspicious. Clear as anything what he was doing. Though the judge didn't help any, not letting evidence come in about other girls York had tried to mess with here. Probably the reason he kept moving."

From the corner of my eye, I was aware of Jennifer giving a slight nod.

"Aunt Gee," Mike asked, "after he was acquitted, did York go back to Texas?"

"He was *not* acquitted. He received a not-guilty verdict. As for where he went, I don't know. Didn't care, either. Wish to high heavens he'd stayed there. Why he ever came back here… Had to know he was hated."

"Some people crave that," I murmured.

She belied the negative shake of her head by saying, "Maybe. Doesn't matter. He was bad. Plain bad. If it weren't for all the trouble to the good people of Cottonwood County and our law enforcement, I'd be just as glad he finally was killed and not worry overmuch about who did it."

Odd to hear that sentiment from the Grande Dame of Cotton-wood County law and order.

Though that attitude would not do for Tamantha. Her goal tolerated no potential lingering doubts.

"What about the rumors that bribery was involved in the verdict?" Mike asked. "Do you believe them?"

Gee sent him a repressive look, but at least she didn't point the knife.

"Rumors are not what modern, professional, and ethical law enforcement are about."

"Rumors can be pointers," he said doggedly.

"If there had been sufficient proof to lay charges against any individuals for circumventing justice in that case, I, personally, would have seen to it. However, even without the legal system, a kind of justice can come about, whether by exile, by not being able to live with the guilt, by finding the hallow of hatred beneath the trappings of worldly success."

"Who are the first two?" Jennifer asked. "Guessing the last one is Norman Clay Lukasik? I've heard his son doesn't like him—" Not naming her source showed growing tact, since she'd heard it from me. "—and his wife couldn't stand him."

Gee's lips pressed tight. "I have said as much as I intend to until I speak with Wayne Shelton. Some might hold I've already said too much. However, you are welcomed to stay for lunch."

"What are you making?"

I quelled Mike with a look, but Gee didn't see it and wouldn't have been quelled regardless. "Chicken salad with spicy-hot almonds."

"Maybe we can stick around..."

My mouth watered despite my stomach loudly declaring itself full. "No. We have a lot to follow up on."

Gee gave me a severe look. "Law enforcement is obligated to look into the death of Furman York, which can only be regarded as an improvement in our county. You are not."

I shook my head. "I am—we are, Aunt Gee. Tamantha's worried about Tom. Who can blame her after last time?"

"My dad was telling my mom he told off somebody at work who was saying they'd always wondered if Tom got away with it last time and if this was another instance..." Jennifer let it fade away as we all turned to her.

Under his breath, Mike uttered a curse. I mentally seconded it. His aunt didn't scold him.

Belatedly trying to stem the reaction, Jennifer said, "And Tom's real worried the sheriff's department has landed on Hiram Poppinger and won't let go."

Gee turned back to her workspace. She covered the bowl, put everything into the refrigerator, except the cutting board and knife, and untied her apron.

"You'll all need to go now. It's clearly high time I report to work."

Chapter Thirty-Seven

"WHAT WAS THAT about people talking about Tom?" Mike demanded of Jennifer as soon as we were outside.

"Just what I said. They didn't say any more. Don't worry. Dad told off that guy."

Mike and I exchanged a look that carried agreement. Neither of us considered it likely that Jennifer's dad encountered the only person in Cottonwood County thinking that way.

He and Jennifer started toward his SUV. I made a detour.

"What are you doing?" Jennifer asked.

"Knocking. I have a question for Mrs. P."

"Aunt Gee's going to be out any second." Mike looked from one front door to the other.

"They're not going to—Hi, Mrs. Parens. I don't want to keep you, but wanted to ask what your school connections think of the new elementary school teacher, Asheleigh Vincennes."

One eyebrow twitched—practically an expression of shock from her. "She is adjusting satisfactorily for a newly minted teacher beginning in the middle of the academic year."

"Anything about her background or her mother?"

"No." And there wouldn't be from that response.

"If you hear of anything..." I started off her front step, then turned back. "Did you know Gee's back? She's going into work now."

Mrs. P looked toward the neighboring house, then to me. "Thank you, Elizabeth."

Back in the SUV and a block away, Jennifer asked cheerfully,

"What next?"

"Gable Lukasik, if we can talk to him away from his father."

"Kind of tough, isn't it, since he works at the family ranch and his father's there. You know, that's interesting, isn't it? Lukasik senior sticking around. Doesn't usually stay here long, does he?"

"That *is* interesting. Something else to talk to Gable about," I said. "Any ideas how to find him away from the ranch?"

"No," Mike said.

A lot of help they were.

Returning to Sherman, I considered that the hunt for Gable Lukasik exposed a gap in my sources.

He had not gone to school in Cottonwood County, didn't participate in civic events or society dos, only marginally participated in the ranching community. He was too old for Jennifer's social connections.

A definite gap.

It left one possibility I could think of.

Gable Lukasik might not cook much, but the guy bought beer and tortilla chips, didn't he?

✧ ✧ ✧ ✧

MIKE AND JENNIFER had to go into the station for work.

First, he was swinging by my house to drop me off.

"What are you going to do?" Jennifer asked. "You have a lot of time before the Pickled Cow opens."

"I want to check some things, before I go out to the Lukasik Ranch again to see if I can catch Gable alone or—Stop. Pull over. Pull over, Mike."

"Why? What—"

"Now. Right here. Pull over."

On second thought, did I need more sources in a town this size? Standing on a street corner might work.

I'd just recognized Gable Lukasik and Asheleigh Vincennes turning off Yellowstone Street into a side street.

"I can't wait long—"

"Don't wait. I don't want them to see you."

"Who?"

I had the SUV door open. Gable and Asheleigh wouldn't hear me if I explained now, but someone on the sidewalk might. "Tell you later."

"But how will—"

"I'll walk home. It's not far."

"—we find out what you're doing?"

Ah. That's what he was worried about. I held up my hand in a phone-you gesture, then waved them on.

As soon as he pulled away, I jogged down the block and turned the corner as the young couple had. A few yards behind my quarry, I eased up, so when I reached them I was at close to natural walking speed.

"Hi, Gable. Nice to see you again. Oh, hello, and you're Asheleigh, right? Asheleigh Vincennes." I had started talking when I was even with them. Turning to see who spoke slowed them, and that let me get ahead and stop. To walk past me now would require circling me in a blatant move. I extended my hand to the young woman. She met it automatically. "I'm Elizabeth Margaret Danniher. We didn't have a chance to get introduced when I ran into your mother yesterday."

"You're a friend of Odessa's?" Gable asked.

"Yes," I said too fast for Asheleigh to disagree, then, holding his gaze, I moved slightly to the side, drawing him around enough that he didn't have a direct line of sight to Asheleigh's face. "I'm interviewing her for the 'Helping Out!' segment. Do you know about the great program her group is doing?"

"I've heard about it."

Not a topic to stick with. I wanted to know about Norman Clay Lukasik, though I'd take some on his son or even Odessa. But what I wanted wouldn't get them talking.

For that, the topic needed to be what interested them. At least to start.

"But what I want to know is about you two. I know Gable volunteered to help coach summer baseball, including my friend's son— Gary Stendahl?"

"Oh, sure. Gary's a good kid. He—"

No. We weren't going down the path of Gary's baseball ability. If it had been Gable alone, maybe, but not with Asheleigh here and suspicious of little ol' me because of her mother's reaction outside the dentist's office. A topic that would disarm both of them was what I needed.

"And the kids were talking about you two and what a great couple you are. Now, how long is it you've been dating?"

"Since April," Asheleigh said.

"Could have started two whole months earlier if we'd been smart, because she moved here to teach at the first of February," Gable said.

"You came in the winter, Asheleigh? You're a brave soul," I said.

"Oh, it's lovely here in winter."

She was delusional. But at least she could enjoy her delusion for a big chunk of each year. Though not, thank heavens, today.

She continued, "I was incredibly lucky that a teaching position came open after I'd graduated from Penn State mid-year."

"Are you from Pennsylvania?"

"I've always wanted to be a teacher."

Yes, I noticed she didn't answer my question.

"And she's a terrific one," Gable said, clearly untroubled by her failure to answer questions. Youth so seldom saw the warning signs. Next thing they knew, they were tied up to someone who made a lousy source. Tragic.

Asheleigh slipped her hand under his arm and leaned against him, leaving me to carry the conversational ball.

"Penn State's a great school."

She nodded and smiled. "Yes, it is. I learned so much."

"Long way from Wyoming."

"I've always wanted to come to Wyoming."

"What about it drew you?"

"And I'm so glad you did." Gable's words and goofy grin ignored another of my questions completely.

So did she. "Me, too." She looked up at him. "The best thing that ever happened to me."

I interrupted love's young idyll. "How did you meet?"

She giggled. "Believe it or not, my mother set us up. She met Gable first."

Finally, an answer to a question.

"How'd you meet her mother?" I asked Gable.

But Asheleigh answered. "Before she took the job she has now, the one you're doing the piece on, Mom went to all sorts of meetings for charities, volunteer openings, and interest groups."

"She was looking for something to do after moving here with you?"

Again, she zoomed past my question. Eager to get back to Gable as a topic? Or away from her mother?

"She came back from volunteering one day and said she'd met someone I had to meet. I did *not* want to meet him. I wasn't even settled into my job and—My *mother*, setting me up. It was weird." She laughed. A real laugh. Not a giggle. "I resisted and delayed and avoided."

"Hey, I wasn't clamoring to go out with you, either."

She swiped at Gable's arm with her free hand. He caught that hand and they smiled into each other's eyes.

Fearing that could go on a long time if I didn't break it up, I asked, "With neither one of you wanting to meet the other, how did it ever happen?"

"Odessa is one persistent woman," Gable said. "We were teamed up together for Shred Day at the library—you know, they do it every year right after tax season. The entrepreneur meet-up group I'm in volunteers to bring machines each year, then we're teamed up with helpers. Odessa was my helper. And she worked like crazy, because I'd volunteered to bring two shredders—we have spares at the ranch. My father's nuts about records for the ranch. He shreds then burns."

I was liking Gable better all the time. He'd not only answered the how did it happen question, he'd tossed in bringing multiple shredders *and* explained his father's shredding and burning practices when all I'd done was arch a brow. He could give his girlfriend pointers.

"So Odessa and I were working away together all day and, after, she insisted I come to dinner at their apartment that night, said I deserved a good, home-cooked dinner for all that work. Sounded real good. I was hungry and I was beat. Heck, she'd worked all day, too, but she was all revved up to cook dinner for me. How could I refuse? And then we get to the apartment and the door opens ... and there's Asheleigh."

Coup de foudre.

The French expression for a lightning strike, also used for love at first sight, whispered in my head. I could practically smell the singe from that moment.

"We talked and ate and talked and ate. All of us, I mean. Then, Asheleigh and I went out for dessert, just the two of us, because Odessa didn't have any in their apartment and—"

Asheleigh laughed. "She did. She had ice cream and cookies. It was all a ploy to let us get off by ourselves."

"Worked for me." He grinned. "We spent hours talking that night."

"And have been together ever since."

Also finishing each other's sentences.

"Odessa sure knew best," he said.

"I generally do," came Odessa Vincennes' voice from behind me, as if she'd come up the sidewalk to join them.

Chapter Thirty-Eight

"MOM."

"Hi, Odessa."

I couldn't interpret Asheleigh's greeting—warning? concern? apology? neutrality?—but Gable's was pure cheerful welcome.

She looked a quick order to her daughter, then focused on Gable. It was an odd look. I couldn't immediately categorize it. Rather than try in the moment and risk cementing a mistaken impression, I concentrated on memorizing it.

I didn't have much time to devote to memorizing, because she quickly turned to me.

But I got in the first word. "How great to see you again, Odessa. About continuing our interview—"

"I can't possibly do that before next week and I can't commit to it then."

"That's a shame." And a change from when I'd first contacted her about the interview. She'd jumped on the first slot I'd offered. "It will postpone getting public support. Especially with this murder—you're aware of that, right?" I asked the two women, getting looks so scrubbed clean of emotion that they must have had the mental equivalent of housemaid hands. "Of course you must be, since the murder victim was Gable's father's ranch foreman. Well, I suspect it will take up a lot of the station's air time, so I don't know when we'll be able to get that segment of 'Helping Out!' on-air if we don't get it going immediately."

That made no sense from a news standpoint. The time devoted to a story generally shrinks after the initial blast. I doubted they knew that, which was good from my standpoint. Not so good, that they apparently didn't care.

Odessa shook her head, the only sign of not being completely at ease the subtle rubbing of her thumb along the side of her forefinger.

My chances of getting her in front of a camera to grill her about her reaction to the news of Furman York being shot hadn't improved one bit.

On the other hand, I had Gable in front of me and he appeared the most cooperative of the three. I didn't hesitate to make a sharp turn in the conversation.

"It was nice to see your ranch yesterday, Gable. I'd heard so much about it."

Ah. I'd pressed the right button. His eyes brightened, the niceness of his face multiplied.

"Your father didn't seem as devoted to ranching as I'd have expected…"

He snatched that worm, along with the hook. "Devoted? No, he's not *devoted*. It's not high profile. Don't get publicity for ranching. Though he did manage to get on TV yesterday, thanks to your colleague."

My micro-expression response to the concept of Thurston Fine as a colleague apparently placated Gable, because he abruptly relaxed.

Before he had a chance to change his mind, I said, "Kesler and Tom said you're heading toward being a good rancher."

"That's what I want. I've always loved it here. As a kid, this started as my place away from, uh, Denver and life there. But it wasn't long before I loved being here for itself. Mom, too. Mom and I spent as much time here as we could. Summers, the holidays, school breaks. Sometimes she'd even take me out of school to spend longer here. She needed it as much as I did. There's something about this place. We could breathe here. Even if my father tried to discourage us."

His grim smile stretched the angles of his face, making it far less cute, though more compelling. It made me aware of strength beneath the softness, like rock under lush grass. I suppose he needed to have underlying strength just to keep upright against the bulldozer who was his father.

"I decided to go to UW—that's the University of Wyoming—" As if I hadn't learned that my first few weeks here or risk being completely lost in half the newsroom conversations. "—to be closer. To come here for breaks. Especially…" He breathed a moment, head tipped forward. "Mom died November 5 in my freshman year. Car accident. Stinking car accident. A couple blocks from the Denver house. A cat was running loose. Mom tried to avoid it. The other car did, too. Didn't even set off the airbags. But she hit her head. Just the wrong spot. They said she'd had a weakness there all her life. Could have lived with it for years if it hadn't been for this accident."

"I'm so sorry, Gable."

As softly as I'd said the words, they still disrupted his remembering.

"Yeah. Thanks. It's been a long time now." Asheleigh's hand tightened around his and he reciprocated.

Odessa never took her eyes off Gable's face, her expression blank.

I said, "I've heard such good things about your mom from everybody."

"Yeah." He cleared his throat. "She was special."

"It must have been very hard for your father," Odessa said unexpectedly.

He swallowed.

"He worked. I was at school."

If that was meant to convey Gable didn't know his father's reaction because they were separated, it failed.

Awkward silence followed.

As if driven to fill the silence, I said, "I didn't have a chance yesterday to ask if you can help fill in gaps we have on Furman York. Who are his friends among the hands on the ranch? No? He doesn't have any?"

He was shaking his head. "He was foreman."

Somehow, I didn't think Furman York's supervisory role explained his apparent lack of friends.

"Friends off the ranch?"

"No idea."

"He must have had some associates, social life?"

More head-shaking.

"He must have talked about those things."

"If he did, I didn't hear it."

This was getting old.

"Did he ever leave the ranch? Have time off?"

"Sure."

"Where did he go, what did he do?"

"We weren't buddies. I don't know."

"Was he a monk?"

His eyes cut toward Odessa, likely in discomfort at letting the mother of his girlfriend know he was aware of any lifestyle outside of a monastery.

"No."

"If you know that, then you must have some idea of what he did and where he went when he left the ranch."

Another look toward Odessa.

But she was looking at her daughter. Issuing some sort of order, if I knew mother-daughter eye conversations. Asheleigh radiated reluctance.

"Other hands talked about him going down to Denver, up to Billings when he had a few days."

That answered where. He wasn't going to explain *what* as long as Odessa was on hand unless York had turned into Mother Teresa on those trips.

"Speaking of the ranch..." Asheleigh's light voice claimed Gable's attention immediately. He smiled at her, apparently missing the clouds in her eyes. "You mentioned having us to dinner at the ranch, Mom and me. Or have you forgotten?"

"That was before—"

"I'd love to meet your father," Asheleigh lied.

It was Odessa who wanted that meeting.

I remembered some of Penny's words.

And the boy. Turned around, though. Happy now. Hope it lasts for him. Not likely, considering the complications. Sins of the father shouldn't, but do, and wider than fathers.

Had she meant Gable? The sins of the father fit. So did the complications. Especially if the *wider* encompassed a pushing mother.

During our abbreviated interview, I'd thought better of Odessa than being someone who pushed her daughter toward the son of a famous—and presumably rich—father. But the mother-daughter interchange, Asheleigh's reluctant maneuvering of Gable, and now Odessa's satisfaction, said otherwise.

"I, uh... We'll do that. Soon. Just now it isn't a good time." Gable had picked up more than I thought, based on his directing his apology to Odessa. "But right now, sorry—I've got to go. I promised Kesler I'd have that tool back to him."

"But lunch," Asheleigh protested with a vague wave toward the sign for a restaurant a few doors away, apparently their intended destination. "You haven't eaten."

"I'll get takeout, eat on the way back. I'll call you. Bye." He squeezed her hand, then released it and turned to go back the way he'd come.

"I better get going, too, if I'm going to have any lunch." I smiled. And blatantly turned to go with Gable.

A few strides up the sidewalk, I said, "Speaking of your father—"

"Please don't."

I let his snapped words ride, curious how he'd react.

Still striding, he glanced at me, then away. "Sorry. It's been a tough time."

"I'm sure it has. Has it made it better or worse having your father around for—how long?"

"Almost two weeks now. And it's made it worse." He muttered something more that sounded like, "It always does."

I led that slide past. "It's unusual, isn't it for him to spend this long at the ranch."

He hesitated just an instant as we turned onto Yellowstone Street, as if to absorb a new revelation to him. "It is. He's usually only here a couple days at a time."

"Well, maybe this will give you time to arrange that dinner, intro-duce Asheleigh and her mom to your dad."

"Yeah." He looked and sounded like a very downhearted preppy at the moment.

I hoped the romance survived Momma trying to advance it by pushing to meet Norman Clay Lukasik. I couldn't imagine he'd be much of a cupid for the young couple.

"I suppose he needs to stay now—indefinitely?—to run the ranch with the foreman dead."

"*Him?*" Did Gable's scoff apply to his father or York or both? "Kesler's running the place. I'm helping as much as I can. Bye, Elizabeth."

He took me by surprise with a dive toward a parked pickup. He and Asheleigh must have just gotten out of it when I spotted them.

I waved goodbye and continued along Yellowstone Street until he was out of sight and I could turn around to head home.

Chapter Thirty-Nine

AS PROMISED, I called Mike as I walked toward my house.

"Hold on a minute," he said immediately. "Better yet, we'll call you back. Couple minutes, okay?"

I reached the side street that formed one edge of Courthouse Square and led to the sheriff's department, tucked behind the imposing courthouse occupying the center of the oversized block.

Looking down the street toward the building housing the sheriff's office, jail, and fire department headquarters, the strangeness of Shelton letting us talk to Hiram Poppinger struck me again.

I hesitated, debating a detour to the sheriff's department.

My phone rang.

I dropped the detour impulse and answered, continuing past the courthouse.

"Okay. We're all in the bigger editing booth and you're on speaker," Mike said.

"We've got to stop meeting like this," Diana said. "Though there's more oxygen without you and Jerry."

"I'm out for a walk on a nice, sunny day. I have plenty of oxygen."

"I wish." Jennifer sighed, deflating my gloating.

"Explain why you bailed on us," Mike said.

I did, along with what happened after I caught up with Gable and Asheleigh, as well as Odessa's arrival.

"She really doesn't want to finish that interview with you, does she?" Diana commented.

"Apparently not."

"She could be afraid her daughter's boyfriend killed Furman York. That would really upset her."

"That's a long shot," Mike said.

"It makes sense of how she looked in the interview tape when you said Furman York was murdered and her staying away from Elizabeth *and* that look on her face Elizabeth just described," Jennifer insisted.

If Odessa had her sights set on her daughter marrying Gable for his family money, ranch, and fame, having him accused of murder would be a real blow to her ambitions.

"We shouldn't get too tied to her expressions," I said. "I once interviewed a law enforcement expert on non-verbal cues. He thought he had an interviewee pegged as having all sorts of guilt about something. Turned out the suspect was coming down with the flu and had to run to the bathroom."

Jennifer argued, "Could've been faking it. Or it was guilt making him sick."

"Then his guilt was contagious, because half the office then came down with the flu."

"Oh."

"So you don't set any store by Odessa Vincennes' expression as she looked at Gable?" Diana asked.

Darn the woman for pointing out the flaw in my dismissing this. "I wouldn't say that."

"So, you *do* set store by it."

"Yes. Fine. I do. But not in any one potential interpretation of it. That expression was there. It was strange. Those two things I'll stick to, but an interpretation? No. So, it does us no good because we don't know what it meant. And that means it doesn't advance us any. If, in fact, there's anything there. I mean, look at it, the person killed is the foreman of a ranch. This is the owner of the ranch's son's girlfriend's mother. That's almost enough degrees of separation to get to Kevin Bacon. Are we going to look into him, too?"

"Protesting too much," Diana murmured.

Jennifer provided the opportunity to ignore that murmur. "I've sent you the trial transcript and articles about the trial, plus the timeline we've got so far on Furman York—those three years are still blank, but we're working on it."

"Great. I'm almost home. I'll start going through what you've sent while I have lunch and decide what to do next."

Mike said, "What about Gable?"

"He *was* more forthcoming now than when daddy was nearby. But showing up at the ranch after just talking to him? More likely to make him defensive than open up."

"Besides, why would Lukasik kill his foreman?" Jennifer asked.

"And his former client," Diana added.

"Not much of a foreman. Guess he was a good client, since that case gave Lukasik his big career break."

Mike shifted gears. "You think Gable will talk to you more openly—"

Pounding sounded in the background and, even more distant, the plea, "Hey, I need the editing bay."

"—if Asheleigh's not around, too?"

"The way those two look at each other, I might never have a chance to find out."

I OPENED THE front door in answer to a knock and froze.

"But... But you're in Cody."

My mother and father smiled at me from my front doorstep— which is *not* in Cody.

"That's a fascinating place and we'd like to go back someday, especially with you, Elizabeth. Maybe when Rob and Anna come with the kids later this summer. But—"

Had that trip gone from a suggestion to a certainty only in Mom's mind or had she already bent my brother and sister-in-law to her will? For their pleasure, of course.

That question got kicked down the expressway in my brain, making room for the vital issue.

But, what?

"—we read the papers in Cody this morning and felt we should be here with you. Hello, baby."

The last was for Shadow, who wagged his tail appreciatively at the crooning and escorted Mom into the house, while I still stood, holding the door wide open.

Dad walked by with suitcases, pausing with a wink that conveyed a sliver of commiseration with me while aligning completely with Mom. How did he do that?

With them both in the house, there was nothing to do but close the door and join them.

Those moments before the knock on the door seemed distant. Way back when I'd been mentally grumbling about the drawback of trial transcripts.

They caught the words, but not the inflection, the cadence, the expression, the nuance, all vital for a performer like Norman Clay Lukasik. I could catch an echo of what it might have been like, but not its full-throated power.

Then came the knock.

My parents were here. In my house.

Being a sucker for lost causes, I said, "There's no reason to cut your time short in Cody. Everything's fine here. Go on back and—"

Mom turned. "I wouldn't call everything fine with a murder happening nearby."

"Oh. That. I'm not even covering it—"

"And Tom mentioned as president of the place where it happened."

"Chairman. Grazing association," Dad filled in.

"That's true. He's talked to the sheriff's department, but the victim wasn't a friend of his—" Or anybody else's, I thought but did not say. "—so as horrible as it is for anyone..."

I'd lost them.

They were looking at my laptop screen, frozen on Odessa's face at that Lady of Shalott moment.

"My. What's happened to her, poor—Well, I was going to say poor soul, but I'm not so sure," Mom said.

I forget sometimes how astute she is about people.

"Does she have something to do with the murder—" If Dad had stopped there, what followed would have been very different. But he added two more words. "—you're investigating?"

Chapter Forty

THOSE FINAL TWO words still echoing in the air, Dad extended a palm-out hand toward me, presumably lobbying I forget I'd heard them.

Then he caught Mom's glare and extended the other palm-out hand toward her.

"Sorry, Cat. It slipped out. But I can't be sorry it did," he said.

I tried. "I don't know…"

Mom arched her brows. "You were better at that look of innocent confusion as a teenager, Elizabeth."

"I had more practice then."

She chuckled. "Oh, yes, you did. A great deal of practice."

I sank to the couch, facing them as they still stood in the kitchen. With the difference in our heights from these positions, it felt like old times—me as the kid, them as the adults. I sat straight, but didn't let myself stand. I didn't need that to be a grownup.

"Mel, I presume," I said, passably calm.

Mel Welch was a lawyer in Chicago who'd stepped in as my agent, despite no experience in that area, out of concern for me.

More germane to this discussion, he was married to my mother's cousin's oldest daughter. He adored and feared my mother in equal parts.

"Mel?" Mom's innocent confusion wasn't any better than mine.

I ignored it. "How long?"

Dad finally dropped his hands and took one of the chairs facing the couch. "Late last summer."

"Did Mel know he gave it away?"

Mom sat in the other chair. "Not a clue, the poor dear. But, then, with that matter involving Bunny—"

Someone I'd known as a kid whom I'd encountered at Yellowstone Park the previous fall. Not a happy reunion for either of us. If she'd blabbed to my parents, I would have no reluctance—

"—it was so obvious it would have been ridiculous to carry on pretending."

"Mel crumbled under the strain of your mother's asking what he was keeping from her. Like an avalanche started by dynamite."

"It was for his own good," Mom said. "He couldn't take the strain any longer. You know how he is."

I knew how he was around her, anyway. She was probably right about the strain on Mel. The question was when to let him know I knew Mom and Dad knew... Decisions, decisions.

"Why didn't you say anything?" I looked from Dad to Mom.

She folded her hands. "Because you didn't want us to know."

She made it a statement of fact. And that's what it was—a fact.

Yet I felt their hurt behind it. I'd expected worry, concern, fear if they ever found out—and those were all there, beneath the surface. I hadn't expected the hurt.

"I didn't want you to worry." Or tell me not to. Or lecture me. Or swoop in and try to stop me. Or otherwise treat me like a delicate, not-too-bright child.

Mom and Dad exchanged a look. "We know, Maggie Liz," Dad said.

"Not knowing is more worrying than knowing," Mom said. "You're our child and we love you. We'll never stop worrying about you. Just as we worry about each other."

Just as we worry about each other...

That gave me a new angle. As if I'd been standing in front of a painting and it pivoted to a side view, showing the foundation lines of the composition and the brushstrokes that created it. They *did* worry about each other. On the other hand, they didn't try to prevent each other from doing what they wanted. Not much, anyway.

"I'm very good at this." No blurt alert warned me those words were coming.

"We know. We've seen the special reports you've shared with Mel. And we're not the least bit surprised." Mom tipped her head slightly. "Are you?"

"I... I don't know."

"You and your friends do this together?" Dad's worry leaked out, along with the hope that a former Chicago Bear and a Lincoln-esque rancher would protect me.

"Yes." I wouldn't mention the protection often turned out mutual. "There's no reason to be worried. We're investigating. It's not like we're involved in gun battles." Although there'd been a time or two... "We're asking questions, talking to people is all."

"All," she repeated. "And by doing that you've discovered a number of murderers."

"Yes." Were they not going to argue I should quit this? Was I setting up for a fall by starting to hope...

"And now there's another, uh, situation you're asking questions about, this shooting a few days ago."

"Yes." I explained briefly, including Tamantha's charge to *fix it.*

"What you're doing," Mom asked, "will help Tom and ease Tamantha's concern?"

"I hope so."

"We hope so, too."

I blinked. Not quite ready to believe.

Mom unfolded her hands and pressed the palms to her knees. I remembered Mom's mother doing that as a precursor to standing up, especially as she got older and her knees bothered her.

Her knees bothered her?

But Mom's—

"We'll get settled. We won't get in your way. In fact, we can help. Your dad saw bushes in back he felt needed trimming—"

"Among other things."

"—and I'll cook something for your dinner."

Mom rose lithely, and I let out a breath. Her knees were fine.

We were fine.

It would take getting used to.

Chapter Forty-One

I MADE AN appearance at the station, timing it so I was there just before Thurston Fine and Les Haeburn returned from one of their lengthy lunches. They'd lunched together less often lately. Their doing so today was fortunate for me, as was getting the message from Jennifer informing me of this.

When they walked in, I was on the phone at my desk, head down, apparently typing notes.

They had no way of knowing if I'd been here for hours or minutes.

Just as they had no way of knowing most of my typing was responding to messages from Diana, Mike, and Jennifer telling me they had assignments that would tie them up until late afternoon. In response, I updated them on my parents being in town.

Les and Thurston went into their respective offices, then popped out again in under five minutes, pretending they weren't checking if I was still around.

Four more times they popped out. The fifth time, Thurston came, but Les didn't. Thurston had that angry rabbit expression he wore when he felt thwarted.

He stalked into the news director's office. Angry voices ensued. Thurston stalked out. He slammed Les' door. Retreating footsteps. Another door slammed. Chuckles from anonymous sources across the newsroom bullpen.

In between, most of my time went to phone calls, starting with nearly identical rundowns with Aunt Gee and Mrs. Parens. Did they know other people who'd known Leah Pedroke or Furman York at the time of the murder? Any acquaintances—asking about friends felt like an overreach—of York's recently? Have experience with Norman Clay Lukasik? Anyone else they thought we should talk to?

All negatives.

I left a message for Tom with the same update as the others when he picked up.

He'd heard my message, he informed me.

"What are you doing?" I asked.

Without lifting my head, I was aware of Les opening his office door and peering in my direction. He retreated and locked his door.

"Putting up fence so Clyde can pasture those valuable Angus within sight of the house. A few of us are here. We're about done. If you want to meet somewhere or—"

"Anybody from the Lukasik Ranch there?"

"Yeah," he said, a question in his voice. "Kesler."

Already standing, I messaged Diana, Mike, and Jennifer where I was going.

"I'll be right out there."

✧　✧　✧　✧

THE WORKERS TRAILED away from their completed job toward pickups parked casually off the road. I parked in the driveway, got out of my SUV, and walked toward them.

I said hello to the Chaneys—Paul and his uncle Otto. Even got a look at a recent photo of Paul's eight-month-old daughter, who looked exactly like him, before they moved on.

Nodded to two young men I recognized from a search last fall known to me only as the Baranski boys, as well as three more I didn't recognize.

Exchanged a few words with Connie Walterston's middle son. Connie ran the road paving company Tom's father established to supplement ranching income. Tom didn't care for the business, but he'd never let it go as long as Connie needed a job. A widow with one son in college and two to go, she'd keep the business going quite a while, I suspected.

Last came Kesler and Tom.

Kesler angled toward the Lukasik Ranch pickup I'd already staked out. Tom steered toward the house, not participating in this questioning.

"Hi, Kesler."

He'd seen me as he came, so I was no surprise. He grunted a possible greeting.

"We didn't get much of a chance to talk the other day. I have a few more questions." Watching him, I added, "Especially after talking with Gable yesterday."

The stoniness of his expression did not miraculously melt. Nor did he fill the opening I left.

I kept on. "He was quite open about not having a good relationship with his father. Wonder how Gable's mother would feel about what's happening with her son. Course she was an outsider here, so maybe nobody would care. Probably gone and forgotten. Nobody—"

"Not forgotten."

He'd opened that crack, but I resisted bulldozing into it. He'd shut down.

"You said she didn't know about ranching. Does Lukasik?"

"She never tried to pretend to know more'n she did."

"Norman Clay Lukasik does?"

"After years and years of playing at being the grand rancher, he knows just enough to be dangerous."

That differed from Lukasik's self-portrayal as not caring about the ranch.

"What about Furman York?"

"What about him?"

"Did he know ranching?"

"Even he couldn't help but pick up a little."

"Did he pretend he knew more than he did?" *While Lukasik pretended to know less than he did?*

"No. Why bother?"

Remembering what Lukasik said, I tossed in, "Could that be why the herd's numbers stayed even?"

I'd hit something. I had no idea what. But this was the most un-comfortable I'd seen Kesler.

"What makes you say that?" he asked.

"The owner of the ranch said it. I'm just repeating it. You think that was a result of York not knowing what he was doing?"

"Hard to say. Lot of things can contribute if that's even so. I don't know. I don't see reports and spreadsheets and all."

Oh, yeah, he was definitely uncomfortable.

"Spreadsheets," I repeated thoughtfully. "Even if Lukasik doesn't know about ranching, he sees and understands the numbers."

Kesler's neutral grunt neither confirmed, nor denied.

"Just like Gable Lukasik will eventually. Was York unhappy with Gable taking on more of a role? Did he worry about his job security?"

This time Kesler snorted dismissively. "That one didn't worry over Gable. Cock o' the walk. That's how he acted."

"But now Gable has a clear path to running the ranch—"

His head jerked up.

"—or he would if his father wasn't staying on."

"Now, that last part, that's what you should be nosing into. Nor-man Clay coming and hanging around like he never has before in all these years, not even early on when she wanted him to. Couldn't be bothered. But now, when it'd be better with him gone, he's staying and staying. Why's that?" He slashed a hand through the air. "I'm goin'. Got better things to do."

He stomped the few more feet to the pickup, got in, and backed out, without ever appearing to check his mirrors for where I was. If I hadn't moved, I'd have been under the pickup's tires.

Chapter Forty-Two

TOM JOINED ME. "You look pretty cheerful for somebody who could've been run over. I know. Worth it because you got interesting points from Kesler."

"I did, but I need to think it through—"

"Think on the way to lunch." He walked beside me toward my SUV. "If you check your phone you'll see messages from the others that we're supposed to meet at Hamburger Heaven."

We occasionally used the back room in that bastion of haute cuisine, thanks to Mike being both a local hero from his football playing days and their best customer.

"Perfect."

ON OUR WAY to Hamburger Heaven in our own vehicles, I thought of what I should have asked Tom. Then I thought how I should introduce it—probably from Diana's influence.

So, after we all were seated in Hamburger Heaven's back room with our late lunches and had brought each other up to date, I turned to Tom.

"That was a good idea asking Kesler to help with the fence. Did you ask him about the case?"

"I didn't ask him to come and I didn't ask questions. We were building fence."

"You didn't ask him to come? But you said you'd make calls and there he was—"

"Clyde called him. To supervise."

"Why?"

His eyebrows rose. "Because he's Clyde's dad."

"*Kesler* is Clyde's father?"

I remembered his "Like who?" when I said he should answer my questions to be sure the wrong person didn't get charged.

"Yep. Just like some of those boys that helped are Clyde's nephews."

"Boys? The Baranski boys are related to Clyde? Kesler, too?"

"Sure. They're all Baranskis."

I looked around to include the others. "Why didn't you tell me they were related?"

Tom raised both hands in partial surrender. "Didn't occur to me."

"If we mentioned every time someone was related to someone else and how many ways, nothing else would ever get said," Mike said.

"Why are you so surprised?" Diana asked.

"Because Kesler works at Lukasik Ranch, where York was foreman, the man strongly implicated in rustling Clyde's cattle."

Tom protested, "You can't think Kesler had anything to do with that."

"With rustling Clyde's cattle? Probably not. But what about if he suspected York was behind the rustling that hit Clyde? Did he know about that check Clyde wrote?"

Tom didn't look happy, but he nodded. "Knew at the time. Told York to keep away from his family. He also gave Clyde hell. But that was seven months ago, like I said before. For it to spark now doesn't seem likely."

At some level I realized he expected me to argue with him. But my thoughts had taken a turn.

I faced Tom. "You said Clyde said your cattle were mixed in with Lukasik's brand. And you saw that, too?"

"Yeah."

"If Lukasik came to his ranch and saw another brand mixed in with his—he's not a rancher like you guys, but surely he knows his own brand—"

"He does," Tom said grimly.

"—he'd spot the brand that didn't fit. He'd have to know something was wrong. Could Lukasik—"

"Might think it was cattle they'd bought and hadn't rebranded," Tom said.

"—be in on the rustling? Or could York be stealing from him, too?"

"If York knew when Lukasik was coming to the ranch, he could move head around..." Mike shook his head at his own words. "Risky if Lukasik isn't in on it. Kesler and Gable, too, along with other hands."

"Wait. Wait." I raised my hand and dropped my head, eyes closed, the better to remember. Not only words. Those came easy. But intonation, body language, expressions. I raised my head, then opened my eyes and lowered my hand. "Lukasik talked about how his herd kept staying the same size, not growing as he'd expect based on births and sales. Remember? It frustrated him the herd didn't grow. Kesler was edgy about that today, too.

"But why did it stay even? Only because York was lazy and a lousy cattleman or a more direct reason? Say he was selling those mismatched calves for his own profit or using them to keep the numbers of Lukasik's herd from actually dropping while he sold Lukasik cattle."

Tom stared at me a beat. "He'd make more money the second way—selling older, bigger cattle for more money, then replacing them with calves. Calves stolen from other ranchers." He thunked one palm on the table. "It's time to visit some feedlots on the other side of the Missouri River."

"I'm going with you," Mike said.

"Me, too," I said. "I want—"

"No." That came from Tom, Mike, and Diana.

Diana was the one who continued. "The people they'll want to see are not the kind to mess with, Elizabeth. Notice I'm not volunteering to go. Yes, I know you've dealt with hard people. But in this case you'd raise their suspicions the instant they saw you. You'd stick out like a sore thumb."

"I can dress like—"

"It's not just cowboy boots and hat. It's a way of moving, of talk-ing—heck, it's a way of looking at the cattle. They'd know you weren't right. And that makes it more dangerous. For all of you."

I could pull it off. I knew I could. And I wanted to be there. To—

"Now you know how I feel when you guys tell me I can't do things," Jennifer said.

That stopped me. For two reasons. When we said no to Jennifer, it was our best judgment it was a bad idea. Shouldn't I accept their best judgment?

Also, because I trusted Jennifer using her computer expertise to get us information without joining her keystroke by keystroke. Shouldn't I respect the others' areas of expertise?

"You're right, Jennifer. I do know how it feels." Her hopefulness crashed with my next words. "And that's why I'm not going. They know what they're doing and I wouldn't." I looked from Tom to Mike. "But you two better bring back a word-for-word report, not missing a syllable, not overlooking a nuance."

"Yes'm," they both said, with not-quite-suppressed grins.

"And if you can get anything on Furman York formerly bringing cattle with the Lukasik Ranch's brand, but on his most recent trip he didn't, that would be a nice, big, fat, red arrow pointing to Norman Clay Lukasik."

"Ah. Because it would mean Lukasik caught him," Diana said.

"Exactly. That ramps up Lukasik's motive. It still could work that York rustled Lukasik's cattle and Lukasik found out *after* Furman York's most recent sale of stolen cattle. Or that Lukasik knew York was rustling, but didn't confront him, possibly waiting to plan a *permanent* solution. But if York had been regularly selling Lukasik's cattle, then stopped, that would be—"

"Big, fat, red arrow. Got it." Mike turned to Tom. "I can drive. Whenever you're ready to leave as long as I can throw some things together."

"I've got chores to take care of before we go," Tom said. "It's not a quick trip and Tamantha—"

I raised my hand. "If you don't leave her with me, my mother will hunt us both down."

He quirked a grin. "Tamantha might join her in the hunt. But your guest room's occupied."

"There's a sofa bed in the sitting area of the master suite."

"It's real comfortable," Jennifer attested.

"There. All settled. How long a trip is it?" I asked.

"Ten hours or so," Mike said.

"*Ten* hours? One way? It'll take twenty hours just to get there and back? And then checking all the livestock markets? You guys won't be back for *days*."

"There aren't a whole lot of likely markets. I'll make some calls, narrow it down." Tom asked Mike, "Leaving in four hours work for you?"

"Sure." He then turned to me. "That's enough time to go see that bartender, catch him before happy hour. I bet the Pickled Cow has a great one."

"I'm still absorbing that it's a ten-hour drive. If you leave in four hours, you'll have to stay overnight somewhere and—"

"Nah. We'll swap off and drive all night. Get there in time to start in the morning."

"You've just made me happy to not be going. Let's go see the bartender."

Tom said, "You still have those clothes in the back of your SUV from horseback riding?"

On our recent picnic date, after riding, I'd changed out of old jeans, shirt, jacket, and new roper boots into fresh jeans, shirt, jacket, and shoes. I hadn't yet acquired a fancy for *eau d' horse* after dismounting. The horsey clothes were all in a tightly zipped tote.

"Yeah." He was monitoring my laundry schedule?

"Put those on before you go in the Pickled Cow."

Chapter Forty-Three

TOM LEFT FIRST. Mike went to settle the bill while Diana, Jennifer, and I finished our drinks.

And while Diana eyed me.

"What's wrong, Diana?"

No, I didn't ask that. Jennifer did.

But Diana addressed me. "You gave up awfully quick—for you—about going with them."

"That's because I thought of something else." No sense fibbing when she had me dead to rights. "This is just for us three for now. The guys go investigating livestock auctions in South Dakota, so we keep this to ourselves."

"This what?" Jennifer asked impatiently.

"This question that occurred to me while we were talking about the possibility that York was stealing from Lukasik. How many defendants end up being part of their lawyer's life for decades? Until the end of York's life, in fact.

"He was not a good foreman, not a good cowhand. He was lazy. Yet he not only stayed on at Lukasik Ranch, he was promoted. Mrs. Lukasik didn't like him. Gable Lukasik didn't like him. The other ranch hands didn't like him. Yet Norman Clay Lukasik kept him on. Why?"

Diana frowned. "And recently York's gone from passively being a bad employee to stealing by rustling. How could Lukasik not have suspected that? Especially with Tom going to him about issues with grazing association members."

"*Exactly.* Lukasik said his herd's been staying even, so he's not a completely hands-off owner. He had to know something was wrong. Yet—"

"He didn't do anything about it," Jennifer completed. "Okay. I've got that. But that's what the guys are checking, right? If York was stealing, including from Lukasik."

"That's not what we're looking into. We're digging into why Lukasik kept York on and—possibly—let York steal from him."

Diana nodded. She had it.

Jennifer worried her lip. Then her head came up. "York was blackmailing him?"

"That's sure one possibility, isn't it?"

"Okay, but how do we look into it when York's dead and Lukasik's not going to tell us?"

"First, by having you and your brilliant minions see what you can find out about Lukasik's financials.

"Second, by putting the rest of your collective wizardry into closing that gap between York being found not guilty and his coming to work at the ranch Lukasik had just bought. We're looking for evidence that York and Lukasik were in contact. Ideally, evidence that Lukasik was paying York."

"Got it. And we're not telling the guys until we find it."

ON THE WAY to the Pickled Cow, Mike and I stopped at his house for him to pack a bag for the trip to South Dakota, while I changed into Tom's specified wardrobe.

Driving east, I asked, oh, so casually. "When you came back here, did you try to buy back your family ranch?"

"Thought about it. Looked at buying the old home place, then leasing the land back to the grazing association, similar to what I do with my place now. Talked to Tom. He was willing, but Lukasik was talking around the county about soaking the football player getting sentimental over a stretch of dirt." One side of his mouth lifted. "Put my back up. Plus, it was just one part of the ranch. Getting all the pieces back, getting it up and running, that's a heck of a challenge.

"Went out there one day. Had a vague idea of taking some of Grandma and Grandpa's things. But when it came down to it, they seemed to belong there, like the roses. Tom came by—still don't know if that was a coincidence or if he knew I was there. Anyway, we talked more. Not about buying the place. About other ... stuff."

Fathers and sons *stuff* and family ranches, I suspected. Tom didn't have the closest relationship with his father, either. And that, too, seemed to center around the family ranch.

"When it first happened, losing the ranch, I swore I'd save every dollar to buy it back. I learned about handling money, I saved, I invested—being careful, limiting risks.

"It wasn't until I stood at what used to be the entry to our home ranch, knowing I *could* do it, that I wondered if I should." He cleared his throat. "There it is, the Pickled Cow."

✧   ✧   ✧   ✧

TO MY RELIEF, the Pickled Cow Bar offered plenty of pickles, but no pickled cattle parts.

However, I wouldn't recommend the pickles, encased in dirt encrusted jars. In fact, I wouldn't recommend the Pickled Cow Bar at all.

Outside, it sat amid bare dirt, with the same color plastered to its walls and roof.

Inside, it smelled. Sweat, old beer, clothes worn too long, things tracked in on boots, topped off by old sweated out beer soaked into clothes worn too long.

It was dark, even on a day when the arc of Wyoming sky seemed to pulse brightness. I was grateful it was dark. I couldn't see the things making it smell.

I felt some making my boots stick an extra beat so it seemed like walking across the sticky side of duct tape.

"You folks in the wrong place?" a sneering voice asked from the darkness behind the bar.

"No," Mike said in a voice I seldom heard him use. I immediately flashed to watching football with my dad and mics picking up players talking trash to each other. "Two beers. Can."

With my eyes adjusting, I could make out the man behind the bar. He had pitted skin, producing an irregular pattern of stubble. His greasy hair was pulled straight back into a stringy rat tail.

One other person was in the place. A man—or a heap of men's clothes—slumped on a stool at the far end. Bar stools don't encourage good posture, but this slump did not appear attributable to the stool.

Without a word, the bartender took two cans from a refrigerator. I hoped age had turned it that dingy gray color. He opened them and placed them on the bar.

Mike gestured to the red plastic bar stool next to the one he took. I hesitated, then sat. We were not getting off these stools without more duct-tape sensation.

I noticed he did not take his hat off—no place safe to put it in this place—though he pushed back the brim as he took a brave drink from the can.

"Hey, you're Mike Paycik, aren't you?" the bartender asked in an entirely different tone. "Watched you score four touchdowns in one game your senior year at UW."

I have never been more surprised or more grateful for Paycik's football hero status.

"He is," I said immediately. He handles it well, often with self-deprecating humor. Not this time. This time he was cashing in. "And the sports anchor for KWMT-TV in Sherman."

"I know. I watch him every night. Can't wait to see more of that interview with John Smith. Seems like a good guy. And he must be rolling in dough."

"Not yet. But he sure should be with his next contract," Mike said.

I settled back—metaphorically only—as they did the mutual sports fans' mating dance. It was an almost immediate match.

The bartender—Nash—turned out to be articulate and quite pleasant. Even to unimportant me.

Mike did a good job steering gradually away from sports. "How'd you come to be working here?"

"Wouldn't be if I had a choice. Place belongs to my step-father. I got into debt with some guys—never gambling again—and the step-father said he'd only bail me out if I worked here two years and lived with them. Two *years*. Got four months left and then they can strike a match to this place and let it burn. Never coming back in that door. Never dealing with these thugs again."

"Thugs?" Mike quirked an eye toward the other customer.

"Oh, him. He's harmless. Some of the others aren't." Nash leaned closer. "You heard about the guy who got shot? Foreman of the Lukasik Ranch? He was in here a lot."

"You knew him, huh?" Mike portrayed someone deeply interested, but too cool to show it. "Did he ever talk about when he was tried for murder?"

Nash rolled his eyes. "Did he ever shut up about it would be the question. And the answer would be no. He'd go on and on about how some TV show nearly got him sent to the gallows—like there is such a thing these days—"

I suspected I knew where he'd gotten the term, though.

"—and it wasn't even like the TV show talked about him at all. It was all about that ancient mess Rock Springs had. So why he kept jawing about it, I never understood. Not that I hung around him trying to make sense of it. Serve the drinks and get away. That's my motto. What I don't hear can't make me want to poison these lowlifes. At least any more than I already want to."

I wasn't entirely unsympathetic with his assessment of his clientele. At first blush, though, it would seem to produce an atmosphere not conducive to repeat business.

On the other hand, there wasn't much competition around.

And Furman York and his buddies might have recognized an upside to a bartender who wanted nothing to do with them—relative privacy.

"Gotcha. Still, interesting to have one of your regulars murdered."

"Yeah, I guess."

"Deputies in asking you questions about him and stuff."

"Yeah, they've been in, but not much I could tell them. Don't know names. Knew the Lukasik truck, but the others are just, you know, old pickups. One guy looks like he takes steroids or something."

"Interesting. Like 'roid rage maybe."

Nash's mouth turned down. "He never lost it or anything, not here anyway. Doesn't say much. The guy who got shot talked the most. The other one who drank with them regular talks about how he's scored lately, getting close to getting a big new truck. You know—" Abruptly, he became more intense. "—another guy who drank with them now and again was busted for selling drugs last fall. Maybe a drug deal gone wrong."

Mike nodded wisely. "Definitely a possibility. Maybe the truck guy's involved with him."

Nash snorted. "If he had drug money he wouldn't still be griping about driving short hauls around here. He'd have the big fancy one he goes on and on about."

Chapter Forty-Four

WHEN WE CAME out, taking grateful deep breaths, we both had messages from Tom.

Mike returned the call, since I was driving.

The miracle of speakerphone let us both marvel at how different Nash turned out to be from our initial impression—though the bar was still foul.

Tom mentioned picking up a lot of road noise. I said, "You'll have to live with it. We've got to keep the windows open to keep that stench from embedding itself in my SUV."

Mike raised his voice to report what Nash said about York, then asked, "Tom, have association members been moving their cattle with their own trucks?"

I cut Mike a quick look.

Tom answered slowly. "No. We've used the same truck to move cattle on and off grazing association lands the past few months. York got a real low price, but only if we all used the same guy."

Mike repeated Nash's comments about York's trucker friend. He concluded, "The trucker's got to be recon and transport for the rustling operation."

"Sure worth looking into, but not necessarily for us. Elizabeth?"

"I agree. Unless there was a falling out among thieves, this doesn't touch on the murder. If one of his accomplices killed York..."

"Sheriff's department's in a better position to catch them." Tom had no trouble saying what stuck in my throat. "Mike, you want to call Wayne or me?"

"You. He'll give what you say more weight."

"Only because he associates you more with Elizabeth," Tom said with a grin in his voice.

"And he doesn't like us beating him to the punch," I retorted.

"Of course." From that deadpan, his next words came more naturally. "Reason I called, got with Jack Delahunt and he narrowed the list of places to check, three prime and a couple others. Said that should cover ninety-eight percent of the likely places, with the other two percent scattered so wide, it wouldn't be worth our while.

"Second piece of good news is he's got a friend who's going to fly us to Sioux Falls and back. Fly there tonight. We can rent a vehicle for hitting those top few, starting first thing tomorrow. Should be back late tomorrow."

"That's great." Anything that compacted the timeline had my vote.

Mike asked, "How small a plane?"

"Not a tin can. Jack said the guy flies big shots with places in Montana. They like their comforts. Good news for you, too, Elizabeth. They're letting you in to talk to Hiram again tonight. Same time. Asked if Diana could take my place and James said sure. He was too stunned by Shelton's cooperation to object to any changes."

I DROVE MIKE directly to Cottonwood County's airport.

More calls occupied the trip, letting my delighted parents know about Tamantha staying overnight, establishing that she'd accompany them to O'Hara Hill for dinner with Mrs. P and Aunt Gee, setting up with Diana for the trip to the jail, and arranging with her and Jennifer to meet at my place after.

To Mike's clear relief when he came out of the airport office restroom after changing for the trip, the plane was more impressive than the airport.

Tom had come with Tamantha, transferring her overnight bag to the back of my SUV. We watched the plane take off together, with her waving her hat as it disappeared into all that blue.

Then she wrinkled her nose at me. "You smell." She sniffed.

"Horses, some, but what's the rest of it?"

Neither Mike nor Tom had tried to hug or kiss me good-bye. I'd thought it was either tact in front of each other or male coolness, since they'd be gone a short time.

This provided an alternate reason.

My agenda expanded to include a shower, change of clothes, and tossing this outfit into the washer. First thing.

✧ ✧ ✧ ✧

I'D EASED HIRAM to the topic of the trial by circling around it first with questions about his *Dateline*-acquired knowledge, experience with jury duty, and knowledge of the case before being on the jury.

"We've heard Lukasik was very skilled in raising inferences."

"More like infernal," he grumbled.

"Such as that there might have been something... improper going on between other men and Leah Pedroke."

His mouth dropped open.

I thought, at first it was shock, perhaps that we knew about that.

I was wrong.

After a moment he closed his mouth, shook his head, and said, "Forgot all about that." He'd been hard at work, searching for memories. "Fool Earl tripped over his tongue like he does. Gee Decker pretty much took care of the idea there'd been any of that nonsense. When we were going through the points in the jury room, that was laughed out of the building right off."

Ah, my opening.

I took it softly. "What happened in that jury room, Hiram?"

"Long time ago. How'm I supposed to remember?"

"You remember." He'd just proved he did.

He grunted and swung away.

I thought that was it. That he wouldn't answer. And with a man like Hiram I'd be unlikely to get a second opportunity.

"Hiram, don't you want to get out of the jail? Don't you have important things to do out of here?"

His neck and the one ear I could see tinged red.

"But even more important, don't you want the truth to come out finally. Keeping quiet isn't protecting anybody, because everybody who was on that jury's suspected."

"Don't care what anybody says about me. I know."

"Do you care that someone else might care what others say about you? Someone who cares about you and can be hurt by what's said about you." Being vague wasn't as easy as Penny made it sound. But just in case Shelton wasn't being honest about not listening in, I played it safe.

His red spread wider.

James gave me a questioning look. I shook my head slightly. Not yet. More patience. As much patience as I could manage.

The silence extended past patience into discomfort.

I picked up a pen.

Diana put her hand on my wrist before I started tapping it.

"It wasn't only him."

Hiram's voice made us all start.

The instinct in a situation like this is to blurt out some variant of *What the hell are you talking about?* But that's the wrong approach.

Talking to a source in a situation like this is the equivalent of dealing with a wild animal.

No sudden moves. Especially not toward them.

Keep your tone calm and neutral.

"Different people say different things," I ventured.

"They say damned wrong if they put it all on him. Anybody says anything that puts it all on him, and I'll tell them to their face they're damned wrong and if they don't back down, I'll do more than that. It wasn't like that. Nothin' like that."

I waited, stretching the moment—no sudden moves, even in asking the next question. "What was it like?"

"He had no choice. No choice at all when you looked at it from where he stood. Not that I did at the start. It was only after—" He broke off, explosively cleared his throat.

Again, I thought the thread was broken, but he picked up, almost as if talking to himself.

"No choice. Not with his girl so sick. And here that snake came danglin' the chance for the doctors he thought could pull a miracle out of their hat. How could he say no? How could any man say no? Even with his friend yappin' at him. Even with his wife sayin' he had to face the truth that there was nothing to be done. He had—he *had.* He'd accepted it and he was takin' each day with his girl and lovin' her, and not thinkin' about what was comin'. And then to have the hope dangled out there in front of him again... It was more than he could bear. More than any man could bear."

He turned his profile to us.

Quietly, I asked, "You knew about it as it was happening?"

"Put it together. Pieces. Saw him talking to somebody I didn't know and we knew everybody the same. Saw the fever in his eyes. The fever of hope. Same time he was sweating like he always did when he'd done something wrong. Got us caught more times than I could count."

His lips twitched, as if they remembered what it was like to grin, but couldn't quite get there.

"He told you?"

"No."

A full stop. A permanent one?

"But...?" I tried softly.

"I asked him what was goin' on. Told me to mind my own business. So I did. Until, in the jury room, when we got the case and started discussin'. Never crossed my mind until I heard him sayin' he had too much reasonable doubt to vote to convict. I didn't want to believe... But there he was, saying those words like he'd memorized them from a poem by the devil. Not believin', but sayin' them just the same. It was like a clap of thunder, then the lightning runnin' right through me, knockin' me off my feet.

"There were a couple other ones. Sayin' about the same words like they'd learned it off by heart, too. But I hardly even heard that. All I could see was Earl. Knowin' what he'd done and why. First chance, I got him off by himself, even though he tried to avoid me. Wouldn't look at me. Wouldn't talk to me. Wouldn't answer me. Told him what

I thought. Told him right out it wouldn't save his girl, but it would damn him to hell.

"We never talked again. Not even at his girl's funeral a couple months after."

Into the sorrowful silence, Diana spoke softly. "But, Hiram, that could make your friend and the others vote for acquittal, but what about the rest of you? If you voted to convict, York couldn't have got off."

Color spread up under his beard, across his cheeks, and even into his forehead. Not the rosy, rather endearing blush when I'd referred to Yvette. But something dark and dire.

"They wore us down. Simple as that. Suppose I stopped carin' after Earl turned the way he did... Doesn't matter. I didn't do my duty. Turned tail and gave up. Remember that every day. More when I saw Furman York 'round here. That would jam it right down my craw. Even now, with him dead, I'll carry that shame to my grave. Right beside my grievin' for Earl.

"He was my friend. Best friend I ever had. And that man ruined him. After the trial, after his girl died, Earl took to drink. Not in a healthy way, mind you."

Presumably that was the way Hiram drank.

"Drank serious. Wouldn't even drink with friends anymore. Not me—we'd crossed each other out, like I said. Didn't mean I didn't know what he was doin' and how he was doin' it. Saw him places. Until he started goin' cross the county line to the Pickled Cow where it's not sociable. Not sociable at all. He'd drink fast and steady, like if he drank enough bottles it would fill his soul back up."

I blinked at Hiram going poetical. Also to hold in sudden tears.

"One night, it was snowin' and blowin', but not a blizzard or nothin'. He left that place. Never got back to Cottonwood County. Found his truck right off. Didn't find him for a couple days."

Diana dropped her hands below the edge of the table, folding them tight enough to whiten the knuckles.

"Deputies said the truck was fine. Nothin' mechanical wrong. Had plenty of gas. ... Said they didn't know what happened. Fools.

Everybody else sure as hell knew what happened. Knew damn right well. He'd reached the end. Couldn't go on another minute. He pulled over and he walked out. Kept walkin' until he couldn't go on with that anymore, either. Then he sat down and died out there. Because it was the only thing he could see to do."

The man's pain was palpable.

He shook his head in sharp anger—at his friend's death, at his own emotions, at us for witnessing them? At all of it, most likely.

"What're you all sittin' there gapin' at me for? Aren't you supposed to be the big high muckety mucks who know everything? Well, now you know Furman York and Norman Clay Lukasik had more to answer for than the murder of that poor girl. They killed Earl, too."

Chapter Forty-Five

"HE WEREN'T THE only one, either. Dick took off from here like a scalded cat after that trial. He mighta had some money, but he lost his home. Hear he died in California—" No worse fate, from his tone. "—five, six years later. Heard he was broke and broken. Called his momma, cryin'. Least he outlasted Earl—"

The door to the interview room opened to Lloyd Sampson.

"Uh, sorry folks. Time's up."

"No," I protested. "We haven't been here as long as yesterday."

Already getting Hiram up from the chair, Lloyd shook his head. "Sergeant says."

He closed the door behind them, Diana, James, and I still sitting where we were.

"You were really getting someplace," Diana said in sorrow.

"Yeah." In my mind's eye, Hiram still sat with his profile to us, letting out what he'd held in so long.

His profile...

Unlike yesterday when he'd been facing us full-on. Us and the one-way mirror.

I jerked my head to look at James, then turned straight ahead before I asked, "Can anybody in the sheriff's department read lips?"

James looked startled. I couldn't blame him.

The lawyer swung his head around and looked at the mirror.

He shook his head, but I noticed he faced away from it before he said, "It wouldn't be admissible."

"Shelton might not care. Get the information first, find another route to it that would be admissible if he needed to."

"I don't know of anyone who can—"

The door opened again to Lloyd Sampson.

"I'll escort you out now, folks."

"SNEAKY." MIKE SOUNDED more impressed than disapproving of Shelton's theoretical tactic.

He and Tom were settled in a Sioux Falls hotel, having secured their rental car, treated the pilot to a steak dinner, and staked him after-dinner drinks while they returned to their room to video conference with us.

Jennifer razzed them about sharing a room. Mike said he'd never minded a roommate even after his veteran status exempted him. Tom said they'd be sleeping most of the time so what did it matter.

I had a fleeting thought that these two guys in a hotel together was a real waste, but kept that to myself.

Tom sat on one bed, pillows behind him, while Mike sat on the easy chair next to it and adjusted the phone as needed, propped on the desk.

My parents, true to their word, left us with dinner—chicken casserole—and a good amount of yard work accomplished when they left with Tamantha for O'Hara Hill. I'd already told Diana and Jennifer about the trip to the Pickled Cow.

Tom got things started. "We plan an early morning to be at the first place when it opens. No late night tonight. What happened with Hiram?"

Mike whistled at the end of our account. After his comment on Shelton, he added, "All these years Hiram wouldn't say a word and you got him to talk about it, Elizabeth. Impressive."

I wondered if it wasn't another woman who deserved that credit.

"You know, that all fits with what Aunt Gee said about a kind of justice happening. Remember?" he asked. "Something about the hollow trappings of success—Jennifer spotted that as Lukasik. Someone in exile's that other guy. And not being able to live with himself, that was Hiram's friend, Earl. So Hiram had a motive."

"His motive, though, is stronger for his wanting *Lukasik* dead than York," I said. "York didn't bribe jurors. He didn't have any money. But Earl was bought with the promise of money to try to cure his daughter. That has to be Lukasik."

"Why would Lukasik go out on a limb like that?" Mike asked. "Especially for Furman York. They didn't even know each other then."

"I think I know why Lukasik would do it."

We all turned to Jennifer.

"It's in those clips I gave you."

Sure, make me feel guilty for not finishing them. "Sorry, Jennifer. I haven't—"

"They all say that case was when he went from small-time lawyer barely making it to big-shot. After he got York off, he moved to Denver. Was the hot defense lawyer. Got big cases. Then bigger and bigger. And every story mentioned it started with the York's not-guilty."

"But he couldn't know that's how it would turn out." Diana waved her coffee mug, which had to be nearly empty or we'd be misted. "I mean, he could hope, but he couldn't absolutely be certain."

"I don't know." Reminded of my own mug, I sipped. "Maybe he couldn't know for sure what winning might mean, but he would have known losing would mean staying where he was, doing what he'd been doing. Or less."

"So, his motive wasn't to succeed, but to avoid failure."

We all let that sink in.

I raised another point. "Aunt Gee said something this morning we need to consider."

Mike nodded. "About having an alibi, I was thinking about that. None of the people we've considered, *seriously* considered," he emphasized, putting his aunt outside that category, "have an alibi that we know about. Lukasik, Kesler, Gable, all out around somewhere on that ranch."

"Clyde and Tom, too. I mean their own ranches." Jennifer looked up. "What?"

"She's right," I said. "The sheriff's department considers Tom a suspect, we should look at what they're considering, too, to fight against it."

"And, of course, Hiram has no alibi, because he was at the scene within the window of when York was shot." Diana cocked her head. Alibis don't eliminate or point to anyone."

"Actually, I was thinking of something else Gee said. *If I could murder, Furman York would have died many years ago,*" I quoted. "But he wasn't killed any time over the past thirty years. He was killed now. And that comes back to Jennifer's excellent question, *Why now?*"

"Geez, if not killing him before rules out people, we don't have anybody left," Mike groused.

Fighting a grin, I said, "Not necessarily. But it does go back to why now. We've asked what sparked Furman York being killed now—"

"And didn't come up with much of anything."

"Exactly, Mike. Let's take it a couple steps back. Instead of *why now*, ask *what's changed?* What was different leading up to the shooting? Without trying to pinpoint whether it caused the killing or not. I'll start by saying one thing that changed is Tom found out about York's rustling scheme with Circle B calves."

I gestured, as if to nudge Jennifer, even though she was out of reach.

"Let's get these down."

Diana said, "Grazing association members had cattle rustled."

Jennifer typed. Fast enough to cover both my point and Diana's.

"And," Diana added, "Tom and others made the connection that grazing association members were being hit by rustlers."

"Which started people suspecting York," Mike said. "But they didn't have proof."

"Let's not get into proof yet. What else changed is Hiram began, uh, courting Yvette," I said.

"Hiram asked Clyde for help with Yvette. And Clyde asked Hiram to put a scare into York, which Hiram was only too glad to do."

After that contribution from Diana, we hit a lull.

Jennifer lifted her head. "Could York have found out Gable directed Clyde to that hidden-away pasture where he had calves from Tom's cows?"

"We can't know if York found out, but it's a change to add to the list that Gable—knowingly or not—opened the door to York's rustling being exposed."

"Norman Clay Lukasik was staying at the ranch," Mike said abruptly.

"That's good." Diana leaned forward. "Everyone's emphasized how he only made flying visits, a few days at a time, but he's been here, what, two weeks or more?"

"That's a change all right. We're not supposed to ask this during this exercise, but it sure makes me want me to ask why he's here," Mike said.

I heard him, but my memory also listened to someone else's words.

"A bunch of what?" Jennifer asked.

I must have said it aloud. I repeated the whole. "*A bunch of bones strung together.* It was something Needham said at our lunch. He said he'd just be a bunch of bones strung together without Thelma."

Diana said, "Not only is that sweet, but it shows how smart he is."

"Yes, yes. But later I remembered the phrase and connected it to Lukasik. Just now, remembering it again, something else struck me hard. From the clips and old video Jennifer sent that I have looked at, Norman Clay Lukasik has always been thin, but not like he is now."

A memory of him facing off with Tom and seeming smaller popped into my head.

"A bunch of bones strung together," Diana murmured. Then she leaned forward and looked up at me. "What are you thinking?"

"That he's not a well man."

Another memory surfaced. At Aunt Gee's, thinking about Furman York's death being part of cleaning the Augean Stables and that if that was so, Norman Clay Lukasik's life wasn't worth much. And how that zinged around my head like the mental equivalent of banging my elbow.

...because Lukasik's life wasn't worth much. Because...

"I think he's dying."

Chapter Forty-Six

"YES."

That confirmation came unexpectedly from Mike.

"That's exactly how an assistant coach looked—great guy—in the last months before he died of cancer. He'd stopped treatment. Said he was done fighting. He was going to live what he had left. He had that same string of bones look... And something in the face."

"It explains why he's at the ranch," I said, "whether from illness or to spend more time with his son."

"But he's not spending more time with Gable," Diana said.

"Doesn't seem to be." I pushed my hair back. "Honestly, I don't know if that advances us any. We'll keep it in mind, but in the meantime, anything else?"

"We made progress on Asheleigh Vincennes today," I said. "Found her birthday—month and date—through social media. The year we figured from what the *Independence* listed in a piece on new teachers. Threw—"

"Don't tell Needham that."

"—in a year either side, just in case. Asheleigh spelled the same way. That made it easy. Tracked down her birth certificate, which gave the father's name. Tracked that back to marriage records. Odessa was married to him when Asheleigh was born, but they divorced two years later."

"Anything interesting about the father?"

She raised one shoulder. "Not yet. No record of him dying, or being in prison in Maryland or surrounding states." She sounded almost disappointed. "Now we'll do the ordinary tracking."

Did I imagine an underlying *bo-ring* in her voice?

"But the marriage certificate gave me Odessa's maiden name and something very interesting."

"That's good work," Diana said.

"What?" Mike and I asked simultaneously, focusing on the *very interesting*.

"There's almost nothing about Odessa under her maiden name, either."

"That is interesting." Thinking it through, I added, "But does that lead us anywhere? Or are we getting lost in the weeds?"

"We are getting pretty far from where we started," Mike said. "And all we had to go on was that woman's weird look. Maybe she knew York from a bowling league or something."

Jennifer wrinkled her nose. "He didn't bowl."

"I mean she could have known him somehow."

"No matter how high the weeds are, I want to know who this woman is," Jennifer said stubbornly. "I have people looking into that name, trying to dig deeper."

"Maybe at this point, we approach Asheleigh. Get an initial take on whether it's worth pursuing."

"I'm gonna find her records anyway," Jennifer warned.

On that note, Tom announced it was getting late and the call ended. Jennifer left almost immediately, eager to get to her computer setup at her parents' home.

DIANA LINGERED. A look in her eye made me edgy.

A feeling totally justified when she asked, "What are you afraid of with Mike and Tom?"

"Nothing."

"Don't tell me, but don't lie."

"I'm not. There's nothing wrong. We get along fine…"

"You could be talking about two old guys playing checkers in front of the fire who get along fine. I thought dating both Mike and Tom was a real step forward and a bold one. But have you had a real conversation with either of them about your feelings for each other since this dating thing started? I didn't think so. They're not pushing to give you time and you're not advancing because you're afraid."

"I'm..." Denial wasn't good enough. Not for the friend Diana had become. I faced her, feeling the hot band at the bridge of my nose that predicted tears. "I'm going to lose one. It can't stay the same. I know that. And I don't want to lose either one."

"You're in love with both of them?"

The threatening tears dried up from shock. Had I even considered if I was in love with one, or both? We'd talked about seeing where things went, and I supposed that meant love at some point. Possibly. Maybe.

"I don't know. I'm not lying, Diana. I'm really not."

"I know you're not. Listen—" She swore. "Your parents and Tamantha are back. This isn't over."

✧　✧　✧　✧

"SHOULD HAVE KNOWN."

Mom's quiet voice made me jump.

Tamantha was sound asleep on the sofa bed, none of the light from my bedside lamp reaching her.

Mom stood at the partially open door. She must have come up the stairs very quietly. I'd swear I hadn't been that absorbed. Lulled to near-unconsciousness, but not absorbed. First by Leah Pedroke's basic data. Then by the list of Lukasik's cases Jennifer compiled. Once his career took hold a few years after he got York off, it was fast-track all the way.

York's timeline still had a gap between his trial and his return to Cottonwood County to work on the ranch.

"I was on the way to the bathroom and saw your light. You're working late."

It was such a Mom comment. A seemingly innocuous statement with layers upon layers of meaning, coming together to draw out deepest, darkest secrets like the inexorable hand-over-hand reeling in of a rope.

"Catching up on work." I closed the laptop lid. "You know how it is."

She looked toward where Tamantha slept. "Let's go downstairs. I'll make you cocoa."

Downstairs, I said, "Sorry. It'll have to be decaf. I don't have cocoa. Or milk."

"Yes, you do." She moved around my kitchen with more certainty of where things were than I had. "Tamantha is a remarkable girl."

"You have only scratched the surface." Temptation to tell her Tamantha got me into this mystery investigating racket came... then went. No reason to dent their connection.

"She and Tom are very close," she said.

"Mmm-hmm."

"Maybe it's impossible for parents to truly see their beloved child accurately." The way she looked at me stung my eyes. "Tom has his blind spots about Tamantha."

"Boy, is that the truth. He *likes* her singing."

She smiled, but it wasn't full-bore.

Impulsively, I said, "I'm glad you and Dad came."

"I'm glad we did, too. If we hadn't, I'd never have recognized what's going on with you and Tom and Mike."

I blinked. The love was still there—now the tough kind now, not the fuzzy kind.

"We're friends. We see each other—"

"Piffle."

"Piffle?" I'd never heard that word from Mom.

She doubled down. "Absolute piffle. You're half in love with both of them, wholly in love with one of them. But you can't tell which because of half of the other one clouds the issue, leaving—"

"Mom, that's four halves, equaling two wholes."

"—temporary lack of clarity."

"Temporary?" That sounded... hopeful.

"Temporary. Until you're forced to face it. Now, drink your cocoa."

DAY FOUR

Chapter Forty-Seven

THEY SAY YOU shouldn't grocery shop when you're hungry.

That made after a Mom meal the perfect time for another trip to the Sherman Supermarket and cashier extraordinaire, Penny Czylinski.

Besides, if I let my stockpile of Double Dark Chocolate Milano cookies dip much lower, I'd be in danger of running out in a month or two, prompting a Pepperidge Farm's stock crash.

Mom, Dad, and I sat at the counter talking for a long time over that meal. I called it breakfast. Mom insisted it was brunch.

Tamantha ate with us, then took Shadow out in the back yard for training. She took this seriously, having read books and studied videos on the topic.

Shadow took it seriously, too, because it involved treats. Lots and lots of treats. As he'd become more social, his willingness to trade obedience for treats had skyrocketed. Or was that vice versa?

My conversation with my parents didn't cover important topics, but was important for the companionship.

All in all, I felt mellow as I walked through the familiar automatic doors of the Sherman Supermarket.

Until Penny yelled at me, "Go. You got plenty of cookies. Go on, get out of here."

I didn't turn and flee before that oddest of greetings.

I've been told plenty of times to get out of someplace in my journalistic career. A few of those places I dearly wanted to get out of. I didn't flee any of them. Wasn't going to start with the Sherman Supermarket.

I stopped in the entry and stared at Penny, *shooing* me with both hands and—most remarkably—not talking at her checkout customer.

"What are you waiting for? She's out there. Musta just missed her."

"Who?" I asked.

"Know you don't need them. You're supplied, and not just cookies. She filled in around the cookies. Don't come in here shopping when—"

Approaching from the service desk, the manager objected, "Penny, you can't tell people not to shop."

We both ignored the interruption.

"My mom filling my freezer? But—"

"—*Love Me Tender.* Right there if—"

Love Me Tender...

"—you get moving. Some things more important. Start bagging these groceries, boy. Now, what was I saying? Asparagus—"

"Thank you, Penny!"

I was already out the door. Clearing the front of the building, I spotted an older woman all in black closing the hatch of a venerable SUV—also black—on a collection of grocery bags. A glance through the front glass into the store showed the store manager—*boy*, in Penny speak—bagging, as ordered.

I left him to his fate and concentrated on the woman, jogging across the lot radiating the sun's heat up through my shoes.

"Yvette! Hi! So nice to see you."

She smiled tentatively at the lunatic running toward her.

"It's Elizabeth. Elizabeth Margaret Danniher from KWMT-TV. We met at—" Darn, darn, darn. Couldn't remember the couple's names. And she still looked uncertain. "—at a wedding a while back. Leona D'Amato introduced us."

All uncertainty evaporated. "Oh, yes. Leona's little friend. How nice to see you."

I had to be half a foot taller than her, but little friend I'd be.

"Yes. That's me. Delighted to see you again."

Her smile slipped as she looked into the SUV at the grocery bags occupying the cargo area.

Ice cream. I saw cartons in at least two bags. No time to waste on finesse.

"I'm so happy, too, to hear about you and Hiram Poppinger." I ignored her mouth forming an O and a blush rising up her wrinkled neck. "He's been quite the romantic courting you, hasn't he? Something about a record...?"

She giggled, the blush still spreading. "He has been romantic. Never thought it of him. You know I love the music of the King?"

"I do remember that about you."

"It's what he doesn't understand. Some call me obsessed, but it was never part of my thought to drive him into hiding and pretending he's dead." Ah. The topic was Elvis, not Hiram. "I've always loved his music too much to lose that, even if it meant sacrificing our ever being together."

I shook my head in sorrow. "Shame that wasn't clear to him."

"I know. Now, perhaps he'll understand, with me pledging to another man. Why, do you know Hiram made sure to call me and tell me he could not make our date the other night because he'd been arrested for murder? I call that gentlemanly."

One of the top ten best excuses for missing a date. It also accounted for Hiram's one call from jail.

"And yet the record...?" I nudged.

"He was so apologetic about that, but the deputies were quite stern and said he couldn't retrieve anything from his truck to send to me. He's promised to bring it to me as soon as he can." She giggled. "He was excited at finding the record after I told him it was the only forty-five of the King's lacking from my collection. It's those little touches that matter, isn't it? Knowing a man is thoughtful."

She sighed gustily. "I do plan to love him tender. As soon as he's out of jail."

Chapter Forty-Eight

WHEN I CALLED, Mike and Tom were arriving at the third livestock dealer.

"First two were clean," Mike said. "Well, relatively."

"Better luck with the third one," I said hurriedly. "What I want to know, Mike, is if the things your grandparents left in the house that now belongs to the grazing association included the record player and old records you mentioned."

Dead silence. Except for road noise from hundreds of miles away.

"Yeah," he said cautiously. "Least they were there last time I was inside, a few years ago. Tom?"

"Can't say when I last saw them but I remember a record player and some of those little records—not albums."

"Forty-fives," I supplied. "Mike, did your grandparents like Elvis?"

"Okay, this is just weird, Elizabeth. What is this about?"

"It's about Hiram not going to the grazing association for a wrench or to kill Furman York. He went there for love."

WHEN I FINISHED explaining—Mike couldn't swear one way or the other about his grandparents' collection including *Love Me Tender*—I drove out to the grazing association.

I made only one wrong turn, and that looped right back to the track I'd been on so didn't go far astray.

The house, the roses, the landscape hadn't changed. The screening and police tape were gone.

I tried figuring out where the body had been by the population of smudged bootied footprints nearby, but there were a number of population centers. I satisfied myself with standing in the middle and looking around.

If Furman York had stood on this spot three mornings ago, he would have seen the front porch of the house, but the house blocked a view of where Hiram parked and of the back door, which was the only one used now.

Surely he would have heard Hiram arrive, though—if he was still alive.

I walked toward the house, stopping where the bootied footprints stopped.

No better view of the house or where Hiram had parked. And this was the best angle, as well as closest.

If not to look at the house, why had Furman York come up here?

I returned to the concentrations of bootied footprints, turning and looking like a lighthouse beam.

The slight elevation gave a better view than being at road level, but view of what? Looking in the opposite direction from the house, two pasture fences came together. That was it. Nothing else to see except pasture land.

I went to the house.

The back door was locked.

I went around to the front, sidling between grabby rose bush branches to get up the front steps. Not all the windows' dust came off, even with several strokes. Still, I saw inside.

To a closed-up vintage portable record player not in vintage condition. A wall rack above held albums. On the floor beside the player, sat a short, square case with a handle on top and clasp on the side. The right size for forty-five records. Its top showed disturbances in the layered dust.

Hiram had been here.

✧   ✧   ✧   ✧

I HAD THE double treat of explaining Hiram's love life to Shelton and

Sheriff Conrad.

I'd taken the precaution of calling Shelton on my way back from the grazing association.

So when Ferrante, from behind the front counter, tried to tell me Shelton wasn't available, he was interrupted by Shelton calling from the door to the sheriff's office, "Elizabeth. Get back here. Now."

Under other circumstances, I might have made him pay for that attitude, but Ferrante's expression marked it paid in full.

I reconsidered that stance when Shelton and Conrad left me sitting in the sheriff's office alone for a full half hour while they went off and did law enforcement stuff.

Or watched me through a secret peephole to see if I'd try to look at papers in Conrad's drawers—there were none on the desktop—or break into his computer. Tempting if I'd had Jennifer along, though it would have seriously undermined my hacking lectures.

I satisfied myself with prowling the bookshelves, stocked with the most boring titles ever, mostly on thick binders.

No apology for keeping me waiting when they finally returned, either.

"I'm here to tell you why Hiram went to the grazing association. It wasn't for a wrench."

Shelton growled. I interpreted that as his having already been aware of that.

"Did you find an old forty-five record by Elvis—*Love Me Tender*—in the truck? That's what he went there for. A courting gift for his lady friend."

Without more pleasantries, I explained succinctly, ready to get out of there.

Conrad looked highly skeptical.

Shelton stared at me for a long moment, then patted the arms of his chair lightly.

"Yvette. Should've known—" He bit that off. Then, as if I were Hiram Poppinger's attorney, he said, "It doesn't clear him."

"It explains a number of odd things about his conduct, which, in turn, lowers the likelihood of him being the killer. Especially—" I stood and smiled sweetly at them. "—since York was shot with his own gun, not Hiram's."

Neither man was the kind to froth at the mouth to prove I was right, but I got eye-narrowing twitches from each as ample reward.

"If you know things about this murder—" Conrad started.

"I just generously shared information I was under no obligation to share. In addition to what Tom Burrell told you yesterday about that friend of York's who hauls cattle being a good person to talk to about the rustling that's been going on around here."

I left before either could outline their view that I should spill everything to them all the time and get nothing in return.

I PICKED UP Diana's incoming call as I walked to my SUV in the sheriff's department parking lot.

She started with, "Hiram took an old record from that house to give to Yvette?"

"Russ Conrad must have you on supersonic speed dial."

"Wasn't Russ. It was Mike, an hour and a half ago. Didn't you see my message? Or Mike's?"

"No." I checked now and saw both messages. Connection could have been spotty at the grazing association and in transit. Or I'd missed the vibrating by leaving my phone in my bag by the chair while roaming Conrad's office.

Diana's message said, "Call me about the Elvis song." Mike's from about an hour ago, said, "Taking off soon. Will call."

"Taking off? In the plane? Or to the next stop? They still had places to check."

"I know. But there's been no answer. Go back—you told Russ?"

"And Shelton. As usual, their gratitude knew no bounds."

She chuckled. "As yours would if the situations were reversed."

"Except they never reciprocate. I know, I know. That's not their job. Where are you?"

"Leaving the station. Thought I'd come be your wingman for the rest of the day. First, though, we better call Jennifer and let her know this development. She won't like being the only one not up to date."

But when Diana added Jennifer to the call, she was uninterested. "I have something good. I'll be at your house in five minutes, Elizabeth. Wait for me there."

JENNIFER HAD THAT found-it glow when she pulled up in front of my house.

I'd stopped on the front steps when Diana arrived and waited for her. Now, drawn by that glow, we both walked toward Jennifer's car parked at the curb.

"I got it," she said, coming around the front of her mother's vehicle. "Followed the trail all the way back to the start and I got it."

"You found York during those three years?" I asked.

"Better. Odessa Vincennes' birth name. You're not going to believe it." She looked around to be sure she had our attention. She did. More from her tone than her words. "She was born Linda Pedroke. She's Leah's younger sister."

Chapter Forty-Nine

IF YOU VIDEOED someone crumbling a jigsaw puzzle to put it back in its box, then reversed it so pieces flowed perfectly into place in the design, that's what I saw inside my head, accompanied by a chorus of *Of course Of course Of course.*

"It's solid. No doubt," Jennifer said, "She definitely hid it, but once I cracked through that last layer, there it all was. The names, the ages, the addresses, all fit. Her parents, Leah's parents—same people. Leaving that spelling of Asheleigh's name was Odessa's big mistake. Should have changed that, too."

"Hard to let a name go when you've found one that feels right," Diana said.

"It's gotta go if you don't want to leave a trail." Even though she'd followed that trail, Jennifer disapproved of slipshod methods. "Glad I did that background work on Leah, too, because the first thing I spotted on this last leg was their mother's maiden name being the same. I should have had all this earlier. You know what Asheleigh's middle name is? Teresa. And Leah's middle name? Teresa. I had them both a *day* ago. And it never *occurred* to me."

"Lots of people have Teresa as a middle name," Diana said mildly.

"I should've spotted it," Jennifer insisted.

"You did amazing, Jennifer," I said. "Amazing. It answers so many questions."

Then Diana immediately asked one it didn't answer. "Do you think Asheleigh knows?"

I shrugged a *Don't-Know.*

Jennifer grinned. "Bet it answers the question of who to talk to next."

It sure did.

"I want to come with. I don't have that York stuff yet, but the guys are working on it and… I want to come," Jennifer said.

"Then you're coming," I said. "Someone else should come, too."

Her face fell. "The guys? But who knows when they'll be back. If we wait for them—"

"No, we're not waiting for them. We'll call them, but the person I was thinking of is Aunt Gee."

"Of course," Diana said. "You call her and I'll try the guys."

DIANA'S CALLS TO Mike and Tom were still not answered. She left a message saying we had news, but no more, so Jennifer could explain her coup herself.

The attempted calls happened while Diana and Jennifer drove to the apartment Odessa—we were sticking with that name—and Asheleigh rented, checking if they were there. We'd decided against calling ahead, believing Odessa in particular would try to avoid us.

Both cars were there.

Asheleigh might be off somewhere with Gable, but it was the best we could hope for.

Gee arrived at my house faster than I'd have thought possible. She must have taken driving lessons from Diana.

I filled her in more during the short trip to the apartment.

The four of us exited the two vehicles in what felt like a not-quite-coordinated choreography for superheroes forming a posse.

The big old house had two apartments downstairs and two up what must have been the original central staircase. This being Sherman, we walked up the stairs to their door.

Before I rang the small bell with Vincennes over it, I took in a deep, slow breath. We were all winded, and it wasn't from the stair climb.

I glanced around at the others, then pressed the bell.

Asheleigh answered.

Her pretty, pleasant face, stiffened.

"Hello, Asheleigh, we'd like to talk to your mother—"

"No."

"—and you. If—"

"No."

"—she's not here—"

We both stopped because of the sound behind me.

It was a low, sharp keening.

Gee, dry-eyed, stared at Asheleigh. She gave no sign of being aware of the sound coming from her.

I took advantage of Asheleigh's distraction, to slip around her and inside. Jennifer followed me.

Diana put one hand on Asheleigh's arm and the other on Gee's back. "She's had a shock. Let's all get in, and..."

She maneuvered her two charges inside, seating them on a loveseat. With two chairs, it formed a U facing a large front window. Diana took the chair closer to Gee, I took the one closer to Asheleigh. Jennifer closed the door, then folded herself onto the floor across a glass-topped wicker basket.

I had an impression of a neat, bright space that matched the daughter, not the mother. But most of my attention was on Asheleigh and her reaction to Gee, who stared at her still, though the sound had dwindled.

Asheleigh touched the older woman's hand. "Are you... Are you okay?"

In her concern for this stranger's distress, she abandoned her defenses.

"You." Gee swallowed. "You are so like her. So very like her."

Asheleigh's eyes gleamed with tears. "I know."

"I knew her. Leah. She lived with me."

Silence seemed to repeat her *I know.*

"Your mother—"

"I'm not talking to you about her. I won't tell you anything."

"Then let me tell you," I said.

"Asheleigh. Go to your room." Odessa's voice came from the kitchen. It was hoarse, raw.

"Mom—"

"Go to your room now." Odessa came into view, her expression blank, her movements slow.

Asheleigh rose slowly, went around the loveseat, and faced her mother.

I couldn't see the daughter's face, but if she was looking at her mother's for a crack, a sliver of uncertainty, she wasn't getting it.

"You're not feeling well, Mom. I—"

"Your room."

Asheleigh turned and went down the short hall behind me. A door closed.

Only when that sound reached us did Odessa come around the loveseat and sit, her hands on her thighs, staring straight ahead.

With no indication that she might ever speak, I said, "We know you're Leah Pedroke's sister. We have proof."

Lifting only the three middle fingers of her right hand she made a lethargic flicking-away motion.

"I was always coming here. I just didn't know it." The words sounded almost drugged. "It ruined my parents. Took the life out of them, though they still breathed. Their hearts beat while they had no heart left."

I heard a door stealthily opening. Quickly, I said, "Your sister's death?"

"No. That they survived. It was here they met ruin. That travesty of a trial. That was their end. The end of my parents. The end of my family."

"You have a daughter."

"Yes."

The single, flat word left me both chilled and uncertain. Every indication to this point had been that she doted on Asheleigh. How did that reconcile with that dispassionate word?

And how would the young woman listening react?

Odessa went on. "My parents still had a daughter. Me. After Leah's murderer went free, I wasn't enough for them to keep living. They were empty. Gone. Even as they breathed and moved.

"My brother went to college far away and never came back. Not for holidays, not for their funerals. He forgot Leah and the rest of us. I tracked him down and contacted him about coming here to deal with the murderers—"

Murderers, plural.

"—he never responded. I don't care. I can handle it. I made my parents live until I couldn't any longer. I had to get out, too. I just didn't know it as soon as my brother. When I married—the first guy who asked—and they no longer had my lifeblood pumping through them, they wouldn't even hold off dying for me to give birth.

"It was only after they died that I knew I needed to be here. To see where she'd been those last months so I'd understand. I'd have peace. But I couldn't come here. I had Asheleigh.

"Then I had my idea. To start, she had to go to college.

"I saved and saved. Years and years. Putting everything I could aside to get Asheleigh through college. A good school. A school that would open the right door for her. And I did it. She got into Penn State, got scholarships. Not enough, but I worked, I squeezed every dime—I knew how to do that—and I got her through. A semester early to save costs. A college graduate.

"And then it was my turn. Finally, my turn. When I saw that job posting, I knew. I knew it would all turn out. I told her. You can go wherever you want later, but first you're going to Wyoming. We're going to Wyoming.

"I tried to find work in O'Hara Hill, but there was nothing. I ate at Ernie's every chance I got. Leah wrote about that place."

Gee frowned. "Your parents never mentioned that. We went there several times and they never said a word."

I'd tensed at the interruption, but Odessa's mouth formed a tight, secretive smile. "It wasn't in letters to them. She wrote to *me* about it. Only to me. She wrote long, wonderful letters to me. Said I didn't have to share them with Mom and Dad if I didn't want to. They were just ours. Reading those letters, it was like I experienced each day with her.

I knew this place, the wildness, the beauty. I loved it as much as she did. I was part of it.

"So, I knew I had to come here, too. And then it turned out I had it all wrong. I thought the place would soothe me."

As she spoke, she rubbed her thumb against her curved forefinger in that now familiar gesture.

A flash of Tamantha's hand in mine at Tom's came to me—a memory that included every nerve's sensation—when she rubbed my hand with her thumb, reinforcing the contact.

Perhaps what a little sister would do when her idolized older sister held her hand, reinforcing their connection, assuring herself of the older sister's presence.

And then, there was only this rub against her own flesh to fill the void.

"But it was the opposite. This place, where she lived, where she died tore at me, splintered...

"And then it was pieces. Little pieces. I didn't even realize I'd heard them until they came together and I realized he was here. *Here*. It was... It was horrible and wonderful at the same time, because it meant I could kill him. No, no, not him—" She scrubbed the words out, jerking her hand back and forth. "Both of them."

Chapter Fifty

"**THE WHISPERS, THE** whispers that I finally realized meant that lawyer who defended him bribed the jury. So, of course, he has to die, too. But then—*then*—even better, to make him suffer first. To have his son fall in love and have his heart broken. For the father to watch that—that was what he deserved. So, I started that right away. Found Gable and got him to love her.

"It gave me time to plan how to kill them.

"The lawyer would be harder, because he wasn't here a lot. But I could take time for that, because he would be in pain from his son's pain, once I had my plan. I could focus first on the murderer. I trailed him. That wasn't always easy. I had to be careful not to get too close, because other workers from the ranch would follow him places for their boring, boring jobs. At least those started in the morning. That was better than when he went places at night and I'd get so tired. But I stayed awake enough to see him go to that bar and sometimes into town to buy liquor.

"That's when I knew it would be simple. Just set up a road block one night and when he stopped, shoot him. Right away. I didn't need to talk to him. I just needed him dead.

"But a week before I had it planned someone else killed the murderer. Someone else…

"I went out there to see his dead body. But I couldn't. They had it covered. Which was more than they did for Leah. I've seen the crime scene photos and they didn't even cover her. And him—the lawyer—he was there crying about how that murderer was treated like an animal.

"And I realized I'd been wrong. I didn't just need them dead. I'd needed to kill them. I lost York, but I won't make that mistake again."

Them.

Sharply, I asked, "What have you planned for Norman Clay Lukasik?"

Her eyes widened unnaturally. "Who?"

I wasn't playing that game. "The rumors say he bribed jurors to get Furman York off. Wouldn't you like to know if that was true?"

"Of course. Wouldn't you?"

"I would. I intend to find out. But what about your daughter?"

She turned those unplugged Lady of Shalott eyes on me. "What about her?"

"She loves Gable Lukasik."

She shook her head. Three, four, five times before she said, "No. She doesn't. She's part of the plan."

✧   ✧   ✧   ✧

THE GUYS HAD landed in Sherman and were driving to my house. "Taking off" had meant the plane.

Waiting messages for Diana and me announced that when we left the apartment.

We would have stayed there if I'd feared anything physical between mother and daughter. On the other hand...

I called Shelton.

Diana nodded approval. Then we got into our separate vehicles.

She wouldn't have been so happy if she'd known the call rolled over to the front desk and Ferrante—gleefully—said he wasn't available.

Gee seemed inclined to take the phone from me and give Ferrante an alternative answer.

It was possible Shelton wasn't available, considering he had a murder investigation going. Didn't matter. There wasn't time to thrash that out or to thrash Ferrante.

I called Richard Alvaro's personal cell phone and barely let him get the H of hello out.

"You need to get to—" I gave the apartment address. "—and question the mother and daughter there—"

"Elizabeth—"

"—about Furman York's shooting. Immediately. The mother is the younger sister of Leah Pedroke—the woman York was accused of murdering. Not only are they integral to a murder investigation, they're dangers to themselves, each other, and others."

"Elizabeth—"

"I am deadly serious. And I do mean deadly, Deputy Alvaro. If you don't do this and something happens to either of these women or someone else, you won't be able to live with it. You hear my voice. Do I mean this?"

The slightest hesitation, then a firm, "Yes."

The call clicked off.

I met Gee's gaze and breathed.

✧ ✧ ✧ ✧

STILL, I FOUND a spot to park behind a hedge that allowed a view of the apartment without giving an arriving deputy's vehicle a view of my SUV.

Alvaro made it in three and a half minutes—good, even for Sherman.

When he went in the building, we pulled away.

Silence continued until we reached my house.

In addition to Gee's vehicle, Tom's truck was there, Mike's SUV— they must have picked it up on the way from the airport—along with Diana's, then the cars of my parents and Jennifer's mother.

"Gee, if you'd like to come in, talk..."

"No. Thank you. I need to return to O'Hara Hill. I work tonight. I... I will take time to consider what we learned—what you discovered. Thank you, Elizabeth. Thank you, very much."

Chapter Fifty-One

I EXPECTED THE house to be crammed. It was empty.

A plastic-wrap-covered spread on the counter featured more healthy options than our usual fare, yet made my mouth water.

The sound of laughter drew me through the house and out the back door. Mike, Tom, Diana, and Jennifer sat at an outdoor table, while my parents occupied lounge chairs, and Tamantha lolled in a hammock, with Shadow nearby. None of which had been here this morning.

"Ah, Elizabeth," my mother called. "You're finally here."

"What is all this?"

"We went shopping," Tamantha said from the hammock. "I said you need roses here. Like the grazing association has. But they said they're too hard to return if you don't like them."

Mom smiled at her while waving off my question. "We'll talk about that later. Your friends have been waiting for you. You all go in now and do your work. We won't bother you. Oh, help yourself to the snacks there for you."

THE GUYS HAD hit paydirt at the third place they'd checked.

Furman York had brought cattle there three times. Twice with Lukasik brands, most recently not. The owner showed them paperwork where York said he was authorized to sell the cattle.

No proof, just York's say-so.

"Still not a sure thing Lukasik caught him," Tom said. "Might not have room in the truck because of cows he took from the rest of us."

"Now tell us about Odessa," Mike said. "And Elvis records."

We did.

"She was *disappointed* at not killing York," Diana emphasized.

"Are we positive she didn't?" Mike asked.

"Acting?" Diana asked. "Sure was convincing. It's what Jennifer said. She was unplugged. What had been driving her all these years was over."

"If she killed him, it could have been a delayed reaction. Like it didn't become real until she heard someone else say it."

"Possible. I find it hard to read her," Diana said. "Her plan for hurting Lukasik through his son—and her daughter—is surreal. Does she change it if Lukasik is dying? Plus, Lukasik's given no indication his son's heartbreak would touch him at all."

"Yeah, and what about her daughter? She doesn't care if It breaks Asheleigh's heart and—?" Jennifer broke off, directing her attention to her phone.

"Revenge or daughter," I murmured.

"Unless Asheleigh doesn't love Gable Lukasik and she is in on it," Mike said.

Jennifer switched from phone to device.

I shook my head. "We could be in trouble if we have to prove who's in love and who's not."

"Not to mention investigating Hiram's love life," Mike said. "But what else do we have?"

Diana's gaze met mine as both of us rebounded from looking toward Jennifer.

"Funny you should mention that," I started. "We do have another angle to consider if—"

But Jennifer raised one hand, capturing our attention instantly. "My guys found interesting things in Lukasik's financials."

"And that's part of it," I said.

"You didn't go digging into his private—"

She cut off Tom's worry. "No. You have no idea how much information is out there. Started with articles ranking regional law firms.

Added firms that had to state incomes and compensation for mergers or divorces. Throw in real estate taxes, organizations that charge membership based on net worth, and a few other sources. Cross-referenced all the numbers with the rankings, so we could slot Lukasik between other lawyers and…"

She looked around to be sure we were listening.

"He's not as rich as everybody thinks. I mean, he's not a pauper or anything. But, still, he's not where you'd expect him to be based on rival firms. If you want to see the numbers—"

"Give us your headlines, first," I said.

"Well, that was one. The other is I found out how much he was paying Furman York."

"How did you find *that* out?"

"He took out a private loan and had to report employee salaries, among a whole lot of other stuff. The group who gave him the loan sold it to another company, which sold it to another company, which … you get the idea. And one of those companies made all their records public accidentally. The idiots. It was sitting there on the web until we found it and reported it—after we copied Lukasik's."

Mike's patience ran out. "How much for York?"

Her figure drew a whistle from Mike, stunned silence from Diana and me, and Tom's, "More than twice what Jack Delahunt gets, three times what a good foreman around here gets."

"Wait a minute, wait a minute." I dropped my head, focusing on a patch of the oriental carpet, blocking out distractions. "Let's look at this chronologically. Lukasik represents York. York gets off."

"Because at least two jurors are bribed," Mike said.

"We think that—okay, we're pretty sure, after what Hiram said. Lukasik represents York, bribes two jurors, York gets off."

"And York goes to work for Lukasik," Mike said. "Blackmail."

My head jerked up. "But York doesn't go to work for Lukasik for three years. Why the delay? If York had proof of bribery in his case, why wait to apply pressure? Why be broke for three years?"

"He got the proof later," Jennifer said.

"How? He wasn't here. And would anyone in Cottonwood County

help him get proof?" I asked.

"Hell, no," Mike said. "The bribed jurors certainly wouldn't. And how could York hold it over Lukasik's head anyway? Wasn't he in nearly as much jeopardy? Lukasik could sure say he'd been involved. How could he prove he wasn't? Even if he turned state's evidence, testified against Lukasik, how many top lawyers would want to try *that* case? Plus, he'd benefited. Wouldn't the authorities find *some* way to punish him for killing Leah?"

That image of the reversed video magically flowing together pieces of a puzzle...

Pieces. ... Pieces coming together.

Something Penny said.

First one didn't do it. Slide, sliding back to where he'd started. Hated that worse than anything. Needed another one and did it again.

Not *didn't do* the murder. But *didn't do* the trick.

Sliding back...

Needed another one...

Did it again...

"A different case," I said. "Lukasik did it again. And York black-mailed him over that. Not his own case. York knew about the bribery in his case, but had no proof. He keeps watching, on the alert for Lukasik to do it again. Making sure to get proof the next time. That explains the three-year delay."

"What proof? Where is it?" Jennifer asked.

"Letters or photos—more likely photos. As for where, someplace York was sure Lukasik couldn't get his hands on it, because he surely tried. If we figure out which case—"

"I can check."

"The ones around three years after the York verdict. That's where it's going to be. An unexpected verdict. Or one for a particularly high-profile client."

Jennifer started immediately, the syncopation of her keystrokes fascinating and taunting.

How long—?

"I hear you people breathing. Go away. Or I'm going away." Jennifer stood before she finished speaking. "Never mind. I'm going. I'll be back—"

"Where? There's not much room with all of us here and—You're not going home, are you?"

"My car. Unless you guys start breathing even louder."

Chapter Fifty-Two

THE REST OF us joined my parents, Tamantha, and Shadow in the back yard for a breather and to admire Dad's yard work. Apparently I'd let spring deadlines whoosh past.

The yard did look trimmer. Happier somehow, too.

Mike excused himself, muttering something about facilities, though I'd bet the buffet remainders also drew him.

After a while, Tamantha went inside to pack her bag.

Returning, I discovered Dad and Tom in a technical discussion about tools and tractors. Mom and Diana compared notes on flowers.

A few minutes of that and the buffet remainders started whispering to me, too.

I went into the house and met Mike, coming around the corner into the living area.

"Hey."

"Hey yourself."

He leaned against the wall. "I was thinking about our talk—the family ranch. How to explain… When family members feel the same about a family ranch, it's a bond that burrows deeper than the roots of any tree. But when the feelings are different, it's like a chasm you try to bridge."

He hitched one shoulder, proclaiming an unknown result. He was talking about his family as much as the family ranch.

"Standing at the old place that day I told you about, it was weird," he continued. "I knew trying to put the place back together would be trying to rewind time, going back to what was.

"In the end, I wanted a place here, a part of Cottonwood County. But I could satisfy that itch while moving forward, not back."

I patted his arm, feeling the strength there.

My hand slid down his arm. Our hands tangled, then caught. Our gazes met as we neared. Then his gaze dropped to my mouth.

Our lips touched as we drew closer and closer, arms encircling, heat building—

"Stop that."

I CAME OUT of the kiss first at that peremptory voice. Mike still had his arms around me, leaning in to resume the kiss.

So I saw the puzzled expression cross his face close-up. He looked down, over his arm, which wrapped around my shoulder and back.

I also looked over his muscled arm and saw the person who went with the voice I'd recognized. Tamantha.

"Did you hit me?" he asked her as I stepped back from his embrace.

"Yes. You're trying to steal my daddy's girlfriend. You're supposed to be his friend."

"I am his friend. And I'm not trying to steal Elizabeth." He still had one hand splayed on my back.

"Stealing is for possessions, Tamantha. People shouldn't ever possess other people." Ethical and moral matters represented the easy route at the moment and that's the one I took.

"Your dad and I are both dating Elizabeth." Mike seemed to think that took care of everything.

It didn't.

"I don't get it," Tamantha informed us with deep disapproval.

Mike opened his mouth. I waited for the words that would wrap up this awkward situation neatly. He closed his mouth.

Finally, he did speak. "You know, Tamantha, I don't really get it, either. This is Elizabeth's idea."

"Hey."

"It's true."

"That doesn't mean..." How could I finish that? That doesn't mean you have to rat me out to a soon-to-be-fourth-grader?

"Why?" she demanded of me.

"To get to know each other better. That's what grownups do. We get real busy with work and other things, so we make special times to get together to relax, to talk, to spend time together—"

Tom came in the back door and stopped, his gaze going from his daughter, to Mike and me, and back.

"—to take our time to get to know each other better and they're called dates."

"I know what dates are," she said scornfully. "Sally's parents do it and it's not to get to know each other better. It's so they can make out in the car and not have the kids bug them."

"Tamantha."

Her father's mild scold had less impact than it might have because I asked a question before he could say any more.

"Sally told you that?"

"No," she said, still in scorn mode. "We saw them. And he had his hand inside her shirt."

"Tamantha." No question, Tom meant that one.

"He did. And she had hers—"

"Not. Another. Word." He held his daughter's gaze. Slowly, she closed her mouth. "You know what privacy is and Sally's parents deserve theirs. You should not have gone spying—"

"We weren't spying. We just happened to go through the garage."

That seemed reasonable to me. But Tom's austere frown remained. "Just happened?"

Tamantha looked away.

Score one for Tom. Actually, score two. One over Tamantha. One over me because he'd spotted the truth and I hadn't.

"In the future, you will avoid just happening to intrude on people's privacy. And should you happen to accidentally witness something that's private, you will not share it with others. Understood?"

Her usual laser focus had returned to her father. "What if I witness something private, but someone's doing something wrong? Because that's what you all do. I know all about that. You find out about things other people want to keep private and bad things they do in private and then you get them sent to jail."

How did she know about that? Who on earth blabbed about our murder inquiries to a kid.

"And then Elizabeth and Mike go on TV about it."

Oh.

We were the blabbers.

"If you witness someone doing something wrong, in private or not, you come and tell me immediately. I'll handle it. That's a father's job. Not yours. Understood?"

"Well, It's sort of Sergeant Shelton's job, too."

I bit the inside of my lip. Mike's eyes were dancing. How I wish Wayne Shelton could know he'd been demoted to *sort of* in Tamantha's organizational chart.

But Tom remained focused and steady. "If you can't reach me, you can tell Sergeant Shelton."

"Elizabeth, too? Because she's on TV about it. And Mike."

"Elizabeth, too. And Mike," he agreed.

I no longer felt like laughing. More like I'd just been sworn in as some sort of law enforcement officer. And not voluntarily.

"Diana?"

That had a one-more-drink-of-water-before-I-go-to-sleep ring to it.

"Tamantha."

"Okay."

"Okay, what?" Tom asked.

That prompt for her to add a "sir" to her response seemed unlike him and unlike their relationship.

"Okay, I am not to just happen to see people in private unless I really can't help it. But if I do see somebody in private doing something wrong, I'm not to talk to people about it, except you. Or Sergeant Shelton. Or Elizabeth or Mike. Or Diana."

I'd missed the boat on his *Okay, what?* He'd been going for something with far broader applications than an added *sir*. But that meant I had been right about my interpretation of it not being like their relationship.

Tamantha drew in a breath and added, "But they can't put it on TV. And he can't kiss Elizabeth anymore."

✧ ✧ ✧ ✧

TOM TOOK TAMANTHA out on the back steps for a discussion.

Mike said he was going to say hello to the Undlins.

Very tactful. He was right. I needed a few moments alone.

Tamantha had seen Mike and me kiss. Awkward, but not the end of the world. Tom had handled it calmly.

Of course he and Mike certainly knew I was kissing the other one.

It can't stay the same…. I don't want to lose either one.

I went upstairs. From a chair overlooking the back yard, I watched Tom go into the garage.

Restlessly, I revisited earlier material Jennifer had sent. The gap in Furman York's timeline from his not-guilty to arriving at the Lukasik Ranch mocked me.

Tom didn't come out of the garage.

Another pass through the timeline didn't change a darned thing. The gap remained.

And Tom remained in the garage.

I went downstairs.

Chapter Fifty-Three

TOM HAD HIS back to me, partially bent over, with a garden tool between his legs while he stretched to reach something behind a dresser that had belonged to the previous owner.

I was enjoying this view a little too much.

"How'd your talk with Tamantha go? Where is she?"

He turned his head, not moving otherwise.

"Give me a minute here."

He focused away from me again. Shifting forward to reach deeper to where I thought I'd once glimpsed pegboard behind all the stored stuff. He came back with what looked like a giant's pair of scissors. Put the other tool back behind the dresser.

He straightened deliberately, stepped back, and—last—faced me.

"Tamantha's taking a walk with your folks and Shadow. Your dad was looking for loppers earlier. Your mom vetoed him using the electric trimmers on the high branches."

"I know. Thank you. Is that the only reason you disappeared into here?"

"No. I would've waited to talk to you until after York's shooting is sorted out." His tone chilled me. "We can still wait."

"No. What's going on, Tom?"

He combed his hair back with his fingers, picked his cowboy hat from where it rested on the dresser, put it on, and met my gaze.

"The other morning here, even with what's going on... Cooking eggs for Tamantha. The three of us in the kitchen. Her happy. You laughing... It's what I want."

I sucked in a breath that turned to fire deep in my lungs. Was he saying...? Was he asking...?

"But I have to look out for Tamantha first. What I want doesn't come anywhere near that. Not even—" His look toward me ricocheted away. "—what you might want. Or what she wants. It's got to be what's best for her."

"Yes." It was all I could dredge up from a lifetime of vocabulary.

"The baggage... She's stuck with mine. But ours—yours and mine... I can't put what I want ahead of Tamantha. I can't."

"No," I said, agreeing.

I'd thought before that Tamantha was the only happiness he trusted. Being right sucked.

"How she was about you and Mike... She's a kid. She doesn't understand. Hell, sometimes I don't, either. It's okay for me to not know. It's not for her. She needs to be sure, to be on an even keel. I can't be making her deal with any more grown-up things."

"I..." I wanted to say I understood. To be gracious and adult. I couldn't say anything.

"I'll explain to her that you and I are friends. Not dating anymore. Can't say she'll be happy." The faintest flicker showed at one corner of his mouth. "Mike might be in for a rough time from her. He'll survive. We all will."

✧   ✧   ✧   ✧

YES. WE'D ALL survive.

It can't stay the same....

Both our phones sounded. He got to his first. "Jennifer says to come in."

Bless her. A need to think, a reason to put off feeling. As long as I could.

I don't want to lose either one.

"I... I better go." I started to leave.

And stopped.

He was behind me.

"What are you doing?"

"Coming with."

"Tom, you don't—"

"We can't take this where I'd like to, but that doesn't mean you're tangling with trouble without me. Not going to happen. I'll leave these loppers for your dad and be in."

He left first, not looking back.

I appreciated that. It gave me the opportunity to wipe evidence from under my eyes before I went in the house.

AS IF MAKING an entrance, Jennifer didn't come in the front door until the rest of us were seated in the living room.

"I got something. That three-year gap for York after the trial? I found him in a little town in Colorado. Bonedrin. Charged with vagrancy."

"Vagrancy. So he wasn't working," Diana said.

Bonedrin.

Why was that familiar...?

"When?" I asked as I reopened the file from Jennifer that included a list I'd just revisited.

"The month before Lukasik hired him for the ranch."

"Elizabeth's got that figured-it-out look," Mike said.

Where was that list? Where—? *Got it.*

"He turned to Lukasik when he was broke and Lukasik helped him?"

"*No.*" I tapped the screen. "York—Tom, what was the name of York's horse? Clyde mentioned it when he was talking about the horse trailer. Called it an ugly brute. What was the name?"

His eyebrows rose. "Same as his previous two horses. Called them all the same—Bonedrin."

"He changed the name of his horses? That's bad luck and—"

"Bonedrin?" Diana repeated, interrupting Mike. "Where York was charged with vagrancy. But—"

"That's it. And the town where York was charged with vagrancy three years after his own trial, the name he kept using for horses—a jab at Lukasik—and—" I jabbed the screen. "—the location of a

Lukasik trial three years after York's trial. In other words, right after Lukasik bought the ranch and right before York started working there—or not working."

"Wait," Jennifer commanded, turning her device's screen toward us. "Here's the headline. That was Norman Clay Lukasik's next big verdict after getting York off. A surprise not-guilty."

Mike flopped back in his seat. "Whoa. Go through that again. I feel like I'm jet-lagged."

"From Sioux Falls?" Jennifer asked.

I didn't mind going through it again, getting it firm in my own head.

"York knew Lukasik bribed the jury to get him off. But as you pointed out, turning him in could have been dangerous to York, too. This next bit is speculation, but considering his later behavior, it makes sense. He tried to coerce Lukasik into supporting him. When Lukasik refused, York reacted just the way he did playing cards. He caught on and didn't let go. He kept track of Lukasik for three years. We can't know if he followed other cases. Maybe Lukasik didn't resort to bribery in any of them, but York was there when Lukasik got that surprise not-guilty verdict in the Bonedrin case."

"Okay," Mike said. "Then York blackmailed Lukasik and he's been blackmailing him ever since in the form of a well-paying job where he didn't work. Kept getting raises, too."

"Exactly. Smart of Lukasik to set it up that way, too. No noticeable payments for nothing, which might look like blackmail. Just overly generous salary as part of the payroll. With York on the ranch, Lukasik kept a comfortable distance, infrequent and short visits. He hadn't counted on his wife and son falling in love with the place."

"Jennifer's question," Tom said. "Why now?"

"Right," she said. "He's been paying blackmail all this time, why kill York now."

"Because," I said slowly. "He's dying. He's wrapping things up."

They all nodded.

"So, now what do we do?" Diana asked.

"We look at all the suspects and all the angles again to be sure. Then we really get to work."

Chapter Fifty-Four

"OKAY, WE HAVE a plan. But before we start, let's take a breath and think this through." It was the last thing I wanted to do right now.

Think? No. That came far too close to feeling.

I wanted to act.

Torpedoes?

Full-speed ahead.

Blowing up something—especially me—sounded good right now.

That's why I had to slow it down. I wouldn't be the only casualty if this blew up.

"There's knowing what happened and there's proving that's how it happened. And if I can't get it over the hump, the other side knows what's coming and can build a stronger defense for any subsequent tries. Shelton would not thank me for that. And speaking of Shelton, we'd need him to have Hiram on hand."

"You've been here before," Diana said.

"I know. But this time it involves playing chicken with Norman Clay Lukasik, one of the top defense attorneys in the country."

"*The* top," Mike said dryly. "Just ask him."

"That could be good. He's full of himself. Cocky. That'll make him easier to take. You can take him," Jennifer said.

Tom was the only one who hadn't spoken.

The others looked at him. I didn't. He said, "I have no right to try to push you."

That had more meaning than the others knew.

"*But?*" I prompted, none too gently.

The driest whisper of a grin touched the corners of his mouth. "But I'll represent Tamantha's interests in this by saying, do it. Go for it, Elizabeth Margaret Danniher."

✧ ✧ ✧ ✧

WE DIVIDED UP.

For the drive to the grazing association, Mike and I were in his SUV, with Odessa and Asheleigh as passengers. All it had taken was telling Odessa that Norman Clay Lukasik would be there.

That left Richard Alvaro free for other duties.

Tom drove his truck, with Clyde, Diana, and Jennifer along. Paul Chaney and his uncle, Otto, were reserves if we needed more on the rustling.

Clyde was to call his father on the way, then have Kesler call Gable or Tom would call him direct. Either way, Gable would be told Asheleigh would be there. We figured that made him a sure-show.

And he was the second lever to get Norman Clay Lukasik over the hump.

I'd applied the first lever. Ego all the way.

"We're bringing together the people from what happened—the important ones. We won't be filming, but working out statements and sequences for later filming for a special we're doing. You might not be aware, spending so much time away from here, that our specials on crimes have been well-received, including national and even international attention." Hey, being aired in Canada qualified as international. "We need to have potential participants on hand at the grazing association now to be included in what airs."

"This is very short notice," came the important man complaint.

Biting back comments about murder investigations seldom allowing time for engraved invitations, I said, "If it weren't vital, we would never ask it of you."

"Well… I'll see."

I was fairly confident I had him.

Shelton was supposed to bring Hiram.

I figured it at fifty-fifty.

"*Reenactment?*" Shelton had repeated when I'd gone to see him at the sheriff's department. He'd spread out the syllables with extra emphasis on the third—*re-en-ACT-ment*—to pile on the disdain.

I'd gone alone, the others busy with the other arrangements.

Besides, Shelton would get his back up regardless, but the fewer witnesses the better.

"Not an exact reenactment," I said mildly, "even though we'll be at the grazing association."

"I don't care where you'll be. I'm not getting involved in amateur theatrics. *Am-a-teur.*"

"I have two cards to play here, Sergeant Shelton. The first—"

"You have no cards, Ms. Danniher. Not a one."

"—is that you've been using me and Tom Burrell and Diana Stendahl and James Longbaugh to get information out of Hiram Poppinger."

Another man would have invited my explanation by asking *How could I have done that when we kept the audio off when you were talking in the interview room?*

Shelton made me plunge ahead, uninvited.

"You've had Richard Alvaro reading Hiram's lips as he answered my questions."

Another man's jaw might have dropped. Shelton's left eyelid flickered.

"I understand the temptation. You never counted Hiram as your prime suspect, but his stubbornness in holding back things slowed your clearing of the underbrush. When James asked to bring in other people to talk with Hiram, you thought, what the heck. It might help.

"Especially with the ace up your sleeve of Richard's ability to read lips. How did he learn? If you say it wasn't from someone in his family, I won't believe you. Someday somebody will do a study of the Alvaros and all their abilities."

Because he knew how easily I could track it down, he answered. "Understand an older sister taught him when she was learning."

"Uh-huh. Well, if he—or you—want to keep his ability a secret, tell him not to let on that he caught a *Casablanca* reference when he was too far away to hear it."

No reaction. Though I suspected Richard would hear about it.

"I don't hold the ploy against you, entirely. However, James might feel differently. And I don't suppose your chain of command would be happy to have it reported on TV. Ah. I see you did not go up the chain of command."

Tamping down triumph, I said, "The second card is that you owe me a favor."

He didn't squirm or deny. "You claiming this favor and canceling out all debt for yourself or for someone else?"

"Someone else."

His steady look demanded more as the price of even possible co-operation.

"Tamantha Burrell."

Chapter Fifty-Five

SHELTON ARRIVED LAST with Hiram, escorted by Richard Alvaro and Lloyd Sampson. Plus another deputy, who stayed with the two official vehicles. That seemed excessive for one portly prisoner.

Portly and unhappy prisoner.

"Up that hill *again*? Wasn't bad enough all the bother it's gotten me into the first time I did it, and now you want me to do it again? York should've been killed years ago, all the upset, irritation, and misery he's caused."

Alvaro and Sampson directed him up the slight rise to where Furman York had been killed.

Shelton and I followed.

Scowl in place, he said, "This better work."

Norman Clay Lukasik, striking a heroic pose at the brim of the upslope, like a captain of a sailing ship, interrupted, "In the future, call ahead of time to see if I'm available."

He didn't realize he came in a distant second to a fourth-grader for authoritarianism.

"Of course." With luck, there would be no need to call him in the future. With lots and lots of luck.

I stopped, gesturing Lukasik ahead of me.

Shelton hung back slightly. Either guarding the pass or disavowing any involvement.

✧　✧　✧　✧

"WHO ARE THESE people," Lukasik demanded.

As arranged, Mike shifted to stand near him in the rough circle we'd created. The lawyer didn't appear to notice the move, but Shelton did. He sent me another sharp look.

Bypassing any prelude, I said, "Most of you know each other. For the others, we'll do introductions as we come to them."

Lukasik had to have a good idea of some, since his son had just taken Asheleigh's hand in his, with her mother on her other side.

"Let's go back to the morning of Furman York's murder. From forensic evidence, we know he was standing approximately there—" I pointed to where the bootied footprints had congregated, now wiped clear by wind-driven dirt. "—when he struggled with someone and was shot with his own gun."

Under his hat brim, Shelton's face was rigid. But I could feel the heat of his fuming over *forensic evidence*. It sounded so much better than inference and deduction.

"As I believe you all know, his body was reported to authorities at approximately nine-thirty in the morning by Hiram Poppinger. York had been dead for a short time."

"See?" Hiram said to Lloyd Sampson. "Killed by somebody else. They go away. Then I find him. Proves I didn't do it."

"The gap doesn't prove you didn't do it, Hiram," I said. "You could have shot him. Been occupied with other things—staging the scene, for instance—and then reported the body."

He started to growl. I talked over him.

"Hiram was here to do a favor for Clyde Baranski—to confront Furman York about suspicions he'd rustled cattle from grazing association members. He'd stolen cattle a couple ways, with Clyde a victim of the direct method the night before. Fence was cut and cattle removed from a field."

I turned to the rancher.

"Clyde, you had other conflicts with Furman York." Before he, his father, Tom, or anyone else could defend him, I added, "I know. Lots of people did. That's why we need to get it all out in the open. He drew you into the fraud by a feedlot operator in South Dakota. You'd written a large check. It was only lucky timing that prevented a major loss. And then he hit you again with direct rustling."

"Was he the only victim of Furman York?" Lukasik asked smoothly. A stab at Tom.

I raised a hand to quiet him.

"Clyde, I've already asked this of most, so I'll ask you now, did you see Furman York the morning he died? And where were you that morning?"

"Didn't see him. Where I was? On my place, examining York's handiwork from rustling my cattle."

"Is there proof of this charge against—"

I cut across Lukasik's belated defense of his former client. "Yes. Shelton has the information. We'll deal with rustling later. Stick with murder for now. Were you alone, Clyde? Can anyone vouch for your whereabouts?"

"Alone."

I nodded. Why should he be any different? "What exactly did you ask Hiram to do for you?"

Clyde shifted his weight and stared at the ground. "Asked him to, uh, talk to York. Tell him to stay the hell away from me and my cattle. I couldn't do it. Couldn't trust myself not to get myself in real trouble. Same reason I wasn't telling my father, didn't want him pulled into my mess."

"Why Hiram?"

He looked up, a glimmer of amusement. "York hadn't responded to reason, wasn't even scared off by law enforcement breathing down his neck about that business in South Dakota. Thought Hiram's, uh, unpredictability might shake him up."

"Before your ranch was hit the night before York's death, you already suspected him of rustling in the area, especially from grazing association members, didn't you?" I asked.

Clyde's gaze shot to his father.

"Yep."

"Your father, Kesler Baranski, who works at the Lukasik Ranch, also suspected Furman York."

As I shifted focus to Kesler, I was aware of Hiram relaxing because

I hadn't asked about Clyde's advice to him on winning Yvette's heart.

"Suspect, yep. No proof," the old man said.

"What about you, Gable?"

He shook his head once. "Didn't know there was rustling going on until... after."

"But you knew." I turned to his father. "Perhaps not that York was stealing from other people, but your own herd... Those flat cattle counts year after year told you something was wrong. That's why you've stayed at the ranch for two weeks, when you usually only come for a few days."

"I have no idea what you're talking about. I needed a rest, I came here for the fresh air and lack of stress. I have no interest in the ranch. I do not deal with such matters as herd count." His mouth twisted on the last two words.

"No interest? Yet you've always seen to the payroll. At least as far as paying Furman York a princely salary."

Shelton became more alert.

Across the circle of people, Jennifer named the sum. That drew a reaction from everyone except Odessa and Asheleigh.

As if that called my attention to them, I said, "Oh, yes, I need to introduce you all to Odessa Vincennes and her daughter, Asheleigh."

"My fiancée," Gable said immediately.

Nobody produced any congratulations, but the couple's hands tightened, they looked at each other, and they didn't appear to need any external approval.

After a slight pause, I added the punchline.

"Odessa was born Linda Pedroke. She is Leah Pedroke's younger sister."

That got reactions, even a few words. Along with instant seethe from Shelton, beside me. He'd make me pay for holding that back ... later.

Diana and I had talked about how to say this next part. If it didn't produce a result, I'd have a steeper climb. If it produced too much of a reaction, everything could fall apart.

"Odessa—Linda—came here to see where Leah lived her last

months."

"I came here to find Leah's murderer and our parents'. I worked to come here. I saved and saved—"

"*We* saved, Mom. I worked, too. All my life. Saving for school and this move."

Gable released Asheleigh's hand to put his arm around her shoulders.

Odessa did not look at her.

The woman had a choice: Daughter or revenge? Though Odessa surely would say she sought justice.

Small compensation for her daughter.

As if the interruption hadn't occurred, Odessa continued.

"York killed my sister." Her thumb rubbed at her finger. "The trial killed our parents. And then I learned here about jurors being bribed to let him go. Those jurors are dead, like York. I cannot kill them." She lifted her head and stared at Norman Clay Lukasik. "But you killed my parents. You deserve to die."

"I have no idea what—"

"He *is* dying." I faced Lukasik. "That's the true reason you've stayed on at the ranch. You must be thinking about what will happen after you die. How the things you established will affect your son, Gable. Because—" I looked around the circle. "—Gable was about to inherit being the victim of Furman York's decades-long blackmailing scheme."

Chapter Fifty-Six

"ABSURD. YOU HAVE no proof. You can't possibly—"

"You think we can't have proof because you're obsessive about getting rid of ranch records, because you thought that was the only way the blackmail could be traced. It's not."

I glanced toward Jennifer. Lukasik tracked that look.

A sliver of confusion came into his eyes.

Of doubt.

"He said—"

"Shut up, Gable. Now."

"But—"

"Not a word." After that cracked-whip order, Lukasik turned to me, trying for his doubt-instilling sneer. "Let Elizabeth Margaret Danniher dig herself even deeper before we end this."

I ignored his implicit threat, and explained to the rest, as quickly and succinctly as I could, how Furman York, knowing Lukasik bribed jurors to win his case, secured evidence when Lukasik repeated three years later, in Bonedrin, Colorado. Then York converted that evidence into a lifetime position of generous guaranteed income, room and board, free transportation, and more.

"Of course, he didn't expect it to end so abruptly," I concluded.

Odessa surged forward, but Tom, stationed beside her, cut her off.

She shouted at Lukasik, directly across from her, "I will kill you. I will kill you for what you have done. You *murdered* my parents."

Asheleigh made a sound. Gable's hold on her tightened.

"Kill me?" Lukasik repeated in nearly his best courtroom voice, turning away from her as unimportant. "You should *thank* me. I relieved you of the task your incompetence kept you from achieving for decades. You and all the rest. None of you acted, for all your whining about Furman York. Only I did."

Norman Clay Lukasik *confessing* to murdering Furman York?

But he'd *never* confess.

That's why we needed Shelton.

We thought—hoped—we could get Lukasik far enough into the corner of guilt with this confrontation that Shelton would take over, using law enforcement resources to fill in our broad outlines.

But this... this didn't fit Lukasik. He would try to outsmart every-one—us, Shelton, the legal system. He wouldn't just give up.

"You? You killed him?" Scorn burned Odessa's words. "And now you think you finally made right all the wrong you did?"

Lukasik spun on her. "Hell, no. I killed him to get him off my back. A bloodsucker who'd been leeching off my blood—and money—far too long. I could never reach around to yank him off me until that day."

"I said it, I said it, I said it," Hiram crowed, jangling the handcuffs like a percussion instrument suitable to a jig. "Said all along Norman Clay Lukasik was the killer. Could've had him in jail days ago. No-body'd ever listen to me."

"Because all you did was say he did it." Shelton said.

"Can't expect me to do *all* your work for you like the little lady does."

Shelton's reaction was like feeling the earth tremble and crack as molten rock surged up inside a volcano, waiting for it to spew lava, ash, and flames.

And then he had himself under control. It would have been a sight to behold, but I was relieved.

We'd needed Shelton more than ever with Lukasik reacting so unpredictably.

I needed to think. Adjust on the fly.

Abruptly Hiram puffed up. "Hey! You meant to frame me." He tried to get in Lukasik's face, but was foiled by Lloyd Sampson's hold and Lukasik staring over his head.

"I had no need to frame you. You shoveled all the doubt yourself, then rolled in it like a pig in a wallow. I simply sat back and watched." With Hiram sputtering himself toward apoplexy, Lukasik swept a contemptuous look around the circle. "You all did. Tom Burrell threatening him—"

Had Lukasik picked the day to kill York because that dispute cast suspicion on Tom?

"—over a few cows—or was there more behind his anger? There were rumors about his former wife and York... Or Clyde, sending Hiram to avoid the temptation of murder—so he says. Kesler would have risen to killing York *if he'd known*. The old cowman, revered by all—how could he not know? This woman. Of loving Gable in his own way *disappointed* she didn't kill the man she proclaims murdered her sister—waiting for decades, she says, yet failing to act when he was right in front of her. Hiram threatening York as he has so many—did he hide a murderous tree among the forest of his threats?"

This was more like it. This Norman Clay Lukasik we could have predicted. A thunderous offering of alternatives, deflecting from him. It's how he'd started.

When had he shifted? When had he stopped denying?

Mike, Diana, Tom, Jennifer, even Shelton watched me.

I should pound Lukasik with questions, get him to make statements, give him no time to regain balance...

But my concentration shuddered.

Something...

"You've got what you need. I've said I killed him. I'm not making any further admissions." Lukasik slashed the air with the edge of his hand. "I have no regrets for what I've done in my life, in my career. If I hadn't won that case, I wouldn't've had the career I've had. Wouldn't've had my ranch to..."

Leave to his son.

Diana jumped in. "You haven't told us about... getting York off." Tactful of her to not bring up bribery.

"Hah. You never figured that out, did you? It doesn't take all the jurors to be with you—"

The latest in euphemisms for bribery.

"—to swing a jury. Juries have a rhythm. They get rolling, like a bicycle. Hit at the right time with a holdout, a vote that switches sides, and it's a stick in the spokes. Instant crash. Right then, one, two in the right place and *boom* it's your jury."

"One or two in the right place because you exploit weaknesses," Diana said. "Someone's greed. Someone's desperation to keep his dying child alive. Not jurors being with you, not persuaded, but bribed. By you. To get a murderer off."

"The murderer of my sister."

"Not proven," Lukasik snapped.

"I *know* it," Hiram shouted. "What it did to Earl. What he did."

Voices exploded. Hiram shouting about his friend. Shelton telling him to be quiet. Odessa not shouting, all the more chilling for it, telling Lukasik what punishment he deserved in this life and the next.

In full oral sail, Lukasik dismissed them, but did not deny his guilt.

He *had* been denying, confident he could not be touched ... and then he stopped. When?

I turned my back to shut out the whirling emotions, so I could think. I had to *think*.

The wind tossed confetti rose petals against the faded house, my thoughts scattering with them. Memories coming instead.

Mike and his family ranch.

Tom, carrying Tamantha's bag.

Tamantha saying, *You need roses here. Like the grazing association has.*

Not now, not now. I needed to think, not remember. Not feel. I needed to figure out when Lukasik stopped denying.

Mom's voice. *Until you're forced to face it.*

Had Lukasik been forced to face something? Forced to feel...

Tamantha's hand in mine. The slide of her thumb.

In that instant, thinking had no power against what burst open. Whatever I felt for Tom, for Mike—and I felt so much for each of them—I loved Tamantha Burrell.

I would do whatever I could to ease her way.

For this girl, I would sacrifice anythi—

My mind flooded with an incongruity—Norman Clay Lukasik and the concept of sacrifice.

When had he stopped denying?

After he told Gable to shut up, which followed…

Words about proof of blackmail, then his son saying *He said*—

Those two words and Lukasik knew.

He knew York. He knew the hold the man reveled in. He knew he would not let it go. He knew York had told his son he would carry the blackmail into the next generation.

In that moment, he knew that his son also knew the burden of this legacy he would carry.

And Norman Clay Lukasik had been forced to face what he felt.

I spun around.

"You didn't kill him. Gable did."

ODESSA GASPED.

But the voice that said, "No. Tell them you didn't," was Asheleigh's.

Gable didn't respond. Might not have even heard. He stared straight ahead.

His silence absorbed all other sounds.

As I'd seen before, the planes of his face shifted, drawing tauter, as if the skeleton of his father surged closer to the surface of the fuller and—even in this moment—kinder face.

I remembered then…

Remembered him saying York must have gotten up early because his truck was gone when Gable left… yet he'd never answered whether he'd seen York.

"He ordered you to come here that morning," I said quietly.

"Don't answer," his father ordered. "Don't say—"

"Usually it's no problem to avoid him, but he was up early that day. He made me climb up here to get my orders. He pointed that gun of his to where two pastures meet and told me to tear down fence so the cattle would mix. I said that would mix Lukasik brand and Circle B. He laughed. Nasty. Said I was a bright one. Started bragging he'd have everybody thinking Tom Burrell was trying to steal Lukasik cattle before he was done. Then he said to get started, because he was the foreman and I was just a hand. I said no. He got—"

"Be quiet, Gable. Shut up now."

I don't think his son heard.

"—real mean and said I'd be taking his orders on more than fences from now on. He said when my father finished dying it would be my turn to take care of him the way he expected, or he'd see to it that everything blew up in my face. I told him I wouldn't pay him blackmail the way my father had for—"

"There's no basis—It's false. He had no knowledge. No basis in fact. Shelton. No motive."

As far as I could tell, no one looked at Norman Clay Lukasik.

Gable held this audience.

"—all these years. All these years him holding the ranch hostage. And there he stood, saying he'd go on doing it. He said he had proof that would take everything away. Everything. The ranch."

I heard Tom's words echoing beneath Gable's.

…like your heart's too big for your chest because it's yours. You're its, too, though. It holds you…

"I said I'd kill him before I let him interfere with the life Asheleigh and I want. He laughed again, the way he did. Then he raised his shotgun and pointed it at me, and said, 'Who's going to kill who?'

"I grabbed it. I suppose that surprised him. Surprised him enough that I got a good hold on it, even with my work gloves on. He—"

Those unlovely work gloves. Spattered and stained. Not only from cows.

"—didn't let go. We fought for it—I don't know how long. And then I had the butt in my hands and got my finger—"

"Ridiculous. I told you. I killed him. I shot Furman York." Even now, Norman Clay Lukasik was really good. The right amount of dismissal, utter conviction. But his words came too late. Far too late.

His power was gone. Shattered by his son.

"—around the trigger and pulled it. He went down to his knees. Exactly like he was praying. Only he never prayed. And he stayed there the longest time, but his eyes... There was nothing in his eyes. Not the meanness, not the calculating. Just... the darkest night you've ever seen, without a single star."

Asheleigh sucked in oxygen, as if she'd held her breath until she couldn't hold it any longer. She hardly seemed to move. No one did.

"I dropped the gun. And when he started to fold down, I pushed it with my foot, under him. Get it out of sight, I guess. And then I looked all around and nobody was there. Nobody else was anywhere. But all those marks in the dust... Didn't look like anything to me, but science can do all sorts of stuff. So, I took my hat off—"

His *hat*.

"—to brush the marks away. I said I wouldn't let him ruin everything. But in the second I pulled the trigger ... I don't know. Maybe I wanted to make up for... Maybe I wanted him gone so her life could be free of him, of my father, of the trial, of her aunt, of her mother, of all of it. Even of me."

"No, Gable. No."

Odessa jerked Asheleigh around by her arm. "You told him?"

Her daughter pulled free.

"Of course I told him. He loves me and I... I love..." Turning to Gable, Asheleigh's voice rose, the words tumbling together. "I do love you. Whatever they did, whatever they planned, it's not us, Gable. It's not *us*. Don't leave me. Please, please, don't leave me."

Odessa Vincennes stared at her, her mouth open, her eyes dead.

Jerry said it when he showed us her footage—*It's all reaction shot.*

Epilogue

MY PHONE RANG as I returned to the editing booth with a food delivery to keep us going to finish our special on the murder by and the murder of Furman York.

I checked caller ID, then answered.

"Hi, Danny. It's Mel," came the familiar voice. "Having a good visit with your parents?"

"It's okay, Mel. No need to worry. I'm still here."

"You're still—? What does that mean?"

"It means I'm still here in Wyoming. Not on my way to Illinois to strangle you."

"Strangle me? Wh—What—? Ha, ha, ha. You're always joking."

"I'm not joking. Mom and Dad told me they know about the murder investigations. Have known. And how they know."

A silence that I dearly hoped was painful on his end followed.

He deserved it for betraying my trust, betraying my confidence as a client. He was lucky—almost as lucky as I was—that it turned out well. But he couldn't have known it would. He was supposed to follow my wishes. No one else's.

I could sense the pressure building in him, until he burst out, "You are more and more like Catherine every day."

I didn't laugh until he ended the call.

THURSTON FINE REPEATED to anyone who didn't get away fast enough that Cottonwood County should be grateful star citizen

Norman Clay Lukasik was cleared of murder.

Fine was happy he got to air another part of his interview with Lukasik. Didn't faze him in the least that it was out of date after being held for breaking news, then our special report. Also didn't faze him that Audrey edited out several bits that made no sense in light of later events. Because Fine didn't watch it.

He also didn't care that *cleared* was an overstatement.

The county attorney moved cautiously on the son's admissions, while the father maintained he did the crime. It was for the legal system to handle now.

Once, Fine tried to corner me—shortly after I'd delivered more brownies and Hamburger Heaven coffee to Jerry—apparently forgetting I was the leader of the Norman Clay Lukasik for Murderer campaign ... until the instant I wasn't.

But I escaped.

And, thus, Thurston avoided me telling him I'd have traded the older Lukasik for the younger one as murderer a hundred times over.

I almost wished...

Except I couldn't wish against the truth.

I thought of Tom's question about whether I'd ever held two contradictory feelings at the same time.

"He could have a case for self-defense," I said to the others when we'd finished the special report and had breath to expend on anything else. "Or manslaughter. He didn't take a weapon. If they can prove a scuffle, that would help."

Diana nodded. She'd had the difficult task of telling her son about Gable's arrest. He was taking it hard. "You know, represented by a good defense attorney, Gable might..."

"Not his father," I objected.

Asheleigh Vincennes had been to see James Longbaugh. Not necessarily to defend Gable on criminal charges, but to ensure his desires weren't swamped by his father.

Odessa remained in the apartment, seeing no one. Except for one visit from Gisella Decker.

"No, definitely not his father. Still, his father has the money and the connections to get him the best," Diana said.

"The money. But the connection might work against Gable. No lawyer would want Norman Clay Lukasik looking over his shoulder every second." Mike said.

Jennifer sighed. "I kind of wish it stayed with Norman Clay being the murderer."

"Sure seems like the son and daughter paying the price for the sins—or at least the obsession in the case of Odessa—of the father and mother," Mike said.

"You can't mean you would rather Elizabeth hadn't figured this out."

Mike didn't respond to Diana's statement, but Jennifer pursued it. "Well, the father *is* dying—" We'd confirmed that in reporting for the special. "—while Gable has a lot of years ahead of him."

"I wonder how much of Lukasik taking the blame was recognition of that," Diana said.

"Whatever else Norman did in his life and whatever lies at his door for setting up the situation, he did not pull the trigger. Gable did."

The silence that followed my grim reminder, spread darkly.

Jennifer brightened abruptly. "You could claim the reward, Elizabeth. It would serve Norman Clay Lukasik right to have to pay when it was his son. You could use the money for something good."

"I'm not claiming the reward." After a moment, I added, "I do hope Gable gets a good lawyer."

I might make a few phone calls myself.

THE DAY AFTER the special ran, Mom, Diana, Jennifer, and I took Tamantha to Cody for a girl's day, including going to a salon.

Persuading her was the easy part. Her father was the tough part.

I left that to my mother. I was working on being around him without the ache swallowing me whole. I'd get there. I had to get there. I wouldn't deny myself Tamantha—or Tom's friendship. I wouldn't deny him, either.

He watched his daughter climb into my SUV like snatching her back was his first choice.

"Nothing fancy. I mean it. Nothing fancy."

Mom patted his arm. "Trust me."

I almost laughed, because he clearly didn't trust her. Or any of us.

While the others loaded up, I said quietly to him, "A haircut won't change who Tamantha is."

I didn't add it wouldn't make her who she wasn't, either—her mother. He'd figure that out eventually, as the changes came over the next decade and he adapted to Tamantha's individual brand of womanhood.

I did add, "Some new clothes won't, either."

If he'd been a horse, he'd have gone wild-eyed and shied like crazy. Instead, he looked grimmer than ever and muttered another, "Nothing fancy. Elizabeth, are you driving or Diana?"

"Me, of course. Why?"

I waited to hear how much safer Tamantha would be with me behind the wheel.

"You'll be gone longer."

❖   ❖   ❖

WE TOOK THE salon by storm.

The stylists had as much fun as we did.

Though the energetic young woman who did my hair was disappointed I wasn't willing to change much. I knew my hair, I knew this style, I knew how to make it work in wildly variable circumstances.

Radical experimentation would have to wait until I retired from in front of the camera.

She did a nice job within my list of limitations, even if she did sigh more than strictly necessary as she watched other stylists giving Jennifer and Diana newer looks. Even Mom, who stuck with her same cut, went for a stylish blowout.

The one we focused on was Tamantha.

Something different, not too different. Flattering, could not require a single styling tool for everyday wear. Satisfying to her and us, yet wouldn't set off a skittish father.

The salon owner pulled it off with a face-framing cut with a few layers to help straight hair curve and move. It played up Tamantha's dark eyes ... which grew larger in a heart-swelling moment when she saw herself in the mirror.

It was like the color explosion suitcase that lived in her soul had brought a manifestation out to where others could see it.

That got another boost from a post-lunch stop at a big-box store for a few wardrobe additions. With my mother and Jennifer unexpected confederates in urging Tamantha to try new fashions, she ventured beyond mom jeans and grandma sweaters. But not far enough beyond to scare Diana or me.

Tom was on his own.

Coming around a low hill, the Circle B Ranch road dipped to a bridge, opening our view to the house and Tom standing in front of it, one hand raised in greeting.

It was as if he'd been there ever since we drove off with Tamantha—not to go to Cody, but back to that first day when the call came that Furman York had been shot at the grazing association.

He didn't move.

Not as we drove up. Not when we all got out of the vehicle—Tamantha last. Like a princess with her grown-up entourage, a half step behind.

Tom stood staring at her, his expression unreadable—darn him.

Without a hint of begging for a compliment, rather in the strict interest of seeking information, Tamantha stepped in front of him and asked, "Do you like this haircut, Daddy? Do I look better than before?"

He swallowed. "I like it because you look more like yourself than ever before and that's exactly what I always love to see."

The man didn't always say much, but he hit it out of the park with that one. As all the moist female eyes proclaimed.

Except Tamantha's.

She looked up at him and said, "Okay. When's dinner? That's hard work, going to a salon. I'm hungry."

✧ ✧ ✧ ✧

AFTER MY PARENTS left to drive back to Illinois, Tamantha, Diana, Jennifer, Tom, Mike, and I went out to the grazing association one morning and cut back, then dug up eight of the rosebushes from around the house's porch. We each took one to plant in our yards, plus one each for Mrs. P and Aunt Gee.

The remaining bushes at the house, we pruned, fertilized, and watered.

The eighth bush we planted in O'Hara Hill in what was now a wild patch at a distance from the road and once had been where Leah Pedroke last breathed.

✧ ✧ ✧ ✧

MIKE KNOCKED ON my front door.

I knew it was him, because he'd called and asked if he could come over after the Ten.

I would have said sure regardless. The house felt rather empty without my parents, Tamantha, and a group of mystery pursuers hanging around.

Shadow might share those sentiments. He greeted Mike with new enthusiasm.

"C'mon in, have a seat. Iris baked cookies and—"

He stopped me halfway to the couch with a hand on my arm, turning me toward him. "Elizabeth, Chicago's offered me a job. A good job."

Immediate, hot weight pressed my eyes. "That's great, Mike. You deserve it. And they're lucky to get you. You'll be terrific."

"Come with me, Elizabeth. My getting the job is only half of it. They're interested in you, too. They were excited when they heard we were working together. They said they wondered where you'd gotten to. You'd have to interview, but they said to tell you they're really interested. You could do the kind of reporting you were doing before. The kind you should be doing. Come to Chicago with me."

Slowly, I pulled in a shaky breath. It came out smooth, steady.

"No." I touched his face.

"It doesn't have to be Chicago. I could try for New York or Washington if that's—"

"No, Mike." I loved this man. I did. But... "No."

"Then I'll stay here. I'm happy here. It's—"

"You will *not* stay here. Not now and definitely not for me. It's what you said about your family ranch. How you didn't want to try to rewind time, about needing to move forward not back. A TV job in Chicago—or any of those other places—is moving forward for you. But for me, it would be trying to rewind time. *This* is moving forward for me."

"Is it Tom?"

My attempt at a smile wobbled.

"No. Tom thinks we're bad for each other. Too much baggage. Or at least that we're bad for Tamantha, which is more important. I understand his point and I certainly understand his protecting his daughter."

My voice caught.

Mike pulled me into his arms, tucking my head under his chin, stroking my back, and letting me cry.

I did love Michael Paycik.

The End

Thank you for reading Elizabeth, Mike, Tom and Tamantha's latest adventure!

After some upheavals in Elizabeth's professional and personal life in Wyoming, not to mention those of her closest friends, she has some recalculating to do. Everything changes, but murder never does.

Body Brace

Enjoy **Reaction Shot**? (Hope so)

Elizabeth and friends ask if you'll help spread the word about them and the Caught Dead in Wyoming series. You have the power to do that in two quick ways:

Recommend the book and the series to your friends and/or the whole wide world on social media. Shouting from rooftops is particularly appreciated.

Review the book. Take a few minutes to write an honest review and it can make a huge difference. As you likely know, it's the single best way for your fellow readers to find books they'll enjoy, too.

To me—as an author and a reader—the goal is always to find a good author-reader match. By sharing your reading experience through recommendations and reviews, you become a vital matchmaker. ☺

For news about upcoming Caught Dead in Wyoming books, as well as other titles and news, join Patricia McLinn's Readers List and receive her twice-monthly free newsletter.
https://www.patriciamclinn.com/readers-list

Other Caught Dead in Wyoming mysteries

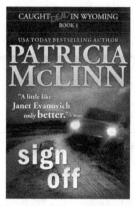

SIGN OFF

Divorce a husband, disrupt a career …
grapple with a murder.

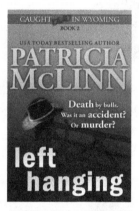

LEFT HANGING

Trampled by bulls—an accident? Elizabeth, Mike and friends dig into
the world of rodeo.

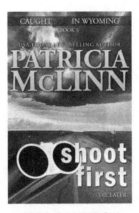

SHOOT FIRST

For Elizabeth, death hits close to home. She and friends delve into old Wyoming treasures and secrets to save lives.

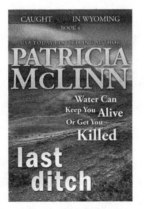

LAST DITCH

Elizabeth and Mike search after a man in a wheelchair goes missing in dangerous, desolate country.

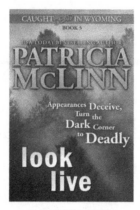

LOOK LIVE

Elizabeth and friends take on misleading murder with help—and hindrance—from intriguing out-of-towners.

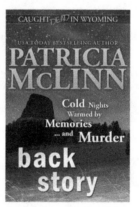

BACK STORY

Murder never dies, but comes back to threaten Elizabeth and team of investigators.

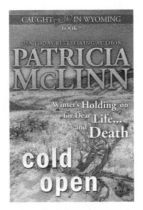

COLD OPEN

Elizabeth's search for a place of her own becomes an open house for murder.

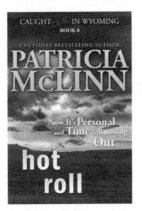

HOT ROLL

One of their own becomes a target—and time is running out.

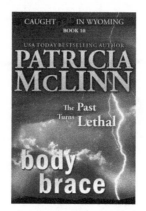

BODY BRACE

Everything can change, but murder still comes calling.

Secret Sleuth series

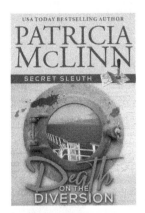

DEATH ON THE DIVERSION

Final resting place? Deck chair.

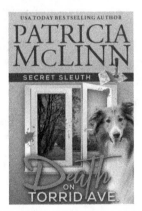

DEATH ON TORRID AVENUE

A new love (canine), an ex-cop and a dog park discovery.

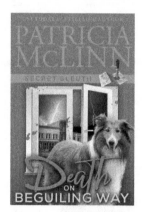

DEATH ON BEGUILING WAY

No zen in sight as Sheila untangles a yoga instructor's murder.

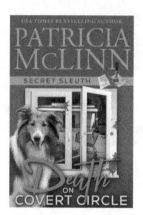

DEATH ON COVERT CIRCLE

Sheila and Clara are on the scene as a supermarket CEO meets his expiration date.

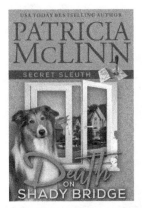

DEATH ON SHADY BRIDGE

A cold case heats up.

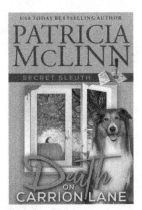

DEATH ON CARRION LANE

More murder is brewing in Haines Tavern.

Mystery With Romance

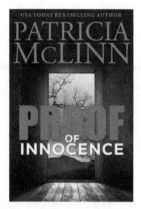

PROOF OF INNOCENCE

She's a prosecutor chasing demons. He's wrestling them. Will they find proof of innocence?

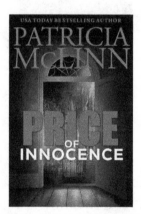

PRICE OF INNOCENCE

To solve this murder Detective Belichek will risk everything—his friendships, his reputation, his career, his heart ... and his life.

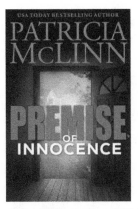

PREMISE OF INNOCENCE

The last woman Detective Landis is prepared to see is the one he must save.

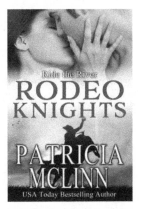

RIDE THE RIVER: RODEO KNIGHTS

Her rodeo cowboy ex is back ... as her prime suspect.

BARDVILLE, WYOMING

A Stranger in the Family

A Stranger to Love

The Rancher Meets His Match

Explore a complete list of all Patricia's books

www.patriciamclinn.com/patricias-books

Or get a printable booklist

patriciamclinn.com/patricias-books/printable-booklist

Patricia's eBookstore (buy digital books online directly from Patricia)

patriciamclinn.com/patricias-books/ebookstore

About the Author

USA Today bestselling author Patricia McLinn spent more than 20 years as an editor at The Washington Post after stints as a sports writer (Rockford, Ill.) and assistant sports editor (Charlotte, N.C.). She received BA and MSJ degrees from Northwestern University.

McLinn is the author of more than 50 published novels, which are cited by readers and reviewers for wit and vivid characterization. Her books include mysteries, romantic suspense, contemporary romance, historical romance and women's fiction. They have topped bestseller lists and won numerous awards.

She has spoken about writing from Melbourne, Australia, to Washington, D.C., including being a guest speaker at the Smithsonian Institution.

Now living in northern Kentucky, McLinn loves to hear from readers through her website and social media.

Visit with Patricia:
Website: patriciamclinn.com
Facebook: facebook.com/PatriciaMcLinn
Twitter: @PatriciaMcLinn
Pinterest: pinterest.com/patriciamclinn
Instagram: instagram.com/patriciamclinnauthor

Copyright © Patricia McLinn
Print ISBN: 978-1-944126-68-1
Ebook ISBN: 978-1-944126-67-4
Large print ISBN: 978-1-944126-90-2
Audiobook ISBN: 978-1-944126-91-9

CPSIA information can be obtained
at www.ICGtesting.com
Printed in the USA
LVHW110226091020
668398LV00001B/273